W9-CMU-161

Someone's going to die.

I took a deep breath, but couldn't stop my hands from shaking. *Please don't be Emma. Or Nash. Or my dad.* I couldn't lose another parent.

I tried to ask—I tried to summon that much strength—but in the end, it just wasn't there. I'd been through so much already in the past few months, and I couldn't stand the thought of losing someone else. Someone I loved.

So Tod answered the question I didn't have the courage to ask.

"It's you, Kaylee. You're on the list."

* * *

Praise for the Soul Screamers series by *New York Times* bestselling author **RACHEL VINCENT**

"*Twilight* fans will love it."
—*Kirkus Reviews*

"The story rocks (for teens and adults, I might add)."
—*Book Bitch*

"Fans of those vampires will enjoy this new crop of otherworldly beings."
—*Booklist*

"I'm so excited about this series."
—*The Eclectic Book Lover*

"A must for any reading wish list."
—*Tez Says*

"A book like this is one of the reasons that I add authors to my auto-buy list. This is definitely a keeper."
—*TeensReadToo.com*

Also by
***New York Times* bestselling author Rachel Vincent**

from Harlequin Teen

Soul Screamers
ebook prequels
MY SOUL TO LOSE
REAPER

MY SOUL TO TAKE
MY SOUL TO SAVE
MY SOUL TO KEEP
MY SOUL TO STEAL
IF I DIE

from MIRA Books

The Shifters
STRAY
ROGUE
PRIDE
PREY
SHIFT
ALPHA

If I Die

RACHEL VINCENT

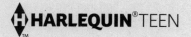
HARLEQUIN®TEEN

If you purchased this book without a cover you should be aware
that this book is stolen property. It was reported as "unsold and
destroyed" to the publisher, and neither the author nor the
publisher has received any payment for this "stripped book."

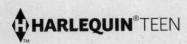 **HARLEQUIN**®TEEN

ISBN-13: 978-0-373-21032-9

IF I DIE

Recycling programs
for this product may
not exist in your area.

Copyright © 2011 by Rachel Vincent

All rights reserved. Except for use in any review, the reproduction or
utilization of this work in whole or in part in any form by any electronic,
mechanical or other means, now known or hereafter invented, including
xerography, photocopying and recording, or in any information storage
or retrieval system, is forbidden without the written permission of the
publisher, Harlequin Enterprises Limited, 225 Duncan Mill Road,
Don Mills, Ontario, Canada M3B 3K9.

This is a work of fiction. Names, characters, places and incidents are
either the product of the author's imagination or are used fictitiously,
and any resemblance to actual persons, living or dead, business
establishments, events or locales is entirely coincidental.

This edition published by arrangement with Harlequin Books S.A.

For questions and comments about the quality of this book
please contact us at Customer_eCare@Harlequin.ca.

® and TM are trademarks of the publisher. Trademarks indicated with
® are registered in the United States Patent and Trademark Office,
the Canadian Trade Marks Office and in other countries.

www.HarlequinTEEN.com

Printed in U.S.A.

This one is for everyone
who wrote to ask what happens next.

Here you go.

Now ask me again. ;)

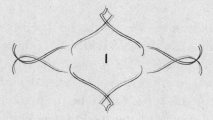

I used to think death was the worst thing that could happen to a person. I also used to think it was the *last* thing that could happen. But if I've learned anything from surrounding myself with reapers, and living nightmares, and my fellow *bean sidhes,* it's this: I was wrong on both counts....

"What are you doing here before the warning bell?" I asked, sliding into my seat in first period algebra II with four minutes to spare. "Isn't that one of the signs of an impending apocalypse?"

"If so, this is how I want to go out." Emma Marshall sighed, digging the textbook from the bag on her lap. "Enjoying the view."

I followed my best friend's gaze to the front of the class, where Mr. Beck—hired in the wake of Mr. Wesner's untimely demise—was writing math problems on the white board with green ink. His numbers were blockish and completely vertical; he had the best handwriting of any teacher at Eastlake. But Emma's focus was several feet below his numbers, where the jeans encouraged by the new "Spirit Fridays" policy proved that Mr. Beck was much more dedicated to physical fitness than the average high school faculty member.

"And I suppose your sudden interest in math is purely academic, right?"

Her grin widened as she set the book on her desk, and it fell open to the place marked with a fat, purple-print emery board. "I don't know if 'pure' is totally accurate, but I haven't figured out how to entirely avoid academia in the school setting. I think the most we can hope for is something pretty to look at, to distract us from the inherent pain of the educational process."

I laughed. "Spoken like a true underachiever."

Emma could have been a straight-A student, but she was satisfied coasting by on effortless Bs, except in French and math, the only subjects that didn't seem to come naturally for her. And the hot new math teacher had done nothing to improve her grades. Thanks to the aesthetic distraction, she was less inclined than ever to pay attention to what was written on the board and in the book.

Not that I could blame her. Mr. Beck was undeniably yummy, from his dark, tousled hair to his bright green eyes and the scuffed sneakers he always wore, even with slacks.

"He's only twenty-two," Em said, when she caught me looking. "Less than a year out of college. I bet this is his first teaching job."

"How do you know that?" I asked, as Mr. Beck set his marker down and dug through his desk drawer for something.

"Heard it from Danica Sussman. He's been tutoring her after school, to keep her eligible for softball."

"Where is Danica?" I asked, on the tail end of the late bell. She'd been out sick for a couple of days, but she'd never missed on a game day before—Danica was supposed to pitch that afternoon.

"Still sick, I guess," Em whispered, as Mr. Beck started taking roll. She unfolded a half-blank sheet of notebook paper. "Did you do the homework?"

I rolled my eyes and pulled out my own work. "What happened to your new interest in math?"

"It doesn't extend to homework."

"Kaylee Cavanaugh?" Mr. Beck called from the front of the room, and I glanced up, startled, certain we'd been caught cheating. But Beck was just standing there with his roll book in hand, waiting for my answer.

"Oh. Here," I said, and he'd called three more names when the door opened and Danica Sussman stepped into the classroom. She was pale, except for dark patches beneath her eyes, which she hadn't even tried to cover.

"Danica, are you okay?" Beck asked, as she crossed toward the front of the room, a blue late slip in hand.

"I'm fine." She handed him the slip, but he balled it up in one fist and dropped it into the trash can next to his desk.

"I haven't called your name yet, so you're not really late," he said, frowning, like he wasn't convinced by her answer.

"Thanks, Mr. B." But when she headed toward her desk, Danica had one hand pressed to her stomach, her face scrunched up in obvious pain.

Halfway through class, as Emma scrambled to finish her homework without ever taking her focus from Mr. Beck's face, a familiar, sharp pain began to scratch at the back of my throat.

No! My heart beat so hard I practically shook in my chair. It *couldn't* be happening again. Not at school. Not just six weeks after the loss of three teachers in a two-day span. My winter had felt like a series of deaths connected only by my advanced knowledge of them. I'd been hoping for a spring reprieve.

But a *bean sidhe's* wail is never wrong. When someone near

me is about to die, an overwhelming urge to scream—to cry out to his soul—consumes me. And the scream clawing its way up my throat at that very moment could only mean one thing.

I clenched my teeth so tight my jaws ached, denying the scream an exit. My hands gripped the sides of my desk, muscles so tense I accidentally pulled it back an inch, and Emma glanced up when she heard it squeal on the dingy linoleum tile.

She took one look at my face and frowned. *Again?* she mouthed, and when I could only nod, her frown deepened. Emma had seen me resist screaming for someone's soul often enough to recognize the symptoms. At first it had freaked her out, and a large part of me wished it still did. I didn't like how accustomed she was becoming to the cocoon of death that seemed to surround me.

Yet there were definite advantages to having a best friend in the know. Like the fact that she didn't panic as she watched my gaze travel over my classmates, waiting for the dark aura to materialize around someone and show me who was about to die. But I saw no aura, and the scream remained a steady, painful pressure at the back of my throat—fairly easily stoppered, since I knew what I was doing—as if the soon-to-be-deceased and I weren't actually in the same room. That thought made me relax enough that I raised my hand to be excused.

Mr. Beck started to nod in my direction, but before he could, Danica Sussman slid right out of her chair and onto the floor. Unconscious.

The entire class gasped, and chairs squealed against the floor as people stood for a better view. I was so surprised my mouth almost fell open, which would have released my painfully shrill shriek into the school.

Mr. Beck stared at Danica, blinking in shock and confusion.

Was it her? Was Danica about to die? If so, why wasn't my urge to scream getting any stronger?

Mr. Beck rushed down the aisle, but before he got there, Chelsea Simms dropped onto the floor and stuck her hand in front of Danica's face, an inch from her nose. "She's still breathing...." Chelsea sat back and glanced over our fallen classmate, obviously looking for an injury. Then she gasped again, sharper than before. "Shit, she's bleeding!" Chelsea scrambled backward on her knees and bumped her shoulder on the nearest desk, as shocked whispers echoed across the room.

Mr. Beck knelt beside Danica, features tense with worry. "Chelsea, call the office from the phone on my desk. Just dial nine." When Chelsea stood, I saw what everyone else had already reacted to: the pool of blood spreading beneath Danica's thighs.

That's when the scream hit me full force. While everyone else whispered and stared, gathering around our fallen classmate until Mr. Beck ordered them back, I sat stiff in my chair, gripping the sides of my desk again, swallowing compulsively to fight back the scream that was scalding me from the inside out.

But Danica was still breathing. I could see her chest rising between the shoulders of two basketball players standing in the aisle. Her breathing wasn't even labored. But the strength of the scream within me said that someone was going to die any minute. If it wasn't Danica, who was it?

"You okay?" Emma asked, leaning close to me, eyes wide, forehead furrowed. "Is it her?"

I could only shrug. The only way I know how to check was...

I let a thin thread of the scream trail from my lips, an emaciated sound so soft no one else heard it over the steady, stunned buzz of the gathered spectators. But it was enough. With that sound calling out to the soul, I would be able to see it when it left Danica's body. Assuming she was the one about to die.

But the insubstantial form hovering over Danica Sussman was like no soul I'd ever seen. Usually, a soul's appearance—merely its representation in the physical world—mimicked its owner's size, at least. But this soul was tiny. No bigger than my fist, and irregular in shape. And Danica's breathing had not slowed.

And that's when I understood. Danica wasn't dying. She was losing her unborn child.

"I don't think I can eat today." Emma stirred a paper bowl of tomato soup with a plastic spoon. "This just isn't in good taste."

I cracked open my soda lid without glancing at her lunch, for fear I'd be sick at the sight. "I'm pretty sure they plan the menu months in advance." But that was little solace after what we'd seen that morning. Somehow, even after all the death I'd both witnessed and heralded, I'd never even considered the possibility of a miscarriage triggering my instinct to wail for a yet-unborn soul. The usual helplessness, frustration and horror that accompanied any death for me were magnified almost beyond my own comprehension. This was a baby. A child who would never be. And I didn't know how to deal with that.

"It does look pretty gory, though," Sabine insisted from across the table, ignoring her own tray as the spring breeze blew long black hair into her face. She tucked the stray strands back, exposing a mismatched set of silver hoops in her upper ear. "So is it true that Danica Sussman hemorrhaged all over the floor in first period?"

"Both true and gruesome." Em dropped her spoon and pushed her meal back as Nash settled onto the bench seat next to me with a cardboard tray of nachos. "I hope she's okay."

An ambulance had come for Danica, and though she was still unconscious, I was long past wailing for her baby by the time they wheeled her away on a stretcher. And I was the only one who knew for sure that she would live—but that a tiny, hidden part of her had already died.

"I hope so, too." Nash slid one arm around my waist and squeezed me, then dug into his chips, and I couldn't help wondering if we would have been able to save Danica's baby, if we'd both been there when it happened. As a male *bean sidhe,* Nash didn't wail for the souls of the dying. His gifts included Influence—the ability to compel people to do things just by speaking to them—and the capacity to guide a disembodied soul. Together, we could reinstate a person's soul and save his or her life—but only in exchange for someone else's. A life for a life. That's how it worked.

But I had no idea if it would work at all on an unborn child, without a fully formed body in which to reinstate the soul. Or if it would last, even if it did work. I mean, miscarriages happen for a reason, right? Because there's something wrong with the baby, or because the mother can't handle the stress. Or something like that. So…really, a miscarriage is a blessing, right?

Or maybe I was just desperate to find a silver lining to go with the single darkest, most horrifying cloud of a death I'd ever witnessed.

"People are saying it was a miscarriage," Emma said softly, and I flinched when a guy in a green-and-white senior class shirt turned around on the bench behind her, his brown eyes shiny with unshed tears, face flushed with anger. Max Kramer was Danica's boyfriend of almost a year, and his pain and anger were so raw I felt like I was violating his privacy just by witnessing them.

"Well, people are wrong," he snapped, and Emma froze, obviously embarrassed, then turned to face him slowly.

"I'm sorry, Max. I didn't mean…"

Max stood without letting her finish, towering over our entire table. "They're all wrong." He didn't raise his voice, but made no special effort to lower it either, so half the quad heard him when he continued. "Danica couldn't have been pregnant. We've never even done it. So find someone else to talk about. Or better yet, why don't you all just shut the hell up."

We stared after him as he stomped off toward the cafeteria doors, and one look at Emma told me she felt just as bad for him as I did.

"Poor fool," Sabine said, one of Nash's cheese-covered chips halfway to her mouth. "I think he really believes that." As a *mara,* Sabine could read people's fears and feed from the nightmares she wove for them while they slept. But even beyond her *mara* abilities, she had an uncanny ability to read people's expressions and body language. To my constant irritation.

"Of course he believes it." Emma would have taken any excuse to argue with the *mara*—Sabine had dragged her into the Netherworld six weeks earlier and almost sold her to a hellion, body and soul. But this time her anger was obviously about more than that; Em felt guilty for passing along what she'd heard in front of Max. "Just 'cause people are saying something doesn't make it true. My aunt had a miscarriage last year, and it looked nothing like that. There was hardly any blood. Mostly just some cramping."

Sabine shrugged, unfazed. "I'm no doctor, but if you ask

me, she was pregnant, and the baby didn't belong to good ol' Max. But he obviously hasn't figured that out yet."

"Well, no one asked you," Emma insisted. "So mind your own business."

The *mara* frowned. "It's not like I was going to tell him!"

"Sabine…" Nash half groaned.

Normally, I like it when he's irritated with her. Sabine was my boyfriend's ex-girlfriend, and she wasn't too happy about the "ex" part.

"She's right," I said, as softly as I could speak and still be heard at my own table.

"How do you…?" Emma asked, and I met her gaze reluctantly.

"Because I felt the baby die."

The silence at our table was almost heavy enough to feel. Then Emma breathed a soft, "Ohhh," of understanding. "That's why you needed to scream. I didn't even think about it, after Danica fell out of her chair. I guess I thought she'd die once she got to the hospital."

"No, she'll be fine, as far as I know," I said, glad to have at least that bit of good news to report. "But she definitely lost a baby, right there in first period. And Max obviously wasn't the father."

"I wonder who knocked her up?" Sabine bit into another of Nash's chips, staring off into the clouds, like she could actually puzzle that one out on her own.

Nash pulled his cardboard tray away from her. "That's none of our business."

"Maybe it is," Sabine insisted. "I bet it was Mr. Beck's."

"You are so full of shit!" Emma snapped, even angrier at having her favorite teacher's name dragged through the mud by her least favorite person.

Sabine rolled black eyes. "It's just a theory. And it's not even that far-fetched. I mean, if he's hiding his species, there's no telling what else he's hiding."

My spoon slipped from my grip and plopped into my own untouched bowl of soup. "Beck isn't *human?*" I demanded, as Emma's brown eyes widened. Even Nash looked surprised.

Sabine shrugged again. "I thought you knew."

"Hell no, we didn't know!" Nash stared at her over the table. "Are you sure?"

"As sure as I am that Kaylee dreams about some very *interesting* things she'd never even consider when she's awake."

Nash pushed aside his lunch and leaned over the table, lowering his voice even further. "How do you know?"

The *mara's* focus tightened on me and her eyes darkened, like a cloud had just passed over the sun. Only the day was still bright and warm, for mid-March. "I played around in her slumbering subconscious a couple of months ago, remember? And in her dreams, Miss Prim-n-Proper doesn't have all those stifling control issues and that pesky trust deficit."

"How do you know about *Beck,*" Nash clarified through clenched teeth, while I tried to redirect the heat in my cheeks into a death ray aimed right at Sabine.

She frowned, like the answer should have been obvious. "I read his fears. He knows this is a hotbed of Netherworld activity and he's afraid of being caught fishing in the communal pond by something bigger and badder before he has what he came for."

"And what's that?" Emma asked, obviously stunned.

"How the hell should I know?" Sabine snatched another chip from Nash's carton. "I'm a *mara,* not a psychic. Not that mind reading would help anyway. It's not like people go around thinking, 'I'm a monster from another world, hell-bent on wreaking havoc. Gee, I hope no one hears my thoughts…'"

"You could have just said, 'I don't know,'" I snapped.

Sabine raised one eyebrow in silent challenge. "I don't know," she said, managing to make her own ignorance sound smug. "But as usual, I know more than *you* do."

I wasn't surprised by her jab, and I shouldn't have been surprised to find out that Beck wasn't human. Especially considering that in the Netherworld—a hellish reflection of our own world, from which all evil springs—our school was the new hot spot for the monster A-list.

After a four-to-eight Friday-night shift at the Cineplex, where scooping popcorn and filling soda cups couldn't drive the image of Danica bleeding on the floor from my head, I pulled into my driveway exhausted, but ready for my second wind. Nash was coming over at nine to watch a movie, and my dad had promised to stay in his room all night. But before I could relax with my boyfriend, I wanted to shower off the scents of popcorn and butter-flavored oil. Also, I should probably tell my dad that my new math teacher wasn't human—that's the kind of thing he usually wanted to know.

I'd just dropped my keys into the empty candy dish on the half wall between the kitchen and living room when the sudden silence made me realize my dad had been talking when I'd come in. *Until* I'd come in.

Hmm…

"Dad?" I kicked my shoes off and dropped them on the floor of the front closet, then headed down the hall toward his room. "You okay?"

"Yeah, I'm fine, hon."

His bedroom door was ajar, so I pushed it open to see him standing in the middle of the floor, his hands in his hip pockets. I'd expected to find him on the phone—he had to be talking to someone, right?

"What's up?" I frowned when he hedged. "Dad...?"

And suddenly Tod appeared in the room, several feet away, staring right at me.

"Okay... This is even weirder than the suspicious silence," I said, expecting one or the other of them to laugh and spit out one of the logical explanations my father always seemed to have ready. But there was only more silence. "Okay, now you two are really starting to scare me."

Tod generally only acknowledged my father's existence when an opportunity arose to drive him nuts. And my dad had no use for Tod at all, unless he needed information only a rookie Grim Reaper could gain access to. So this private powwow had to be about something important.

"Guys? I can only stand here pretending you're not scaring me for another second or two before I completely lose it. T minus five...four..."

"It's nothing, honey," my dad started to say, but the scowl on Tod's face exposed the lie before my father could even finish it.

"If you don't tell her, I will," the reaper threatened.

"Tod, I can handle this—"

Tod turned his back on my father and met my gaze with a frighteningly honest weight. "Kaylee, the new list came out today." By which he meant the reaper list, detailing every death scheduled in his district in the next seven days.

Oh, shit. Someone's going to die. I took a deep breath, but couldn't stop my hands from shaking. *Please don't be Emma. Or Nash. Or my dad.* I couldn't lose another parent.

I tried to ask—I tried to summon that much strength—but in the end, it just wasn't there. I couldn't stand the thought of losing someone else. Someone I loved.

So Tod answered the question I didn't have the courage to ask.

"It's you, Kaylee. You're on the list."

2

"Where's Styx?" I turned my back on my father and the reaper and closed my eyes, trying not to let them see how shocked I really was. Fear would kick in soon, surely, once the reality had set in. But for the moment, I was numb and oddly chilled, like I'd jumped into the lake instead of letting my body adjust to the temperature a bit at a time.

"Kaylee?" My dad's footsteps thumped behind me as I stepped into my room, questions whirling around in my head so fast I got dizzy, just standing still. "Did you hear Tod?"

"Of course I heard him." Though, admittedly, that was never a guarantee. Reapers could choose who they wanted to be seen and heard by, on an individual basis, and Tod had an irritating habit of appearing to just one person in the room at a time—usually me.

"I think she's in shock," the reaper said as I scanned the floor, the rumpled covers, and the laundry piled in my desk chair, looking for a breathing lump of fur.

"Styx?" I called, but nothing moved. Tod materialized at the foot of the bed, studying me closely for my reaction, and I jumped, startled by his sudden appearance. "I'm not in shock. Not yet, anyway." At a glance, he looked nothing like his brother, beyond their similar athletic builds. Tod had his mother's blue eyes and blond curls, while Nash obviously took after his father, who'd died long before I met either of the Hudson boys.

"For the moment, I am firmly entrenched in denial, which—honestly—feels like the healthiest stage of acceptance. And I'd really appreciate it if you'd let me wallow there for a while." I brushed past my father into the hall, headed toward the kitchen. "Styx!"

"I let her into the backyard," my dad said at last, following me into the kitchen. "She doesn't like Tod."

"That's because Tod never brings anything but death and bad advice," I snapped, beyond caring that I was being un-fair—it wasn't the reaper's fault that my number was up.

"That's not true." Tod tried to grin, and I had to respect his effort to lighten the mood. "Sometimes I bring pizza."

Because the reaper gig—he extinguished life and reaped souls at the local hospital from midnight to noon—didn't pay in human currency, Tod had begun delivering pizza for spend-ing money during his free time. At my suggestion.

At first, I'd been amused by the fact that you could get both death and a large pepperoni delivered by the same person. But after Danica Sussman's first period miscarriage and the news of my own impending demise, nothing seemed very funny at the moment.

"Styx is probably starving," I mumbled, pulling open the fridge. My father's warm hand landed firmly over mine on the handle and he pushed the door closed.

"Kaylee, please sit down. We need to talk about this."

"I know." But I was terrified that if I stopped moving for more than a second, that cloud of denial would clear and leave me staring at the ugly truth. And I'd already faced more than my share of ugly truths in the almost-seventeen years of my life.

Finally I nodded reluctantly. For all I knew, I didn't have the luxury of avoiding the truth for very long.

I opened the fridge again and pulled out a can of Coke, then followed my dad into the living room, where Tod was already seated in my father's recliner. For once, Dad didn't yell at him to move. Instead, he sat on the couch with me, and I could see that he wanted to hug me, but I couldn't let him, because that gesture of grief would make it real, and no matter how little time I had left, I wasn't ready for that. Not yet.

So I would focus on the facts, rather than the truth. Because no matter what it sounds like, there's actually a very big difference between the two.

"Are you sure?" I asked, holding the cold can with both hands, relishing the discomfort because it meant that I was still alive.

Tod nodded miserably. "Normally I don't see the names more than a day or two in advance, but because you're already on borrowed time, your name came on the special list."

Special...

I was on borrowed time because I'd already died once. I was only three at the time, and thirteen years later, I only knew what I'd been told long after the fact: I was scheduled to die that night, on the side of an icy road in an accident. However, my parents couldn't stand the thought of losing their only child, so my father tried to exchange his death date for mine. But the reaper was a vicious bastard, and he took my mother's life instead.

I'd been living my mother's life—literally—since I was three years old. And now her lifeline was coming to its end. Which meant that I would die. Again.

"Aren't you just a rookie?" My father frowned skeptically.

"How do you even have access to this special list?" Normally, my dad wouldn't hesitate to question the reaper, based solely on the fact that they didn't get along. But his disbelief this time had a deeper root. One I understood.

If Tod was wrong, or even lying for some reason, then maybe I wasn't going to die. Maybe my borrowed lifeline wasn't really sliding through my fingers faster than I could cling to it.

"That's the weird thing," Tod said, unbothered by my dad's skepticism. "Normally, I *wouldn't* have access to it. If I'd known it was coming up, I could have looked up the specifics on the sly." Tod had his boss's passwords because he'd set them up in the first place—he was one of only two reapers in the district young enough to have grown up with computers. "But this time I didn't have to. When I went in this afternoon to pick up my own list, Levi sent me into his office for something. And the special list was sitting right there on his desk, in plain sight."

"And naturally, you read it," my father added.

"I'm a reaper, not a saint. Anyway, I think he wanted me to see it. Why else would he have left it out, then sent me in alone with it lying right there?"

"Why would he want you to see it?" I asked, curious in spite of the huge dark cloud hanging over my truncated future.

Tod shrugged. "I don't know. Maybe he likes me. Maybe he likes *you.*" I'd only met Levi, Tod's boss, once, but he *had* seemed impressed with my ingenuity. Impressed enough to give me a heads-up about my own death? Maybe, but…

"Why?" I asked, focused on Tod's eyes in search of an answer. If I'd been looking at Nash, I'd have known what he was feeling just by watching the colors twist in his irises. But, like my dad, Tod was too good at hiding what he was feeling.

He rarely ever let his emotions show through the windows to his soul.

"Why would he like you?" Tod's eyes held steady. "Well, you do have this sort of magnetic effect on the darker elements of life. And the afterlife." As evidenced by Avari the hellion's obsession with claiming my soul. "And Levi's definitely on the murky side of things."

I had no idea how old Levi was—though my best guess was in the mid-triple digits—but he looked like an eight-year-old, freckled, redheaded little boy. That, combined with the fact that all reapers were technically dead, made him hands down the creepiest reaper I'd ever met. And, unfortunately, in the last six months, I'd had occasion to meet several.

But that wasn't what I'd meant.

"No, why would he want me to know? Why would *you* want me to know? Nash said we're not supposed to tell people when they're going to die, because that just makes their last moments miserable. And I gotta say, he was right." I didn't know my exact time of death yet, but just knowing it was coming was enough to make my stomach revolt against the entire concept of food.

"In general, that's true…" my father began, but Tod cut him off, sporting a characteristic dark grin.

"But you seem to be the exception to so many rules, why should this one be any different?"

"Does that mean you want me to suffer through anticipation?" I asked, hoping I'd misinterpreted that part.

"No." My dad shook his head. "It means that forewarned is forearmed. We couldn't have fought this if we didn't know it was coming."

"We're going to fight this?" That possibility hadn't occurred to me. I mean, someone had *already* fought that battle for me once, and won. I'd been saved, at the expense of my mother's life. As badly as I wanted to live, it hardly seemed fair for me to cheat death again. No one else I knew had even had *one* second chance, much less two.

Then there was the other problem. The big one: extending my lifeline—again—would mean killing someone else instead. Again. And I couldn't live with that.

"Of course we're going to fight it!" my dad insisted. "There are ways around death, at least temporarily. We know that better than anyone. We've done it, once."

"That's the problem," Tod said softly, his grin notably absent. "One of them, anyway."

My father scowled at the reaper. "What does that mean?"

"The rules are very clear about second extensions." He hesitated, and I heard what he was going to say next before he even formed the words. "There are none."

For a long moment, there was only silence, and the deep, cold terror that settled into my chest was like hands of ice massaging my heart. In spite of my determination not to let anyone else pay for my continued existence, the death of that possibility echoed into eternity, like no fear I'd ever felt.

"There have to be exceptions," my father insisted, as usual, the first to recover his voice after severe systemic shock. "There are always exceptions."

Tod shook his head slowly, and a single unruly blond curl fell over his forehead. "Not for this. I already asked around, and…well, it just doesn't happen. It can't."

"But you're a reaper!" My dad stood, his voice thundering throughout the room. I felt like I should do something. Make him stop yelling, or at least try to calm him down. "What good are you if you can't even help out a friend?"

"Dad…" I protested, uncomfortably aware that he'd never referred to Tod as a friend before. But I guess that's what they say about desperate times…

"Kaylee, this is your life we're talking about," my father said, and a chill raced through me when I realized his hands were shaking. "We're not going to let this happen. We'll do whatever it takes. *I'll* do whatever it takes."

And suddenly I understood what he was saying. He'd tried to give me his lifeline before, and he'd do it again without a second thought.

"No, Dad..." I whispered, fear and shock rendering my voice a pathetic whisper.

My father ignored me and turned to look at Tod. "But I can't do it without help." The blues in my dad's eyes churned with desperation, the strongest emotion I'd ever seen displayed there, and I was only seeing it now because he couldn't hide it. He'd lost control, and that scared me more than anything. "Please, Tod." My dad sank onto the opposite end of the couch, elbows on his knees, scrubbing his face with both hands. "I'm begging you. I'll do whatever you want. Please make an exception for my daughter."

Tod looked almost as stunned as I felt. I'd never heard my father beg for anything, not even for his own life, when Avari dragged him into the Netherworld, using him to get to me.

"Mr. Cavanaugh, I'd do it in a heartbeat." Tod looked so earnest and frustrated that *I* wanted to comfort *him*. Especially when he turned those sad blue eyes on me, silently begging me to believe him. "Kaylee, I'd do it if I could. You know that. But it's not up to me. I'm not your reaper."

For one surreal moment, I wasn't sure whether to be relieved or upset about that.

"They don't let rookies reap under special circumstances. They'll call in an expert. I don't even know what zone you're actually supposed to be in when...when it happens," he finished miserably.

I sucked in a deep breath, trying to process everything I'd

just heard. Trying to push past the tangle of frighteningly use-less words and grasp something I could actually use. "Who?" I said at last. "Who will they bring in? Libby?"

Libitina was the dark reaper—one of the oldest in existence—who'd come to execute Addison's death and dis-pose of the Demon's Breath that had kept her alive in place of the soul she'd sold. Libby had done what she could to help us return Addy's soul, but in the end, she'd also done her job. She'd taken Addison's life and damned her disembodied soul to eternal torture.

I wouldn't find leeway with Libitina.

"I don't know," Tod said. "If the reaper's been chosen, I haven't heard about it."

But at least I wouldn't have to worry about Tod killing me, which seemed like an odd thing to be grateful for.

"How?" I set the sweating soda can on the end table and clasped my hands in my lap to keep them from shaking. "Do you know how it'll happen?" I asked, not sure that I really wanted to know. Knowing too much could make me para-noid—would I walk around staring up to avoid anvils falling from the sky?

But Tod shook his head. "We never know that, because the method isn't predetermined. Sometimes there's an obvious choice. Like, if it's an old man with a weak heart, the reaper will just let his heart stop beating. But with young people, it's usually an accident, or an overdose, if there's no preexisting illness. We work with what we have. It's easier for the family and the coroner if they have something to blame it on."

"Wow. You make death sound so courteous."

Tod exhaled slowly. "We both know it's not."

Yeah. I knew.

"So…" I stared at the floor between my feet, and I couldn't stop my leg from jumping as I worked my way up to the question I'd been avoiding. "Do you know when? Does the list at least tell you how long I have?"

I was avoiding my father's gaze—my own fear was hard enough to swallow at the moment—but I could see in my peripheral vision that he was watching Tod closely, waiting for the answer just as nervously as I was.

Tod cleared his throat, avoiding the question.

"Tod...?" My father's voice was barely a whisper.

"Next Thursday," the reaper said finally, looking right into my eyes. His irises roiled with a sudden maelstrom of pain and distress, and I was pretty sure he was watching the same storm rage in mine. "You're going to die in six days."

3

I stood so fast the room spun around me, and it felt like my head was going to explode.

Is this how I go? A stroke in my own living room, when the stress of knowing I'm going to die becomes too much? Could knowing I was going to die actually bring about my death? And if so, did that make it Levi's fault? Or Tod's? Or my dad's, for letting him tell me?

But the truth was that it was no one's fault. I'd overstayed my welcome, and death had finally caught up to me. There was no more natural, more necessary part of life than this end to the whole thing. Yet I was overwhelmed by the need to stomp my feet and pound my fists and shout *it's not fair!* at the top of my fearsome *bean sidhe* lungs.

"Kaylee...?" Tod repeated, when I didn't answer my dad.

Six days...

I headed down the hall and into my room, where I pulled my shirt over my head without remembering to close the door. They both followed, and when my dad realized I was changing, he stepped out of the doorway and shoved a very corporeal Tod farther down the hall.

"Kaylee, say something," he called, but I couldn't. I barely even registered his voice. All I could hear was the raucous clamor of panic in my own head, insisting I do something—anything—to take my rapidly fracturing mind off the fact that I had less than a week to live.

No senior year.

I unbuttoned my uniform pants and let them pool around my ankles, then stepped into the pair of jeans draped over my bed.

No graduation.

I pulled open the second drawer of my dresser and pawed through the contents for my favorite blue ribbed T-shirt.

No college.

I pulled the shirt on and tugged my hair from the collar, then stepped into a pair of sneakers.

No career. No family. No anything, beyond whatever catastrophe next Thursday had waiting for me.

"Kaylee, where are you going?" my father demanded as I stomped past him and Tod on my way to the front door.

"Out." I turned to face them as I scooped my keys from the candy dish, and the panic clear in my father's expression could have been a reflection of my own. "I'm sorry. I have to… I can't think about this right now, or I'm going to lose my mind. And I don't want to spend my last week on earth in a straitjacket. I'll be back…later. Could you feed Styx for me, please?"

Without waiting for an answer, I opened the front door and jogged out to my car. A moment later, I glanced up as I backed down the driveway to find them both standing on the front porch, staring after me.

As it turns out, you can't outrun death. No matter how fast you drive, you can't even outrun *thoughts* of death, when you know it's coming for you. *Is this how Addy felt?* Like she couldn't breathe without choking on the knowledge that she'd soon be breathing her last?

I drove for nearly forty minutes, paying little attention to the direction, blasting music on the radio in an attempt to drown out my own thoughts. But none of it worked, and by the time I'd made my way back to familiar surroundings, I'd realized that the only way to get my mind off my own problems was to focus on someone else's.

When I glanced up, I realized the hospital was several blocks ahead, as if my subconscious had known where I was going the whole time.

I found front-row parking in the visitors' lot, which was nearly empty because visiting hours were over. The lady at the front desk gave me Danica Sussman's room number, but warned me that I wouldn't be able to see her this late. I thanked her and headed back toward the parking lot—then looped around to another entrance, where I took an elevator up to the third floor.

There was only one person at the third floor nurse's station, and it was easy to sneak past when she got up for coffee. Room 324 was around the corner and four doors down. I hesitated, loitering outside Danica's door for a couple of minutes, trying to dial up my courage and think of an opening line that wouldn't make me sound like a nosy gossip in search of tomorrow's high school headline. But when shoes squeaked from around the corner, I hurriedly pulled the door open and stepped inside.

After all, what was the worst that could happen? I'd babble like an idiot and get tossed out of her room? The embarrassment could only last six days, max, and after that, nothing would matter anyway.

The hospital room smelled sterile and felt cold, and it was lit only by a horizontal strip of light over the head of the bed.

Danica was asleep on her right side, facing me. She looked pale and small beneath the thin covers. Too young to have been a mother. Not that that mattered now.

I watched her sleep for several minutes, thinking about how very different our lives must be. She'd obviously done at least *one* thing I hadn't, and that had led to pregnancy—another experience I would never have—and to a loss I could never personally understand.

But Danica would live. If she wanted another baby, she'd have time for that, whenever she was ready.

I would not. I wouldn't have time for anything. No more firsts, and only one more last. My time was up.

What the hell am I doing here? I couldn't help Danica. It was none of my business who her baby's father was, even if he *was* a teacher, on the odd chance that Sabine was right. Even if that teacher wasn't human. I was just using Danica and her problems to distract myself from my own, and that wasn't fair for either of us.

Half ashamed of myself and half irrationally irritated, I had one hand on the door handle when the bed creaked behind me.

"You're not a nurse."

I turned slowly, suddenly nervous. I had no idea what to say to her. How to explain my presence. We weren't friends. I didn't have any similar personal experience or wisdom to share with her. I was just snooping. And now I'd been caught.

"Kaylee Cavanaugh?" Danica squinted into the shadows beyond her bed, and I nodded.

"Yeah. Hi."

"What are you doing here?"

"I was…visiting a friend. Then I remembered you were here, and thought you might like some company."

She didn't smile and wave me over. But she didn't yell for security, either. "Isn't it kinda late for visitors?"

I shrugged and came forward slowly, my hands in my pockets. "Yeah, but I can hang till I get caught, if you want."

Danica stared at the hands she was twisting together, and I knew she was going to tell me to get lost. But then she looked up, and there were tears standing in her eyes, and I realized that maybe her problems *were* as rough as mine. Maybe even rougher—after all, mine would soon be over. "That'd be cool. If you want."

I sat in the armchair by the window, and we avoided looking at each other, neither of us sure what to say. But finally Danica sighed and pressed the button to raise the back of her bed, then she leaned against the pillow and rolled her head to face me. "So, I guess everyone's talking about what happened?"

"Well, it's probably safe to say that the girls' quarter-final basketball loss is no longer big news."

Danica nodded slowly. "What are they saying?"

"The most extreme theory I've heard so far is that you're dying of colon cancer." Another shrug. "But most people think you had a miscarriage." Which I knew for sure.

Danica rubbed tears from her eyes with the heels of both hands. "Everything's so messed up...."

"Messed up seems to be my natural state of being. But if it makes you feel any better, Max has your back. He's telling everyone you couldn't be pregnant, 'cause you guys never..." I let my words trail off toward the obvious conclusion, and Danica's eyes overflowed again.

I felt bad about manipulating her. I really did. But I couldn't tell her I knew the rumors were true, because she'd ask how I knew. So I needed her to tell me herself.

"Yeah. Max doesn't have my back anymore," she sniffled.

"He came to see me after school, and I had to tell him the truth." Another sniffle, and this time she reached for a tissue from the rolling tray table.

"The truth?" I held my breath. She wouldn't tell me. I mean, *I* wouldn't tell me, if I were Danica. She didn't owe me any answers.

"I was pregnant. But it wasn't his."

I actually glanced around the room in surprise, looking for evidence of medical malpractice in the form of unregulated, judgment-impairing pain medication. But then I saw her watching me, looking for something in my expression, and I realized that she wasn't overmedicated. She just needed a friend.

"Wow." And suddenly I felt guilty for pumping her for information just to distract myself from my own encroaching expiration date, when all she wanted was a friendly ear. "So... how'd he take it?"

I can do this. It didn't have to be either-or, right? I could listen like a friend and still dig for answers like...um...an ill-fated amateur detective trying to solve one last case before she kicks the proverbial bucket. Right?

Danica wadded her tissue in one hand, then dropped it onto her lap. "At first he just looked at me, like he wasn't sure he'd heard me right. Then he got this awful heartbroken look, like I'd told him I murdered his puppy. Then he just turned around and walked right out the door without a word." She sighed and tossed the tissue toward the can, where it landed a foot and a half shy. "The only visitor I've had, until you, and he leaves hating me. But I guess I deserve that."

Her only visitor? "Your parents didn't come?"

"My mom's...sick. And my dad won't talk to me. The doctor told him what happened, and he left without even coming in to say hi. Because, you know, the shame is contagious."

For a moment, biting sarcasm eclipsed the obvious pain in her voice, and I found myself hating a father who wasn't mine. A man I'd never met. "And now I've lost Max, too. And I don't even know how this happened!"

"You don't...?" I started, brows raised, but Danica rolled her tear-reddened eyes.

"I mean, I *know* how it happened. I just can't figure out *why*. I remember...getting pregnant. But I can't remember what I was *thinking*. I don't *do* things like that. I love Max, and I can't remember why I was willing to throw him away for one stupid night...."

"It was just one night?" I said, stunned by the thought that a single mistake could throw her whole life into chaos.

Danica nodded miserably. "Less than that, really. It was just a couple of hours about a month ago. Afterward I tried to put it behind me and move on, but every time I see him, I want him all over again, even though I hate myself for what I did to Max. How horrible does that make me?" She covered her face with both hands. "Why can't I get him out of my head?"

I waited, hoping she'd let a name slip, but when her hands fell, she only stared at the wall across from her bed, shoulders slumped, eyes starting to lose focus. Maybe she was a little medicated after all.

"Did you know you were pregnant?" I whispered, wondering if I'd worn out my welcome. She looked like she wanted to go back to sleep for a long, long time.

Danica nodded slowly. "I found out last week. That was the only bright spot." She blinked, then faced me again. "I was going to keep it. I don't know how—my dad would rather kick me out than claim a bastard grandchild—but I would have found a way. Then this morning, I passed out in first period and woke up in the hospital, and bam, my whole life's ruined." She let the tears fall that time, and they rolled down her face to drip on the white blanket.

I leaned forward, hurting for her and desperate to help. But I was in over my head. I had no experience with peer counseling, and no matter what Sabine had to say about my inexperience and naivety, I wasn't exactly a shining example of the adolescent ideal. Just ask my dad.

"Your life isn't ruined, Danica," I insisted, scrambling for something to support that statement. "Max might get over this, if you tell him how much he means to you. And even if he doesn't, you have a whole lifetime to decide who you want to be with, and if you want kids later, you can…"

"No, I can't." Danica stared down at her fingers, shredding a second tissue all over the bedspread, and the flat, dead quality of her voice sent chills through me. "I can't have kids, Kaylee. Not anymore. Whatever went wrong with this one ruined it for the rest of them."

Ohh…

I leaned back in my chair, devastated for her and stunned beyond words.

"I know I wasn't ready," Danica began, and this time her voice was alive with bitter pain. "It was probably stupid of me to think I could handle it. But now I don't even have that option. What kind of screwed-up world is this, when the doctor can stand there and tell a seventeen-year-old that her insides are so messed up that she can't support life. Ever. And they can't even tell me why. That's the real bitch."

I nodded for lack of a better response, oddly relieved to find her anger outshining her grief. "They don't know what happened?"

She shook her head miserably. "They have more tests to run, but all they know now is that this morning I was pregnant, and now I'm not, and I lost a ton of blood in the process.

That doesn't usually happen in a first trimester miscarriage, according to the doc, but I needed a transfusion."

She got quiet then, with her head against the pillow, and I thought she was falling asleep.

Last chance, Kaylee...

"Danica, who was the father?" I whispered, leaning forward in my chair again.

"Doesn't matter," she whispered back, her eyes closed. "Not anymore." She fumbled for the controller and pressed a button to lower the head of the bed again. "I need to sleep now," she mumbled, clearly exhausted by the visit. "Thanks for coming..."

I stood and watched her doze for a second, then I was heading for the door when Danica groaned, and I glanced back at her.

"Maybe this would have happened later anyway," she mumbled, so low I could barely hear her. "Maybe I wasn't meant to have kids. But I wanted this one..."

"Visiting hours were over two hours ago," a sharp female voice barked as I closed Danica's door, and I spun around to find an elderly nurse—her name tag read Debbie Nolan, RN—in pale purple scrubs frowning at me.

Oops. Busted...

"Sorry. I didn't get off work in time to visit, and she's my cousin, so..." I was almost disturbed by how easily the lie flowed. When had I gotten so good at that?

"Oh..." Nurse Nolan's frown melted into a bruising look of sympathy. "I'm sorry. It's so sad, with her so young." She glanced behind her, like someone might be watching, then gestured for me to come closer as her voice dropped into a conspiratorial whisper. "Do you want to see your aunt, too, while you're here?"

"My...?"

My aunt was suffering an eternity of torture in the Netherworld at the hands of the hellion she'd sold her soul to. But Nurse Nolan meant Danica's mom. When Danica said her mother was sick, I'd assumed from the way she said it that "sick" was a euphemism for drunk, or stoned, or psychotic.

"Sure..." I said at last, hoping the nurse hadn't followed the progression of my thoughts across my expression. What kind of fake cousin would I be if I didn't visit my fake aunt while I was there?

"Room 348, at the end of the hall," she said, still whispering. "I'll give you ten minutes, if you promise not to tell...."

"Of course. Thank you." I'd hoped to sneak out when she went back to the nurse's station, but I never got the opportunity because she escorted me down the hall to a perfect stranger's hospital room, while my heart pumped panic-fueled fire through my veins.

How the hell am I going to explain this to my not-aunt? If Mrs. Sussman ratted me out, my dad was going to be pissed. Especially considering I hadn't yet told him about the gruesome miscarriage or my nonhuman math teacher, or Sabine's theory about a possible connection between the two. *I wonder if encroaching death is a plausible excuse for temporary insanity?*

I held my breath as Nolan opened the door, scrambling for some way to explain and excuse my intrusion. But if hearing about Danica's private pain and loss was heartbreaking, meeting her mother was downright creepy.

Mrs. Sussman—Amanda, according to the bracelet on her wrist—was sleeping. Deeply. So deeply that her chest barely moved with each breath.

"How long has she been like this?" I asked, and the nurse looked at me strangely, like I should already know the answer to that. "The days all run together...." I said, scrambling to fix my mistake.

"It's been almost four weeks now," the nurse said as we stood at the bedside, shaking her head over the tragedy. "Her daughter comes in on the weekends, and her ex-husband has even come a couple of times. But there's nothing any of us can do for her."

"What happened?" I asked, before I realized that a real niece would already know the answer to that. Fortunately, Nurse Nolan thought I was asking for medical specifics.

"The doctors aren't sure. And they've brought in several of them. She came in like this—your cousin found her, you know."

I nodded, like I'd really known.

"Brain-dead from the moment she arrived, but she keeps breathing, and as long as they keep feeding her—" Nolan ran one hand gently over the tube protruding from Mrs. Sussman's left arm "—she'll be here just like this."

"How awful..." At least my mother'd had a clean death. This was... I didn't even have words for what this was, though it had to come close to my own aunt's eternal torture. "Thanks, but I... I have to go." I backed away from the bed, suddenly grateful for the knowledge that I wouldn't have to linger like this. At least, not for more than six days.

In the hall I jogged for the elevator, running away from pain and anguish that put my own into startling perspective, and ran right into Tod. Literally.

"You okay?" he said, and I knew without asking that no one else could see or hear him, though he was fully corporeal for me.

"What are you doing here?" I whispered, tugging him toward the elevator, grateful that Nurse Nolan had evidently found something to do in Mrs. Sussman's room.

Tod dug for something in his pocket while I jabbed the call button. "Your dad asked me to find you. You forgot your phone." He handed me my cell, and when my fingers brushed his, there was a sudden swell of color in his eyes—not quite a swirl, but…something. "And that's not all you forgot…."

"Huh?" I stepped into the elevator, and he stepped in after me, grinning, the teasing light in his eyes comfortable for its familiarity when everything else around me now felt cold, and foreign, and sharp.

"You forgot your date."

Crap! I closed my eyes, cursing myself silently. I'd forgotten all about Nash.

4

"What were you doing at the hospital?" Tod asked, as I shifted into Reverse and backed out of my parking space.

"Trying to distract myself from the fact that next week, my address changes from a house number to a plot number." But that distraction had proved temporary, and without Danica's problems to occupy my mind, my own tumbled back in, clamoring for attention like a dog willing to howl until it's fed.

Tod chuckled, and oddly enough, coming from a reaper, laughter in the face of death didn't seem terribly inappropriate. "Yeah. Been there."

And suddenly, as I pulled out of the lot and onto the street, I realized Tod was the only person I knew who might possibly understand how I felt.

I glanced at his profile as I braked for the stop sign at the corner. "Did you know you were going to die before it actually happened?" My voice was barely a whisper—a trembling reflection of the quiet terror lurking at the back of my mind, leaping into the spotlight every time a failed distraction left me vulnerable.

"Only for about five minutes."

"Were you scared?" Because I felt like the pendulum on a grandfather clock, ticking toward my last seconds, dizzy from the motion, but unable to stop....

"Like I've never been, before or since."

I had a million other questions, but his answers wouldn't help me. They probably wouldn't even be relevant, because my death wouldn't mirror his, or anyone else's. I was on my own, in death. I knew that, if little else.

"Kaylee?" Tod said, as I turned the corner into my neighborhood.

"Yeah?" I was hardly listening now, lost in my own thoughts, and the effort not to think them.

"I'm scared *now.*"

Something in his voice made me look at him, in the fading glow from a passing streetlight. Then something in his eyes made me pull over, two streets from home, in front of a house I didn't recognize.

"Why are you scared?" I asked, and suddenly the night seemed so quiet, beyond the soft rumble of the engine.

"Because I can't fix this." He swallowed thickly, one hand braced on the dashboard. "There's nothing I can do, and that's hardly ever true for me, and I hate how helpless and useless it makes me feel. But at the same time, *that* makes me feel human, and I haven't felt human much lately, either."

"Because Addison's gone?"

He nodded slowly, like there was more to it than that, but he wasn't ready to elaborate. "I did everything I could for her, but sometimes everything you can do isn't enough, and you just have to...let go."

"I'm not ready to let go of life," I whispered.

"I'm not either—for you *or* for me. But knowing I have no power over death this time makes me feel terribly, wonderfully normal. And some deep part of me likes that. And that scares me."

I blinked, trying to make sense of the tangle of words that had just tumbled from his mouth. "You hate feeling useless, but you like that feeling useless makes you feel human?" I asked, fairly certain I'd missed something.

Tod thought about that for a second, then nodded. "Yeah. Does that make any sense?"

I could only shrug. "Right now, nothing makes much sense to me, so I may not be the best judge." I stared at my hands, tense around the wheel. "I don't expect you to fix this, Tod. It doesn't make any sense for you to put your job—" and thus his afterlife "—in danger, when I'm going to die no matter what you do."

"Kaylee..." he said, but I interrupted, determined to have my say.

"I heard what you said earlier. And I totally respect the 'no second exchanges' policy." Even if it killed the only ray of hope trying to shine on what remained of my life so far. "But my dad doesn't. I need you to promise me that you won't let him trade. Because he's going to try. And if you let him, I swear I'll haunt your afterlife for all of mine."

"It's not going to be an issue," Tod assured me. "He'll never even see your reaper. No dark reaper worth his job would ever appear to a grieving relative."

"Good." At least I could stop worrying about that part of it.

I shifted into Drive again, and Tod's hand landed on mine, still on the gearshift. "Kaylee," he said, and I turned to meet his gaze. "If there was anything I could do, I would do it."

"I know." And in that moment, that was about all I knew.

Styx lifted her head from Nash's lap when I opened the front door. *Some guard dog.* But then, she was supposed to guard me from hellion possession, not boyfriends I'd forgotten about. He stood, and Styx hopped down from the couch and trotted toward me, half Pomeranian, half Netherworld… something or other. And all mine. We'd bonded while she was an infant—she wasn't much more than that now—and she would obey no one else's orders until the day I died.

Which had seemed like a much better deal, a couple of hours earlier.

"Hey," I said, and Nash folded me into a hug so tight, so desperate that I couldn't breathe.

"Are you okay?" He finally let me go, but only to stare into my eyes, looking for more than he should have been able to see there.

"They told you?" I bent to pick up Styx, petting her frizzy fur out of habit.

"I thought you'd want us to," my dad said, and I looked up to find him in the kitchen doorway, cradling a steaming mug of coffee, in spite of the late hour.

Did I? Did I want Nash to know? There was nothing he could do, and I couldn't imagine keeping a secret that big from him. But now he was looking at me like I would break if he so much as breathed on me. Like I was fragile and must be protected.

"Yeah. Thanks," I said, to keep from hurting my dad's feelings.

The front door closed at my back, and I turned to thank Tod for bringing my phone—but he was gone.

"You hungry?" my dad asked, and I could only stare at him for a moment, until I understood what he was doing. He was taking care of me, the only way he knew how. He couldn't save my life—not this time—but he could solve my hunger.

"No. Thanks, though." I set Styx down, and she hopped

onto my dad's chair and stared out at the room, on alert from this new height.

"No popcorn for the movie?"

"I'm not really in the mood for a movie anymore." A sappy tearjerker just wasn't a good way to follow the news that you're going to die. "I think we're just going to hang out in my room." I tugged Nash toward the hall and he came willingly, but looked like he couldn't decide whether I'd just come to my senses or lost them completely.

"Leave the door open," my dad said, the second most common warning in his arsenal. Right behind, "Nash, go home."

I wanted to laugh at the absurdity of it. I had six days to live, and he was worried about an unsupervised visit with my boyfriend?

I dropped Nash's hand and crossed my arms over my chest, trying to figure out how best to say what needed to be said. "Dad, this is no slight against your parenting skills, which are seriously formidable. No worries there. But I've only got six days to live. I'm never going to turn eighteen. I'm never even going to turn *seventeen*. The only part of my adult life I'm going to get to experience is the part I can claim in the next week. So I'd kinda like to spend these next six days—my *last* six days—as an emancipated minor." Or at least an honorary adult.

"Kaylee…" His voice was deep with warning, yet a little unsteady.

"I'm not talking about moving out, Dad," I insisted, hoping to avoid a parental meltdown—I really didn't want his last memories of me to include a temper tantrum. "I'm just saying I don't want to spend my last week on earth following a bunch of rules that don't even really apply to me anymore. I mean, would you tell an eighty-year-old woman with terminal cancer to leave her door open?"

"You're not going to die, Kaylee." My dad was scowling now, his arms crossed to mirror my own.

I lifted both brows in challenge. "You know somethin' I don't?"

"I know I'm going to find a way around this, and we're going to laugh about it when you're a very old woman. And yes, if you're still living here when you're eighty, I will damn well tell you to leave the door open."

My chest ached fiercely and I had to swallow to speak past the lump in my throat. "I tell you what—if I'm still alive on Friday morning, you can consider me happily un-emancipated."

My dad's frown deepened and his irises churned slowly in a rare display of fear and frustration, but he didn't object when I tugged Nash down the hall and into my room. Where I closed the door behind us. Then had to open it again to let Styx in.

Nash sank into my desk chair looking up at me, and though his irises held steady—obviously a struggle—his eyes were… shiny. "Why'd you let your dad tell me? Why didn't you tell me yourself?"

I blinked, surprised by the amount of pain in his voice. "He beat me to it. I would have told you." But I'd needed some time to process the information myself before I had to consider anyone else's reaction.

"This is messed up, Kaylee." He pulled me closer and wrapped his arms around my waist, clutching the back of my shirt, his face pressed into my stomach. "Scott, and Doug, and now you… Why is everyone leaving me? What the hell am I going to do without you?"

He was going to lean on his mom, and Tod. And Sabine. The three of them would do anything to protect Nash, and they'd be there for him when I couldn't be. I was much more worried about my father.…

"Don't think about that right now," I said, talking to my-self as much as to Nash. I stepped back so that he had to look up at me. "Think about all the privacy I just bought us. Too bad I waited until the week I'm gonna die to join the teenage resistance, huh?"

"That's not funny." Nash frowned as I sat on the edge of the bed.

"I wasn't joking."

"Your dad thinks he can stop it."

"Yeah, well, Tod says he can't." I leaned back on the bed and let my legs dangle over the side while I studied my ceiling. How had I never noticed that crack, directly over my pillow? How often had I stared at that very spot and never noticed it?

Nash swiveled toward me and the chair creaked. "And you believe him over your dad?"

"Do I believe the reaper with insider's knowledge on how death works over the desperate *bean sidhe*? Yeah. I do."

"Why are you acting like this?" he demanded, walking the rolling chair forward until his knees hit the mattress.

I rolled onto my side to watch him. "My expiration date didn't come with instructions. What am I supposed to be act-ing like?"

Nash sighed and leaned forward with his elbows on his knees. "I just don't understand how you can take this so lightly."

"What do you want me to do, slap on some black eye shadow and host my own wake? I'm gonna die, Nash. There's nothing anyone can do to stop that. But I've got six days left, and I don't want to spend them thinking about how it's all gonna end."

I sat up on the bed and studied him, trying to see him like I had six months earlier, when we'd first started going out. Be-fore he'd betrayed me to feed an addiction to Demon's Breath that was my fault in the first place. I'd spent the past month and a half learning to trust him again—letting him convince me that was possible—but now I was out of time. As with everything really good in life, I'd have to either jump in head-first, or not at all.

"What?" Nash said when I just stared at him, thinking. Wondering if I could really go through with the idea taking root in my brain. Or maybe someplace a little lower. "You better not be thinking something stupid, like breaking up with me now will make next Thursday easier for me."

"Nash, if I thought there was any way to make my death easier for you, we wouldn't be together in the first place. I just... I don't want to dwell on all the things I'm not gonna get to do." I took a deep breath and ignored my racing pulse. I couldn't choose when or how my life ended, but I could choose how I spent what time I had left.

I can do this.

I took his hand and pulled him out of the chair. I didn't have to pull very hard—it was more an issue of guiding him where I wanted him. Onto the bed. With me. "I wanna do some of them, before it's too late."

I scooted backward and he crawled over my legs and up my torso as I lay back on the pillows, and my heart beat so hard I could hear it echo in my ears.

"This is why you closed the door?" he whispered, dropping a series of tiny kisses at the back of my jaw.

"It wasn't premeditated...." I breathed, running my hands over the front of his shirt, feeling the planes beneath. Was his heart beating as hard as mine? Was that even possible?

"Coulda fooled me."

"Shut up." I slid one hand behind his neck and pulled him down until his mouth met mine. His lips were warm and soft, and the taste of him brought back nothing but good memories—the only advantage to having been possessed by a hellion is that you don't actually remember what happened while you were away from your body. Which made it just a *little* easier for me to push aside the knowledge that he'd been less than trustworthy in the past and just *decide* to trust Nash now.

I'd been unable to do that completely so far, but knowing I was going to die soon—knowing I was about to lose my chance—made me bold. Not quite fearless, like Sabine, but definitely brave. And more than a little eager.

My mouth opened beneath his, and Nash kissed me deeper. His weight settled onto me, heavy and warm, and very, very real. A nervous tingling started in the pit of my stomach and spread like pins and needles everywhere Nash touched me. I'd never felt more alive, and the irony in that thought did not escape me.

This is going to happen. I was ready, mostly because there was no more time to not be ready—not unless I wanted to die a virgin. And of all the things I still wanted to do before I died, this was the only one within reach.

Nash's mouth trailed down my throat, and I closed my eyes, concentrating on the electric feel of his hands, the scalding heat from his lips. Letting it all overwhelm the sharp edge of fear holding steady like the eye of the storm raging around me. I had a lot of things to be scared of—*real* things—but this wasn't one of them. And slowly, I let my hands trail down from his chest to the waist of his jeans.

I gave the top flap of denim one sharp tug, and the button slid through the hole.

"Whoa...!" Nash rolled onto his side, staring down at me in confusion. "What are you doing?"

"I think you're pretty familiar with the concept...."

His gaze searched mine. "Is this a test? Should I ask what color your first bike was?"

I laughed. Six weeks earlier, I'd used that question as a sort of password, to make sure I wasn't talking to a hellion who'd hijacked my friend Alec's body. "I'm not possessed." I looked up at him from the pillow, letting him see the truth on my face. "I'm just ready."

"You weren't ready last week." Nash sat up, frowning down at me from the edge of my bed now. "And the only thing that's changed is…"

"The only thing that's changed is that now I'm dying. I'm out of time, Nash, and I want to do this. Now." Before I got nervous, or scared, or started to feel really, really embarrassed by the fact that *I* was having to convince *him*.

"Your dad's in the other room."

"So let's go to your house."

He shook his head slowly. "My mom's home."

I shrugged. "Fine. Let's go the lake."

"Kaylee…" Nash scrubbed his face with both hands, then looked at me with the most conflicted regret I'd ever seen. "You know I want to, but…"

I sat up, and I could feel my cheeks flaming. Was he turning me down? After all the times he'd hinted, and asked, and outright pushed? "But what?" I demanded, and I could hear the bite in my own voice.

"Not like this. You don't really want this. You're just trying to avoid thinking about next Thursday. Or maybe you're trying to cross things off some kind of morbid checklist. Either way, this isn't really what you want, and—"

"Don't tell me what I want!" I snapped, but he only put his hand over mine and leaned closer, so that I had to see the depth of the regret swirling in his eyes.

"—*and* I swore to you once that I knew you well enough

to know when you want to stop, even if you can't tell me. Don't make a liar out of me, Kaylee. Not again."

He was right. Damn it.

"Okay, I get it. But things have changed." I sucked in a deep breath and looked right into his eyes, begging him silently to understand. "Everything's changed, Nash. I do want you. And you want me. You've wanted this for months, and now we've only got six days to make it happen before we both lose our chance."

He closed his eyes, and I realized that was to prevent me from seeing whatever he couldn't stop them from showing. When he finally opened his eyes, they shined with good humor, and only the lines in his forehead told me it was forced. "How did this turn into you begging me for sex?" He grinned, and I laughed out loud.

"You're not gonna let me live it down, are you?"

Nash's smile faltered. "No more life and death jokes, Kaylee. This is hard enough as it is."

"They say humor is the best defense."

"No, they say the best defense is a good offense. But you can't take the offensive with death. Though he's awfully easy to piss off sometimes…" Meaning Tod, of course. Though, honestly, Nash usually meant to piss him off.

"Whatever. Where do we stand on the subject of my dying wish?" I leaned back against the pillows again, hoping to tempt him.

"I'm your dying wish?" He lay down next to me, and I lifted my head so he could put his arm behind it.

"Well…not quite. My dying wish is not to die. But you're a close second. So where do we stand?"

He ran one hand down my arm and my pulse spiked when his fingers splayed across my stomach. "We stand…"

My desk chair creaked, and I looked up to find Tod sit-

ting in it backward, facing away from us—the most courteous entrance he'd ever given us as a couple. And while most
of me was frustrated by the disruption, some tiny part of me
was also a little relieved—and confused by the discrepancy in
my own emotions.

"Hope I'm interrupting something." The reaper swiveled
to face us and Nash sat up, cheeks already flaming.

"Get. Out," Nash growled.

Tod rolled his eyes. "I made Kaylee a promise. As usual,
I'm just the messenger."

"What's up, Tod?" I laid one hand on Nash's arm before
he could say anything else.

"Mom's in the kitchen with your dad, trying to talk him
out of doing something stupid. It sounds like she could use
your help."

5

"There's always an exception, Harmony," my father said, and the raw pain in his voice stole my breath with an almost physical force. I was scared, and pissed off, and riding an unforeseen wave of sexual resolve in the face of certain death. But my father was in serious pain over a loss he refused to accept as inevitable.

The fact that *I* was that loss was almost too much for me to wrap my mind around.

I inched down the hall silently, aching to see my father's face, but if they knew I was there, they'd stop talking, and I'd lose this glimpse into his true emotional state.

"Aiden." Harmony's whisper was so soft I almost didn't recognize it. "I am so, so sorry. I wish I could say I know how you feel, but I didn't have any warning with Tod."

"There's nothing to be sorry about," my dad answered, his voice hard now, like he could hold off the unavoidable with nothing but sheer will. "There's a way out of this, and I'm going to find it."

I peeked through the living room and into the kitchen just as Harmony scooted her chair closer to my father's. They sat at the table with their backs to me, and I could only see them from the shoulders up, over the half wall separating the two rooms.

"Aiden, there's nothing you can do." She slid one arm around his waist and leaned her head on his shoulder, and I held my breath to make sure I could hear the rest. "Do you really want to miss your daughter's last few days of life to chase answers that just aren't there?"

"I don't want to miss anything. And I don't want her to miss anything, either—that's the whole point. I've been such a fool, Harmony. I wasted thirteen years of her life letting my brother raise her because it hurt to look at her. Every time I saw her, I saw her mother. I only got Kaylee back six months ago, and now she's being taken away. Six months isn't long enough!"

"No one's taking her away," Harmony insisted gently. "Her time's up. It happens to everyone."

"What would you do?" my dad demanded, pulling away from her. "If you knew Nash was about to die, would you ever quit looking for a way to stop it? Would you give up on him?"

"I…"

"It doesn't matter what she would do." I stepped around the wall, and Tod appeared at my side. Nash's footsteps squeaked on the hall tile behind me, even though I'd asked them both to stay in my room.

Harmony and my dad stood facing us, but they were both too good at hiding their feelings for me to read anything more than general angst. They were better at that than I would ever be, considering how little time I had left to perfect the art.

"Dad, don't do this," I begged, frozen where I stood. "You can't change this, and if you try, you'll only be putting yourself at risk. Do you really want me to spend my last six days worrying that we're *both* going to die on Thursday?"

"I don't want you to worry about anything." He ran one hand through hair that showed no sign of graying, less than a month before his one hundred thirty-fourth birthday. "I want you to finish high school, and break curfew, and keep giving me excuses to toss the Hudson boys out of the house, not necessarily in that order. I want you to have a normal life. A long one."

I bit my lip, trying to hold back tears as he crossed the room toward me. "Well, that's not going to happen. And I'm not going to be able to enjoy what life I have left if I'm worried about you getting yourself killed trying to do the impossible."

"Kaylee…" He reached for me, but I stepped back and crossed my arms over my chest.

"Promise me, Dad. Promise you'll leave this alone."

"You know I can't—"

"Promise," I insisted, and his stoic expression crumpled beneath a burden of pain and responsibility I couldn't imagine.

"Fine. I promise," he said at last, and I let him fold me into a hug.

And as he squeezed me, his heart beating against my ear, I knew only two things for sure: I was going to die, and my father was lying.

I stood on the front porch and knocked again—there was no doorbell—then stared down the rough gravel road at a series of run-down houses and old cars, their age and ruthless depreciation exposed by harsh March sunlight. My own neighborhood was dated—the houses were small with one-car garages and tiny yards. But compared to living in this part of town, I had nothing to complain about.

Finally, the door opened and Sabine raised one dark brow at me, her hand still on the knob. "You look like shit."

"I wish I could say the same." And I really meant it. I'd

barely gotten any rest the night before—frankly, wasting what little time I had left sleeping felt almost criminal—and I was paying the price with pale skin, dark circles and a generally exhausted appearance. Sabine, on the other hand, only required four hours of sleep a night, yet she constantly walked the fine line between unconventionally hot and darkly captivating. A fact which fascinated and irritated me to no end.

"Any chance you're here to admit defeat and hand over your boyfriend, like the good little *bean sidhe* we both know you are?"

My temper flared, but I held it in check, because of what I had to say next. "Actually, I need a favor."

Sabine turned around and stalked into the darkened house, and I decided the open door was as much of an invitation as I was going to get.

"Is your foster mom home?" I followed her into a living room barely furnished with threadbare furniture smelling vaguely of old sweat.

"Rarely. She stays with her boyfriend most nights. Always comes back to collect the reimbursement check, though."

"So you're all alone?"

Sabine propped her hands on hips half-exposed by the low waist of her jeans and the short hem of a thin black tank top. "I'm a nightmare, Kaylee. Anyone who breaks in here would leave screaming. Or not at all." She sat on the arm of an old brown-and-yellow striped couch. "Besides, I didn't come here for parental supervision—I came for an address in the Eastlake school zone." The *mara* had scared and manipulated her way into this foster home just to be near Nash. And evidently to drive me insane. "Now, if you would just step down and relinquish the prize...."

"Nash isn't—" but before I could finish insisting that my boyfriend wasn't a prize to be won, a fierce, low rumbling

rolled over the room, raising hair all over my body. I turned
to find Sabine's dog—Styx's littermate—growling at me from
the kitchen doorway, his tiny body tensed and ready to attack.
Nothing that small and fluffy should have been able to make
such a threatening sound, but thanks to their Nether-hound
father, the entire litter sported teeth that could easily shred
flesh and jaws that could snap most human long bones.

"What's his name again?" I asked, careful not to make any
threatening moves until Sabine had called the little monster
off.

"Cujo."

Of course it was Cujo. "Any clue why Cujo looks like he
wants to chew my face off?"

"Probably because he wants to chew your face off."

"Funny. Could you call him off?"

Her satisfied grin grated my nerves like nails on a chalk-
board. "Only because I'm curious. Why the hell should I do
you a favor, when you consistently deny me the one thing I
want?" She snapped her fingers and Cujo followed her into a
tiny galley-style kitchen, where she pulled a package of raw
hamburger from the fridge and dropped it on the floor without even pulling back the plastic. Cujo dug in like he'd never
seen meat before, though he looked pretty well fed to me.

I stood at one end of the kitchen, trying to decide if I
should sit at the table or wait to be invited. Which probably
wasn't gonna happen. "Because..." I hesitated, trying to make
up my mind while she dug a can of generic soda from the
snot-green fridge. Then I sucked in a deep breath and spit it
out. "Because I'm going to be dead in five days, and whether
I like it or not, you're the one Nash is going to turn to when
he's half out of his mind with grief. Which means I'm practically doing *you* a favor." If my death would benefit anyone, it

would be Sabine. "That means you owe me. And considering the timetable I'm on, I'm gonna need payment up front."

Sabine popped the tab on her can and stared at me. "You're dying? For real?"

"Not till Thursday." At first, the thought had made me sick to my stomach every single time it crossed my conscious mind. But after contemplating my own untimely demise roughly four thousand times, the original terror and denial had given way to a hollow, distant acceptance. Thinking about my own death now had about the same effect on me as thinking about the eventual incineration of planet Earth, as it's consumed by its own sun.

"You're lying." Sabine laughed like her life was a joke and I was the punch line. Then she drained half her can and brushed past me into the living room.

I followed her and perched on the edge of the ugliest, most ancient brown recliner I'd ever seen. "Why would I lie?"

She shrugged and set her can on the milk crate serving as an end table. "Habit? You're not exactly a pillar of truth."

I wanted to argue, but I couldn't without proving her point. But to my credit, my lies were really more half truths, and they were always intended to help someone. Whereas Sabine's compulsive truths were usually intended to hurt someone else or to entertain her.

"I'm not lying." Another deep breath, and I nearly gagged on the acrid stench of stale cigarette smoke. Which I then spat out, along with an offer I *really* didn't want to make. "Read me."

Sabine sat up straight, her black eyes suddenly bright with interest. "Seriously?"

No. I shuddered, then swallowed my own bitter fear. "If that's what it takes for you to believe me."

She shrugged. "The offer itself was enough to make me

believe you. But you can't take it back now." She crossed the small room in an instant, and my jaw clenched involuntarily when she dropped onto her knees in front of me. "You know I have to touch you, right? The stronger the contact, the better the reading."

"Great." I held out my hand and she wound her fingers around mine, like I'd once seen her do with Nash when neither of them knew I was watching. Their contact had looked intimate. Comfortable. I wondered if ours would look the same from the outside.

I started to close my eyes, but Sabine shook her head and leaned closer for a better look. Her hand was warm and dry, her grip firm. And as I watched, her pupils bled into the near-black of her irises, and the whole room seemed to dim around us.

A cold wave of fear swam over me, consuming me. It was uncomfortable, like being the center of attention in a room full of hellions.

Then that fear came into focus, and suddenly my own death was the only thing I could think about. Would it hurt? Would there be blood? Would anyone else have to see me die? Would I see them cry?

Would I die alone?

The lack of answers scared me almost worse than the questions themselves. But it was over in a second, and when Sabine let go of my hand, I realized she could have held on much longer.

"Holy shit, you're gonna die." She looked stunned. "You're really going to die, and you're terrified of death."

"Is there a more rational reaction?"

The *mara* frowned, and her eyes darkened again. "Also, you're planning to sleep with Nash before you go, and you're scared you won't be any good."

Damn it. I could feel my cheeks burn. "Let's just keep that bit between us, okay?"

Her dark brows rose. "Is that the favor?"

I scowled. "No."

"No promises, then. And just FYI, you *won't* be any good. Not the first time, anyway." I started to stand, my cheeks flaming now. Why couldn't she help me, just this once, without throwing my own fears into my face? But Sabine put one hand on my arm and pulled me back onto the chair before I could stomp off. "You won't be any good, but he won't care, Kaylee. Because he's a guy, so any sex is good sex. And because he loves you," she added, lips curled like the words were bitter on her tongue.

I blinked away unshed, angry tears, but couldn't bring myself to thank her for softening the blow. Why was she antagonizing a dying woman anyway?

"You know I can't let this happen, right? You can't sleep with him, Kaylee. You have to break up with him."

I rolled my eyes. "Okay, if I haven't handed him over to you yet, why the hell would I do it now?"

She blinked at me, like the answer should have been obvious. "Because he loves you, and you're dying. If you don't dump him now—make a clean break—you're always going to be the tragic lost love. How the hell am I supposed to compete with a ghost?"

"I don't care how you compete!" But didn't I, at least a little? As weird as it was to think about the two of them together, I wanted Nash to be happy after I died. I wanted him to be able to move on. But I couldn't hurt him to make that happen.

"Fine. Then think about him. He won't see it now, but you'd be doing him a favor. Helping him move on."

"It's not going to happen, Sabine."

"Is this about sex? No one should die a virgin—I agree with you there. But you don't need Nash for that. I could make a phone call. Of course, you'd have to break up with Nash for this to work..."

My head spun, and I didn't know what to yell at her for first. So I decided to ignore the whole thing and focus on the favor I needed.

"Sabine. As much fun as these little forays into my personal life always are—" fun, like public incontinence "—I really need a favor."

"Beyond me facilitating the timely loss of your virginity? 'Cause I think that's a pretty generous offer."

"Yeah. You're a walking charity. But I need you to find out what Mr. Beck is. And obviously I don't have a lot of time."

Sabine watched me while she took a long drink from her can, pointedly not offering me one. "Why?"

"Because I went to see Danica Sussman in the hospital, and she admitted that the baby wasn't Max's. And the nurse said the miscarriage nearly killed her, which is evidently pretty rare."

"Well, aren't you the little sleuth?" Sabine raised both brows, reluctantly impressed. "I'd start calling you Veronica Mars, if you weren't quite so mousy." She grinned when I ground my teeth together, determined to bite my tongue until she agreed to help me.

"So I was thinking maybe you were right. Maybe Mr. Beck is the father. I mean, if he's not human, the baby wouldn't have been fully human either, right? And that could explain why her miscarriage was so...awful. Right?"

"I guess." Sabine set her can on another milk crate and crossed her arms over her chest. "But I hope you're not basing this on what I said at lunch. That was just a theory. I have lots of time to think those up while people are cowering away from me in the halls and avoiding my eyes in class." Because unless she was careful to keep it in check, creepy vibes emanated from Sabine like BO from an unwashed jock. "Wanna hear this theory I have about Tod? I think you're gonna like it...."

"No." I shook my head sharply and held her eye contact, determined to get through my request with the bare minimum of Sabine's nosy, spiteful tangents. "I don't want to hear any more of your theories. I just want you to follow up on this one, as a favor to a dying classmate. Please."

Sabine watched me in open curiosity. "Why do you care? I mean, you're going to be dead in a few days. Do you really want to spend your last few days tracking down whoever Danica Sussman cheated on her boyfriend with? Don't you think it's possible you're grasping at a problem that doesn't really exist to distract yourself from a reality you're not ready to face?" Sabine stopped and grinned, obviously pleased with herself. "Damn, that was perceptive of me. And I didn't even get that from reading your fear!"

I sighed. "I fully admit that's what I'm doing. Don't you think you'd want a distraction if you found out you were going to die before the end of the week?"

"Hell yeah. But I'd find it in Nash's bed, not in Danica's possibly skeleton-bearing closet."

Sabine's eyes widened. "You already tried, didn't you?" When I didn't answer, her smile grew. "Nash turned you down? Wow. That's unexpected. And *really* satisfying..."

"He didn't turn me down. We were interrupted," I insisted, but as usual, she refused to rise above her own moment of triumph in the rivalry she'd decided we were in.

"And he didn't want to pick up where you left off? Try not to read too much into that. It isn't necessarily because you don't know what you're doing..."

My temper flared, and my jaw ached from being clenched. "Okay, look." I leaned forward in the chair, capturing her gaze in spite of the discomfort of looking directly into the *mara's* eyes. "I get that you want Nash. And as much as it kills me to admit this, you're going to get a shot at him in a few days. I can make that easier for you. Or I can make it very, very hard."

Sabine's eyes narrowed and darkened, and suddenly the room felt colder. "Are you threatening me?"

I shrugged. "Yeah. Kinda."

Her brows rose. "I should be pissed off, but this is actually kind of funny."

"I'm serious. If you don't leave me and Nash alone for five more days, I will make it clear that I can't possibly rest in peace knowing the two of you are together, and you really will be competing with a ghost. How's that for a threat?"

She nodded solemnly. "Not bad, for a first attempt. So what do I get if I do let you…have him?"

"A truce. I agree not to stand in the way of your relationship with Nash once I'm gone, and you agree not to stand in the way of our relationship until then."

"But I want him now."

I shrugged. "And I want to live. Looks like the universe mixed up our wish lists. So what do you say? Truce now, and my blessing for the two of you, once I'm gone?" I'd thought saying that would make me want to rip my own hair out, but it was actually a bit of a relief. Because the truth was that after I was gone, Nash would need her. Resisting addiction wouldn't be easy for him, coupled with grief, and she could help keep him straight.

Sabine blinked, and I could practically see the gears turning behind her dark, dark eyes. She knew what I was offering— Nash would let himself be happy with her if he didn't think

I'd object. "Fine," she said finally. "But I think I'm getting the better end of this deal."

The scary part was that I believed her. "Whatever. For now, I really need you to find out about Mr. Beck."

Sabine's gaze narrowed on me in sudden suspicion. "Are you sure you don't have a more personal interest in this? I know you're trying to lose the big V before you meet the big D, and since Nash isn't sounding incredibly interested, you may be looking into some other options. And I have to respect your taste. Beck would be one yummy hunk of flesh, even if he didn't have a fear in the world. But why don't you try looking a little closer to home—"

"Ew, Sabine, I don't want to sleep with Mr. Beck!" I couldn't stop the shudder of revulsion crawling up my spine at the thought that he might be connected to what happened to Danica. "And Nash *is* interested."

"But you haven't done it yet...?"

"That's none of your business." I started backing toward the front door.

Sabine shrugged, and I wanted to smack the smug look off her face. "He'll tell me all about it once you're gone, and I can wait a few more days for that."

"Do you even *have* a heart in there?" I demanded, one hand on the front doorknob.

"Not anymore. I gave it to Nash before he even met you." She couldn't quite hide a flash of true pain, but for once, I was unaffected by someone else's suffering. Like she'd said, I'd be gone in a few days, and she could wait that long to pick over my corpse and claim what I'd left behind.

"Just find out what Mr. Beck is—without letting him know you're not human. Can you find some reason to touch him and read his fears a little more in depth?" Thanks to the braided bracelets we both wore—woven strands of *dissimu-*

latus, to keep hellions from identifying us from the Netherworld—he'd never know either of our species unless we gave ourselves away.

"If you think he's really screwing students, finding a reason to touch him will be the easy part." Sabine leaned back on the couch, making no move to show me out.

"Yeah. For you, I guess it will be."

Her brows rose again, in challenge. "You calling me a slut?"

"No." I sighed, trying to push aside thoughts I really didn't want to think. "I think you're fanatically loyal to Nash, at least in your heart." And when I was gone, that loyalty would probably be mutual.

"Sabine?" I said, and her focus narrowed on me, her attention as serious now as my tone of voice. "I know you'll be there for him when I'm gone." In more ways than I wanted to contemplate. "But don't even think about touching him until I'm cold and in the ground."

Sunday morning, I woke up alone. My dad had left a note on the fridge, telling me he'd be back for dinner. No explanation. But I knew what he was doing. He was looking for a way to save my life. I also knew that if he found one, he'd take it, no matter what it cost him, or anyone else.

What it cost me was obvious. Why did my father always seem to demonstrate his love for me through his own absence?

I ate a pint of Phish Food for breakfast—why worry about either calories or poor nutrition when I wouldn't be there to suffer from either one?—then got showered and dressed on autopilot. After half an hour of flipping through TV shows I had no interest in, I picked up my phone to call Emma—then remembered that she was working. But before I could slide my cell back into my pocket, it started playing Nash's dedicated ring tone.

I smiled and flipped the phone open.

"Hey," Nash said into my ear, his voice deep and gruff, like he'd just woken up. "You busy?"

"Got nothin' scheduled till sometime Thursday. Why? What'cha got in mind?"

Bedsprings groaned, and Nash's voice got louder. "Lady's

choice. Lunch? Movie? Hell, skydiving? You name it, and I'll do it."

I hesitated for one heart-thudding moment. "My dad's out. I could use some company...."

Silence, but for a single exhalation over the line. "Seriously?" he asked. But we both knew what I was really saying. "You sure you're ready?"

"Yeah." *No.* But I'd run out of time to get ready. "Bring protection." 'Cause I sure didn't have any.

"Give me half an hour."

I closed my phone and slid it into my pocket, suddenly so nervous I couldn't even breathe properly. Every breath seemed to come too early or too late, like I was alternately suffocating and hyperventilating.

Was that normal?

Feeling clueless and stupid, I squelched the urge to call Emma for advice—she wouldn't have her phone behind the counter at work anyway—then stood and stared around my living room like I'd never seen it before. I felt like I should do something to...prepare. But damned if I knew what.

To distract myself from the endless list of things I suddenly realized I didn't know about sex—not the science stuff, the real stuff; stuff I'd never really contemplated, but that now seemed vital—I made my bed. Then brushed my teeth. Then changed out of my boring cotton underwear for a pair of slightly less boring cotton underwear, silently cursing the embarrassment that had kept me from buying actual grown-up clothes when Emma had dragged me into Victoria's Secret a couple of months earlier.

When none of that helped, I glanced at the clock on the kitchen wall. T-minus nine minutes, and counting. It would take five just to boot up my laptop. So I sat on the couch and pulled out my phone. Then did the unthinkable.

I called Sabine.

The *mara* answered on the third ring. "School doesn't start for another twenty-one hours, Kaylee," she groaned. "I haven't had a chance to talk to Beck yet."

"I know. I, um…I need some advice." I closed my eyes and put one hand over them, silently cursing myself.

"From me?" She couldn't have sounded more surprised if she'd woken up bald and toothless.

"I wouldn't have called you if I had any other options, but Emma's at work, and my mom's dead, and Harmony's…well, she's Nash's mom, so that's out of the question. And that only leaves you."

Bedsprings creaked again—was I the only one who got up before lunch?—and her hand scratched the receiver as she covered it. I couldn't make out whatever she yelled at her foster mother, but it definitely wasn't…polite.

Then a door slammed and most of the background noise died. And Sabine was back.

"I'm assuming this is about sex. If I'm wrong, correct me now, or this conversation is going to get really weird."

"You're not wrong. I have questions, and I need answers, fast. Nash will be here in—" I glanced at the clock again "—seven minutes."

"Cutting it pretty close, aren't you?" She sounded distinctly unhappy to hear that I was minutes away from sleeping with Nash, and I choked back the sudden fear that her answers would sabotage my first—and likely only—sexual experience.

"The opportunity came up kind of fast."

"What aspect of our relationship made you think I'd give you advice on sleeping with Nash?"

"We have a truce!" I fell back on the couch in exasperation.

"I said I wouldn't get in your way—I never said I'd help."

"Please, Sabine. You're going to have him for the rest of your life, but I may only get this one shot." When that didn't work, I sighed and tried from another angle. "You were right. I don't know what I'm doing. Please help me." Even I could hear the anxiety in my voice, so I wasn't surprised when Sabine laughed.

"Okay," she said, and suspicion lingered on the edge of my mind. Why would she agree so easily? "But first, breathe, Kaylee. He's not even in the room yet, and you sound like you're about to pass out. "

"That's *your* fault." I sucked in a deep breath and held it for a couple of seconds. "You told me I wouldn't be any good."

"Yeah, and I also told you it wouldn't matter."

But it would. I stretched out on the couch with my eyes still covered. "Look, I don't have time to get good at this and I'd like to avoid humiliating myself. Just this once. Are you going to answer my questions, or do I need to go create the most embarrassing Google search history known to womankind?" Not that there was time for that anymore.

"Fine." I could practically see her pouting, in my head. "What do you want to know?"

Another deep breath. "Don't laugh, but…what am I supposed to *do?*"

Sabine didn't laugh, and I almost died of shock. "Anything," she said. "Nothing. Whatever feels right."

"That's a nonanswer." And it only made me more nervous.

The *mara* sighed. "It's the truth. If you don't know what to do, don't worry about it. Nash knows what he's doing. Trust me."

My stomach clenched around my ice-cream breakfast. "Could you please not remind me of the two of you together?"

"Who's asking who for help here?"

I was regretting asking already. But there was no one else. "What about my hands? What do I do with them?"

That time Sabine laughed, but she sounded genuinely amused, not cruel. It was a nice—if suspicious—change. "Touch…whatever you want to touch."

I groaned and squeezed my eyes shut tighter. "Anything more specific?"

"Use your imagination. But really, you can't go wrong. He's going to *want* you to touch him." I started to ask another question, but she spoke again before I could. "Fortunately for you, the process is kind of foolproof, Kaylee. The basics, anyway. People have been doing it since the beginning of time—with no instructions. Just keep it simple."

Right. Simple.

"Do you know how the French describe an orgasm?" Sabine asked, and the familiar edge of mischief in her voice was almost a relief.

"How the hell would I know that?" Sexual euphemisms weren't covered by Mrs. Brown's French II class syllabus.

"They call it *la petite mort*. The little death. I think there's irony in there somewhere. At least for you."

"Wow. Thanks for that," I snapped. "I love being reminded that I'm about to die."

She exhaled heavily. "You know how much this sucks for me, right? I have one thing with Nash that he doesn't have with you. One thing. And you just called me for advice about how best to take that away from me. If we hadn't just called a truce, I'd think you were finally learning how to play the game."

"I'm not—" But before I could finish insisting that I hadn't meant to rub it in her face, Nash knocked on the door, and I stood so fast my head spun. "He's here. Gotta go."

"Swell," Sabine said, and her voice cracked a little on that one syllable. "But call Emma when you want to talk about it afterward. I'm not that kind of friend." She hung up and I slid my phone into my pocket. Then I wiped sweat from my palms onto my jeans and opened the door.

Nash stood on the porch, smiling. Waiting.

His smile slipped a little when he saw my face, and a thread of doubt swirled through his eyes before he could squelch it. "Are you sure about this?"

"Yeah." I grinned nervously. "Yes. Come in." I grabbed his hand and pulled him into the house without stepping back, so that he was pressed against me when I swung the door shut. "I want this." *It's now or never.*

"Me, too. You have no idea how badly I want this." Nash kissed me, and I forgot to be nervous. I forgot about everything except him, and the heat between us, and everything that had seemed forbidden before but was now suddenly available, and irresistible, and…right in front of me.

I backed slowly across the living room, still kissing Nash. Breathing him. Tasting him. I let him guide us through the doorway and down the hall, one hand around my waist while mine slid around his neck. I clung to him like the safety bar on a roller coaster, hurtling down the track fast enough to steal my breath and scatter my doubts. And that was the whole point, right? To put aside fear and let myself *feel* something, before I'd lost that chance.

When we crossed into my room—I knew by the change in light and the feel of carpet beneath my toes—I pulled his shirt over his head and dropped it on the floor.

My pulse roared in my ears. I'd seen him shirtless a million times, but never like this. Never with such a storm of need and blatant lust churning in his eyes, so hot that smoke should've been rising off his skin. Never with the understanding that we weren't going to stop there.

I was already out of breath when Nash stepped back and his scalding gaze met mine. He lifted one brow in silent question, and when I nodded, he slid his hands beneath my shirt, warm against my sides. His hands skimmed up my skin slowly, dragging the material with them, leaving chills in their wake. I raised my arms and he pulled the shirt over my head.

I didn't see where my shirt fell because he was kissing me again, and his arms wrapped around me. My bra pulled tight for a minute, and I gasped against his lips when the material suddenly fell to the floor between us. Then we were chest to chest, skin to skin. For the first time.

At least, that I remembered…

But I pushed that thought away. So what if he'd already been this far with me before, when I wasn't in possession of my own body? That nonmemory didn't matter anymore, right? Thanks to my truncated lifeline, *nothing* mattered anymore, except how I spent the next five days. And I wasn't going to spend them being ruled by fear.

I pulled Nash down for another kiss, the only reliable cure for encroaching panic. His hands fell away from me, and a moment later we were on the bed, and his pants were gone, though I had no memory of that happening.

I lay back on the pillow and closed my eyes, and the world was reduced to his lips, and hands, and a flood of sensations that were nothing like I'd imagined, yet somehow even better. I got lost in the feel of him—everywhere all at once—and only found myself when he unbuttoned my jeans.

Startled, in spite of my own intentions, I sat up, and his hands fell away again. Nash studied my surely churning irises, watching me closely. "You want to stop?" He would take no chances this time, and that meant the world to me.

"No." My voice was a shaky whisper. "Don't stop."

He smiled—a burst of heat before the flames rolled over me—and I lay back again, staring at that crack in my ceiling as he slowly slid my pants over my hips, leaving my underwear in place. For now.

This is going to happen. My choice. I wanted it.

But when Nash's face appeared over mine, his weight settling onto me gently, I couldn't breathe. He was naked. Completely.

"You okay?" he whispered, kissing the sensitive skin below my left ear.

"Yeah. Yes." I nodded, just in case I wasn't clear, running my hands over his chest.

He kissed me again, and his knee slid slowly between mine. I listened to my heart pound in my ears, wondering if he could hear it. Wondering if he could *feel* it.

His lips traveled south of my collarbone and I threw my head back, and—

Someone knocked on my bedroom door.

I sucked in a cold, shocked breath. Nash rolled off me and sat up, breathing too fast. Already reaching for his pants. I flipped the edge of my comforter up to cover myself, my face flaming. Thursday be damned, my dad was going to kill me *now.*

Right after he killed Nash.

"Just a second!" I yelled, then I held one finger to my lips, warning Nash to be quiet. Saying I was an adult for the next five days didn't mean my father was going to play along with my decision. Or that Nash would live long enough to see me die.

"It's me," a voice called from the hallway, and Nash threw his pants at the floor instead of pulling them on.

"Tod, get the *hell* out of here before I kill you myself," he growled. "And this time, you won't be coming back."

"I need to talk to Kaylee." Tod's syllables were bitten off, like he was speaking through clenched teeth. "Just be glad I'm not her dad. You guys aren't exactly stealthy."

"We're not in the mood to talk." Nash sat on the edge of my bed and slid one arm around my bare back while I clutched the covers to my chest, mortified beyond speech.

"It's important," Tod said through the door. "Get dressed. I'm coming in."

"Damn it!" Nash swore, pawing through the tangle of material on the floor for his boxer briefs. I stood and scanned the room for my clothes, and Nash spat profanities at his brother while I fastened my bra and pulled my shirt over my head.

"Time's up," Tod said, and an instant later he appeared at the foot of my bed. He glanced at me long enough to realize I wasn't wearing pants, then turned around while I pulled them on.

"What the hell is wrong with you?" Nash snapped. He bent to pick up his pants again, then straightened, his gaze narrowed on Tod in anger and suspicion. "How did you know to knock?" Nash demanded, and my cheeks flamed like hot coals when I followed his logic. "You usually just blink into the room, right? How did you know not to this time?"

I zipped my pants and Tod turned to me, dismissing his half-naked brother. "Sorry, Kay. I wouldn't be here if it wasn't important."

"What's wrong?" I couldn't manage any more than that as I pushed hair back from my face, trying to pretend he hadn't just seen me in my underwear.

"I got your reaper's name." He glanced at the ground for a moment before meeting my gaze again, and I felt my heart

stop. "It's him, Kaylee. The same one as before. They're bringing in the reaper who killed your mom."

"Does my dad know?" I stared at the kitchen floor, trying
to wrap my brain around the facts. Minutes earlier, I'd been
seconds away from losing my virginity and concerned with
nothing else. Now I sat at the kitchen table, virginity frustrat-
ingly intact, embarrassed beyond belief, and suddenly scared
of my approaching death for a whole new reason.

My mother's reaper. Now *my* reaper. Again.

"No one knows, except you two." Tod leaned against the
refrigerator, watching me, probably wondering if he should
have said anything at all. Knowing who would be coming for
me didn't exactly lessen the stress of my last days. But I was
glad he'd told me.

"How could this even happen?" I demanded, as Nash paced
back and forth between me and Tod. "This reaper—what's
his name?"

"Thane," Tod said, watching me from across the room. "If
he had a last name, it's long gone now."

"Thane." Once I'd heard it, I had to say it. I had to try out
the name of the man who'd taken my mother's life out of spite
when he was denied mine.

I shook my head to clear it and found both Hudson boys
waiting for me to finish my thought. "Shouldn't this bastard
be on the run or something. I mean, he's psychotic, right? He
tried to kill me again while I was still in the hospital, before
my mom was even buried!"

"Yeah, and if he'd actually been caught with an unauthorized soul, he'd have been fired on the spot," Tod said. "But
your dad stopped him before he could kill you again. The
bright side, obviously, is that you're still alive—at least so far.
But the not-so-bright side is that Thane got away with at-

tempted murder and potential soul trafficking because no one in the afterlife knew he'd tried it. Your dad didn't even know he *could* report the incident, much less who to report it to. So, from what I can tell, Thane's spent the past thirteen years in another district, where he continued reaping off the record, but was never caught."

"So you're saying the only way to keep him from killing me this time is if he'd succeeded in killing me last time?" My life had already been a nightmare. I probably shouldn't have been surprised that my death was becoming one, too.

"Yeah." Tod shrugged miserably.

"But there's no proof he did anything, after he went after Kaylee, is there?" Nash said. "If there was proof, they'd have repossessed his soul and sent him on to a true death, right? So how sure are we that he's ever even reaped off the record?"

Tod exhaled slowly, then met his brother's gaze. "Not sure enough to openly accuse him, but sure enough to have caught Levi's attention. Turns out he was Thane's supervisor when Kaylee died the first time. He didn't like Thane, but he didn't have proof of anything, so he had him transferred out of the district. Then, when Levi saw Thane listed for your reaping the other day, he did some digging. There are no official complaints, but there are a few discrepancies in Thane's last district. No one's associated them with him yet, but then, they don't know what he tried to do to you. He's never been caught in the act, or with an unauthorized soul."

"So, how did he wind up in line to kill Kaylee again? Legally, this time?" Nash asked, sinking into the chair next to mine. "The bastard actually got promoted?"

"Not yet. This is something like a courtesy call, if I understand correctly," Tod explained. "Thane is up for advancement—proof positive that the system is flawed—and since Kaylee was supposed to be his kill in the first place, some idiot higher up in the chain of command has decided that she should be his test case. A chance to finish what he started and secure a promotion."

And that's when I truly understood why Tod had considered his news important enough to interrupt me and Nash, even knowing what we were…up to. "So, if my death is the key to Thane's promotion, there's no way he's going to let my dad do anything to mess that up."

"That's right." Tod's eyes were eerily, frighteningly still, and suddenly the "grim" descriptor seemed to fit him perfectly. "And if Thane gets this promotion, he'll be working without a regular schedule, which will leave him plenty of time and opportunity to reap souls off the record, for profit or his own amusement. And what would amuse him more than reaping the soul of a man who's gotten in his way not once, not twice, but three times before?"

That man, of course, would be my father.

"No." *No!*

"Kaylee, it's going to be all right." Tod started across the room toward me, but stopped when Nash scooted closer to rub my back.

"No, it's not. He's going to kill me. That sucks, but I could almost deal with that, because I thought that after Thursday, all my problems would be over." Nash would have Sabine to lean on, and I wouldn't care what they did together, because I wouldn't even exist anymore. My dad would be sad, but he'd still be alive, and eventually he'd deal.

But Tod's bombshell had changed everything.

Tears filled my eyes, and I scrubbed my face with my hands to hide them. But I could still hear them in my voice. "If my dad makes trouble and Thane kills him, what will he do with his soul?"

Warm hands wrapped around my wrists and gently pulled my hands away from my face. I blinked, expecting to see Nash's hazel eyes staring into mine—but I saw blue instead. Tod knelt in front of me, holding my arms, staring straight into my eyes. "That's not going to happen."

"Don't promise her things you can't deliver," Nash snapped from the chair to my left, and I could hear anger in his voice, just as thick as the tears were in mine. "We all know how well that worked out for Addison."

Tod's jaw clenched, but his attention never left me. "I can't stop whatever's going to happen on Thursday, Kaylee. More than anything in the world, I wish I could." I nodded, sniffling. "But Levi said if I can get proof that Thane's been reaping off the record, he'll take it to his boss, and at the very least, we can get him removed from your case and held for review. And that should protect your dad. No promises..." The reaper glanced pointedly at his brother, then met my tear-blurred gaze again. "But I'll do what I can."

"Thank you." I wiped away more tears, trying to balance overwhelming fear and frustration with the bone of hope he'd just tossed me.

"How do you know all this already?" Nash's gaze narrowed on his brother when the reaper finally stood and stepped back. "You popped in here like you had urgent news, but if it was so urgent in the first place, how did you and Levi have time to work this out?"

•

I glanced at Nash, surprised by his anger. "He's just trying to help," I insisted, sliding my hand into his.

"Don't you think his timing is a little convenient?"

Tod actually laughed. "Little brother, the last thing I was trying to be was convenient."

Something silent passed between them. Some kind of un-spoken challenge that made my stomach pitch. "What am I missing?" They'd never been best friends, but I'd rarely seen them openly hostile.

Nash never even glanced at me. "You've delivered your news. Now go deliver some pizza."

I glanced at him in surprise. "What's wrong with you?"

But when Nash didn't answer, Tod did, his eyes darker than usual, but still steady. "He wants to pick up where the two of you left off."

I could feel myself flush, and Nash's hand tightened around mine. But he was watching his brother again. "Do you have a problem with that, Tod?"

That sick feeling in my stomach grew stronger, and I looked up to find the reaper watching me, like he was waiting for some kind of signal. And when I didn't give him one—when I couldn't even fully understand the words they were saying, much less the ones they weren't—he exhaled heavily, holding my gaze. "Not if that's what she wants. At least this time she's actually in there and able to speak for herself." He tapped his head to illustrate his point, and I struggled to breathe through a complicated mix of embarrassment and squirming discomfort.

I didn't like the reminder that he knew what had happened. What Nash had let happen when he was high. I didn't want to think about it, and I didn't want to know that anyone else ever thought about it.

Nash went stiff at my side, and I could practically feel his temper rolling off him in waves. "Get. Out."

Tod watched me for another second, while I tried desperately to calm the storm of confusion battering my heart from all sides. Then he disappeared.

"I can't believe he said that to you." Nash pulled me up by the hand he still held, and I let him tug me toward the living room.

"He was talking to you," I said softly, as I sank onto the couch next to him, and Nash went very, very still.

It was the thing we didn't talk about. It had happened, more than once, and it had broken us up for a while, but he felt horrible about it, and the whole thing was behind us now. And I was fine as long as I didn't think about it. About what was said and seen and done while I wasn't in control of my own body.

Nash looked straight into my eyes with an intensity and sincerity that made me catch my breath. "It's never going to happen again. Not even if you lived to be a thousand. You know that, right?"

"You're here, aren't you?" I said at last. Wasn't that proof enough that I was trying to move past it?

But I couldn't get Tod's expression out of my head. There'd been just a flash of motion in his irises—a swirl of blue too quick to interpret.

I closed my eyes and tried to clear my head. Tried to get back to the place Nash and I had been an hour before, alone, in my room, where thoughts didn't matter—it was all about feeling. But when I met Nash's gaze, I knew the moment was over. He was still mad at Tod, and hurt by the reminder of things we'd put behind us. And maybe I was, too.

"He did this on purpose." Nash let his head fall against the back of the couch. "He dredged up old problems to start new trouble." And this time I couldn't argue.

As it turns out, there's no greater impediment to *la petite mort*—the little death—than a visit from the real thing.

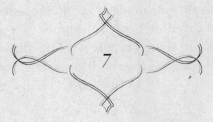

7

I blinked in the dark, confusion covering me like a blanket over my head. Why was I awake? Then Styx growled, and I realized two things at once: I was in my room, and I wasn't alone.

I sat up, heart pounding, pulse whooshing in my ears. Light from the hall painted a strip of color over one corner of my desk and the end of my bed, while the rest of the room stood shrouded in shadow. Styx lay near my footboard, curled up like she was still asleep, except for her raised head, shining black eyes, and sharp teeth, exposed as she growled in warning.

Avari. Harmony had said Styx would wake up if a hellion came anywhere near me, even from the other side of the world barrier, and though I'd managed to piss off two other hellions—Belphagore and Invidia—in the six months since I'd learned I was a *bean sidhe,* Avari would always be my default guess. My go-to bad guy, a title awarded on the basis of persistence alone.

It creeped me out to know that Avari was wandering around the Netherworld version of my house—a field of razor wheat—with nothing separating us except for the world barrier. Was he trying to possess me again? He couldn't take over my body while I was conscious, which is why Styx's job—half guard dog, half security alarm—was so important. And that was also why I was under orders to wake my dad up if Styx so much as growled in her sleep.

I crawled out from under the covers and stretched to reach her fur, stroking her in reward for a job well done on my way out of bed.

"Well, look who's all grown up."

I jumped at the sound of an unfamiliar voice, then sat up slowly, skin crawling as I reached for my bedside lamp. It wasn't Avari. It couldn't be—unless he'd possessed someone else and broken into my house.

Shit, shit, shit! I flipped the lamp switch and every dark silhouette in my room was thrown into full color, the sudden light blinding me for one long moment. I blinked rapidly, fighting off panic as I waited for my vision to adjust, but when it did, it brought no answers—only more questions.

A man sat in my desk chair, watching me silently, arms crossed over the front of a white button-up shirt. His dark eyes glittered with some perverse version of anticipation or amusement, as if he knew me and was waiting for a familiar reaction. But I'd never even seen him before—I would have remembered that face. Smooth and young, with a strong chin and wide forehead. If I'd seen him at a party, I would have watched him—or watched Emma fawn over him. But in my room, in the middle of the night...?

"Get out." I slid off the mattress on the opposite side, and squatted to pull an aluminum baseball bat—one of Nash's spares—from beneath the bed. I was no stranger to late-night unwanted company.

"Do you even know who I am?"

"Don't know, don't care." Unscheduled visitors rarely

brought good news—just ask Jacob Marley. "Get out now, or I'll yell for my dad."

The stranger settled farther into my chair, getting comfortable. "How *is* your dad?" he asked, still watching me eagerly, like he'd rather read my thoughts than hear me speak. "I haven't seen him in, what? Thirteen years?"

No, no, no... I shook my head, but I couldn't deny the swift understanding and terror colliding within me. "Thane?" I whispered, suddenly cold all over.

He was early.

"No. You can't be here yet." I glanced into the hall and started to yell for my dad—until I remembered what Tod had said. If my dad got in Thane's way, Thane would kill him. That would give us proof enough to get Thane fired, but my dad would still be dead.

Instead of shouting, I backed slowly away from the bed, tightening my grip on the bat, for all the good it would do. I could handle this myself. "I still have four days, and you're not gonna—"

"Relax." Thane smiled, and no matter how pretty he was, I couldn't shake the certainty that kittens everywhere were suddenly screeching in pain from the mockery of joy that had just settled onto his face. "I just thought we should formally meet, since I'm going to be the last thing you ever see."

I took a deep breath, trying desperately to focus on the fact that he hadn't come to kill me—yet—instead of on the fact that he'd come at all. "Do you always show up early to taunt your victims?"

"You're not a victim, you're an assignment," Thane said, watching as I made myself climb back onto the bed and lay the bat at my side on the comforter, as if I wasn't terrified and in shock. "Do you always act like having a reaper in your bedroom is a matter of course?"

Show no fear.

I shrugged and tucked my legs beneath me, glad I'd slept in pajama bottoms. "I know interesting people."

"Of course. Because you're a *bean sidhe,* right?" the reaper said, as if he'd just remembered. "And that makes me one very lucky worker bee. The average reaper will go his entire afterlife without ever encountering a nonhuman soul, and here I've got the opportunity to reap yours for a second time. It doesn't get much better than this..." Thane rolled the chair close enough that his knees touched my mattress, still eyeing me boldly, studying me. "Except for reaping your mother."

My hand flew before my brain caught up with it. A second later, my palm throbbed, and an angry red patch marred his smooth, stubbleless cheek.

Thane threw his head back and laughed, and I glanced at the door, hoping my father would sleep through the whole thing. Hoping Thane was audible—and inexplicably corporeal—only to me.

"Well, aren't you fun!" he said, raising one hand to his cheek. "Who would have guessed that the toddler who once died without a whimper would grow into such a hellcat!" He leaned closer, and I held my breath. "It's almost a shame I have to extinguish such a bright flame, but it's true what they say about life being unfair. Death, however, is the great equalizer. Death comes to everyone, eventually, and *you* have the honor of meeting him twice." Thane leaned back in my chair and recrossed his arms. "Lucky, lucky girl..."

"Get out." I picked up the bat again, thrilled to find fury overwhelming my fear. "Get the hell out of my room and don't come back."

"Or what? You'll sic your father on me?" He raised both brows in silent challenge, and I wanted to hit him again. With the bat this time. "He's a sad, desperate man, with the potential to become a real thorn in my side. But you have to respect his determination to save his daughter. Too bad it's not going to work."

I didn't really want to know, and I certainly didn't want to prolong Thane's visit or admit my own ignorance. But I had to ask. "What's he doing?"

"He's been hanging around the local reaper office for two days, begging anyone who'll listen to let him trade his expiration date for yours. It's not going to matter, though. Your file has a big red 'special circumstances' sticker on the front, and the notation inside states clearly that you've already had one date exchange and are thus ineligible for another."

Uh-oh.

"I don't suppose you know how he found the local headquarters, do you?" Thane asked, and I shook my head, though it had to be Tod. Who else could have told him? Who else would even know?

Thane looked like he didn't believe me, but didn't really care one way or another. "As amusing as the whole thing would be, if it weren't so pathetic, if he doesn't back off soon, he might find his expiration date exchanged for someone he's never even met."

"Is that why you're here?" I asked, fury burning bright behind my eyes, a headache in full bloom. "To threaten my dad?"

The reaper laughed again, softer this time, and I already hated the sound. "That's just a bonus. I'm here to get to know you. By my count, we have several days to spend together before our business is concluded, and I say we make the most of it. How do you feel about Mexican takeout?"

Was he serious? "Why are you doing this?"

He shrugged. "I've never reaped a soul from someone who knew what was coming, so I look forward to observing your last days, studying how you cope as you count down the hours. Like a fish in a glass bowl…"

"You're psychotic."

Another shrug. "Nah. Just bored. But don't mistake my interest for sympathy. Nothing will stop me from ending your life when the time comes."

"When is that?" I asked, trying hard not to reveal how desperate I was for that nugget of information. "When am I supposed to die?"

For a moment, he only watched me, and I got the feeling he was trying to decide whether I'd suffer more from knowing or from not knowing. "I think this will be more fun as a surprise," he said finally, and I groaned on the inside. "See you soon, Kaylee."

Then he was gone, and I was alone with my own fear and anger. And with Styx, who glanced around the room, sniffed the air once, then curled up and went back to sleep, secure in the knowledge that the big bad reaper was gone.

But I couldn't sleep—not after what had just happened. Not knowing it could happen again, at any time. Not knowing my father had spent the entire weekend painting a target on his own back, for me.

I lifted my cell from the charger on my nightstand and autodialed Tod. He answered on the first ring. "Kaylee?"

"Did you tell my dad how to find the local reaper office?" I demanded, without a greeting.

Tod sighed. "You in your room?"

"Yeah."

Another pause. Then, "Are you dressed?"

For just a split second, I considered saying no, and I wondered if he'd take that as deterrent or motivation. Then I came to my senses. "Pjs."

He appeared at the foot of my bed an instant later, already

sliding his phone into his pocket as he pushed Styx over and sank onto the mattress. She growled at him until I patted a spot next to my right hip, and she curled up there, content to watch him in threatening silence.

"I'm sorry," Tod said, one bent leg on my comforter. "I was trying to help."

"How is telling my dad where to go beg for my life possibly helping? You know they're not going to make the trade."

"That's why I sent him there. Because they won't do what he wants, but they won't hurt him, and Thane's not going to make a move on him while he's in a building full of other reapers." He shrugged, and it got a little harder for me to stay mad at him. "Besides, that way I know where he is, and I can check up on him without having to hunt him down."

"Oh." When he put it like that, it sounded kind of…smart. "Well, then…thanks for keeping my dad out of trouble."

Suddenly nervous, for no reason I could pin down, I fidgeted with the handle of Nash's bat, and Tod noticed.

"You know, most girls sleep with a teddy bear or an extra pillow. But I gotta say, that's kinda hot…"

My cheeks blazed on the lower edge of my vision. "Nash gave it to me. But I wasn't sleeping with it. I…" I shook my head and started over. "Thane was here, Tod. That's how I knew Dad was at your office."

"Thane was *here?* In your room?" He sat up straight, eyes churning with cobalt streaks of anger like I'd never seen from him before. "Please tell me you bashed his skull in."

"No, but I did slap him. He's planning to watch me to see if I crack up, knowing I'm going to die in a few days. Can he do that?"

His dimple disappeared beneath a dark scowl. "Yeah, but he's not supposed to tell you he's doing it. You're never supposed to see your own reaper."

"Would that be enough to get him fired, if I told Levi?"

Tod shrugged. "If he were a rookie and you were a clueless human, yeah. But since he's not, and you're not, it'd probably just derail his promotion and get him knocked a peg or two down the ladder. Which would piss him off."

"I don't suppose you're any closer to proving he's done anything else?"

"Not yet. I'll get him, though, Kaylee," Tod said, and that look was back. His irises were too still, like there was something he didn't want me to see. And when I realized how badly I wanted to see it, I glanced down and noticed I was playing with the bat again.

My weak laugh sounded nervous, even to my own ears. "I guess I should tell Nash he was right about the bat. It did come in handy."

Tod leaned forward to catch my gaze, and a blue twist of fear churned in his. "Kaylee, you can't tell him about Thane. Anyone Thane sees as a threat is in danger. The irony there is that if he killed Nash, or your dad, or whoever, we'd be able to catch him with an unauthorized soul. But it'd be too late for whoever he took."

A chill ran the entire length of my body. I'd known that, of course, but I hadn't actually thought it through that far. No one else could know about Thane. No matter what.

"You want me to stay the night, in case he comes back?" Tod asked. I glanced at him in surprise, but he was serious.

"Don't you have to work?" He was less than two hours into his shift.

"I could ask someone to cover for me."

I stroked Styx's fur, but she refused to sleep as long as he was there. "I thought you were out of favors."

"Yeah, now I'm taking on debt," he admitted. "But I can handle it."

"Would Thane be able to see you, if he comes back?"

Tod nodded. "Reapers can't hide from one another. I can't, anyway. Maybe if I had more experience…"

"But if he sees you here, he'll know you know about him, and your investigation will be hosed," I said. Tod started to argue, but I cut him off. "You have to stay away from him and find proof. I'll be fine—till Thursday, anyway."

He nodded again, reluctantly, this time. "I'll let you know when I find something. Until then…keep sleeping with the bat."

When Tod left, Styx went back to sleep, like her night had never been interrupted.

I lay awake for another hour and a half, listening to her breathe.

Sabine was waiting by my locker on Monday morning—not the beginning I'd hoped for on the third-from-final day of my life. But honestly, considering my luck, it fit.

"So, how'd it go?" she asked, leaning against the locker next to mine while I entered my combination, and for several seconds, I thought she was talking about the unscheduled appearance of my own personal reaper. Then I remembered she didn't know about that…

Sabine was talking about me and Nash. He obviously hadn't told her that our plans had been interrupted. Again.

"I thought we weren't that kind of friends." My locker clicked open and I shoved my French text inside, then pulled out my algebra book.

"We're not. I just…"

When she hesitated, I glanced up to find her avoiding my gaze. Sabine wouldn't lie to me—that would violate whatever kind of screwed-up moral standard she subscribed to—but that didn't mean she necessarily liked the truth.

I sighed and slammed my locker. "We didn't do it. Happy now?"

The hallway seemed to get a little brighter, and her black eyes actually shined. "More like satisfied. For the moment, anyway. But honestly, I'll be a lot closer to happy on Friday. Not because you'll be dead, but because Nash won't be tied to you anymore."

I rolled my eyes and resisted the urge to smack her. I'd done it once, and that fact seemed to make subsequent urges harder to resist. But giving in would break our truce and probably affect her willingness to help me with Mr. Beck. Also, she'd hit back, and I was less than confident in the local undertaker's ability to hide a broken nose with pancake makeup.

"Why did you even give me advice, if you don't want me to sleep with him?"

Sabine frowned, like *I* made no sense. "It's like we were born on different planets. Is your world really that black-and-white?"

"What does that even mean? And I don't have time for one of your speeches right now."

"It means that even though I'm willing to go through you to get Nash back, I like you, too. That's a little bit of a conflict for me."

I slammed my locker shut and faced her directly. "Why do you like me, Sabine?" I couldn't figure that one out. I would have been perfectly fine with her hating me, so long as that didn't put me in the direct line of fire from the creepy-vibes she leaked whenever she got mad. Or from her killer right hook.

"I'm not sure." Sabine tossed long, dark hair over her shoulder and the cartilage piercing in her left ear shined in the overhead lights. "You don't have any outstanding qualities, other than a gritty determination I can't help but relate to."

"Meaning…?"

"Meaning, you tend to grow on people. Like some kind of persistent fungus."

It was very clear, however, why *I* didn't like *her.*

"So, you give me vaguely girlfriendly advice about sex, then cross your fingers and hope I don't have it with Nash. Is that how this plays out in that warped, shriveled little cerebrum of yours?"

She shrugged. "More or less."

I couldn't shake the feeling that it was actually "less," and I knew that if I pressed for details she'd give them to me—along with significant TMI about her former relationship with Nash. But life—especially mine—was too short to waste time picturing her making out with my boyfriend. So I changed the subject.

"You're still going to talk to Mr. Beck today, right? When do you have him?"

"Sixth period. And yeah, I'm actually looking forward to your cheesy little spy mission." She glanced around the hall like a bored housewife tired of her own décor. "This place has been dull as shit since we got rid of the hellions."

"Okay, first of all, 'we' didn't get rid of the hellions." I zipped my backpack and slung it over my shoulder. "*You* tried to sell me and Em to them."

Sabine rolled her eyes. "I *said* I was sorry about that…."

"And second of all, they're not gone—they're just stuck in the Netherworld. Which is why you are *not* supposed to make people cross over in their sleep."

She actually grinned. "Damn, how long can you hold a grudge?"

"Four days more. Then you're in the clear. Bonus points if you figure out what Mr. Beck is *today.* I'm kinda short on time."

"I'm all set to feel him out."

"Feel who out?" Nash asked, sliding one arm around me from behind.

"Beck." Sabine's grin widened. "Kaylee wants to know what he is, so I'm going undercover. Maybe literally."

"She's kidding about that last part," I insisted, setting my bag on the floor so I could slide closer to Nash.

He huffed. "No she's not."

I glanced at Sabine, and the *mara* shrugged. "I'm gonna play that part by ear. I figured I'd start with a little dyslexia, then move on to a basic incomprehension of functions. It'll soon become obvious that I need more help than he can provide during class, so he'll ask me to drop by after school. He'll explain patiently, I'll stare adoringly into his eyes and take every possible chance to touch him, letting him know in no uncertain terms that I am—tragically—available."

Nash exhaled, long and low. Like he was grasping for patience, and it was too slippery to hold. "Sabine, you can't hit on a teacher." He sounded frustrated, but not really surprised.

She frowned. "Yes I can. The taboo you're thinking of is the reverse of that. Which'll probably also happen, if I do this right."

"That's not just a taboo, it's illegal," I said. She was already planning to go further than I'd intended.

"For him, not for me," Sabine insisted, and when neither of us conceded her point, she propped both hands on her hips, where a ring of bare flesh showed above the low waist of her khakis. "Look, if he's a good guy, he won't take the bait. If he's not, regardless of species, he deserves whatever he gets. But you'll never know for sure unless we give him a chance to actually *take* the bait. Right? Fortunately for you—" her gaze narrowed on me and her grin grew "—I'm willing to take one for the team. But only because he's hot. If we were

talking about Coach Rundell, you'd have to find yourself another underage carrot to dangle."

Nash groaned, and I twisted in his grip to find him frowning at me. "I just wanted her to find out what he is, I swear,"
I said. "She's improvising."

"I know." He pulled me closer and refocused on the *mara*.
"This is a bad idea, Sabine. What if he's something dangerous? He obviously doesn't wanna be outed.…"

"*I'm* something dangerous." She shrugged. "Besides, if he
sticks to math and stays away from my anatomy, he won't be
outed. He'll never even have to know what I know."

Nash's frown deepened, and I recognized the concern
swirling slowly in his eyes. He was worried about her. "You
have an amazing ability to gloss right over the point."

The *mara* tugged her backpack strap higher on one shoulder. "It's a gift."

"How did Kaylee talk you into this, anyway?"

She lifted one brow at me, like we shared some special secret. "Advance payment for the favor she'll be doing me on
Thursday."

The blood drained from Nash's face, and I wanted to melt
into the floor. "That's messed up, even for you, Bina," he
snapped. "This is hard enough for me to handle without the
two of you joking about it."

Sabine frowned, clearly confused by his reaction. "We're
not joking. She dies, I inherit you. We've got it all worked
out."

Nash glanced back and forth between us, obviously at a loss
for words.

"It's okay, Nash." I swallowed the lump in my throat, and
it hurt going down. "Look, I don't want to die, and I don't
want you to wind up with someone else. But I'm not going
to ask you to spend your whole life mourning me. I saw what

that did to my dad." It took another deep breath to prepare me for the rest of what I had to say. "Besides, I know I'm the only thing keeping the two of you apart, and I know you'll eventually wind up together again with me gone. I'm making peace with it. Just promise you won't go over to the dark side until after the funeral."

"Kaylee, what the hell is wrong with you?" Nash demanded. "This isn't funny. This is your life!"

"No, this is my *death*," I whispered, well aware that people were glancing at us now, on their way to class. "And I'm dealing with it the only way I know how. I'm providing support for the people I'm leaving behind. I'm crossing things off my very last to-do list. And I'm desperately trying to distract myself from everything else by focusing on other people's problems."

Nash stared at me like he'd never seen me before. "I don't want to think about what life's going to be like on Friday, and I don't understand how you can be so calm about this!"

Fighting fresh tears, I pulled him into the alcove by the restrooms, and Sabine followed at an almost respectful distance. "How am I supposed to react?" I dropped my bag on the floor again and stared up at him, silently challenging him not to look away. "You want me to pull out my hair and start wailing for myself? I'm trying to accept this with dignity and good humor. You're only making that harder."

"That's because this *is* hard," Nash insisted. "It's supposed to be. We were supposed to have hundreds of years together, and now we don't even have hundreds of hours. I'm not okay with that, and I'm not going to pretend I am."

The first hot tear rolled down my cheek, in spite of my determination not to cry. "Fine. I understand. But I have to deal with this my way, and you can either be a part of that or you can walk away."

Please, please don't walk away... The only thing more terrifying than knowing I was going to die was knowing I'd be alone when it happened.

"I'm not going to turn my back on you, Kaylee."

"Thank you." I stood on my toes to kiss him and blinked away more tears. "Because this is really scary for me, and no matter what else I fill my head up with, it's always there, in the back of my mind, just waiting for a chance to shove everything else over and take center stage." As Thane had shown me less than six hours earlier.

Nash's arms wound around me again and he held me close enough to whisper in my ear. "Well, maybe I can take your mind off it for a little while tonight, if your dad's going to be out again."

"He won't be home till dinner," I said, and my pulse jumped a little at just the thought of finishing what we'd started.

Sabine cleared her throat to get our attention, but it was too late. Coach Tucker, the girls' softball coach, was marching across the hall toward us, pink detention pad in hand. "I saw that, Mr. Hudson," she called, already scribbling on the pad with a red pen. She stopped two feet away, ripping the first slip off the pad, and handed it to Nash. "And you, Ms. Cavanaugh. Kylee..." she thought out loud, already writing on the next sheet.

"It's Kaylee," I corrected.

"My mistake." She scribbled through whatever she'd already written and started over. "And *your* mistake was the public display on school grounds. That'll get you a detention apiece."

I glanced at Nash to find him grinning at me, the browns and greens in his eyes swirling with mischief. I shrugged and went up on my toes again, speaking to Coach Tucker even as my lips met Nash's. "Better make it two."

It's not like I'd be there to serve them.

"What are they for?" Emma whispered, staring at the detention slips I was now using to mark chapter fifteen in my algebra book.

"Public display."

"Both of them?"

I'd made Nash and Sabine promise not to tell Emma that I was days from death, in spite of our new "full disclosure" policy, because it seemed cruel to make her anticipate what was coming for days in advance. That was hard enough for me and Nash—Sabine didn't seem to be suffering—and I wouldn't put my best friend through it, if I could possibly spare her. And I have to admit, it felt good to talk to someone who didn't get sad and overprotective the minute I walked into the room. So she didn't understand my new cavalier approach to the school's code of conduct.

I shrugged, grinning from ear to ear. "I guess we didn't look sorry enough after the first one."

Emma gaped at me, and I almost laughed out loud. Knowing I was going to die changed everything. Consequences no longer mattered, so long as they didn't hurt anyone else—and Nash's detentions didn't count. There was no way they'd make him serve them while he was mourning the death of his girl-friend.

I could do whatever I wanted. And that incredible liberty—the only thing even *approaching* a bright side to the terrifying reality of my own death—left me feeling light-headed. And maybe a bit reckless.

I could stay up till four in the morning and eat pizza and ice cream for every meal. I could stay out all night. I could get drunk. I could have sex. I could get a piercing or a tattoo. I could stand up in the middle of sixth period and tell Mrs. Brown that the past perfect conjugation of irregular French verbs would never come in handy for me at all, and yes I *did* know that for a fact!

Next week, no one would care whether I'd gained weight or fallen asleep in class, or skipped school entirely. What did it matter if I failed French, or my piercing got infected, or I got pregnant?

But thinking of pregnancy killed my rebellion buzz with a single, gruesome mental image of Danica Sussman bleed-ing on the floor. Which reminded me of Mr. Beck, and when I looked up, he was walking down the aisle toward me and Emma, a stack of graded quizzes in hand.

For a moment, I couldn't breathe, afraid that he'd take one look at me and know exactly what I was thinking. That was entirely possible; we still didn't know what he *was*. So when he put a quiz facedown on my desk, then moved on to the next student, I exhaled with relief.

Okay, I guess some *consequences still matter…*

I flipped the paper over. Eighty-two. Normally, that would bother me. I was pulling a high B in algebra II and I'd hoped to push that into the low A range by the end of the term, mostly because Nash's grades—at least, pre-frost addiction—

made me look bad. But now, a low B was the last thing on my mind.

Mr. Beck came back up the next row and put a paper face-down on Emma's desk, but instead of moving on, he leaned over and whispered something to her. Something I couldn't hear. Emma nodded. And when he walked away, she was grinning from ear to ear.

"What'd he say?" I asked, leaning across the aisle as he headed toward the whiteboard at the front of the room. Something had gone wrong on a cosmic level if Em had aced a quiz I'd barely pulled a B on.

She turned up one corner of her paper so I could see her grade. Fifty-four.

"Since when is an F a good thing?"

"He wants to talk to me after class," she explained, eyes bright with excitement that gave me chills. Em had failed the quiz.

And caught Mr. Beck's attention.

"What'd he say?" I fell into step with Emma as she left Mr. Beck's room several minutes after class, acutely aware that though she had a late pass, I did not. Then I remembered that didn't matter. Next week, instead of serving detention, I'd be taking the great dirt nap.

"The usual. I'm a smart girl, but I'm not applying myself. Math *is* relevant to my future…."

She kept talking, but her answer faded into the ambient hallway chatter when a familiar set of dark eyes caught my attention, and goose bumps popped up all over my body. Thane stood across the hall, leaning against a bank of lockers in black jeans and a plain black T-shirt, still and silent against the rush of traffic and noise. He watched me, smiling intimately about the secret we shared. The future I would not have. The last moments of my life, which he would no doubt savor.

"Kaylee?" Emma elbowed me in the ribs. "What's wrong?"

"Nothing." I made myself turn away from the reaper, confident no one else could see him. And absolutely certain that he was still watching me. "What were you saying?"

"Mr. Beck said that maybe I just need a little extra help to get all caught up."

"That's it?" If that was it, why was Em practically glowing, like she did at parties, when every head in the room turned to watch her dance?

Emma pushed open the door to the bathroom and I followed her inside as the second period late bell rang. "Yeah. He thinks I could bump my average up to a B with a little tutoring."

"Who's the tutor?" *Please, please say it's a senior with mad math skills...*

"That's the best part. He's gonna tutor me himself. After school." She grinned at me in the mirror, pulling a tube of lip gloss from her purse. "And I suspect it just might take me a while to pick up on the more complicated concepts." Her eyes glittered with excitement, and my stomach churned. Something was wrong.

I leaned against the wall, clutching my books. *Sabine* was supposed to draw a foul, not Emma. Sabine could take care of herself, but Emma had no defensive abilities whatsoever, beyond a blinding distraction of cleavage, and she had no concept of how dangerous the world really was, even knowing that humans weren't alone in it.

"Em, this is a bad idea," I said, squatting to peek beneath the row of stalls to make sure we were alone. All good, unless someone at Eastlake had developed powers of invisibility. "Why don't you just go hit on someone in honors calculus?"

"Because there's no one hot in honors calculus," she said without moving her lips, as she dabbed clear gloss on over her lipstick. Then she eyed me in the mirror, screwing the lid back on the tube. "What's the big deal, Kay? It's an hour after school, twice a week. In a *classroom.* If I *have* to learn function notation, shouldn't I at least have something pretty to look at until my brain self-destructs?"

I dropped my backpack and leaned with both hands on the edge of the sink, staring at her reflection in disbelief. "Em, he could be dangerous. He's not human!"

"Neither are you!"

"Yeah, and I'm *dangerous!* How many times have you almost died because of me?"

She dropped her gloss into her purse, then set her purse on the stack of books balanced on the edge of the next sink. "Why do you have to be the storm cloud, always raining on my parade? Why can't you let me pretend—just this once—that someone smart, and hot, and thoroughly post-pubescent could possibly be interested in me?"

"Because you don't need to pretend. He could *totally* be interested in you, and that's the problem."

"It's just tutoring, Kaylee."

"The last girl he tutored nearly bled out on the classroom floor," I said, and Emma blinked, like she wanted to say something, but couldn't quite put it into words. "Sabine's going to figure out what he is and I'm going to find out whether or not he knocked up Danica Sussman." And Emma was going to stay away from him, whether she liked it or not.

"Okay, don't take this the wrong way, Kay, but how is it any of your business who Danica sleeps with?" She crossed her arms over her chest. "What are you now, the monogamy police?"

"Emma, he's a teacher!"

"I know, and normally that'd be really creepy. But he's twenty-two, and she's eighteen. They're only four years apart, and she's a legal adult. If this were June and she was out of high school, we wouldn't even be having this conversation."

"But it's barely March, and she's still in school. And he's an authority figure," I pointed out, frustrated and beyond bewildered by her argument. Was it really so hard to understand that a teacher sleeping with a student was *bad,* no matter how old either of them was? "At the very least, this could get him fired."

"Assuming it's true. And at this point, it's just a theory, right?" she asked, and I nodded reluctantly. "So how 'bout this…" Emma turned from the mirror to face me directly. "I promise not to sleep with the hottest teacher on the face of the planet—math facts and harmless fantasies only—and you promise to tell me if he turns out to have horns or a forked penis. Deal?"

"No! No deal!" I snapped, gaping at her now. "You've seen the Netherworld. How can you not be freaked out by even the possibility that he could be some kind of monster? That forked penis thing could be *true,* you know."

"Just because he's not human doesn't mean he's a monster, Kaylee. You, of all people, should know that." She shrugged and continued before I could argue. "Besides, Avari and Invidia were scary as hell, but hellions can't cross into the human world. And Mr. Beck isn't scary. He's just…hot."

I knew that look. That was the look Emma got every time her mom told her to be home by midnight. Every time her sister forbade her from borrowing her clothes. Hell, every time our fifth grade teacher told her to stop charging the boys in our class a dollar apiece for a peek at her training bra.

I exhaled, long and slow. "You're gonna do whatever you wanna do anyway…"

"How well you know me…" She smiled and slid her purse strap over one arm, then picked up her books. "Hey, have you noticed you're ten minutes late to chemistry?"

"Yeah. I don't care," I said, pushing the door open.

Emma frowned and studied me closer. "Since when do you not care about being late to class?"

"My priorities have recently undergone realignment."

Her frown deepened. "What does that mean?"

"I'm tired of playing by the rules."

"So?" I said, as Sabine slid onto the bench seat across the table from me and next to Emma. School had been out for half an hour, so the food court across the street from our campus was packed. I would have been happier in the quad or the parking lot, but Sabine was hungry. And thirsty. And in possession of information I wanted.

"Is that mine?" She reached for the paper bowl of frozen yogurt in the middle of the table and scooped a spoonful of nuts and berries off the top.

"Extra large, double raspberries." I scowled into my own kid-size helping. "I make minimum wage, you know. You're gonna break the bank."

"Can't take it with you," she pointed out, and my frown deepened at the reminder of my own impending death.

"Where's Nash?" The *mara* glanced around like he'd simply materialize in front of her.

"Baseball." Nash was the starting pitcher. He'd offered to skip practice, determined to spend all of what time I had left with me, but I'd told him to go on. Sabine and I—and now Emma—had work to do anyway. "What'cha got?"

"Well…no luck scoring private time with Beck." Sabine shrugged. "Evidently I'm not believable as a remedial math student."

"That can't be right," I said, and the *mara* scowled while Em laughed, a spoonful of chocolate yogurt halfway to her mouth. "What's your average?"

"Eighty-nine. I'm not stupid," Sabine snapped, and Emma bristled, no doubt thinking about her own seventy-eight average. "My only problem with math is that the very concept of homework violates one of my most strongly held beliefs."

"What belief?" Emma said. "That you're too special to work like the rest of us?" Like *she* did homework.

"The belief that homework should be optional for those of us who already understand the concepts."

"I like it," Emma said. "You should run for student council."

"No," Sabine muttered, around another bite of yogurt. "I really shouldn't."

"Okay, so he won't tutor you..." I said, redirecting the conversation. "We can work around that. You can still flirt with him, and try to read—"

"No way!" Emma slapped her palms flat on the tile-top table, and I flinched, hoping she hadn't drawn attention from the crowd all around us. "You'll let her *hit* on Mr. Beck, but you don't even want me to be tutored by him?"

"I'm not *letting* her do anything," I insisted, but Sabine spoke over me.

"Kaylee's not the boss of me. Hell, she's not even her own boss most of the time."

I rolled my eyes. "Thanks for yet another unsolicited amateur psychoanalysis." Then I turned to my best friend. "I'm sorry, Em, but Sabine can hold her own against...well, pretty much whatever's out there. And if I can't stop her from throwing herself at Nash, how am I supposed to stop her from hitting on Mr. Beck?"

"You can't, on either count," Sabine said, and Emma

shrugged in concession, still pouting. We both knew there was no taming this particular shrew. "Doesn't matter anyway. I already tried and failed to flirt my way in. I don't think he knows what I am, but he was definitely creeped out when I read his fears."

The *dissimulatus* bracelets we wore would disguise our psychic signatures, but if we used our abilities and they were recognized…we were screwed. And we couldn't chance letting Beck stumble over our secrets before we'd uncovered his.

"You read him? In class?" I snapped. Was she *trying* to get caught?

"Yeah, and I probably won't get another chance." She shrugged, and a sly grin blossomed. "So I guess it's a good thing I got what I needed on the first try, huh?"

Em stuck her spoon into her yogurt, where it stood straight up. "You know what he is?"

"Why didn't you say that in the first place?" I demanded, crossing my arms over my chest.

Sabine huffed. "Because this is a favor, not a charity. Nothing's ever really free, Kaylee."

"You're a credit to capitalism. Now spill it."

Sabine leaned over the table, and I scooted closer to hear her when she lowered her voice. "Okay, I'm about eighty-percent sure—"

"Eighty percent?" I bit back a groan.

"Reading fear isn't an exact science, Kay," Sabine snapped. Then she frowned and seemed to reconsider. "Okay, it kinda is, but it's *fear* reading, not *mind* reading. The only things I know for sure are what he's afraid of."

Em waved her hand in a "get on with it" gesture. "And that would be…"

"Failing to procreate."

"What?" Emma and I said in unison.

"He wants a baby. Specifically, a son."

"Okay, I think he's a little young to be so desperate for kids, but reproduction isn't exactly the most dastardly of deeds," Emma said.

But my stomach had started to pitch and a chill was crawling up my spine. Mr. Beck wasn't human and he wanted a baby, but he was afraid he wouldn't get one. Danica Sussman had just suffered the gruesome miscarriage of a baby that wasn't her boyfriend's, leaving her insides permanently damaged.

"He's not young," Sabine said, but I could barely hear her over the horrible conclusion building to a crescendo in my head. Beck—whatever he was—was preying on teenage girls. "In fact, he's afraid he's waited too long, and that he won't live to see another fertile period."

"Fertile period?" Emma echoed, and the picture refusing to come into focus in my head grew a little darker.

"What is he?" I stared at the table beneath my hands, concentrating on the grout between the tiles to focus my thoughts.

Sabine exhaled and crossed her arms on the slick four-inch tiles. "My best guess is...incubus. Our new math teacher is a no-shit, in-the-flesh lust-demon. What are the chances?"

"Pretty damn good, considering Eastlake High makes Buffy's hellmouth look like a crack in the sidewalk." I shoved hair back from my face and met Sabine's black-eyed gaze, which practically sparked with anticipation—the sure sign of an adrenaline junkie. "What exactly are you basing this assessment on?"

"Other than the fact that he's not human, but he lives on this side of the barrier?" she asked, and I nodded. "Mostly the fertile period part. Incubi are only capable of breeding, like, once a century. Or something like that. And if he's afraid he's too old, I'm guessing that rumor about him being twenty-two is *way* off base."

"Wait, incubus?" Emma said, glancing back and forth between us, desperately trying to keep up. "Like, the band?"

I was starting to *really* regret my promise of full disclosure. "No. Like the psychic parasite."

"Psychic...parasite?" If Em frowned any harder, her face would cave in on itself. "So, what? They drink thoughts?"

Sabine rolled her eyes. "The only thing worse than working with one clueless do-gooder is working with two." She twisted on the bench to face Emma, and I leaned closer to listen. My knowledge of incubi was limited to a couple of stories from our mythology unit in English the year before, and if those were as inaccurate as the stories about "banshees," then I really knew next to nothing.

"Psychic parasites feed from human energy, in one form or another. An incubus, specifically, feeds from lust."

"Please tell me this means you've come up against one before," I said, hoping for a ray of sunshine in what was otherwise turning out to be a very cloudy day.

"As interesting a story as that would have been...no." Sabine actually sounded disappointed. "I did meet a succubus once, though. That's the female version of an incubus," she added, glancing at Emma. "We did *not* get along."

"Color me shocked."

"Okay..." Emma frowned at Sabine. "Incubi and *maras* both feed from human energy, right?" she said, and Sabine nodded, already scowling in advance of Emma's point. "So that makes you different from Mr. Beck *how?*"

"When I feed, I don't kill people," Sabine snapped.

"Well, neither has he," Em insisted. "We don't even know for a fact that Danica's baby was his."

"Like I said, I'm eighty-percent sure of his species, and if

I'm right about that, the probability of that being his baby is closer to ninety-nine percent."

And if he'd lost both the baby and the ability to have another with Danica, would he be looking for a new potential mother from among his remaining students? Maybe…students who needed help with math?

"Can we please forget the percentage points?" Em groaned. "This is already too much like school."

"And if he's as old as I think he is, he *has* killed," Sabine continued, ignoring Em's complaint. "Otherwise he wouldn't have survived this long."

"But he's obviously not feeding where he…*breeds,* or else we'd have heard about the deaths." I closed my eyes, far from relieved that my distraction had actually turned into something big enough to eclipse my own problems. "Any idea how often he has to eat?"

Sabine shook her head. "Sorry. I exhausted my incubus knowledge with that fertile period thing."

"Well, you knew more than I did. What else did you get from reading him?" I asked, while Em listened with a frown, obviously reluctant to believe anything bad about Mr. Beck.

"Um…he's afraid that the girls are too old, though I'm not sure I understand that, if he's targeting his students." Which seemed to be the case, if we were right about Danica. "And he's afraid that even if he gets a baby, it won't be a boy. He's scared of a lot of things," Sabine said, and when I looked up, I realized she was talking to me, not Em. "But do you know what he's not afraid of?"

"Clowns?" Emma said, throwing her hands in the air in exasperation.

Sabine never even glanced at her, and I shook my head in reply. I had no idea.

"Getting caught." The *mara's* eyes gleamed with a dark malevolence I found oddly comforting, since she was on my side this time. "It hasn't even crossed his mind that there might be a consequence in this for him, other than not getting what he wants. How do you feel about that, Kay?"

"Pissed off." I was almost as surprised by the anger in my own voice as I was by the actual words I hadn't intended to say. Until I realized they were true. I *was* pissed, on Danica's behalf, and on behalf of anyone else who may have suffered like she did.

Sabine nodded sharply, and her earrings glinted in the sun from the skylight overhead. "I say we take the bastard down."

9

Emma had to leave for work straight from the food court, but Sabine insisted on following me home in her car so we could start researching incubi in general, and Mr. Beck in particular. She claimed dedication to the mission, and I'm sure that was part of it—she typically cured boredom with chaos—but I wasn't fooled; we could have researched separately and combined info later. Sabine was coming over so that when Nash arrived after practice, we wouldn't be alone.

And honestly, I couldn't blame her.

I pushed the front door open and was surprised to find Alec sitting on the couch, obviously waiting for me.

"Hey, what are you doing here?" I held the door for Sabine, then closed it behind her. "And how'd you get in?" As happy as I was to see him, I couldn't help being suspicious. It turned out that about half the time I'd spent with Alec when he was staying with us had actually been spent in the company of Avari, the hellion of greed who'd been possessing him and using him to kill my teachers.

But then I noticed Styx curled up asleep on the couch next to him, and both my suspicion and fear slipped away. She would never sleep through a hellion possession.

Alec stood and held his arms out for me. "Your dad dropped by my place on his way to work this morning with a key and a strongly worded request that I come keep you company tonight. He's not gonna make it for dinner." I let him fold me into a hug, and I knew by his tight grip and reluctance to let go that my dad had filled him in completely—and that he was now off looking for some way to save my life. "Four days, Kay? Why didn't you tell me?"

Before I could answer, Styx's head popped up and a low growl rumbled from her throat. Sabine stiffened and I backed out of Alec's brotherly grip, all three of us instantly on alert.

"Yeah, why didn't you tell him, *Kay?*" Thane said, and I whirled around to see the reaper standing in the kitchen doorway, eyeing me in mock concern. "Don't you think your friends should know you're about to leave them?"

"What's wrong?" Sabine had noticed me staring toward the kitchen, and Alec was just watching me, waiting.

"Nothing," I said, hyperaware of Tod's warning about putting our friends in danger. "Styx is probably just mad that we interrupted her nap."

"Yeah, that's it...." Thane said from behind me. I actually heard his clothes rustle as he came closer and because I didn't trust him at my back, it took every bit of self-control I had to keep ignoring him. "Where'd you get that thing, anyway? I've never seen one of those yappy little monsters on this side of the barrier."

"I didn't tell you because there's nothing you can do," I said to Alec, struggling to concentrate on the conversation I was actually having, rather than the one I was boycotting.

"Damn right..." Thane sat on the arm of the couch, and Styx stood on the cushion to growl at him.

"There's nothing *anyone* can do," I continued, determined to ignore him. "So I'm just kind of...trying not to think about it." And thanks to Thane, I was failing miserably, in spite of the scary new distraction Mr. Beck had provided. Knowing my death was coming was like tumbling into a deep, dark pit in slow motion. The world above me narrowed into an ever-smaller point of light as I fell further and further from its influence.

And I fell faster every time Thane showed up.

Sabine dropped into my father's recliner like she owned it, eyeing Alec. "So you're, like, the babysitter? What, Kaylee can't even be trusted to die on her own?"

Thane laughed. "I like her!"

Completely oblivious to the reaper sitting feet away, Alec sank onto the couch and pulled me down next to him, brows raised at Sabine. "Wow, you're about as warm as a frostbitten toe."

I leaned back with my feet on the battered coffee table, hands folded over my stomach. "Sabine has frostbite of the *heart*. Unfortunately, her mouth is perfectly functional."

"As is my brain. Let's get started."

She was right—time was my enemy. Well, time and Thane. I twisted to look up at Alec, who towered over me even when we sat side by side. "My dad's just being overprotective. You can go if you want," I said, in spite of the voice in my head insisting that I not be left alone with Thane. "Obviously I won't be wasting away here by myself…" I glanced pointedly at Sabine. "And Nash is coming over after dinner, so I'll be in good hands."

Sabine gave a harsh laugh. "She'll be in more than just his hands, if you leave them alone together. So feel free to hang out and keep them from getting naked." Since she'd promised not to stand in our way.

"Oh, goody, a show!" the reaper cried, and because I

couldn't yell at him, I had to take my frustration out on the *mara*. Who probably deserved it anyway.

"Sabine!" I snapped, before I realized that rising to her bait was as good as admitting my intentions.

Alec's surprise slid quickly into amusement. "*That's* why your dad really sent me...?"

"No." *Probably.* I could feel my face burn, and I could have *killed* Sabine for giving the reaper that little glimpse into my life—even though she had no idea what she'd done. "And my sex life is none of anyone else's business."

Sabine laughed out loud. "Your sex life is fictional."

"Okay, get out." I stood and gestured toward the door on my way into the kitchen, talking to her, but glancing pointedly at Thane. "If you aren't going to help, then just go home."

"Oh, calm down," Sabine called from the living room. "And let Alec stay, too. We could use him."

"Use me for what?" Alec asked, as I dug in the fridge for three cold sodas.

"Nothing like what you're probably thinking," Sabine said. "Though I do have four more days as a free woman, so long as you're just lookin' for a little fun...."

I tossed a soda at her, secretly aiming for her head, and the *mara* caught it one-handed, shooting me a challenging grin. I brushed past the reaper no one else could see and Alec frowned as I handed him a can and sank onto the couch again, this time facing both him and Sabine. "Does that mean what it sounds like it means?" he asked.

"Yes." I could only shrug and pop open my drink. "In one sentence, she managed to proposition you, call dibs on my boyfriend, and remind us all—again—that I'm going to die."

Sabine grinned. "I'm an acquired taste."

"Well, my tastes run more toward comfort food, but thanks

for the offer," Alec said, and Sabine shrugged off the dismissal while he turned back to me. "I hesitate to ask—I'm not sure I want to know what put the two of you on the same side of an issue—but what's going on? What were you going to use me for?"

"Yes, what *are* you up to, little *bean sidhe...?*" Thane taunted, leaning back to watch the show, like he was our own live studio audience.

"I had no plans to drag you into this, but since you're here...what do you know about incubi?"

Alec stared at me for a moment, his brown eyes wide with surprise. Then narrowed in concern. "Do you ever ask for help with anything normal?"

I lifted one brow at him. "There's a Netherworld guard dog curled up in my lap and I'm going to die in four days," I said, my stomach pitching at the very thought. *And I'm being stalked by the reaper assigned to kill me.* "I don't even remember what normal looks like, Alec."

"You're taking this death thing pretty calmly," he said, his voice soft, his gaze searching mine for signs of a crack in my composed facade.

"I believe he's right." Thane leaned in closer, staring at me in imitation of Alec, and the urge to punch him was almost as strong as the fluttering panic his presence—another re- minder of my own impending death—spawned deep in my chest. "Can't have that, now can we? Hmm..." Then he dis- appeared, and I sighed in relief, in spite of his ominous exit.

Styx put her head down on my knee and went to sleep while I refocused on the conversation, determined to push my own problems aside for just a little while longer, a luxury that was rapidly expiring, along with my lifeline.

"I'm only calm on the outside. What can you tell us about incubi?"

Alec frowned over my reply, but didn't push the issue. "What do you already know?"

I set my soda on the coffee table and began ticking points off on my fingers. "They're always male. They feed from lust. They go into some kind of weird fertile period every century or so. And…there's one teaching math at my school."

"Whoa…" Alec sat up straight, glancing from me to Sabine and back. "One of your teachers is an incubus? How are you just now figuring this out?"

"Because he doesn't stand at the front of the classroom chanting 'I'm a sex demon, please come vanquish me,'" Sabine said, popping the tab on her soda.

"He's only been there six weeks," I added, still stroking Styx's fur while she slept. "He's Mr. Wesner's replacement. Sabine knew he wasn't human, but we didn't know anything was wrong until Danica Sussman had a miscarriage in the middle of first period on Friday, and it turns out the baby wasn't her boyfriend's," I said, trying not to remember her on the floor, bleeding…

"Uh-oh." Alec scuffed one hand over his tight, dark curls. "Okay, let's start with the facts." He popped his can open and took the first sip, then set it on an end table. "Incubi *are* all male, and they *do* feed from lust, either indirectly—kind of like sunbathing on a bright day—or directly, which involves… pretty much exactly what you're thinking."

"Ew!" I tried and failed to purge the visual of Mr. Beck feeding during sex, but Sabine only shrugged.

"At least you'd die happy." Her brows rose. "Hey, maybe that's how you're gonna go, Kaylee…."

I shook my head, firmly denying the unease crawling slowly up my spine. "No way. No." But I couldn't deny the coincidence. Our new math teacher was a psychic leach and

I was scheduled to die in four days. *Please, please, please don't let those two things be connected...*

"Don't worry." Alec leaned forward to scratch behind Styx's ears. "I doubt his charm would have much of an effect on either of you, considering you're not human."

"Charm?"

"It's like sexual charisma, or some kind of strong, supernatural pheromone. He can direct it, to a certain extent, but a little bit of it is always going to leak out and draw people to him. And he, in return, can feed indirectly off the lust those people feel for him."

"So, every time some poor student gets a crush on her math teacher, he has a little snack?" I said, horrified by the very concept.

"Yeah. Only he's not limited to students. Or girls."

"Lucky bastard!" Sabine set her can on the floor. "He doesn't even have to wait for anyone to fall asleep."

"Yeah. *That's* the part of this that's messed up." I turned to Alec, trying to forget how much Sabine had in common with Mr. Beck, at least on the surface. "Any other incubus facts?"

"Well, you're right about the breeding. The incubus fertility cycle lasts a hundred to one hundred twenty years, but they're only actually fertile for twelve to fourteen months of that. The exact length of time varies, like a woman's menstrual cycle."

"That is *nothing* like a menstrual cycle," Sabine said, and for once, I had to agree with her.

"So, what you're saying is that Mr. Beck is ready to have kids for the first time in roughly a century, and he picked Danica Sussman to be the mother?"

"Well, I doubt she was the only one," Alec said. "Incubi can breed with human women, but it takes a *lot* of work to produce just one little baby incubus."

"What does that mean?"

Alec shrugged. "I don't have concrete numbers, but from what I've heard—" and because he'd spent a quarter of a century in the Netherworld, Alec's information was the best we'd have access to "—for every dozen or so girls he gets pregnant, only one will give birth to a healthy baby boy. The rest will either miscarry or give birth to a girl."

"So then Danica was just the first, right?" I asked. "There will be more like her?"

"Yeah, or there may already have been. He could have a whole string of miscarriages and pregnant girls behind him, but based on the fact that he's still trying, I'm guessing he doesn't have a son yet."

"Who cares if it's a boy?" Sabine asked. "What, he's a *sexist* lust-demon?"

Alec actually laughed. "Only the boy babies are incubi. Girls share their mothers' species and are usually considered worthless."

"So, you can't put an incubus and a human girl together and get a succubus?" I asked, sorting through the details in my head.

"Nope." Alec shook his head. "They're two completely different species. And consider yourself lucky you're dealing with an incubus, because the only thing scarier than a succubus trying to get pregnant is a succubus who's already pregnant. Talk about hormonal..."

"What did you mean about the girl babies being worthless?" Sabine asked, her eyes going dark again, and I realized he'd hit one of her hot buttons. As a toddler, Sabine was abandoned by her parents on a Dallas church doorstep, and after that, she'd bounced from one foster family to the next, for most of her life.

Alec shrugged. "They're almost always abandoned by the

incubus. As recently as a few decades ago, it was difficult for a mother to raise an illegitimate child alone, so the baby might have been abandoned by the mother, too. That's not much of an issue today, though."

The *mara* didn't answer, but I could see anger simmering quietly in the dark depths of her eyes.

"So, how does this charm work?" I asked, trying to redirect the discussion.

Alec shrugged. "I've never actually met an incubus, and I'm not sure his charm would work on me even if I liked guys, because I'm half-hypnos." His father was a minor Netherworld creature who fed on the energy from sleeping humans, as it bled through the barrier between worlds. "But from what I understand, just being around him makes people…well, *want* him. If he's reining it in, which he probably is in a public place, it'll exaggerate the symptoms of physical attraction. Students may start competing for his attention. They'll flirt and try to impress him. They'll touch him and try to get him to touch them. They'll become infatuated with him very quickly and personally offended by criticism of him."

Uh-oh. That sounded like Emma already.

"It'll be strongest with those who are already attracted to him, but it could have a light effect on just about any human," Alec continued. "But when he finds someone he wants, either to impregnate or to feed from, he'll turn it on full-strength, and the lucky girl will… Well, she'll need him. Desperately. Like a craving she can't control."

"But it's like some kind of spell, right?" I said, uncomfortably reminded of the strength of Nash's Influence, when he lost control of it. "She doesn't *really* want him, she just thinks she does, because of this charm crap. Right?" I said, thinking back to Danica's physical obsession with her baby's father.

"I don't know, Kay," Alec said, obviously reluctant to voice whatever was coming next. "I think it's less like a spell and more like primal physical attraction. It's hormonal, and it's very strong."

"Do they actually fall in love with him?" Sabine asked, her nose wrinkled in disgust, and I was relieved to realize we were on the same page for once.

"No," Alec said. "And most of them have no delusions about that—at least, the older, more experienced women. They know they don't love him. They may not even like him. But they physically have to have him, like they have to have food and air."

"So...sleeping with him is consensual?" Sabine asked.

"No," I said, just as Alec said, "Yeah."

I turned on him in surprise. "No, it's not. It can't be. This 'charm' of his is like a...a drug. They're not in their right minds. Right?"

"I don't know, Kaylee. I think they really want him. In fact, some young incubi have been mobbed, like celebrities."

"Do they have a choice?" Sabine asked. "Can girls fight his charm?"

"Yeah. It takes a lot of willpower, but yes," Alec said. "Definitely."

"They shouldn't *have* to fight," I insisted, struggling with a squirming discomfort the entire discussion dredged up in me. "The fact that they have to proves that it's not consensual. Not really. And you're not going to change my mind."

Alec nodded. "I'm not even gonna try."

"So...any idea how to stop him?"

He shrugged. "I don't know how to get rid of an incubus, other than giving him a son. Ask your dad for help?"

I shook my head. "Can't. He has his hands full trying to save my life right now."

Alec frowned. "How can he...?"

"He can't. But telling him that does no good. I've tried, and so have Tod and Harmony. Feel free to add your voice to the chorus."

"So anyway, we've only got four days to take this murdering, daughter-abandoning bastard down." Sabine hesitated, then shrugged. "Well, *you* only have four days. *I* have as long as it takes."

The truth of her statement hit me like a brick to the forehead, and the room swam around me. I set Styx on the couch and stood, staring straight into the *mara's* eyes. "Sabine, I think he's going after Emma. You have to promise me you'll watch out for her if I die before we get rid of him. Don't let her wind up like Danica. Please."

Sabine frowned, staring up at me. "At this point, I think *you* actually owe *me* another favor, *bean sidhe...*"

"Promise me!" I grabbed her arm and hauled her to her feet, almost as surprised as she was by my strength. "She's human, and she's defenseless, and she's my best friend, which has already gotten her killed, and possessed, and on the radar of two different hellions. You're not leaving this house until you promise me you'll protect her when I'm gone. You can inherit her just like you will Nash. You need a real friend anyway."

Sabine stared at me like I'd lost my mind. "Emma doesn't even like me."

"I don't care! I swear if you let her get hurt, I'll haunt your ass for eternity. I'll turn up in the room every time you're alone with Nash, and you'll never get another taste of him. Ever."

Her pierced right brow rose in interest. "How are you gonna do that?"

"I'll find a way..."

"Jeez, settle down, Mama Bear, I'm not gonna let Emma get hurt." Sabine pulled her arm from my grasp and dropped back into my dad's chair, grinning up at me. "I just wanted to see how good your threat would be."

I had to concentrate to unclench my jaw. "How'd I do?"

Her head bobbed, almost respectfully. "Not bad."

"Not bad, nothin', that was *badass!*" Alec said, and I turned to see him watching me, already on his feet, ready to come to my rescue if Sabine had decided to bite back. "That was great, how your voice got all deep and scary."

"It did?" *'Bout time my voice did something helpful for a change.* I sank back onto the couch next to Styx, who yipped and watched me until she was convinced I was okay. Then she curled up in my lap and went back to sleep again. "Okay, so we know Beck's hurting people, but we don't know how to get rid of him…" I began, making a conscious effort to guide us all back onto the subject.

"Short of killing him? No," Alec said, plopping onto his end of the couch again, soda in hand.

"Well, that's a moot point anyway, 'cause I don't think I could kill someone." Except maybe in self-defense. Or Emma-defense.

Sabine shrugged. "I could." I glanced at her in disbelief, but she only rolled her eyes. "What? He's a bad guy."

"By whose definition of bad?" Alec asked, and Sabine and I shot him twin looks of disbelief. Alec sighed and sat up straighter. "Look, I'm not saying he's a saint, but I've seen plenty of *real* bad guys in the last quarter century, ladies. Monsters who would do much worse than what Beck's done, just to watch some poor girl suffer. But so far, it sounds like your math teacher's just trying to feed himself and propagate his own species, both of which are rights the two of you take for granted."

"Nuh-uh." Sabine shook her head vehemently. "I'm a parasite, too. If I can control myself during a meal at seventeen years old, then he can damn well do it at…however old he is."

Alec nodded, conceding the point, but his gaze held Sabine's firmly. "And you have no evidence that he hasn't. All you have is a teenager's miscarriage. I'm not saying that's not horrible, because it is. But he didn't mean for that to happen. Your incubus wants that baby even worse than its mother probably did, yet you're willing to kill a man because his lover had a miscarriage?"

Sabine leaned forward in her chair, and the lights in the room seemed to dim as her eyes grew darker. "You're twisting it all around to make it sound innocent, but it's not," she insisted. "This is a very old man taking advantage of teenage girls, using some kind of supernatural charisma as a weapon. That's messed up, no matter how you look at it."

I frowned at Alec, turning on the couch to face him more directly. "You can't seriously think what he's doing is justified?"

"No. And I never said I did. I'm just saying that the punishment ought to fit the crime. You're talking about killing this man, and you have no evidence he's actually taken a life."

Crap. "He's right," I said, and Sabine turned on me in surprise. I shrugged. "I'm not saying we should drop the issue. I'm not even saying you can't kill him." If he lay one hand on Emma, I'd be right there behind Sabine when she threw the first punch—or whatever. "But before we condemn a man to death, we need to know that he's actually taken a life. Otherwise…we're going to have to find some other way to get rid of him." Some way that wouldn't just push him into the next school unlucky enough to have a midsemester job opening.

"Okay, so we find his victims," Sabine conceded, obviously confident that there actually *were* victims. "How do we do that? Look for other pregnant girls?"

"Well, unless he's a moron—and he's isn't, or someone would have caught up to him by now—he's not going to feed from anyone carrying his child, 'cause that would drain the baby, too. Right?" I asked, and Alec nodded. "So, basically, we're looking for dead un-pregnant women."

"Can't think of any of those, recently," Sabine said.

"Me, neither. So we stick with what we know, which is that Danica probably isn't the first girl he's knocked up during this fertility cycle. Maybe if we find the others, and search the obituaries in their towns, we'll be able to put together a pattern."

Sabine nodded, brows raised. "Not bad, *bean sidhe!*"

"Not bad at all," Alec agreed. "And maybe I can narrow your search a bit... Incubi—and succubi, too, if memory serves—tend to return to the same breeding ground cycle after cycle. If he's breeding here now, then this is his territory, and you're probably going to find most of his other conquests in this general area."

"Same breeding ground, cycle after cycle..." I said, thinking aloud. "And if he's teaching now to get to teenage girls, maybe he taught somewhere else before Eastlake."

"So, what are you gonna do?" Alec asked. "Go question every principal in the metroplex about former teachers?"

"Poor Alec, you've missed so much in the last quarter of a century." Grinning from ear to ear, I set Styx down and bent to pull my laptop from my bag on the floor. "Most schools don't put students' yearbook photos online, but lots of them have pictures of the faculty..." I set the laptop on the coffee table and turned it on, then sipped from my can while the system booted up.

With any luck, the face that had probably brought girls

flocking to him for centuries would now lead us to his previous victims, along with the evidence we'd need to get rid of Beck for good.

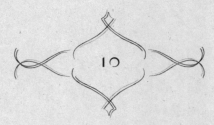

10

Sabine didn't have a laptop, and mine was a one computer household, so going through the local school districts took a while. And a lot of them didn't post pictures of their teachers. But finally, after an hour and a half of searching and two bags of microwave popcorn—I'd sworn off everything but junk for what remained of my life—we found him.

During the fall semester, our Mr. Beck had taught advanced math at Crestwood High. Only the Crestwood students had called him Mr. David Allan.

"That's him!" Sabine said, and I nodded while Alec leaned over my shoulder for a better look. "Does it say why he left?"

"I doubt they'd put that on the website. But..." Crestwood's student newspaper was online, so I did a quick search for his alias, looking for some mention of why he left—or was fired.

I found it in the November 3 issue. Mr. Allan had left his position as a first-year math teacher after one semester to pursue a graduate degree, and he hoped to be back in a couple of years, better able to serve the students of Crestwood.

Yeah, right.

I was about to close the tab when a familiar—and horrifying—place name caught my attention from the short mention just below Allan's article.

Our thoughts and prayers are with senior honor student Farrah Combs, who was admitted to Lakeside Hospital last week. Get well soon, Farrah!

What the editor of the *Crestwood Observer* obviously didn't know—if she had, the mention probably never would have run in their paper—was that Lakeside wasn't a regular hospital. It was a mental health facility, attached to Arlington Memorial. The very same mental health facility—psych ward, to the uninformed—where I'd spent a week of my life, a year and a half earlier.

Lakeside was only fifteen miles away. Maybe Farrah Combs—assuming she was still there, and marginally coherent—could tell me something about Mr. Allan. And whether or not any of her fellow students had gotten pregnant or died while he was teaching there.

But I couldn't tell Sabine my idea, because she'd insist on tagging along, and I was *not* taking a living nightmare into a mental health facility.

I glanced at the onscreen clock before closing my laptop and was relieved to realize it was almost six o'clock. "Okay..." I stood and slid my computer back into the bag. "I'm gonna find something to eat and *you're* going to go home."

"Why?" Sabine said, physically resisting as I tried to guide her toward the door. "We're on a tight schedule here, Kaylee. I thought you wanted to nail this bastard."

"I do. Figuratively. But I can't think when I'm hungry, so why don't you go home and go online and see if you can find any more of Beck's former employers."

"I don't have internet at home."

"Then go to the library. Sometimes people fall asleep

there—I'm sure that's an untapped market for you. We can exchange information in the morning."

"What information are you gonna have?" she demanded, as I pulled the front door open and pushed her half-empty soda can into her hand.

I scrambled for another well-meaning lie until my gaze settled on an obviously amused Alec, and the answer slid into place. "Alec's going to help me come up with a plan B for getting rid of Mr. Beck, in case murder starts to look a bit extreme."

"That's not gonna happen," Sabine insisted, eyes narrowed at me now from the front porch.

"Well, just in case. I'll see you tomorrow." Then I closed the door in her face.

Alec laughed out loud. "What was that all about?"

"You have to take the direct approach with Sabine—she doesn't understand subtlety." I peeked through the blinds until her car drove away, then I turned to Alec. "Your turn. How'd you get here, anyway?"

He crossed both arms over his chest and suddenly embodied the immovable object. "I took the bus."

"Good. I think there's another one at six-fifteen. You need change?"

Alec frowned. "I'm gainfully employed, Kaylee. And I'm not leaving. I promised your dad I'd stay with you."

"I don't need a babysitter, Alec."

"I know. But your dad's afraid that whatever's supposed to kill you could hit early and leave you lingering on the brink of death for the next few days. And he's pretty determined not to let that happen."

"Then he should be at home, not out chasing possibilities that don't exist."

"You can't rationalize with grief and denial, Kaylee."

"I'm trying to rationalize with *you*. I have something important to do, and I need you to go home."

Alec dropped into my dad's recliner, and I knew with one glance that he wasn't going to be moved until he was damn well ready. "If this is about Nash…you're as grown as you're gonna get and it's not my place to tell you what not to do with your boyfriend. You two can go back there and close the door and make the whole damn planet quake for all I care. I'll even wear earplugs, if you think it's gonna get loud, but—"

"No! This has nothing to do with Nash." In fact, if I told him, he'd try to talk me out of it. I sighed and sat on the edge of the coffee table. "I swear, I'll kill you if you tell my dad, but…I'm going to sneak into Lakeside and talk to Farrah Combs. And I need to be back before Nash comes over, so you have to go!"

"You're gonna sneak into Lakeside? I thought you hated that place."

"I do." *With a fierce and glorious passion.* "But that's my best chance of finding the bodies in Beck's closet, and I am *not* going to die without knowing he's no threat to Emma, or anyone else at school."

"Fine. I'll go with you."

"You can't. It'll be hard enough to get myself in, and bringing you will only double our chances of getting caught."

He shifted in the chair and it groaned beneath his weight. "How are you going to get in?"

I stared at my hands in my lap, avoiding his gaze. "I have an idea, but it only works for one person. Me."

"*Please* tell me you're not going to get yourself committed." He leaned forward with his elbows on his knees, trying to catch my gaze. "I'm pretty sure your dad would actually kill me if I let that happen."

"No! How am I supposed to help *anyone* if I'm tied to a stretcher?"

"They really tied you down?"

"We have that in common," I said, and he burst into laughter, no doubt remembering what was probably the most embarrassing moment of either of our lives.

I couldn't quite decide why I was reluctant to admit the next part, but when I realized he wasn't going to go without more information, I knew I had no choice. "I'm going to see if Tod can get me into Lakeside without being seen."

"Are you sure that's a good idea?" Alec asked softly, watching me closely, and I couldn't tell if he meant breaking into the hospital, or asking Tod for help.

"I'm not sure about anything anymore, Alec. Except that I'm going to die. But not before I take Beck down." I stood and gestured toward the front door. "Now *please* go home so I can be reckless and brave for possibly the last time in my tragically short life."

Alec rolled beautiful brown eyes. "No fair playing the death card."

"No fair having it to play," I shot back, holding the front door open.

"Fine." He stood and shoved his hands into his pockets. "But if your dad finds out, tell him you overpowered me and left me for dead."

"Got it." I pushed all six-foot-two, one hundred eighty-plus pounds of him over the threshold with both hands.

"Be careful, Kaylee," he said, and I nodded solemnly as I closed the door in his face. He hadn't even made it to the sidewalk when I pulled my phone from my pocket and auto-dialed.

"Kaylee?" Tod answered on the first ring. "What's wrong?"

I hesitated on my way to the kitchen with Alec's empty soda can. "How do you know something's wrong?"

"You only call me when you want something Nash can't do for you."

My face flamed, and I was suddenly glad he couldn't see me. That I knew of. "That is *not* true."

"Oh, yeah?" he teased, and I could hear the challenge in his voice. "So…you don't need anything?" Was it true? I *had* kind of come to count on him…

A smile snuck up on me, in spite of his valid point and the grave reason for my call. "As a matter of fact, I was going to offer *you* something."

For one long moment, the only sound over the line was the soft whisper of his next inhalation, then his voice sounded a little scratchier than usual. "What did you have in mind?"

"A field trip. You interested in doing something dangerous, and possibly illegal?"

"Does it involve underage girls, broken curfews and assorted fruit toppings?"

I dropped the empty can into the recycling bin and leaned against the kitchen peninsula, grinning like an idiot. "Two of the three. And I could probably scrounge up some strawberry jam, if you're desperate."

"I'm *never* desperate," Tod said, only his voice hadn't come from my phone. I whirled around to see the reaper standing behind me, still holding his cell. "But for the record, I prefer apricot."

"Yuck. Nobody likes apricot jam."

Tod shrugged and pocketed his phone. "Sure, strawberry is the more obvious choice, but I submit that apricot has a more complex, unusual flavor, with just enough tang to keep things interesting…" He raised one brow, grinning more with his eyes than with his mouth, and I had the sudden inexplicable urge to look away, before I saw too much. Then Tod blinked, and whatever I'd almost seen was gone. "So...what illegal adventure will I be aiding and abetting today?"

I closed my phone and slid it into my front pocket. "Remember when you snuck me into Nash's room to watch him and Sabine?" At the time, he'd said it was so that I could better understand their friendship, but in retrospect, I think it was so that I could see for myself how connected they were. Tod had made no secret of the fact that he thought his brother and I were a bad match. It was one of the few things he and Sabine had in common.

"Are we playing spy again? That's my second favorite game." Tod followed me down the hall and into my room, where I pretended I didn't want to know what his first favorite game was while I dug in the bottom of my closet for a pair of laceless, slip-on canvas shoes. If I got caught, shoelaces would be a dead giveaway that I didn't belong at Lakeside—strings of any kind were banned from the facility.

"More like detective. I need to get into a secure building."

His brows rose in interest. "The police station? Did Sabine get arrested again?"

I stepped into the first shoe. "If she had, I'd be laughing from afar, not busting her out. We're breaking into Lakeside."

Tod dropped into my desk chair and it bobbed beneath his very corporeal weight. "Don't most people try to break *out* of the psych ward?"

"I'm not most people." I stepped into the other shoe and slid my ID and a twenty-dollar bill into my back pocket.

"That's what I like best about you. So why are we breaking into the loony bin?"

"I need to talk to one of the patients. And I figured I should check on Scott while I'm there."

"Scott's at Lakeside?" Tod appeared in the living room

ahead of me, and when I tried to grab my keys from the empty candy dish, I found them dangling from his index finger instead.

"Your mom said he was moved there for long-term care last month."

Scott Carter was Nash's best friend and fellow frost addict. But because he was human, the drug had affected him much faster and stronger than it affected Nash. Scott suffered a psychotic breakdown and irreparable brain damage from his addiction, and he now had a permanent, hardwired mental connection to Avari, the hellion of avarice, whose breath they'd both been huffing.

Nash had visited him several times in the hospital, always hoping for improvement that never came, but he couldn't get in to see Scott at Lakeside, where visitors had to be approved individually by the attending physician.

"You wanna ride with me, or meet me in the parking lot?" I asked, plucking my key ring from his finger. Obviously, it'd be faster for him to just blink himself there, but he didn't yet have the strength—or maybe the skill—to materialize that far away with a passenger, so I'd have to drive myself.

Tod crossed his arms over his uniform shirt, a blue polo with a stylized pizza embroidered on the left side of his chest. "I haven't said I'll do it yet."

I frowned, one hand on the doorknob, trying to decide whether or not he was joking. "What if I said this is my dying wish? You know, one last request?"

"Your last request is to break into a psychiatric hospital?"

I shrugged. "I'm kind of operating under the assumption that I get one last request from everyone who gives a damn that I'm dying." I shoved my hands into my pockets and stared straight at his eyes, demanding the truth from them in a sudden surge of reckless courage. "Do you fall into that category?"

"Don't play that game, Kaylee. You already know the answer to that." There was just the slightest twist of emotion in his blue eyes, and my pulse spiked when his voice went deep, like his response meant more than the sum of the individual words.

"Then will you help me?"

"You know the answer to that, too," he said, and I smiled in relief, then almost laughed out loud over the absurdity of that. You'd *have* to be crazy to break *into* a psychiatric hospital.

I held the front door for him, then locked it behind us, and when I looked up, Tod was already sitting in my passenger seat waiting for me, with all four doors locked. "You know, you'd make a great thief," I said, sliding into the driver's seat next to him.

"I'm a man of many talents."

"Thanks for doing this," I said as I backed down the driveway.

"I was bored at work anyway." He shrugged as I shifted into Drive and took off toward the highway.

After several miles of me watching the road and him watching me, I finally huffed in exasperation. "What?"

"What'd you want from Nash, Kaylee?"

"Huh?" I glanced at Tod and found his irises holding steady in spite of clear tension in the line of his jaw.

"Your last request from my little brother. What did you ask him to do for you?"

My grip tightened around the steering wheel, and I could feel my face flush. "That's none of your business, Tod."

In my peripheral vision, he nodded stiffly. "That's what I thought."

"What, no lecture about how I'm too young, or I'm not ready?" Or I shouldn't be with Nash in the first place?

"I've already said what I have to say about you and my brother." Tod stared out his window, and it irritated me that I couldn't see his face. "If that's really what you want, go for it. I just thought…"

"What? You thought what?" I demanded, further irritated by his tone—which I couldn't quite interpret.

Finally he turned to face me again, and my focus shifted back and forth between him and the barely past-rush-hour traffic. "I just thought… I thought you'd have something better to do with these last few days than spend them in bed with your boyfriend."

I couldn't think beyond the sting of his words, each like a needle puncturing my heart. Or maybe my pride. But then my surprise—and yeah, a tiny hint of shame—morphed into anger, sharp and clear. "Did you die a virgin, Tod?" I demanded.

He rolled his eyes. "No."

"Then where the hell do you get off telling me I should?"

He sighed and leaned his chair back a little as I passed a slow-moving station wagon. "That's not what I'm saying. If you wanna sleep with Nash, then sleep with Nash. You wouldn't be the first to make that mistake."

Anger made my heart beat harder. "Why are you so sure it'd be a mistake?"

"Because I know you! You've waited this long because it's important to you and you want it to mean something. And if it's with Nash, I think you'll regret it later, when you realize the two of you don't belong together."

His insight scared me, and for a second, I couldn't think beyond the shock of hearing some of my own thoughts coming from his mouth, albeit colored with his usual anti-Nash perspective. Then the reality of what he'd said kicked in and fear-fueled anger flared in me like living flames.

"There isn't going to *be* a later, Tod! These next three days? That's my life. That's all I get. I'm not going to live to regret *anything*."

"So—just to be clear—you're doing it for the novelty of the act? Not because you love him or because it means some-thing—just so you can say you've done it?"

Yes.

"No!" I shook my head, trying to jostle my conflicting thoughts into some semblance of order. "You're such a hypo-crite! Did your first time *mean* something? Did a choir of an-gels set the mood with an a cappella fanfare celebrating your union?" I demanded, and Tod just stared at me, his expres-sion caught somewhere between surprise and regret. "Why do you even care if I sleep with Nash?"

Why did I care that he cared?

He turned to stare out his window again. "I just assumed you'd have something a little more meaningful on your last to-do list."

And that's when I realized he had no idea why we were breaking into Lakeside. "Not that it's any of your business, but this little field trip we're on has a purpose. I'm hoping a psych patient named Farrah Combs can give me the informa-tion I need to get rid of the incubus posing as my math teacher so that he can't seduce and either kill or impregnate my best friend after I'm dead. Is that noble enough for you?"

Tod blinked. Then he blinked again, clearly stunned. "Yeah, actually. That's more like what I thought you'd be doing."

"Well, don't read too much into it. I'm not a saint, and I don't want to be. I just want to be *normal*. I want to have fights with my dad, and secrets with my best friend, and sex with my boyfriend. But most of all, I want to not be dead in a few days. I'm not done living! And I can't fit everything else I want to do into the next ninety-six hours, and no matter how many dying wishes I make, that's not going to change. And I *hate* it!"

Tod laughed, and my teeth ground together as I swerved smoothly onto the exit ramp. "Why the hell is that funny?"

"It's not. It's just a relief to hear you sounding less than rational and perfectly accepting of your own death. For a while it looked like you were going to 'go gentle into that good night,' or whatever. And that's not you, Kaylee."

I glanced at him, brows raised in surprise. Tod rarely ever said what I expected to hear, but poetry was new, even for him. "You like it better when I 'rage, rage against the dying of the light?'"

"I like it when you 'rage, rage' against anything. It makes you look fierce and...*alive*." The blues in his eyes started to swirl. "And if you tell anyone I quoted Dylan Thomas, I'll... Well, I won't have to do anything, because no one will believe you."

The light ahead turned red, and I slowed to a stop in the left turn lane, then laid one hand over my heart and gave him a cheesy, wide-eyed double-blink. "I will take your secret to my grave."

"I wish you didn't have to."

"Yeah, me, too." My chest ached just thinking about it.

The light changed and I turned left, then pulled into the parking lot on the right. Lakeside was attached to Arlington Memorial, the hospital where Tod worked as a reaper— unbeknownst to the living—and his mother worked as a third-shift triage nurse, but it was a separate building, with a separate entrance and better security.

I parked in the last row and killed the engine, then sat there staring at the building for a minute, trying to calm the flut-ter of panic the sight of it raised in my stomach, even though I had no memory of being taken in. I'd just woken up inside, all alone, strapped to a bed in a featureless white room.

"You sure about this?" Tod asked, watching me.

"Yeah. Thanks for helping, even if it's just to fulfill my last request," I teased, trying to lighten the mood.

"How is it fair that you get, like, five dying wishes and I didn't even get one?"

"No dying wish?" I frowned. "That's criminal."

Tod shrugged. "One of the many downsides to an unex-pected death."

"Better late than never," I said, pushing my car door open. "I officially owe you one dying wish."

Tod's pale brows arched halfway up his forehead, and he looked suddenly, achingly wistful. "She knows not what she says…"

Maybe not. But I was starting to get a pretty good idea.…

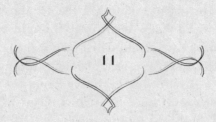

11

"So what's the plan?" Tod asked, as we stared at the building, sitting side by side on the hood of my car.

I shrugged. "Nothing complicated. You get me in, we find Farrah, I ask her questions."

"Sounds simple enough."

"If you don't count the million and one things that could go wrong. How long can you keep me invisible?"

"As long as we're in physical contact."

My throat felt suddenly dry. "Holding hands?" That's how we'd done it last time.

"Unless you had something else in mind."

"I…" Words deserted me until he grinned, and I realized he was kidding. "No wonder you and Nash can't get along."

"We get along." He brushed that one stubborn curl back from his forehead. "We just don't agree on anything."

"That doesn't make any sense."

"It would if you had a brother."

I could only shake off confusion and change the subject. "Last time we did this, you couldn't keep me invisible and inaudible at the same time. Has that changed? Do you think you could make sure only Farrah can see and hear us?"

Another shrug. "Only one way to find out…" He stood and I slid off the hood, my palms suddenly damp from nerves, in spite of my determination to do what needed to be done. To protect Emma by getting rid of Mr. Beck and to face this, my worst fear, before I faced death. The thought of which was rapidly becoming my second worst fear.

Tod was already walking toward the building—no doubt moving corporeally for my exclusive benefit—but when he realized I wasn't with him, he turned. "It won't be like last time," he said, with one look at my face.

"You don't know what last time was like." My hands started to shake at the memory of waking up strapped to a tall bed in an empty room.

"I know you couldn't leave, and you didn't know what was happening to you. And I know you're more scared of going back in there than of crossing into the Netherworld."

I stared at him, confused by the ache in my chest, like my heart suddenly needed more space.

"This time, you can leave whenever you want," Tod said. "You just say the word, and I'll make the rest of the world go away. I'll take you someplace safe, where no one else can reach us."

I couldn't see anything but his eyes, staring into mine. I couldn't take a breath deep enough to satisfy the need for one. I kept waiting for him to laugh, or grin, or do something to break the moment stretching between us. And when he didn't—when he let that moment swell into something raw, and fragile, and too real for me to think about, I crossed my arms over my chest and scrounged up a challenging grin to lighten the moment. "You think I need to be rescued?"

"I think it doesn't hurt to let someone else do the rescuing every now and then, when your own armor starts to get banged up."

Maybe he was right. "And you think you're up to the challenge?"

Some nameless emotion swirled in the blues of his eyes for just an instant. "I'm up to any challenge you could throw down. And several you've probably never thought of."

I laughed out loud. "I'm starting to see the family resemblance."

Tod frowned. "That's not funny."

"I know." That time I took the lead and we stopped twenty feet from the back door, where the serene, manicured greenery gave way to cold concrete and two industrial trash bins.

"You ready?" Tod held his hand out and I took it, twining my fingers around his. His palm was warm and dry, and I tried to ignore the wave of confusion and possibility that crashed over me. There was no time—and no real purpose—for either one.

"Close your eyes," he whispered, and I was happy to comply, because I couldn't deal with what I might still see in his. Not now, anyway. "Here we go…"

My stomach pitched with the sudden sensation that I was falling. I fought the urge to grab on to something and clung to Tod's hand instead, surprised that it still felt warm and solid while my own body felt oddly insubstantial.

Then the world seemed to settle around me and I felt the floor beneath my feet. The air was cold and had that distinctive hospital smell, somehow both sterile and stale at the same time. Tod squeezed my hand and I opened my eyes.

And the fears of my present slammed into the terror of my past.

Nothing had changed. Lakeside still looked and felt exactly the same.

We stood in the open common area of the youth ward, where patients gathered to eat, watch TV, play games, and have group therapy. The nurse's station was only feet away, and the girls' wing stretched out on my right. At the end of the hall was the room I'd occupied, and I was overwhelmed with the perverse need to go see who lived there now, and whether her delusions could hold a candle to my own.

You're not crazy, Kaylee.

I had to remind myself, because just being back in that place blurred the line between delusion and reality for me. The last time I was there, I hadn't known I was a *bean sidhe*. I'd only known that I was seeing things no one else could see—dark, horrifying auras surrounding certain people, and odd smoke, and things skittering through it. I'd fought, and failed, against an overwhelming need to scream, and it was those fits—what I thought were panic attacks—that landed me in Lakeside in the first place.

"I don't suppose you know her room number?" Tod said, and his volume alone told me no one else could hear him. I shook my head, unsure whether or not that benefit of his abilities extended to me. "I think you can talk," he said, and I lifted both brows, silently asking if he was sure.

Tod shrugged. "Give it a shot. Even if someone hears you, he won't be able to see you, and I bet half of these people are here because they already hear voices."

But I wasn't particularly eager to add my voice to the general din of insanity.

The hall was empty, except for the canned laughter of whatever was playing on the common-room TV and the clatter of plastic utensils, which told me we'd arrived at the end of dinner. Any minute, the residents would emerge from the dining area and begin whatever doctor-approved leisure activities were currently available. But it wouldn't be enough. Not even a lifetime of books, puzzles, or games could make them forget where they were or that most of them would only ever leave when they were transferred to one of the adult wards.

And nothing could make the time pass any faster.

"In here," Tod said, tugging me toward the nurse's station, which was temporarily empty.

He glanced around for a second, then zeroed in on a chart hanging on the wall. "What was her name?"

"Farrah Combs," I whispered, terrified that the nurse on duty would hear me and step out of the break room. Maybe we should have tested this plan in an unsecure part of the hospital first...

"Room 304," Tod said, and I scanned the chart long enough to see that he was right. And that Scott was in the first room on the left in the boys' wing.

We headed into the girls' wing, but before we were halfway down the hall, footsteps squeaked on the tile ahead and a woman in purple scrubs emerged from one room carrying a clipboard with a pen chained to the metal clasp. I stood frozen in the middle of the hall, suddenly sure she'd see me, in spite of Tod's assurance to the contrary.

"Relax." He squeezed my hand. "She can't see either of us, and I don't think she can hear you, either." When the nurse got too close for comfort, I stepped out of her way, still clinging to Tod's hand, and was both fascinated and a little scared of the fact that she obviously had no idea we were there. She didn't hesitate or look up from her clipboard. If she got any telltale chills or weird feelings, I saw no sign. It was like Tod and I existed in our own world, population two, surrounded by the real world, but not a part of it.

"Is it always like this for you?" I asked in a spontaneous moment of bravery, and I couldn't resist a sigh of relief when the nurse kept walking. She hadn't heard me.

"Like what?" Tod asked from inches away, and suddenly

I was very aware of his hand in mine, his fingers rough and real against my own, in spite of how very tenuous the rest of reality felt in that moment.

"Like this." I gestured at the rest of the building as the first residents stepped into the hallway, girls with stringy hair and sweatpants, most wearing slippers or laceless shoes. Dinner was over. "Like you're alone in a crowd. Like you're not really here at all."

Tod stared at me like I wasn't making any sense. Or like I was making *too* much sense. "Yeah. Most of the time. But I've never been more *here* than I am right now." His hand tightened around mine again, and my pulse raced, running from something I couldn't think about yet.

As the girls shuffled toward us, a couple blinking in medicated dazes, several guys headed in the opposite direction, toward the boys' wing, and I glimpsed a dark head that might have been Scott's. Or might not have been. I wanted to check on him, but business came first.

Still holding Tod's hand, I stared into the faces of the girls as they passed me, waiting for one of them to turn into room 304. I had no idea what Farrah Combs looked like—she could have been any one of the girls passing us. A couple of the faces did look familiar—it creeped me out to think we may have been residents together.

But none of them went into room 304, and before I could pull Tod into the room to wait for its resident, the woman in purple scrubs stepped in front of me and knocked on that very door. Surprised, I pulled Tod with me as she pushed the door open and stepped into the doorway, just far enough into the room to get the resident's attention.

"Farrah?" she said, and my heart leapt into my throat. If there was a reply from inside, I couldn't hear it. "You didn't even touch your tray today. The doctor says if you don't eat, they'll have to feed you intravenously. You don't want that, do you?"

Again, there was no audible response, and based on the nurse's frown, there was no silent gesture, either.

I edged down the hall toward 304, my pulse racing fast enough to make me light-headed and Tod came with me.

"Normally we don't make these kinds of accommodations," the nurse said. "But considering your situation... Is there anything I can get you? Anything you'd particularly like to eat?"

Again there was no answer, and I was actually starting to feel sorry for the nurse. And to wish there'd been more like her when I was there...

"Okay then," she said, in response to nothing I'd heard. "Please let me know if there's anything I can do to make you feel better."

Wow. She was really going out of her way for one resident.

I flattened myself against the wall when the nurse headed down the hall again, but Tod let her walk right through him. "What does that feel like?" I asked, whispering out of instinct. Talking when no one else could hear me felt weird.

He shrugged, looking right into my eyes. "Right now, this is all I feel." He held our intertwined hands up for me to see and I wanted to look away, but I couldn't break the hold his gaze had on me, like he could see more than anyone else saw. Things I couldn't even see myself.

I didn't know what to say—I could hardly remember how to take my next breath—but then he looked away first, like maybe he wished he could take it back. So I let him tug me toward the open door still swimming in confusion.

I stepped inside first with Tod close at my back. The room was a double, with two identical low beds against opposite walls. There were two sets of metal shelves bolted to the walls in place of dressers, and a door on the left led to a tiny private bathroom.

The bed on the right was empty and sort of haphazardly made, the plain white blanket pulled up and the pillow tossed on top. But Farrah Combs—it had to be her—sat cross-legged on the other mattress, white sheet and blanket shoved to the bottom of the bed, waist-length, greasy brown hair hanging like a curtain over her face and half her body. She stared at a book open on the bed in front of her, and I desperately wanted to see her face.

"Can you let her see and hear us?" I asked Tod, acutely aware of his hand in mine. "Just her?"

He nodded, and I turned back to the girl on the bed. "Hi, Farrah," I said, and she looked up slowly, like she'd heard me on some kind of a delay. Her face was gaunt and deeply shadowed, her arms thin and knobby at the wrists and elbows. When my gaze met hers, I realized two things immediately about Farrah Combs. First, she was sick, and not just mentally.

And second…she was very, very pregnant.

Oh, wow. Questions flew through my mind so fast I couldn't harness them. Was this Mr. Beck's baby? If so, why had he tried again with Danica? Was one kid not enough? Was this one not a boy?

"Farrah?" I said, finally. "Are you Farrah Combs?"

"I used to be," she said, her voice higher and sweeter than I'd expected.

I glanced at Tod, but he could only shrug.

"So…you're not Farrah Combs now?" I asked, and she shook her head slowly. "Then who are you?"

"No one," she said. "I'm not real." Her brown eyes widened in sudden interest. "Are *you* real?"

"Yeah. For a few more days, anyway…" I said, and Tod's

hand squeezed mine again. "Farrah, can I talk to you about your baby?"

She shrugged and glanced at her round belly, barely covered by the T-shirt stretched over it. "He's not real, either. Feels real, though." She flinched and pressed one hand against her bulging stomach.

"Can you tell me who the father is?" I asked, and she shook her head solemnly. "Please, Farrah? It's very important."

"I can't…" Her voice faded into a whisper on the last sound.

"Why not?"

"Because he's real." She barely breathed the words, and the tears standing in her eyes made my heart ache. "He's still real, and I was real when he touched me, but he doesn't touch me anymore. But I remember being real." She looked at her book again and turned a page she couldn't possibly have seen through her tears.

"Why do you think you're not real, Farrah?" I asked, dropping into a squat next to her bed with Tod at my side.

"He told me. I'm not real, and this place isn't real, so none of this matters. Soon it will all be over."

Over? My stomach clenched around nothing, and anger on Farrah's behalf blossomed like a fresh bruise on my soul.

"Are you sure you're real?" she asked, and I could only nod, still trying to understand what she wasn't really saying. "What about him?" She looked right at Tod and he gave her a small smile.

"Yes, Farrah, I'm real, too."

Her frown was a child's pout, innocently skeptical. "You ask a lot of questions for real people."

"Yeah, I guess we do," I said, though I had no idea what she meant. "Farrah, what can you tell me about your baby's father? Can you tell me his name?"

She shook her head again, and long brown hair fell over

her face, half hiding one brown eye. "The baby isn't real," she said. "So he doesn't get a name, either."

I stood, frustrated, and nearly jumped out of my own skin when cloth rustled behind me.

"Hope you're not expecting any of that to make sense," a new voice said, and my grip on Tod's hand tightened as I whirled around to find another resident in the doorway. Her bright blue eyes—shadowed by dark circles—seemed to watch the entire room at once, but never quite focused on us, and I realized she couldn't see us. Maybe she couldn't even hear us. But she clearly knew we were there.

"There's no message in her madness." The new girl stepped hesitantly into the room, like a blind woman afraid of running into a wall. "No hidden code. She's been told she doesn't exist, so she believes it." She took another step forward and I almost felt sorry for her, wandering around in the dark. Figuratively. "I tried telling her she does exist, but since I'm evidently not real either, she doesn't believe me. I don't think she even hears me."

"She can't see or hear us," Tod whispered, and I knew by his volume alone that he was unnerved. "How the hell does she know we're here?"

"Maybe you're not as good at this as you think you are," I whispered, my gaze glued to the new girl. Who was starting to look vaguely, uncomfortably familiar.

He shook his head. "I'm every bit as good as I think I am."

"If you're going to hang out in my room, show yourself. Loitering unseen is rude, you know."

I glanced at Tod and he shrugged, waiting for my opinion. And finally I nodded.

I knew the moment Farrah's roommate saw us because she gave a startled little yip and kind of jumped back, bumping her hip against the shelves bolted to the wall. "Two of you. Didn't see that coming."

"Sorry," I said, and the roommate's gaze narrowed on me like my face was a puzzle she needed to solve.

"Thanks for...showing up. I was starting to think I really was losing it."

"Are you sure you're not?" Tod asked, and I elbowed him in the ribs. No fair making the residents doubt their own sanity. They got enough of that from the doctors.

"As sure as I am that you're standing there," the roommate said. Then she laughed at her own joke, and discomfort crawled over my skin. I hate nut-job humor like Emma hates blond jokes.

"How did you know we were here?" Tod asked, his grip tight around my hand, suspicious frown trained on the newcomer.

"Because Farrah doesn't talk to herself. She doesn't talk to anyone, actually. At least, no one the rest of us can see. And I've seen enough to know that just because I can't see something doesn't mean it isn't there." Her focus shifted to me again, and again she seemed to be looking for something in my eyes. "You don't remember me do you?"

"Should I?" I asked, my discomfort bloating like a corpse in the sun.

And then suddenly I did remember...something.

"Lydia..." I whispered, and she nodded, obviously pleased, while Tod's focus shifted between us. "You were here when I... And you...did something. You helped me."

"I tried," she admitted, and her small smile faltered.

"And now you're Farrah's roommate?"

"Yeah. The staff thinks they're doing us a favor. The residents think it's a joke. You know, the two mute girls sharing a room…" She shrugged and sank onto her bed staring up at us.

"Because Farrah only talks to 'real' people, and you… You didn't talk either, when I was here." Or had she? My memory of Lydia was fuzzy, but her voice wasn't unfamiliar. And the confusion I couldn't quite see past made me worry that I might not be done with Lakeside after all….

Lydia shrugged. "I don't say much to the staff because when I do talk, they tend to extend my stay. But you're not staff."

"Maybe she can help us. With Farrah," Tod suggested, and Lydia's eyes widened in interest.

"We need to know about her baby's father," I said, wishing I could sit, but unwilling to let go of Tod's hand. I didn't want to be seen by the next aide to walk down the hall. "Do you know who he is?"

Lydia shook her head. "She talks to someone at night sometimes. Someone I can't see or hear. I'm assuming it's him, based on the things she says." Lydia glanced at the floor, cheeks flushed, and I realized she'd gotten quite an earful from the side of the conversation she could hear. "At first, I thought she was talking to him just now, but obviously I was wrong. Unless you…?" She glanced at Tod, and he shook his head once, sharply. I almost laughed.

"If you've never seen or heard him, how do you know he's really there?" Tod asked, and Lydia frowned up at him.

"I know, because she talks to him like she was talking to you guys, and *you're* really here." Lydia turned to me. "How did you do that, anyway? You're a *bean sidhe,* right? But *bean sidhes* can't…be invisible."

She knew what I was. She'd probably known before I had, back when I was still a Lakeside resident. Why did it always seem like everyone else knew more about me than I did?

"I'm a reaper," Tod said, and Lydia's eyes went round

with the first sign of fear I'd seen from her. "Don't worry," he added before she could freak out too badly. "I'm off the clock."

Lydia nodded hesitantly, like she didn't quite believe him, and I got the feeling she'd liked him better when she couldn't see him.

"Does anyone else ever visit Farrah?" I asked, drawing her attention away from the reaper. "Anyone other people can see?"

"Her dad came once, but her mom's dead, and I get the impression her family doesn't want anyone to know where she is. Or how sane she isn't. Not that I blame them."

"This is so messed up!" I glanced back at Farrah and that ache in my heart flared to life again. "If everyone else could see who she's talking to, they wouldn't think she's crazy!"

"Oh, she *is* crazy." Lydia folded her legs beneath herself on the bed. "She just doesn't hear voices. And that baby's killing her." She rubbed both hands over her face, and I realized she was almost as pale as Farrah, the hollows beneath her eyes and cheekbones almost as dark. "I've taken what I can, but if I keep that up, the kid'll just kill us both."

"What did you take from her?" Tod asked, and Lydia turned to me instead of answering.

"Do you remember?"

"No." But I was starting to. "You took something from me, too. Pain," I said, struggling to pull the buried, fuzzy memory to the surface of my mind. "I needed to wail for another patient, and it hurt all the way down..." My free hand found my throat, and I could almost feel the echo of that old agony, so much worse back then, when I hadn't understood it and couldn't control it. "You took the pain, and that helped me hold it in." And if I'd screamed again, they would *never* have released me. "You got me out of here..."

"I just did what I could," Lydia insisted. "But there's not much more I can do for Farrah." She sighed, and the pain in that sound was beyond the physical. "Maybe I shouldn't have done anything. She would have lost the baby if I hadn't helped in the beginning, but at least *she* would have lived. Now it's too late for both of them."

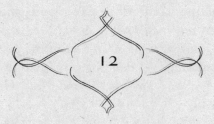

12

"She's going to die?" My voice was barely a whisper, and I couldn't stop staring at Farrah, who still flipped pages in her book as if we weren't even there. She'd tuned us out as soon as we started talking to Lydia—evidently we were now "unreal" by association. "Are you sure?" I asked, and Lydia nodded.

Tod glanced at Farrah. "Why do they keep her here, if she's so sick?"

"They don't," Lydia said. "They take her over to Memorial when she gets too weak, but all the doctors can do is feed her. The tests all come back negative. They have no idea what's wrong with her. But some of the older nurses say she's just lost the will to live. They're kind of right."

"Because she doesn't believe she *is* living," I said, and Lydia nodded. "But it's more than that. It's the baby," I insisted, flashes of Danica's miscarriage connecting the two girls in my mind. "Farrah would have lost her baby early, just like Danica did, if not for you. How far along is she now?"

"The nurses say she's twenty-eight weeks. Why?" Lydia asked, her focus shifting between me and Tod. "What's wrong with the baby? And who's Danica?"

"She's a senior at my school. I think her baby and Farrah's

baby had the same father." And I was really starting to wish I'd printed the faculty picture of "Mr. Allan."

Wait a minute... I turned to Tod, acutely aware that we'd now been holding hands for at least twenty minutes. "Does your phone get internet?" Mine didn't.

He nodded, already digging it from his pocket with his free hand. "I splurged—I don't have many bills." He handed it over, and it took me a minute to find the site I wanted, typing with only my left thumb.

"Farrah," I said, when I'd found the faculty images on the Crestwood website. She didn't even look up, so I tugged Tod closer so I could kneel by her bed again. "Farrah, is this your baby's father?" I zoomed in on Allan's face and held the phone in front of her book. Farrah tried to shove my hand out of her way, but I just pushed back. "Look at him! Is this him?" I demanded, and finally she looked.

And her brown eyes watered. "David," she whispered, and my short thrill of triumph was swallowed by anger on her behalf.

"It's him." I stood, already turning back to Tod, but Farrah grabbed my hand, holding the phone firmly in front of her face.

"Who is he?" Lydia asked, while I stood hunched over, so Farrah could get another look.

"I don't know his real name." I dropped onto my knees again to get more comfortable. "But he's an incubus in heat. He taught at Farrah's school just long enough to get her pregnant, and now he's at my school. And since Danica just miscarried his demon seed, I'm pretty sure he's set his sights on my best friend. But I'm not sure why, since Farrah's pregnancy seems to be progressing in spite of...everything."

"Insurance," Tod said, kneeling next to me. "Most human women can't carry an incubus baby to term, so he's increasing his chances of a successful harvest by planting as many seeds as he can."

My rage knew no limits. "And with each one, he's damaging a teenage girl, or abandoning his own newborn daughter, or both at once, with no guarantee that he's even spawning a son."

"My baby's a boy," Farrah insisted, still staring at Tod's phone, and my arm was starting to cramp from holding it out. "Not a real boy, though."

What, was she carrying Pinocchio?

"Did the doctor tell you that?" I asked, gently pulling the phone from her grip. I stood and handed Tod's cell back to him, and her gaze followed it until it disappeared into his pocket. But then she went back to her book, dismissing us as "unreal" once again.

"She's right," Tod said. "She wouldn't be in here if she was carrying a girl. Girls are born human, from normal pregnancies. Boys are incubi, and if the pregnancy doesn't kill the baby, it usually kills the mother slowly, both body and mind." He shrugged when I just stared at him. "I thought you knew that."

"I didn't." And I was starting to think that ignorance was at least somewhere in the neighborhood of bliss because the more I knew, the angrier I got.

"Me, neither," Lydia said, and after a long, awkward moment of silence, I looked up at Tod.

"Well, I guess I have what I came for," I mumbled, trying to swallow the sick feeling I got every time I looked at Farrah, knowing what was going to happen to both her and her baby.

"Wait, you're leaving?" Lydia stood, eyes wide in panic. "Take me with you," she insisted, when I stared at her in surprise. "Or at least get me out of here."

I glanced at Tod, but he only shrugged. "Your call."

Why was it *my* call? "Lydia, I can't. What about your parents?"

"They put me in here. Please, Kaylee." She stood, eyeing me desperately. "I'm a syphon. Do you know what that means?"

I shook my head, fairly certain she wasn't offering to steal gas for my car in exchange for orchestrating her escape from a mental institution. 'Cause that would be...crazy.

"I take things from other people. Anything. My body has an innate need to maintain balance between what I'm feeling and what's being experienced around me, and when there's an imbalance, I get the urge to take some of whatever there's too much of, to even things out. I've spent my whole life fighting that need for balance to keep from poisoning myself with other people's problems, and this is where it landed me." She spread her arms to take in all of Lakeside.

I could certainly sympathize.

"I took your pain, and I've been taking some of Farrah's illness," she continued, as sympathy for her swelled inside me. "I can syphon some things on purpose, to help, like I did with you, but I don't always have a choice. When there's too much, resisting it is like trying to swim with your hands tied. I can't do it." She grabbed my free hand and held on tight, like I could somehow pull her above that brutal tide. "Farrah's going to die, and if I'm still here when that happens, she'll drag me down with her."

"It wouldn't matter if we got you out," I said, heartbroken that she and I might be facing parallel ends. "If it's your time to go, you'll go, no matter where you are."

"Maybe not," Tod interrupted, and I turned to him in confusion while Lydia's eyes shined with hope. "And not for *her*, either," he added, glancing at Farrah. "An incubus pregnancy is...well, it's a sort of supernatural intervention, like Doug dying from a frost overdose. It trumps the natural order of things. Same thing for Lydia, if she becomes collateral damage. This probably isn't when or how they're supposed to die. Either of them."

Ohh. I glanced at Lydia in growing horror. "So, leaving her here is like murder?" I asked, and Tod shrugged.

"You're not pulling the trigger. But you're not taking the gun away, either."

"Please, Kaylee," Lydia begged. "Get me out of here. I did it for you. You owe me."

She was right, and I was rapidly running out of time in which to repay my debts. "Will you do it?" I asked Tod, and he nodded. "I can't take you both at once, though, so I'll have to come back for her."

"No, take her first," I insisted. "I have a couple more questions for Farrah, and I still want to check on Scott. I'll wait here for you."

"You sure?" Tod knew how much I hated Lakeside, and that the thought of getting caught there terrified me.

"Yeah. Just make sure you come back for me."

"Nothing could keep me from it," he said, and I believed him.

I let go of his hand, and mine suddenly felt cold. And empty. And when he reached for Lydia, I had a sudden mad urge to slap her hand away and reclaim his for myself, in spite of what I owed Lydia, and my genuine need to help her.

"You ready?" Tod said, and she nodded, taking his hand.

"What are you gonna do?" I asked, trying not to see where they touched each other, or wonder what it meant that I cared. "You can't go home, can you?"

She shook her head. "They'd just send me back. But I'll be fine. It can hardly get worse than dying in here, right?"

she said, glancing around the space she shared with another mental patient in a secure facility. I knew how she felt, but I also knew that starving—or being attacked—on the street wouldn't be any better.

I glanced around the room until I found a pencil on her desk, then pulled the twenty-dollar bill from my pocket. "This is all I have," I said, scribbling my number on a scrap of paper from my pocket. I wrapped the money around it and handed it to her. "Call me if there's anything I can do to help. I gotta warn you, though, this offer expires on Thursday."

She frowned in confusion, but took the twenty and my number and shoved them in her pocket. "Thanks."

I nodded, and Tod met my gaze. "Be right back." Then they both disappeared, and sudden panic nearly overwhelmed me. Anyone who walked in would see me. I could be arrested, or even mistaken for a resident by some eager new staff member. Neither of those catastrophes would last once Tod came back for me, but that knowledge did nothing to calm me.

So I focused on Farrah, who didn't seem to know Tod and Lydia were gone.

I sank onto the end of her bed, facing her. "Farrah?" She didn't look up. "I'm real, remember? You can talk to me."

She shook her head without looking up. "Real people don't talk to Lydia. She can't hear them, 'cause she's not real."

"You're not real either, right?" I said, hating myself a little for stepping into her psychosis. "But you hear real people. It's the same for Lydia."

Farrah seemed to think about that for a minute, her hand frozen in the act of turning a page. Then she looked up and met my gaze. "Oh. Yeah."

"Since I'm real, just like David, do you think you could tell me a little more about him?" I held my breath, sure she wouldn't fall for that one. But then...

"He's *beautiful*," she said, her gaze losing focus, as if she could see him in her mind.

"Yes, he is." Blanket policy when talking to the insane victim of incubus procreation: agree with everything she says. "But I was hoping for a little more than that. Do you know if any of your friends know him? Like you know him? Are any of them having babies, too?"

"Erica tried," Farrah said. "But she got sick, and her baby died. It must have been real."

"How awful," I said, as she flipped more pages. "Anyone else?"

"Tiffany. But I haven't seen her in a long time. She's not real. But her baby is. It's a girl."

"How do you know it's a girl?" I asked, as chills broke out on my arms. I hoped Tod would be back soon.

"David told me. He was sad."

"Do you know where David lives?" I asked, and Farrah shook her head.

"He doesn't take students to his house. That would be inappropriate."

"Of course." But evidently sleeping with them wasn't. "So you only saw him at school?"

"Except when he came to my house."

I sat straighter in surprise. "Mr. B—I mean David came to your house? Were your parents okay with that?"

"My dad wasn't home. But my mom didn't mind. She liked David."

Uh-oh. I closed my eyes and swallowed the sick feeling creeping up from my stomach. "Farrah, Lydia said your mother died. Was that *after* David started coming to your house?"

"Yeah. Doesn't matter, though, because she wasn't real. So she didn't really die. I won't, either."

"Because you're not real?"

"Right. You're going to die, though," she said, looking right into my eyes, and my chill bumps doubled in size.

"How do you know that?"

Farrah shrugged. "Because you're real. Everything real dies."

Thoroughly creeped out, I stood and backed away from her bed, and Farrah went back to her book, like I'd never been there at all. And for a moment, I envied her effortless ability to simply move on, like nothing she'd heard mattered. At first, I'd thought facing death would do that for me, but somehow, the less time I had left, the more there seemed to be to do. And it all mattered.

Nervous now, I crossed the room and opened the door enough to peek into the hall. It was empty. I glanced at my watch to see that nearly five minutes had passed. How long did it take to blink into the parking lot, then blink back? Was something wrong?

Tod would never leave me there. Not if he had any choice.

Five minutes later, I'd gone through most of Farrah's stuff without learning anything new, and I *had* to get out of that room. Every passing second brought the next nurse check closer, and I could *not* be found at Lakeside, in the room of a missing resident.

Finally desperate, I took off my shoes and put on the plain white bathrobe Lydia had left behind. Then I pulled the ponytail holder from my hair and shook my head, leaving my hair down to half-hide my face, and knelt by Farrah's bed one last time.

"Do you know Scott Carter?" I asked, and she nodded.

"How...um...?" Turns out there's no polite way to ask exactly how crazy someone is. "How is he?"

She looked up at me slowly, eyes wide, expression more coherent than I'd seen from her so far. "He's real, but he doesn't know it. So don't tell him. He might not wanna know he's going to die."

That made two of us.

"Thank you, Farrah." I stood and took one last look at her, wishing there was something I could do to help her. Then I sucked in a deep breath and stepped into the blessedly empty hallway.

I'd gone four steps when a door opened at my back and soft-soled shoes squeaked on the floor. I didn't turn. Unless she got a good look at my face, whoever was behind me wouldn't know I didn't belong. I could have been any brunette mental patient in a bathrobe—a fact which unnerved me enough to make my hands shake. So I shoved them into Lydia's pockets.

My heart pounded with every step, and when I stepped into the open common area at the center of ward, agoraphobia crashed into me like a hit from Eastlake's defensive line. The light felt too bright and the tile floor seemed to go on forever. People milled around like living land mines I had to avoid, without looking like I was avoiding them.

When I passed the TV room, my fists unclenched in my pockets. When I passed the dining area, I exhaled slowly. But I didn't dare look up from my feet until I'd passed the nurse's station without triggering any alarms. And even then, I could still hear my pulse rush in my ears, each surge counting down the seconds until I might be caught.

I leaned against the wall next to the visitor's bathroom and snuck several furtive glances around to make sure no one was watching me. No one was, but my luck wouldn't hold out forever, and Tod had yet to make an appearance. If I wanted to talk to Scott, I was on my own, at least until then. So in my head I began a countdown, starting with three, trying to slow my racing heartbeat with each number.

When I got to zero, I glanced up one more time, then stepped around the corner into the boys' hall. Scott's room was open, and I could hear him talking, but I couldn't see him, or whoever he was talking to. In a sudden burst of courage—or desperation—I dashed across the hall and into his room, then eased the door shut and stood with my back against it, sagging with relief.

"What's she doing here?" Scott's room was a single. He sat sideways in his desk chair, staring at me, and if I didn't already know where he was, I might have thought nothing was wrong with him. He wore his usual jeans and a T-shirt displaying the logo of some band I'd never heard of. He looked the same, if a little thinner. And maybe he was a little paler than the last time I'd seen him—no more football practice in the sun.

But if not for the fact that he was in Lakeside and that he was talking to himself—or maybe to no one—I might have thought he was…sane.

"You see her?" Scott said, still staring at me, but clearly talking to someone else. He looked confused, but not really surprised, and I wondered how often girls appeared in his room without explanation. "She's not real!" He closed his eyes and punctuated the last word with a blow to the side of his own head, and I sucked in a sharp breath. "If she's not real, but I see her, does that mean I belong here?" Another self-inflicted punch, and I jumped, but didn't know what to do. "No, no, no. It's not *seeing* things that makes you crazy—it's *hearing* things. So *don't talk to me!*" he hissed, opening his eyes to glare at a spot near the right-hand wall.

"Scott?" I said, and his head swiveled so fast I was afraid he'd hurt his neck.

"Nononono, you can't talk because you're not here, and

I can't see you, and I can't hear you, 'cause if I can then I'm crazy, but I'm not crazy. Right?" he demanded, looking at that same spot again. Whatever he heard must have made him happy because he nodded decisively, then turned to stare down at his desktop.

And my heart broke for him.

Scott Carter and I had never been close. In fact, before too much frost had cracked his sanity, I'd thought him shallow, rude, arrogant, spoiled and selfish. But he'd been my boy-friend's best friend and my cousin's boyfriend, so our paths had crossed fairly often.

But now, watching him try to convince himself that I was no more real than whoever else he was seeing and hearing, it was hard to feel anything other than pity and sympathy for the boy who'd been one-third of the social power trifecta at Eastlake High.

"I'm real, Scott. And I'm really here."

He shook his head again and this time covered his ears with both hands, like a stubborn toddler. "That's exactly what a hallucination would say. You think I'm gonna fall for that just because you look like Kaylee and sound like Kaylee? I see Kaylee Cavanaugh every day, and she's not real, and you're not real, either. You're just another one of his tricks. So why are you talking?"

What? He saw me every day?

I wasn't sure how to feel about being a regularly featured guest star in Scott Carter's hallucinogenic existence. But it wasn't his fault. Because of their hardwired connection, Avari could make Scott see or hear whatever he wanted, and the more Scott suffered, the better Avari fed.

And considering how messed up Lakeside's newest resident obviously was, the psychotic hellion bastard was probably glutted on his energy alone.

"Shut up," Scott said to the wall. "How can I freak her out if she's not really here?" He moved one finger over the surface of his empty desk, like he was finger painting. Or trying to write something. And suddenly I realized why he had no pens, pencils, or anything else that could be used as a weapon—he'd tried to stab me the day he was arrested and he was later declared mentally incompetent. But surely they'd keep him somewhere else—somewhere more secure—if he was still considered dangerous. Would he try to hurt a hallucination?

Maybe I shouldn't have come without Tod….

"I don't *know* why," he said without looking up, and I was starting to feel like a Peeping Tom, watching uninvited as he spoke to himself. Or Avari. "Her cousin's hotter, but it's always Kaylee Cavanaugh." Scott stopped for a second, listening to something I couldn't hear, his fingertip still on the desktop. Then he shook his head. "Nothin'. She doesn't do a damn thing but stand there and watch me. Or she'll sit on the toilet when I need to go. Or lie on the bed when I'm tired, knowin' I'm not gonna lay down next to some ghost, or hallucination, or whatever the hell she is. Kept me up till three in the morning last time. But she never says a damn word." And suddenly he turned to me. "You're not supposed to talk!"

I could only stare at him. I don't know what I expected, knowing some of what he'd been through, but this wasn't it. And I didn't know what to say to him. So I started with the most basic question, and one he was probably tired of hearing. "Scott? Are you okay?" I asked, my palms pressed against the door at my back. I wished I could melt through it, like Tod could, then wander around, invisible, until he came back.

"I'm crazy, how do you think I am?" Scott snapped. "Were you this crazy when you were in here? Did I come and stare at you all day, watching you sleep, and eat, and piss?"

I shook my head, and he stood, shoving his chair out with the backs of his legs.

"No. Because that wouldn't make any sense, would it? So why the hell are you always here? Why does he put you here day…after…day? Because I couldn't take you to him? That's it, right? He wanted you, and I couldn't deliver you, so now he rubs my face in you all…damn…day." His words ended in a whimper, punctuated by three more blows to his own head, and when he came closer, fists still clenched, I inched away, desperately wishing I'd stayed with Farrah.

Then he glanced at the wall again, and his eyes narrowed. "I can't hurt her. She's not here."

I stared at the wall, trying to see what he saw. Avari had messed with the shadows before, making Scott see and hear things in them, until he'd started screaming and cowering away from at the slightest shade. But the only shadows here were beneath the bed and dresser. Just like in the hospital, the staff at Lakeside kept his room lit from all four corners to chase away as many shadows as possible. Just to keep him functional.

He was staring at the wall again, his head slightly tilted. Like he was listening. "Why should he?" Scott asked no one. "He wants to know what's in it for him."

"For who?" I asked, and Scott glanced at me.

"For *Avari*. Pay attention!"

Crap! Did Avari know I was there? Could he see what Scott saw? Is that who Scott was talking to?

No, it couldn't be. He was talking *about* Avari. Or maybe *for* him. But who was he talking to? Or was he completely imagining the other half of the conversation—not beyond the realm of possibility for someone who regularly saw people who weren't there.

"Scott, I can't hear whatever you're hearing. I can't see your hallucinations."

He laughed out loud, and the bitter cackle caught me completely off guard. "*You're* the hallucination. The rest of us are real."

The weird parallel between his psychosis and Farrah's chilled me from the inside out, but arguing with him would do no good.

"No way." Scott shook his head, talking to the wall again. "He wants more. Something bigger." He paused as the wall presumably answered, and the smile that crawled over Scott's face then made me want to hold my breath and throw salt over my shoulder. "Now you're talkin'."

"Scott, who are you talking to?" I asked, creeped out to realize that whatever he was talking about was starting to make a weird kind of sense. Nothing I could quite understand, but definitely not lunacy.

"I don't know!" he shouted, and I jumped, then glanced at the door, worried it would fly open and the room would be overrun with needle-bearing aides. "I'm not talking to you," he insisted, a little quieter. "Because you're *not supposed to talk!* Go away! Goawaygoawaygoawaygoaway!"

I opened my mouth, but before I could think of what to say, the door flew open and a large male aide—Charles, according to his name tag—burst into the room. I stood frozen, pulse racing so fast my vision was starting to blur. I'd been caught. I'd be arrested, and handcuffed, and driven to the police station in the back of the car.

"Okay, Scott, calm down…" Charles started, both hands outstretched, and I realized this was a familiar performance for them both. But when he saw me, the aide's voice faltered, and I was pretty sure he was doubting his own sanity in the brief silence. Then, "Who are you? You're not a resident."

They never called us—er, *them*—patients. Always residents, like people resided at Lakeside by choice.

My hands opened and closed. I was starting to sweat, and my chest ached until I realized I wasn't breathing. I opened my mouth and sucked in a deep breath, but that didn't fix anything. Tod wasn't back. I was still trapped.

"She's not real," Scott whispered, glancing from me to the aide, then back. "Make her go away."

Charles scowled at me, part confusion, part anger. "You can't be here. How did you even get *in* here?"

"I…" But that's where my words ran out.

I could run, but I'd never get past Charles. He was big, and part of his job was restraining residents, when the need arose. And even if I got past him, I couldn't get out of the locked ward.

Each breath came faster than the last, but I couldn't stop them. Couldn't even slow them. There was only one way out, and I desperately didn't want to take it. If hellions and assorted monsters hung out across the world barrier from the high school, I didn't want to know what was lurking in the Netherworld version of a mental health facility. *Insane* hellions? Was there any other kind?

I closed my eyes, trying to block out the entire room and both of the other occupants. Pulse racing, I tried to think about death. To remember those I'd witnessed so that my wail for them would help me cross into the Netherworld.

But the only death I could think about was my own, and I can't wail for myself.

"Security!" Charles shouted, and I squeezed my eyes shut tighter, still trying.

A warm hand took a strong grip on mine, and I screamed and tried to jerk away. But he held tight. An instant later, the hum of the air conditioner faded into silence and my ears popped.

Then, suddenly the world felt warm and humid. Cicadas chirruped all around me, and that hand still held mine, its grip confident, but looser now.

"You okay?" Tod asked, and I opened my eyes to find him watching me, dark blond brows drawn low over blue eyes still brilliant in the setting sun. We were in the parking lot, by the trash bins, almost exactly where we'd stood half an hour earlier.

"That was… What *was* that?" I demanded, as my pulse finally began to slow.

"That was me taking some of the tarnish off this old armor." He pretended to brush dust off the front of his shirt.

"You call that a rescue?"

Tod frowned. "You don't?"

"That aide was about to haul me out of the room!" I pulled Lydia's robe off in several angry movements, surprised to see that my hands were still shaking from the close call.

"It's more fun when you're almost caught."

"That's not almost. I *was* caught." As evidenced by the remnants of panicked adrenaline still burning in my veins.

"Well, now you're *un*-caught. And for the record, you're the second chick I've snatched from the jaws of the mental health industry tonight." His eyes shined in the dying light, and I couldn't resist a small smile. Yes, I'd been caught and nearly suffered a fatal aneurysm from the shock—several days early, by my count—but it was over now, and I'd gotten what I needed.

"So, you what? Just blinked us both out of there? So that aide saw us disappear?"

Tod's brows rose. "What kind of amateur do you think I am? He only saw *you* disappear. He never saw me at all."

"That makes two of us. I was starting to worry about you."
I dropped Lydia's robe on the sidewalk and headed for my car.

"Sorry." Tod fell into step beside me. "It was a little more complicated than I expected."

"But she's okay?" I asked.

"She...? Oh, Lydia." Tod brushed one stubborn blond curl from his forehead. "Yeah. I mean, she's scared to be on her own, but anything's better than that place." He glanced over his shoulder at Lakeside. "And she has your number, right?"

"Yeah." As I drove home, I played with the idea of inviting her to stay at my house. In a perfect world, that would have been...perfect. My dad needed someone to take care of, and he was about to lose me. Lydia needed to be taken care of, and she couldn't go back to her own parents.

But if we lived in a perfect world, I wouldn't be days from death and Lydia wouldn't have been locked up in the first place. The reality was that she could never take my place, and my dad would probably be in no shape to take care of anyone for a while after his grand scheming failed and I died.

How could there possibly be so many things left to fix, and so little time in which to fix them?

"You wanna come in?" I asked, as I pulled my key from the engine.

Tod looked at me in the light shining through the windshield from the porch light. "Don't you need to do some homework, or get a good night's sleep, or something equally wholesome?"

I pushed open my car door. "I am no longer attending school for the purpose of education. At this point, I'm only showing up to keep an eye on Mr. Beck. And speaking of evil demon sires, I have a theory I need to verify. Interested in helping?"

The reaper shrugged. "I have nothing else planned till mid-night."

"Good." I got out of the car and shoved my door closed as he stepped right through his. "That gives us five hours to…" Oh, crap. I glanced at my cell phone screen again, then groaned. It was just after seven.

I'd stood Nash up. Again.

I took several steps toward the house, then froze when my gaze landed on the front porch. Where Nash sat watching us.

"You know, pretty soon I'm going to start taking this per-sonally."

13

"Hey, I'm sorry. I lost track of time."

Nash stood as I unlocked the door, but instead of following me inside, he stepped into the doorway, one hand on either side of the frame. Symbolically blocking Tod from entering, since he couldn't physically keep the reaper from doing anything. "I need to talk to Kaylee."

"So talk." Tod disappeared from the front porch, then reappeared next to me in the living room, and when Nash turned around, his eyes were flashing in anger.

"This is private."

Tod opened his mouth, then seemed to change his mind about whatever he was going to say and looked at me instead, brows raised in question.

I nodded. "I'll see you tomorrow. Thanks for…everything." But I owed Nash both an apology and an explanation.

Tod disappeared from my living room as fast as he'd appeared, and Nash closed the front door and leaned against it, watching me. "What happened?"

I collapsed onto the couch next to Styx, and ran one hand over her fur. "Sabine figured out that Beck's an incubus, and Alec said that if he's in heat, or whatever, Danica probably isn't the first student he's slept with, so we did some research and figured out—"

Nash shook his head. "I know all that. I talked to Sabine while I was waiting on your front porch. For almost an hour." He dropped into my dad's armchair and stared at me across the coffee table. "What happened with Tod?"

"With Tod?" I said. And then his meaning sank in, and my gaze dropped. I hadn't done anything wrong—other than breaking into Lakeside and springing a patient—but I couldn't deny that I knew what he meant. Not anymore.

"Don't let him do this, Kaylee."

"I'm not letting him do anything," I said, as exhaustion, confusion, and fear crashed over me, drawing all of the day's overwhelming risks and revelations into one sharp point of focus. "What good is it going to do for us to have this conversation? I'm sorry I stood you up, but nothing happened with Tod."

Nash blinked. "But you know how he feels?"

"I kinda figured it out." But not as soon as I should have. Maybe if my life wasn't full of nightmares, and hellions, and incubi, I would have had time to stop and notice what was going on with the people in my life who weren't trying to kill me.

"Then why are you still hanging out with him? How am I supposed to take that?"

"He's my friend, Nash." Styx twitched in her sleep beneath my hand, and I watched her, wishing my life was as simple as hers. Eat. Sleep. Growl at everyone you don't like. There was something to be said for simplicity.

"No." Nash shook his head and leaned forward in the chair, elbows on his knees, trying to catch my gaze. "He's in love with you, Kaylee."

"That's…" Wait. *What?* I hadn't thought it through using those words. I hadn't realized…

My heart pounded, and I didn't know how to interpret the sudden lurch of my stomach into my throat.

"No," I said, trying not to remember Tod holding my hand in the adolescent ward, or pulling me out of the Netherworld right before Avari could grab me, or staying all night with me and Emma to make sure no one tried to possess her again. Or telling me I don't belong with Nash… "But even if he is, what does it matter, Nash? Really. I'm going to die in a few days, and after that, none of this will matter."

So can't we just go on ignoring it for a little longer…?

"It'll matter to me." He looked like I'd just punched him. How could things suddenly be so complicated?

"I'm sorry. I didn't mean it like that." My head felt like it was going to explode. "I just meant—"

"I don't like you hanging out with him alone."

My temper spiked, and my apology died a swift death on the end of my tongue. "You mean like you hang out with Sabine alone, even though she's in love with you?"

Nash rolled his eyes and leaned back in his chair. "That's different."

"You're right." I pulled Styx into my arms and stood with her, stomping toward the kitchen. "Sabine hijacked my dreams and tried to feed me to the Netherworld to get to you. Everything she says is intended to either drive a wedge between us or put herself in your bed. But Tod's never tried to hurt you and he's never even come close to pulling his clothes off and jumping me. So yeah, I guess that *is* different."

The recliner creaked, then Nash's footsteps followed me into the kitchen. "The difference between Tod and Sabine is that she's honest about it. You know what she's up to, and you know why, but you'll never see the strings Tod's pulling behind the scenes until suddenly you're just magically where he wants you to be."

"He isn't pulling any strings, Nash. He's just helping me with something very important. And if I wind up somewhere other than where I am now, it won't be because he wanted me there. It'll be because *I* want me there." I set Styx on the floor and stood to find Nash watching me, arms crossed over his chest.

"What the hell does that mean?"

What *did* that mean? I hadn't thought it through, I'd just... let it out.

I exhaled slowly, trying to push everything irrelevant—everything I knew I wouldn't have time to really address—to the back of my mind. "It doesn't mean anything except that I needed help, and he came through. That's what a friend does."

"If you needed help, why didn't you ask me? Why don't you ever want my help anymore, Kaylee?"

"I..." The words died on my tongue, my answer as incomplete as the thought behind it. I'd asked Tod and Alec for help with Beck. Hell, I'd even asked Sabine for help. But I'd told Nash to go to baseball practice while the rest of us researched and plotted. Was he right? Had I been excluding him?

Not on purpose. In fact, I hadn't even thought about him not being there, because I was focused on Mr. Beck and Nash couldn't help with that. He couldn't read Beck's fear to ID him. He couldn't give us background info on incubi, and he couldn't get me into the mental health ward unseen.

"You couldn't help me with this," I said, finally. "I needed Tod." My logic was sound, so why did I feel so guilty about the truth?

Nash's irises churned in anger. "You needed Tod. Do you hear yourself? You're supposed to need *me*."

The ache in my chest grew into a throbbing so fierce I

could hardly breathe. "That's not what I meant." Things were falling apart. In spite of my best effort to hold everything together until the end—until my end—my life was unraveling faster than I could grasp at the threads, and I could see chaos bulging through the seams.

Nash watched me, waiting for more, but Styx started whining then and glanced from me to the fridge, where I gripped the door handle much harder than necessary. She was hungry. As usual. And taking care of her was easier than taking care of Nash.

I pulled open the fridge and took a package of raw sirloin from the bottom shelf. Styx preferred venison, but we were out, and beef would do in a pinch. Nothing ground, though. Styx didn't just want to eat—she wanted to tear flesh with her tiny little teeth.

Maybe that was why Cujo was constantly pissed off.

"Do you like him?" Nash demanded, leaning against the peninsula, and I closed my eyes, wishing I could erase this moment forever, like it had never happened. But when I opened my eyes, that moment was still there, taunting me with its stamina.

Styx went crazy at my feet as I peeled clear plastic back from the beef. I dropped a small hunk of meat into her bowl, and she dug in, growling like her meal was still alive and kicking as she ripped small chunks from it and swallowed them whole, more like a cat than a dog.

"Uh-oh, trouble in paradise?" a new voice said, and my head popped up in surprise. Thane sat on the small table in our dining nook, and Styx hadn't so much as acknowledged his presence. "Yeah, evidently fresh meat outranks even the dreaded reaper," he said, when he noticed me frowning at the dog.

"Kaylee." Nash stepped into my line of sight to reclaim my

attention, though he had no idea what had stolen it. "Do you like him?"

"Like who?" Thane slid off the table and walked right through Nash, and I shuddered, revolted and horrified by the sight of them…blended together.

"Does it matter?" I wrapped the remaining meat up, trying desperately to pretend that the man assigned to kill me wasn't getting yet another unauthorized peek into my private life.

"Of course it matters," Nash snapped. "Why wouldn't it?"

I shoved the meat into the fridge and spun to face him, struggling not to vent my fury at Thane on him. "Because in three days, I'm going to be dead, and this'll be the mootest point of all time."

"Well said!" Thane shouted, and his voice echoed around the room like thunder, though only I could hear it.

"It matters to me," Nash insisted. "And the question won't be moot in three days, because Tod will still be here, and every time I look at him, I'm going to know how he felt about you and wonder if that was mutual. If my own brother was trying to steal my girlfriend. So answer me! Do you like him?"

"Oooh, there's a brother?" Thane demanded, standing inches away, his chest practically brushing my right shoulder. "Drama, drama, drama."

I did my best to ignore the reaper, and focus on Nash. "First of all, I'm not a piece of property that can be stolen."

"That's not what I meant," Nash began, but I cut him off.

"And second of all, Tod isn't trying to steal anything from you. You and your mom are all he has left in the world, and I don't think he'd ever intentionally hurt you."

"You know, Cain and Abel were brothers…" Thane said, and I whirled on him, fury sparking like fire in my veins.

But before I could say a word, Nash followed my gaze and found…nothing.

"Is that him? Is he *here?*" Nash demanded. "Is he talking to you, now?"

"Why would this Tod be invisible?" Thane asked. "Don't you have any human friends?"

I ignored him and focused on Nash. "No, it's not Tod. It's—"

"Uh-uh…" Thane taunted, crossing in front of me slowly, his nose brushing my cheek on its way to my ear, and I shuddered in revulsion. "If you tell him, I'll have to kill him. And once I've broken one rule, I'm on the run anyway, so what's to stop me from breaking another one and taking you *right… now…?*" He circled behind me, and his hand trailed across my lower back. I closed my eyes, fighting nausea at his touch.

"Kaylee!" Nash shouted. "Answer me!"

But I couldn't. I could barely even think past the terror and loathing crawling through me.

"So this'll be our little secret, right, Kaylee?" the reaper whispered into my other ear, as he completed the circle around me.

"Tod!" Nash growled through clenched teeth, glaring at random spots in the empty room. "Get the hell out of here."

"It's not Tod!" I said, and the reaper stiffened at my side, until I continued. "It's not *anyone.*"

"Good girl…" Thane whispered. "Until next time…" Then he disappeared, and I leaned against the kitchen counter, sagging with relief.

"Then what's wrong?" Nash asked, and my brain raced as I tried to refocus on him in the aftershock of Thane's invasion.

"I don't know, Nash. I don't know if I like Tod."

The truth was that I hadn't even considered the possibility until a couple of hours earlier, because it hadn't seemed real.

I wasn't Emma or Sophie. I didn't have C-cups bouncing in front of me with every step and I didn't dance around in tiny skirts. Guys didn't fight over me. Nash was an anomaly. I never would have been on his radar if we didn't share a species, so it had never occurred to me that I might be on anyone else's.

In fact, the reverse had always seemed much more plausible—that someone else would steal *him* away from *me*.

"Do you like Sabine?" I asked softly, silently daring him to tell me the truth, in the face of his own accusations.

Nash turned and stomped into the living room. "This isn't about Sabine."

I followed him, truly irritated now. "Maybe it should be. You wanna know what I think?" I asked, then gave him no time to reply. "I think you *do* still like Sabine, at least a little bit. I think you like it that she still wants you, and you like flirting with her when I'm not there, dangling the possibility in front of her. Playing her game." I sucked in a deep breath, surprised to realize that I was now *thoroughly* pissed at what amounted to his hypocrisy.

"But I think it goes beyond that. I know how serious the two of you were, and I don't think you can ever really get over something like that. Not completely. And you know it. But you still hang out with her, alone, in your room. Practically daring each other to take things beyond friendship. Then you have the nerve to ask me if I like Tod, three days before I'm going to die?"

How could the four of us *possibly* be so tangled up in one another? And how could I not have seen it coming?

Nash stared at me, stunned. "I'm sorry," he said. "I'm so sorry I opened this can of worms, especially now. I swear I have no intention of taking things beyond friendship with Sabine, but this is the second time this week you've stood me up, then turned up with Tod. And I know he wants you, and it was starting to look like that might be mutual...?"

His voice went up on the end in question. He was still asking. And I didn't want to lie. But did it really matter? So what if Tod was funny, and unpredictable, and there every time I needed him. So what if he liked it when I "raged" against things and didn't think I was crazy for wanting to break into Lakeside? So what if he'd spent months hanging out, getting to know me instead of trying to feel me up the first week we met.

What did that matter? What good was the possibility—the life-changing, love-wrecking possibility—when I wouldn't be around to explore it?

Should I admit that I might—*might*—like Tod back, when that would wreck everything between me and Nash for no reason at all?

It would be different if I weren't dying. If I was going to have a chance to decide how I felt and think about the long-term consequences. But since that wasn't going to happen...

"Nash, why would I be with you, if I liked him?"

Instead of answering, Nash pulled me closer, staring into my eyes, and for a moment, panic consumed me. Then I swallowed my panic and steadied my breathing, focusing on how desperately I didn't want to hurt Nash.

"So, we're okay?" he asked, and I realized I'd controlled the telltale swirling in my eyes, possibly for the first time in my life.

"Yes, we're fine."

"Well then," Nash said, brows arched in challenge, like he wasn't sure he completely believed me. "I can't help noticing that we're all alone here." He squeezed me tighter and whispered into my ear, though there was no one else to hear him. "I say we go to your room and start granting wishes..."

A couple of hours earlier, I would have led him to my room with my head spinning, the rest of me on fire with anticipation. But now, it didn't feel right. Tod was right—I did want to sleep with Nash just to say I'd done it. To know what it felt like. But Nash would think it meant more than that.

Lying to avoid hurting him felt bad enough, and I was only doing it because I'd be gone in a few days, but Tod wouldn't, and three hundred years was a long time to hate your own brother.

But sleeping with Nash for the wrong reason was something else entirely. I couldn't use him like that. So I lied again.

"It's been a really long day, and I'm kind of starving. Why don't we order Chinese and watch a movie? Your choice."

Nash frowned. "I thought you wanted to."

"I did. I do. Just…not tonight." Not that there were many nights left, but I'd deal with those as they came.

"Are you still mad because I asked about Tod?"

"No. Nash, this has nothing to do with Tod, and I'm not mad at you. Everything's fine." Surely the biggest lie I'd ever told.

He looked unconvinced, but dropped a kiss on my forehead anyway and tried to hide his disappointment. "You order the food, I'll find a movie. It doesn't matter what we do. Just being with you is enough for me."

My guilt was like the ocean, swallowing me whole.

"When you were little, you used to call those 'pop hearts,'" my dad said, and I looked up from my blueberry toaster pastry to find him standing in the kitchen doorway.

"Hey. Where were you last night?" He looked like hell. Bloodshot eyes, dark circles, pale skin.

"Out looking for a miracle." My dad sighed and trudged toward the coffeepot.

"Okay then," I said as he poured. "Where were you all day yesterday? Mr. Ryan left a message on the machine. He says if you don't come in today, you're fired. Have you even been to work this week?"

He took the first sip of black coffee without bothering to replace the pot. "I have more important things to worry about right now, Kaylee. But the universe seems adamant that you are the only miracle I'm going to get."

I nodded slowly, fighting to keep my eyes from watering. "The universe is always right, Dad. There's nothing you can do."

He just looked at me over his steaming mug, refusing to admit defeat. Then, finally, he sighed and leaned against the counter. "You wanna skip school today and hang out? Just the two of us? There's an *Alien* marathon on all day, all the way through *Alien vs Predator: Requiem.* We could order pizza and revel in the carnage."

I wanted to cry. He wouldn't admit he couldn't save me, but an offer to play hooky for father-daughter time spoke volumes. And I really wanted to say yes. To stay in my pjs and watch TV with my dad all day, for the last time in my life. But... "Can't," I said around the last bite of blueberry filling. "You have to go to work." And I had to go to school and plot the destruction of a Netherworld monster posing as my math teacher.

"Tonight, then?" He tried to hide his disappointment, but the rare swirl of color in his eyes spoke the truth. "I can set it to record."

"No you can't." We'd had the DVR on the living room TV for a month, and he still hadn't figured out how to change the channel. "But I can. Come home with pizza, and I'm all yours." I wouldn't be doing any more homework anyway. For the rest of my life.

"Deal." My father smiled and looked a little less than exhausted for a couple of seconds. But then he sipped from his mug again and I could see how tired he was and how hard the past few days had been for him, and for the first time, it occurred to me that I may have gotten the good end of the deal. In a couple of days, my troubles would be over. But my dad would have to live with my death—with failing to save me—for the rest of his life.

I started to say something else—to try to put into words how much I loved him—but the doorbell rang before I could come up with the first word.

My dad frowned, his mouth already open to ask who was at the door, but I jogged past him to open it before he could speak. Nash and Sabine stood on the front porch, her car parked at the curb. I stepped back to let them in while my dad poured the rest of his coffee into a travel mug.

"Hey, Mr. Cavanaugh," Sabine said, plopping next to Nash on the couch.

"You're all up early today. What's going on, guys?" My dad held his work gloves and keys in one hand, his mug in the other. He tolerated Sabine in spite of the creepy vibes she leaked when she got angry or upset because he didn't know what she'd been willing to do to me to get to Nash. And because he felt sorry for her, stuck with a foster mother who only wanted to draw a government check. But what he didn't know was that Sabine relished the freedom apathetic parenting afforded her.

What *no one* knew—except maybe Nash, and he wasn't talking—was where she'd gotten her car, with no job and very little spending money.

"We're working on something for school today," I said. And technically, that wasn't a lie. But if I told him the whole truth, he wouldn't go to work, then he'd lose his job, and after I died he really would have nothing left to live for.

"Okay." My dad watched me from the entry, one hand on the doorknob. "Now tell me what you're *really* up to."

I should have realized he knew me well enough now to recognize my half-truths. "You don't want to know."

"Tell me anyway."

"Emancipated minor, remember?" I said, daring a grin he didn't return. "Besides, how much trouble could I possibly get into in the next two days?" But he didn't seem very pleased by the reminder.

"If I recall, this emancipation expires in less than forty-eight hours. I expect to hear all about this over breakfast Friday morning."

"Deal."

None of us said what we were all thinking—that this time, I wouldn't be around to 'fess up and get grounded.

Alec knocked on the door minutes after my dad's car disappeared down the street, just like I'd planned. "Okay, I'm here," he said, brushing past me into the living room. "What's with the summons?"

I pushed the door closed behind him. "I talked to one of Beck's other victims last night at Lakeside, and we were hoping you might have some more answers for us."

Alec just looked at me. Then he looked at Sabine and Nash. Then back at me. "You're not going to give this up, are you?" he asked, and I shook my head. "Fine. But you're gonna have to feed me. I haven't even been to bed yet." He worked third shift at the same factory where my father worked.

"Pancakes?" I offered.

"And lots of coffee."

Nash made a fresh pot while I nuked an entire box of frozen chocolate chip pancakes, three at a time. "The girl I went to see last night is named Farrah Combs, and she's very, very pregnant with Beck's baby. According to Lydia, the nurses say the baby's a boy. Which means it's an incubus. Right?"

Alec nodded around his first bite, then licked a smear of chocolate from his lower lip.

"Who's Lydia?" Nash asked, sliding into the chair between me and Sabine with a plate of his own.

"Farrah's roommate. I met her when I was at Lakeside."

"Okay, so Beck's about to get his baby." Alec shrugged and picked up his mug. "It sounds like this mess is about to clean itself up. Once he gets what he wants, you'll be rid of him, at least for the next century."

"No way." Sabine shook her head firmly. "He doesn't get a happy ending. He has to pay for what he's done."

I refrained—barely—from pointing out that she hadn't paid for what *she'd* done, which added a hollow note to her righteous anger, at least in my ears.

"He's not getting a happy ending *or* a son," I said. "According to Tod, incubi babies are really hard to carry to term. The few that aren't miscarried either drive the mothers insane—literally—or kill them. Farrah got the worst of both worlds. The only reason she and her baby have both survived this long is because Lydia's a syphon and she's been kind of splitting the burden with Farrah. But now that she's gone, Farrah and the baby are both going to die, and Beck will be back to square one. Which means he's still dangerous, and we still have to get rid of him."

"Wait, where did Lydia go?" Nash asked, absently cutting his pancakes into small triangles.

"Um...Tod and I kind of...broke her out."

"You broke a psych patient out of the hospital?" Alec's fork stopped halfway to his mouth, dripping syrup onto the edge of the table.

Sabine leaned back with her chair balanced on two legs. "Playin' a little fast and loose with the rules lately, aren't you?"

"She didn't belong there any more than I did," I insisted, and the *mara's* brows rose.

"Interesting phrasing, Kay…"

I glared at her, but refused to be distracted. "The point is that Farrah can't hold on to the baby without Lydia's help, and as soon as Beck realizes he's going to lose his son—if he hasn't already—he's going to step up his game. I figure if Farrah's seven months pregnant, assuming she was one of his first tries, he's already more than halfway through his fertile period with no luck so far. That has to be making him kinda desperate, and possibly careless, and the last thing our school needs is a rash of demonic miscarriages."

"Though miscarriage seems to be the lesser of several evils, considering how dangerous the pregnancies are," Sabine said.

"I don't know," I said, thinking about what Danica had told me in the hospital. "Danica's messed up so badly that she can't have kids. Ever. And now I'm wondering whether her case is a rarity, or just another awful part of the pattern." I turned to Alec as he swallowed another bite, and Sabine and Nash followed my gaze.

"That's pretty typical of an incubus miscarriage, and it would have been worse a couple of centuries ago." Alec shrugged without setting his fork down. "Before modern medicine, your classmate would have bled to death. At least this way she's still alive."

"Yeah. I'm sure Danica will be thrilled to hear how lucky she is." I pushed my own plate away, untouched.

"Damn," Sabine swore softly. "I have to feed to survive, but I never did *anything* that messed up. I swear."

I tried not to remember how hard she'd tried to break up me and Nash, which I'd personally found pretty messed up.

"Is that how you think about me?" she demanded softly, like she might not really want the answer. "Like some kind of monster?"

"No," I said, and she pretended to believe what I pretended was true. But she looked more wounded than I'd thought possible.

"The internal damage is an unfortunate side effect for women not strong enough to carry an incubus's baby to term," Alec said, obviously trying to draw us back on track. "That's why they usually target younger, healthier women, who are more likely to survive the pregnancy."

"Which is why he's teaching high school," Nash said. But that rationalization did nothing to soften my horror.

Alec shrugged. "The age thing probably doesn't mean anything to him. A couple hundred years ago, girls in his target age range were considered marriageable."

I crossed my arms over my chest. "Yeah, well, now we're jailbait."

"That won't matter unless he's a complete idiot," Sabine said. "And if he were an idiot, we'd have heard about him hitting on students before one of them miscarried in his class. And anyway, if Danica's any indication, he's picking juniors and seniors—girls at or past the age of consent. Which is seventeen, in Texas, in case you were wondering."

I scowled at her. "I wasn't wondering."

"My point is that even if he was scared of the human justice system—and he's not. Hell, *I'm* not—he's not doing anything illegal, technically. He could get fired, but I seriously doubt he gives a shit. He wants a son, not a pension."

"Okay, so we agree that he's going to try to spread his seed beyond just Emma," I said, thinking aloud.

"And the next girl will probably be a junior or a senior," Nash said, glancing at Sabine to acknowledge the age range she'd provided.

"She'll be one of his own students," the *mara* added. "Someone having enough trouble in math to warrant personal attention, which will make his interest in her look like legitimate academic concern."

"And opportunity," Nash said, pushing his empty plate away. "He'll be looking for someone whose parents aren't going to get in the way. You said Farrah's dad's a trucker, so he's gone a lot, right? And didn't you say her mother's dead? And Danica's mom's been in the hospital for a while, so she wasn't there to notice anything going on."

"Yeah, but Mrs. Sussman's only been in a coma for four weeks, and Danica said she spent one night with the baby's father about a month ago," I said. "So it's entirely possible that Danica got pregnant before her mom got sick. Or at least right around that time…" My voice trailed off as another possibility clicked into place in my head.

"What?" Sabine called when I pushed my chair back and headed for the living room, to grab my laptop from my bag.

I set the laptop on the table and turned it on as I pulled my chair closer. "Danica's mother's brain-dead, according to the nurse, and Farrah's mother is just plain dead."

"You think that's more than a coincidence?" Nash asked, scooting his chair closer so he could see the screen as I opened my web browser.

"What have we learned about coincidence, boys and girls?" I typed the keywords: *Combs, Farrah, obituary* and *Crestwood, Texas* into the search engine and hit Enter.

"There's no such thing," Nash mumbled as results began to fill the screen. The third link led to the *Dallas Morning News* online obituary page entry for Lynne Combs. "There." Nash pointed and I clicked, and Sabine and Alex got up to look over my shoulder as I read aloud.

"Lynne Erica Combs, 38, passed away in her home on August 29. She is survived by daughter Farrah Combs and husband Michael Combs, of Crestwood, Texas, and sister Emily Meyers of Dallas, Texas."

"August," Sabine said, as I pressed the print screen button. "Almost seven months ago."

"Lydia said Farrah was twenty-eight weeks pregnant." I closed my laptop without bothering to shut it down. "That's seven months, right?"

Nash nodded. "Are we all thinking the same thing?"

"He fed on the mothers and bred with the daughters." My stomach pitched with disgust, and suddenly I was glad I hadn't eaten anything. I twisted in my chair to face Alec, who looked as grim as I'd ever seen him—which said a lot, considering how he'd spent the last quarter of a century. "Is that proof enough for you? Has he earned a permanent end?"

Alec nodded, glancing around at each of the three of us. "Take him down."

14

"So, I'm meeting Mr. Beck after school today," Emma announced, a bottle of Coke halfway to her mouth.

"No you're not," I said, and Sabine choked on a laugh.

Em set her bottle on the picnic table and glared at me. "Does the phrase, 'You're not the boss of me,' mean anything to you?"

"Nope. Nothing." But I softened my hard line with a smile.

"Nothing what?" Nash slid onto the bench seat next to me with a tray full of chicken nuggets and mashed potatoes and Em turned to him, like she'd just discovered an ally.

"Mr. Beck's tutoring me after last period today…" she began, and Nash looked at me over a spoonful of potatoes.

"You really think that's a good idea?"

"Why are you asking her?" Em demanded, and Sabine just watched, enjoying the show.

"Sorry." Nash dipped a chicken nugget into a puddle of gravy and glanced at me again with his brows raised. "I wasn't sure how much…?"

"She knows everything. About Beck…" I qualified, when his brows rose even higher. I'd given Em the basics before first period, hoping to arm her with knowledge. But I still hadn't decided what to tell her about Thursday. I didn't want her worrying about me for the next two days, but I didn't want my death to take her by surprise, either.

"Okay, look, it's not like you're swimming in options here," Em pointed out, as Nash shoved the entire nugget into his mouth. "You guys need me. Sabine can't get close to him and even if Kaylee's math grades were bad—and they're not—she's not exactly seducible."

Sabine laughed so hard she nearly inhaled a corn chip.

"What's that supposed to mean?" I demanded.

The *mara* cleared her throat, eyes still watering. "She means that you're a solid, respectable seven on a scale of ten. But Beck's gonna be looking for an eleven." Sabine shrugged while I glowered at her. "That, or your ironclad virginity's a deal-breaker."

"That's not what I meant..." Emma started, but I was too furious at the *mara* to listen to anything else until I'd had my say.

"Shut up!" I snapped at Sabine, and they all three stared at me in surprise, not because Sabine didn't deserve it, but because I rarely let her have it. "Just shut the hell up until you have something helpful to say. I'm trying to do something really important here before I..." I trailed off with a glance at Emma. "Before anyone else gets hurt. And I'm sick of Sabine taking cheap shots at me. I'm sick of school, and bells, and classes that don't matter. I'm sick of waiting for the inevitable."

My voice was rising, and people from other tables were starting to look, but I couldn't stop. There were too many things taking up space in my head, and the only way to relieve some of the pressure was to let them spill out of my mouth. And spill they did....

"I'm pissed off about all the things I'll never see and do, and

I'm furious about the fact that I don't have time for anything I *want* to do, because I have to spend seven hours a day here, learning things I'm not going to use just in case I get a chance to do what really needs to be done. And even if I manage to actually *do* that, no one's ever going to know about it. Which shouldn't matter. This isn't about me anyway, right? But the selfish part of me wants to be remembered for doing something good. Something *important*. But in the end, I'll just be gone, and the world will go on like I was never here, and I won't even be around to be pissed off about that."

Sabine and Emma gaped at me, and on the edge of my vision, my cousin Sophie stood from her table and stomped into the cafeteria, probably mortified by the spectacle I'd made of myself, and of her by extension.

Screw Sophie.

Nash slid one arm around my waist and started to whisper something in my ear, but before he'd said more than my name, someone started clapping. I looked up just as Thane appeared on the bench across from me, next to Emma.

Startled, I yelped and jerked away from the table. Nash tried to catch me, but I fell over the bench and landed on my back on the grass, stunned and out of breath.

Laughter echoed all around me, but I barely heard it. Em and Sabine stood to make sure I was okay. Nash pulled me to my feet and brushed grass from my back, but I couldn't focus on what he was saying, because when Emma sat, Thane scooted closer to her. So close that if he'd been corporeal, she'd have felt his warmth against her arm.

"Entertaining as always, Kaylee..." Thane said. "If I ask nicely, will you scream for me when it's time?" Then he disappeared and my hands shook at my sides as the rest of the quad roared back into focus, now that the reminder of my own mortality had gone.

And there, leaning against the brick wall across from my table, stood Tod, scowling furiously at the spot where Thane had just been. He met my gaze and held it for just a second, then blinked out of sight.

"Kaylee, are you okay?" Emma asked, as I sank onto the bench seat again.

"Yeah." I ran my hands through my hair to tame it, and debated hiding behind it instead. People were still staring. I could feel them.

"What was that all about?" she asked, while Sabine just watched me, without her usual smirk for once.

"Nothing. Sorry. I'm just stressed about Beck and I didn't get much sleep last night."

Em looked unconvinced. "Maybe you should go home for a nap," she suggested. "I'm sure Nash could talk them into letting you check out." Every now and then his Influence actually came in handy.

"I don't have time for a nap. I'm fine."

"What do you mean, you don't have time?"

Crap. *Get it together, Kaylee.* "Are you seriously going to see Mr. Beck after school today?" I asked, and for a second, she looked thrown by the change of subject.

Then Emma nodded. "If you're done bossing me around."

I exhaled, long and slow, then met her gaze. "Em, I'm just trying to protect you. But if the threat of pregnancy, infertility and death isn't enough to give you second thoughts about playing bait...I guess I can understand that."

My dad had been trying to protect me from the Netherworld ever since he'd come back from Ireland, and I'd sidestepped every effort he'd made, because my own safety—hell, my own life—didn't seem worth protecting if I wasn't willing to risk it for something important. If Em felt the same, who was I to stand in her way?

"But I'm sure as hell not going to leave you alone with him." She had no resistance to his lascivious charm, and her intentions would melt into memory once he unleashed the onslaught of lust she wasn't prepared to resist, no matter how hard she dug her heels into the dirt. In fact, he may already have started. Was that why she was insisting on playing bait? To stay close to him? "So I don't have time for a nap."

"Thanks." Em looked relieved, in spite of her bravado. "You three aren't the only ones pissed off about what he did to Danica, and I may not be able to cross into the Netherworld or make people do whatever I say, but I *do* know a thing or two about fending off wandering hands. But I do have one question before I totally commit to this, my first supersecret spy mission," Em said, her eyes sparkling with good humor. "Did we ever find out for sure about the possible forked penis?"

I stared at the clock for most of last period, waiting for the hands to move, but they seemed sluggish at best, and by the time class ended, I'd had as much French as I could take. When the bell finally rang, Emma stood so fast her chair skidded on the floor and she was in the hall before the ringing echo faded from my ears. She was definitely eager to get to Mr. Beck's room, and her unbridled enthusiasm made me very, very nervous. I tried to follow her, but Mrs. Brown stepped in front of me before I made it to the end of the aisle.

"Miss Cavanaugh, this is the second day in a row you haven't had your homework."

"I know. I'm sorry." I glanced into the hall and could just see Emma's blond ponytail bouncing out of sight. "Can we talk about this later? I'm kind of in a hurry."

"We can talk about this now." Mrs. Brown reached for the door like she'd close it, trapping me. "You know I have a zero-tolerance policy for missing assignments, and I don't think you've missed one all year until this week. Is something wrong, Kaylee?"

"No, everything's great. Really. It'll never happen again, but I have to go now. I'm late for...something." Mrs. Brown called my name, but I was already out the door, clutching the shoulder strap of my bag, forcing my way against the flow of traffic toward the parking lot. I dodged every familiar face for fear of another delay, and when the hall finally cleared, I jogged left around the corner—just as Mr. Beck pulled his door closed.

Crap. I'd hoped to beat him there, so I could hide in the storage closet and keep an eye on Emma. The plan felt a little juvenile, but Nash and Sabine knew where we were, just in case something went wrong.

But now the door was closed, and I couldn't get in without being seen. Unless...

I set my bag on the floor in the hall and dug my phone from my pocket to text Tod.

@ SCHOOL. NEED UR HELP

Tod always answered instantly, probably because unless he was reaping a soul or actually delivering a pizza, he had nothing else to do. But this time, when Emma needed us both, he was out of reach.

I stood on my toes to peek through the window in Beck's classroom door just in time to see him gesture toward the rolling chair behind his desk. Emma smiled up at him, then sat, and he pushed the chair forward. Then he leaned over her shoulder, pointing at something in the textbook open on his desk.

I wanted to vomit. He hadn't done anything overtly evil, but just being alone in a closed classroom with a female student was borderline inappropriate, and out of character, based

on what Farrah had told us about his determination to maintain the appearance of propriety.

Beck was getting desperate. He was rushing things. And
based on the stoned-out-of-her-mind expression on Emma's
face—she was watching *him,* not the book—she was falling for
it. Falling for him. Even knowing what he'd done to Danica
and Farrah, and countless other girls our age.

Beck looked up, and I ducked beneath the window, heart
pounding, fingers crossed that he hadn't seen me. The hallway
was empty, but it probably wouldn't be for long, and Tod still
hadn't responded. Sabine and Nash were in the quad, waiting for word from me. Not that they could help. I needed to
borrow reaper abilities, and in the absence of those, my own
were the next best thing.

But that wasn't saying much.

Throat tight with dread, I stepped into the middle of the
hall, glancing back and forth to make sure I was alone. So far
so good.

I didn't want to cross into the Netherworld. And I especially didn't want to cross over in my school, which I knew
for a fact to be Avari's new base of operations, unless something had changed in the past six weeks. But I wasn't going to
hang Emma out to dry, even knowing that crossing into the
Netherworld could mean forfeiting my last two days of life.

Fortunately, with no mental patient yelling at me and
no hospital aide shouting for security, I might just be calm
enough to put aside fears of my own demise long enough to
focus on one from my past.

Sucking in a deep breath, I closed my eyes and thought back
to the last death I'd seen—the last soul I'd sung for. Other
than Danica's baby, that was Mrs. Bennigan, who'd died in her
classroom the day after Mr. Beck's predecessor had died at his
desk. While she'd breathed her last, I'd hidden outside with

Nash, trying to hold back the song my body demanded I sing for her. The song that now echoed inside of me, in memory of her.

The clawing pain in my throat was both familiar and welcome, because with it came the first thin tendrils of sound—a muffled version of the fabled *bean sidhe* wail—which wanted to burst forth full-strength from my mouth. But this occasion called for stealth on both sides of the world barrier, so I swallowed all but a soft, high-pitched whine which resonated in the windowpane in the door to my left. It was a sound no human could have made, but it was quiet enough to go unnoticed.

A second after my wail began, the gray fog rolled in out of nowhere. The Nether-fog was liminal—a visual representation of the barrier between worlds—and while I stood in it, I wasn't fully present in either the human world or the Nether. I was caught between, kept company by only the slithering, skittering creatures crawling through that fog, their very presence a constant warning to move on, in one direction or the other.

I took one step away from the wall, and with a single thought of clear intent echoing in my head—*I intend to cross over*—the fog around me dissipated and the Netherworld came into startling, horrifying focus.

The first glimpse is always the worst—until you blink, and see it all for a second time, and you realize it's not going to go away with just a click of your heels.

The building around me hadn't changed. Because it was heavily populated during the school year, Eastlake High bled through into the Netherworld almost exactly as it existed in the human world. The real difference lay in what the Nether *did* with that building.

In the Netherworld version of Eastlake's math hall, the

walls were *crawling* with Crimson Creeper, a mass of slithering, dark green vines sprouting red-edged variegated leaves every couple of inches. The vines were carnivorous, of course, and they'd snatch anything edible within reach, which was why I'd crossed over in the middle of the hall. But the real danger was the thousands of needle-thin, titanium strong thorns. One prick would inject a predigestive poison to begin dissolving the victim's organs from the inside out. And all the vine had to do then was coil around the body and wait for its liquefying meal to soak in like plant fertilizer.

I'd been stuck by an infant vine once, and the pinprick scars around my ankle were a lasting reminder never to tangle with it again.

Unfortunately, lengths of the vine crisscrossed the open doorway, blocking the Netherworld version of Beck's classroom, beginning a couple of inches from the ground. I couldn't get to the closet, where I'd planned to cross back over, without getting rid of the vines. And every minute I wasted in the Netherworld was a minute Emma was alone with Mr. Beck and his incubus charm.

For one long moment, I stood still, listening for evidence of any Nether-life. When I heard nothing immediately threatening, I jogged down the hall, careful to avoid twisting vine feelers and to peek into open classrooms before I passed by them. I turned right at the corner and ran past the foreign language labs and into the science wing, and only released the nervous breath I'd been holding when I saw that one of the three chemistry labs was open and free of Creeper vines, except for one stretching across the top corner of the doorway.

The usual stools were missing from the lab, but the high, black-topped lab stations were still there, and so far unmolested by the Netherworld population and plant life. I opened several drawers and pawed through piles of useless pencils, erasers, pens, rulers and the occasional stirrer without finding anything useful. All the good stuff was locked in the cabinets at the back of the room.

But when I glanced up, I realized that the padlocks hadn't bled through from the human world. Did that mean the supplies weren't there, either?

Conscious of the clock ticking steadily in my head, I raced across the room and threw open the first cabinet—then grinned like a fool at the full shelves.

I pulled on a pair of thick neoprene gloves from the third shelf, then pawed through a series of Bunsen burners and test tubes before stumbling upon a basket full of scissors on the far right. I grabbed the biggest pair I could find, then tugged a pair of goggles into place over my eyes, just in case. Then I ran, my sneakers silent on the linoleum. I was several feet from the hallway intersection when a familiar voice spoke from a classroom to the left, and I froze in terror.

"I believe this is the second such gift you've brought me," Avari said, and tiny icicles formed in my veins. "One might think you were paying tribute. Or trying to appeal to my mercy."

"Can't appeal to what doesn't exist," a second voice said, and my chill bumps sprouted chill bumps. *Tod.* No wonder he hadn't answered my text; cell phones don't work in the Netherworld.

"Mmm," Avari said, as I tiptoed toward the hallway juncture. "You are not quite as foolish as you appear."

"What's that, the evil version of a compliment?" Tod said, and even though I couldn't see him, I could picture the sarcastic lift of one eyebrow, based on nothing but his tone of voice. "Are we buddies now?"

Avari made an unpleasant noise in the back of his throat. "I retract my last statement."

"Whatever. Just…take him, so I can get out of here."

"This isn't what you offered, and I don't yet have what you asked for."

"This is worth more than I offered, and I no longer need what I asked for. Which means you're getting the better end of the deal. And you should do whatever you're going to do before he wakes up, or you'll never be able to keep him here."

What the hell were they talking about? Who had Tod brought to Avari? Why would he make a deal with the hellion who'd made it his life's goal to possess me, body and soul?

I stood in the middle of the hallway junction, exposed and vulnerable from four different directions, should anyone step out of a classroom. And I probably looked like an idiot in lab gloves and goggles, carrying a giant pair of scissors. But I couldn't decide which way to turn. I could go right, and cross over to watch out for Emma. Or I could go left, and sneak a peek at whoever Tod had delivered into the third room on the right.

I'd be safer in the math classroom, and Emma would be safer with me there. But I couldn't quite escape the brutal curiosity pulling me to the left—did this have something to do with me?—even though my exchanged expiration date meant nothing in the Netherworld. Here, I could die anytime, by any means. Or I could suffer eternity at Avari's hands instead, and wish for death until the end of time.

I knew I was making a mistake, even as I turned left and took those first steps, rolling my feet for a silent approach, glad I'd worn sneakers instead of clunky flats.

"You don't want him? Fine," Tod said, when Avari made no reply. "I know a couple other hellions who will appreciate the value you're passing up."

"Leave him," Avari said at last. "But I offer nothing in exchange, other than the safe passage you've already negotiated for yourself. It has not escaped my notice that *I* am doing *you* a service by taking him. But indulge my curiosity for one moment before you go," Avari said, as I peeked cautiously into the first open doorway, careful to avoid the tendrils of Creeper vine curling around the door frame. The desks and chairs inside were stacked in a bizarre, complicated arrangement, like a pyramid of Cirque du Soleil gymnasts about to topple, but the room itself was blessedly empty. "How does this benefit our lovely Addison?" the hellion continued. "You've neglected to negotiate for time with her, and it's much too late now...."

"This has nothing to do with Addy," Tod snapped, and the pain in his voice echoed deep within my own chest.

"Some imbecilic human sage once said that absence makes the heart grow fonder, and though I must confess to absolute incomprehension of the very concept of 'heart' it appears to me that you fall under a contradictory philosophy. With Addison out of your sight, she is clearly also out of your mind. Which is fitting, because since you last saw her, she's been mostly out of her own mind, as well..."

Don't listen to him, Tod, I thought, as I crept past the second door, now only feet from the room where they both stood, along with whoever Tod had dragged into the Netherworld. *True or not, he's only saying it so he can feed from your suffering.* If I'd learned anything since discovering my nonhuman heritage, it was that pain of any kind was the currency of choice in the Netherworld.

"There's nothing else I can do for Addy," Tod said, an angry undercurrent threaded through his voice now. "You've made sure of that."

"And you've moved on quite readily. I know precisely what bringing me this tribute does for Ms. Cavanaugh, and by extension, what it does for you."

I froze at the sound of my name, less than a foot from the

open doorway. My heart beat frantically, and I was afraid to breathe for fear of missing the next words spoken.

"What do you care, so long as you're well fed?"

Avari actually laughed. "I will be better fed from your pain when you understand how futile this noble deed is. You know this won't change anything, don't you, reaper? This won't even delay the inevitable. Your heroic gesture is rendered completely useless by the irony of poor timing and inexorable fate. She will die—right on time—without ever knowing about your failed attempt to save her."

My heart leapt so high I could practically taste it on the back of my tongue.

I dared a long, silent inhalation to keep from passing out, but that didn't stop the building from spinning around me. Confusion, anticipation and a strange plummeting feeling deep in my stomach kept me off balance, my very existence hinging on whatever words would come next.

And when Tod finally spoke, I realized my world might never stop spinning at all.

"This isn't about saving her," he said, his voice strong and steady, even though he was powerless in the Netherworld. "I know my limitations. This is so that bastard can't ever put his hands on her again. So her last moments won't be spent in terror. This is about making damn sure his face won't be the last thing she ever sees."

He? I took that last step forward, pulse roaring like the ocean in my ears, heedless of the danger for one moment as desperate, blinding curiosity overwhelmed every need I'd ever felt. Tod stood in the middle of the bare floor, facing the half of the room I couldn't see. And when I saw what lay at the reaper's feet, still waiting to be claimed by the hellion, understanding clicked into place in my head, like someone had thrown the breaker in my skull.

Thane. Unconscious and crumpled like a feed sack on the floor, one eye swollen and black above the massive blue bruise his cheek had become.

But even with that new information, I still had no real answers to the questions I couldn't even properly form through the haze of gratitude and amazement now swirling around me like the Nether-fog. Tod had found Thane, knocked him out, dragged him into the Netherworld and given him to Avari to dispose of. Or maybe to feed from.

All to make my last days as peaceful as possible. Was he even going to tell me?

Tod crossed his arms over a plain white T-shirt. "Just bind him, or lock him up, or do whatever it is you do to keep people here." Because reapers could cross over anytime they wanted. "I'm done with you both." Tod shoved Thane with his foot, and the unconscious reaper rolled onto his back, revealing another dark bruise on the right side of his face, disappearing beneath his hairline.

I stifled a gasp, but Tod must have seen my hand fly to my mouth in his peripheral vision, because he looked at me, then immediately returned his attention to the half of the room I couldn't see.

For one long, terrifying moment, I was afraid Avari had seen his glance into the hall and figured out what it meant. I stepped away from the doorway, and when no one emerged to rip me limb from limb, I let myself breathe again. A little.

"Our business is concluded," Avari said, and Thane's feet—all I could still see of him—slid across the floor and out of sight. "Unless you're willing to present my offer to Ms. Cavanaugh. One century of life in the Nether, untouched in both body and mind, in exchange for her soul."

"She'd rather die than be your ward in hell," Tod spat, and in my heart, I cheered.

"Two centuries. You could be with her every day. I've seen her lifeline, reaper, and in the Nether, it could stretch into forever. You could greet eternity together…"

"You will *never* have her," Tod said, and as his footsteps thumped across the floor toward me, Avari's reply echoed in my head, so soft I wondered if he'd actually said it out loud.

"We share that misfortune, reaper…"

A second later Tod was in the hall, taking my arm above the rubber glove, and that same fog rolled over my feet before I could protest. Before I could do anything but close my eyes. When I opened them an instant later, I stood in the human world, in the middle of the hall, staring at Tod in amazement, my heart still pounding from our narrow escape.

I pulled my arm from his hand just as a group of girls in Eastlake softball uniforms came around the corner carrying equipment bags and duffels. Several of them laughed at my chemistry safety gear, but I hardly noticed. And when Tod reached up to pull the goggles from my face, I only vaguely realized that meant they could see him, too.

"Why are you dressed like a mad scientist?" he whispered, dropping the goggles on the floor between us.

"Why did you give Thane to Avari?" I countered, as he pulled my first neoprene glove off slowly, as if baring my hand meant more than it should have.

"I think you know why." He took the scissors from my other hand and slid them into his pocket, and when his gaze met mine, he let me see the blues swirling madly in his irises. "I think you heard most of that."

"You made a deal with him to get rid of Thane?"

"The deal was for *evidence* against Thane." Tod pulled my remaining glove off. "If I could find one of the souls he was supposed to have turned in, we'd have proof that he sold it instead. Avari was going to see if any Thane's recent reapings had turned up in the Netherworld."

"In exchange for what?"

Tod dropped the second glove on the floor at my feet, but his gaze never left mine. "There's this guy in the county jail, waiting for his trial. I reaped the soul of the girl he killed. I saw what he did to her. If anyone deserves eternity at Avari's hands, it's him." Tod shrugged. "Now the courts will get that bastard, and Avari gets Thane's older, more powerful soul."

My head was still spinning. I could hardly wrap my mind around it all. "When did you set all this up?"

"In Scott's room, at Lakeside." He glanced at his feet for a minute, then back at me. "I was there when you came into his room, negotiating with Avari through Scott."

I blinked, stunned. Scott *had* been talking to someone else! "Why didn't you tell me?"

Tod's brows dipped low over bright blue eyes. "I didn't want you to know about any of this."

"Why not?"

"Because it doesn't fix anything. Avari's right—I can't save you. But I saw Thane tormenting you at lunch, and I couldn't wait for evidence that may never come through. That psychotic bastard shouldn't be anywhere near you, and he damn well shouldn't be the last thing you ever see." He glanced at the gloves lying between us on the floor, and when he looked up again, the fierce ache in my heart swelled until I thought it would burst, and that falling feeling was back, like I might never regain my balance. So I did the only thing I could think of to bring the world back into focus and make sense of the waves of confusion lapping at me from all sides. I stood on my toes and wrapped my arms around his neck.

Then I kissed Tod.

15

Tod's arms slid around me like they were always meant to be there, and that sense of belonging was so strong that it took me a second to realize what I was doing. And to remember I wasn't supposed to be doing it.

I stepped back and stared up at him, and one hand went to my mouth automatically, like covering it up would erase what I'd just done.

"I'm so sorry…" I took another step back, drowning in confusion and guilt, and in the giddy, reckless joy that threatened to overwhelm them both, in spite of my best effort to deny it. "I shouldn't have done that."

What the hell am I doing? And why didn't it feel *wrong?* Vaguely I was aware that we were both fully visible, in the middle of the school, and those were just two of the many problems with what had just happened.

"Did you mean it?" His eyes churned urgently now, a collision of hunger and uncertainty. "Was that real, or were you just granting my last wish?"

"That was your last wish? A kiss?" Most guys would have wished for…more.

"I could have kissed you months ago, but it wouldn't have

meant anything. I wished for you to *see* me. And want me. So…did you mean it?" Fragile hope peeked out at me from behind the smug self-assurance I now recognized as his mask. As armor, against a world that no longer claimed or understood him, and suddenly I realized he wasn't breathing. He was just waiting. For me.

"Yes," I said, and some unnamed tension inside me eased. "I see you, Tod."

And in that moment, I saw nothing else in the world.

Tod kissed me, and I fell into that kiss like Alice into Wonderland, headfirst and flailing, heart pounding the whole time. The world spun around me and still I fell, and I only crashed down to earth again when someone called my name.

"Kaylee?" Nash said, and I jerked away from Tod so fast I nearly tripped over the rubber gloves at my feet.

Nash stood at the end of the hall with Sabine, his phone in hand, like he was about to dial. Or like he just had. And before I could even complete that thought, my phone buzzed with a text message, probably a check-in from Nash, who'd thought I was watching Emma and Beck.

Shit! Emma…!

Nash stared at me, his expression cycling through pain and anger so fast I could see the tempest churning in his eyes from down the hall. "You said you weren't… You said there was nothing…" Then he stopped, like the words had gotten tangled up in his mouth, and he couldn't spit them out straight.

"There wasn't," I said, struggling for a deep breath against the tightening in my chest. "It just happened. I'm so sorry." Tod had risked his afterlife to give me peace, and suddenly I saw what had been there all along. But the timing could not have been worse.

"I told you he'd do this." Nash turned his fury on Tod. "How could you *do* this?" he shouted, storming toward us without waiting for an answer, and a door squealed open around the corner as some after-school club heard the very public fallout of my not-so-private life.

I stepped into his path, trying to hold him back from Tod with both hands on his chest. But Nash just kept coming, and I had to walk backward with him.

"Sabine, a little help?" I called over his shoulder, but she only crossed her arms.

"Nah, I think I'm gonna sit this one out." Blatant satisfaction glittered in her black eyes, like she'd known about Tod the whole time. Like she'd been waiting for this.

"Nash, please calm down," I begged softly, mortified to realize the Mathletes could hear us now. They wouldn't know exactly what had happened, or who Tod was, but rumors would fly the next day—Wednesday. Not that it would matter. With any luck, by Thursday my death would eclipse even the worst of the gossip. "Let's go outside and talk."

"It's okay, Kaylee," Tod said from behind me, and I could hear the strain in his voice. "You can let him go. He has a right to be mad."

Nash finally stopped trying to push past me and glared at his brother over my head. "Don't tell me what I have a right to feel. And don't talk to her like she should listen to you. You don't get to talk to her, and you damn sure don't get to kiss my girlfriend!"

My cheeks burned. So much for no one knowing what had happened...

"Nash..." I said again, trying to get his attention. "We didn't plan this."

"You might not have, but *he* did," Nash whispered fiercely through clenched teeth, either because he'd realized people were listening, or because he couldn't manage any more volume. "He hates me, because I lived and he died."

"You don't know what you're talking about," Tod said softly behind me, and I turned to look at him, drawn by the complex threads of emotion woven through his voice. I'd seen Tod mad, and I'd recently started seeing something else when he looked at me. But this was neither of those. Or maybe it was both. It was guilt, and loyalty, and anger, and fierce, protective love, all so tangled up I couldn't tell them apart, and I doubted he could, either.

Tod was wrestling with more human emotion than I'd ever seen from him or any other reaper, and for one horrifying moment, I was afraid that it was too much for him. That after only two years dead, he'd lost the ability to process so much at once.

I wasn't sure *I* could process it all.

"The hell I don't!" Nash shouted, and my focus volleyed between them. And vaguely I was aware of the spectators inching closer, trying to hear. "You're trying to take Kaylee so I'll be as miserable as you are."

"Oh, hell, let him have her!" Sabine said, and several of the Mathletes laughed, but Nash and Tod didn't even look up.

"Nash, listen to me," I said, fighting for his full attention. "I'm so sorry. But your happiness doesn't depend on me." It shouldn't, anyway. It *couldn't,* because no matter how this little disaster ended, he'd be without me forever in two days. And I really needed to know that he could handle that.

He frowned down at me from inches away. "What does that mean? Is this what you want?" he demanded, gesturing behind me at Tod. "You want *him?*"

I opened my mouth, but nothing came out. What *did* I want? Did what I wanted even matter, with so little time left in which to want it?

"You call it, Kaylee," Nash demanded, when I didn't—when I *couldn't*—answer. "Me or him?"

Tears burned in my eyes, and I could barely see past them. Everyone was watching me. Waiting. Listening. And most of them had no idea that no matter what I decided, it would all be over in two days. Which was why I'd tried so hard to make sure Nash would be okay. Because we'd been through a lot together, and I *did* care about him.

But wasn't it a little easier than I'd expected, thinking of him and Sabine together after my death? Didn't it mean something that I kept forgetting about him when I was with Tod? And that I was embarrassed, but not really disappointed every time sex with him failed to happen?

Had Nash and I ever really gotten back what we'd had in the beginning, or had I just held on to him out of habit? Or some misplaced sense of loyalty?

My voice came out thick and half-choked from holding back sobs. "I'm so sorry, Nash," I said, hyperaware that there were at least a dozen people watching us, which meant there would be at least that many versions of this making the rounds the next day.

Nash blinked, surprised and hurt, and I realized I hadn't said what he'd expected to hear. Then defensive anger took over, and his irises churned with it as he turned on Tod. "You *suck* as a brother. Stay away from me, or I'll kick your ass into the next life myself."

Tod exhaled slowly. "Nash, wait. I know you don't believe me, but this isn't what I wanted. Not like this."

"Whatever. This was inevitable, right? What difference does two more days make?" Nash said, and Sabine gave me a satisfied, almost respectful nod, like I'd orchestrated the whole thing just to please her. After all, she'd gotten what she wanted—now she'd be competing with the memory of a cheating ex instead of a tragically lost love. Nash glanced angrily at the crowd of spectators, then back at me and Tod.

"Have a nice life—what little you have left." Then he turned and stomped off with Sabine at his side.

"Kaylee, I'm so sorry," Tod said when they were gone, but his gaze kept flicking from face to face, and I realized he was uncomfortable being visible to this many people at once. He probably hadn't felt so exposed since the day he'd died.

"It's my fault." I blinked back unspent tears and glared at the onlookers, daring them to comment. "Don't you guys have something to calculate?"

Rebuked, the Mathletes wandered back to their club meeting, already discussing what they'd seen, and most of the solitary onlookers faked disinterest by digging in their lockers or loitering at the water fountain.

"I have to check on Emma," I whispered, trying to ignore the stragglers. "And you should probably go."

"Can I come by later? To talk?" Tod asked.

"Yeah. That'd be…good." I understood that what he'd done to Thane wouldn't change the bottom line for me—I was still going to die. But I was convinced that this would change at least a few of the smaller details, like who my reaper would be, now that the chosen one was presumably out of the picture. And who knows, Tod might have even changed the location and timeline by a little bit.

"Okay. I'll see you later." His arms hovered at his sides, like he wasn't sure whether we should part with a hug or a handshake. Or nothing at all.

But if there was a protocol for how to say goodbye to your newly ex-boyfriend's dead brother, right after you kissed him and probably sent your ex into the arms of his willing ex-girlfriend, I didn't know what it was.

"This isn't one of the things they train reapers to handle," Tod whispered in acknowledgment of the awkward circumstances, and I laughed in spite of eyes still damp from tears. But the last notes of my laughter sounded hollow.

I'd ruined everything.

"Later, then," Tod said, and I laid one hand on his arm before he could disappear out of habit.

"Walk this time," I whispered, with a pointed glance at the sophomore watching us around her open locker door. "You're visible."

"Oh, yeah." He winked and took several steps backward, then shoved his hands into his pockets and spun on one heel.

When he turned the corner—without looking back—I took a deep breath and mentally shoved the drama to the back of my mind, where it would no doubt fester until I had time to truly deal with it. Then I picked up the chemistry gear and started down the math hall, pointedly ignoring the stragglers. Mr. Beck's door was closed, which meant he and Emma either hadn't heard the spectacle or didn't care enough to check it out.

Either way, something was wrong.

I dropped the gloves and glasses and grabbed my book bag—still lying by the door, where I'd left it—then backed up several steps and walked past the classroom, glancing through the window at just the right moment. Emma still sat in the teacher's chair, but now Beck sat on the edge of his own desk, and they weren't even pretending to do math anymore. He'd gotten bold and careless. Had losing Danica's baby made him that desperate?

I doubled back to pass the room again, and this time I stopped for a better look, because he had his back to the door. Em would have seen me if she'd looked up, but that clearly wasn't going to happen. She looked practically enthralled.

Emma laughed at something he said, and he leaned forward to brush a strand of hair over her shoulder. His hand brushed her cheek and lingered while she stared up at him, and anger flared to life inside me, burning just beneath my skin. He shifted slightly on the desktop, his left thigh flexing and relaxing, and it took me a second to understand what I couldn't see very well from my current position—he was slowly swinging his left leg, running his calf back and forth against her outer thigh.

Those flames of anger roared into a full-blown blaze, roasting me alive.

I pulled the door open, and they both looked up. "Hello, Ms. Cavanaugh." Beck smiled at me without bothering to stand, and Emma looked first confused to see me, then irritated that I'd interrupted, then surprised when she glanced at the clock over the door.

Yup, she'd been charmed. Time to extract her from danger without looking like I knew she was in danger.

"Hey, Mr. Beck." *Keep it light and casual, Kaylee. Nothing's wrong, you're just bored...* "Can Em come out and play now?"

"We're kind of in the middle of a lesson. High scores in math are crucial if you want to get into a good college."

Scores, huh?

I propped both hands on my hips, half flirt, half challenge, stealing a page from Emma's playbook. "Mr. Beck, are you aware that recent studies suggest a link between math overload and a variety of unfortunate medical conditions including restless leg syndrome, mad cow disease and erectile dysfunction?"

Beck burst into laughter. "I'll be careful," he said, still chuckling, and I had to remind myself that he was a predator. That whole "young, approachable teacher" act was like wearing camouflage in the woods—his prey would never see him coming.

"Seriously, though, if you're done with her...? We're gonna

be late to work," I lied. Our shift didn't start for another hour and a half.

"You two work together?" Beck asked, finally standing to wave me into the room. I stepped inside and the door swung closed behind me, without the rubber wedge to hold it open. Emma and I were alone with Mr. Beck—and suddenly I had an idea. The kind of idea I would never have even tried if I had more than two days to live, or any dignity left, after the spectacle I'd just caused in the hall.

The kind of idea that never would have worked if he'd had other options—I wasn't gorgeous, as Sabine had pointed out. But I was *there,* and Beck was getting desperate, so if I were willing, and easy, and ready to share...

I pasted on my best Lolita smile and propped my hands on what little hips I had. "We do *everything* together, Mr. Beck."

Emma's eyes nearly popped out of her skull, and she seemed to shake off a bit of that charmed daze in surprise.

"Do you now?" His brows rose in interest like he'd just noticed me for the very first time, and when he glanced from me to Emma and back, I knew I had him.

I nodded slowly, staring straight into his green eyes, and tapped my fingers on my own hip bones to draw his gaze where I wanted it. Where it probably would have landed anyway, eventually. I'd learned that from Emma too, but never expected to actually use it.

"Two's greater than one, Mr. Beck," I said, tilting my head to the right. "Shouldn't a math teacher know that?"

"With absolute certainty." He didn't gawk or proposition me, like a guy my own age would have, and he certainly didn't look me in the chest, not that there was much to see there. But he had the ironclad confidence of a man who's never been turned down in his life—for a very good reason.

Even without the hedonistic pull of his incubus charm, I

could see why girls would fall all over him. Mr. Beck radiated
a maturity and skill high school boys couldn't compete with.

He was dangerous. He was a predator. He was…looking
right at me.

"Kaylee?" Beck frowned. "You okay?"

"Yeah." I blinked, then crossed the room without breaking
eye contact. "I just never noticed how much gold there is in
your eyes. You can't see them very well from the back row."

At the last minute, I veered away from him and toward
Emma, who was staring up at him again. I leaned down to rest
my chin on her shoulder and wrap my arms around her waist.
"You ready, Em?" I whispered, still holding Beck's gaze.

He looked *starved*.

"Um…yeah, I guess." But she made no move to stand so I
pulled her chair back and closed the book on the desk.

"I don't think we're quite done here," Mr. Beck said, and
my pulse spiked almost painfully. "Emma needs some more
practice. I could fit you in tonight…" he suggested, as I slid
her textbook into her bag.

Em started to nod, her eyes lighting up again with eagerness, but I cut her off before she could agree.

"We have to work," I reminded him, and he scowled—as
close to irritated as I'd ever seen him. "Tomorrow night?" I
said, dangling the jailbait in front of him. "I think I could
benefit from a little private instruction, too. You could teach
us both at once—if you're up for it."

She frowned over my intrusion, but the heat in his eyes
could have melted iron. "Around eight?"

Em nodded eagerly and slid one arm around my waist.
Either she was playing along, or she'd decided that sharing
him was better than not getting him at all. "My house. Do
you need the address?" she asked, as I guided us subtly toward the hall.

"I can get it from your file." Surely a violation of school policy. But then, so was sleeping with students.

"Then we'll see you tomorrow." I pushed the door open and tugged Emma into the hall. The door swung shut behind us and I threw my backpack over one shoulder and half pulled her toward the parking lot. When I glanced back, I found Mr. Beck watching us through the window in his door.

The trap was set, the bait in place. But I still had no idea what to do with him once we'd caught him.

Emma turned on me the moment the heavy glass door swung shut behind us. "What'd you do that for?"

"Why did I save you from tortures untold at the hands of our evil math teacher? Because I'm your best friend."

Em sighed and clutched the strap of her backpack. "I'm pretty sure nothing that man's hands do could be described as torture. I had him right where we wanted him!"

"Right. I could tell from the way your eyes go out of focus every time you look at him. He charmed you, Em. He was touching your hair when I came in, and—"

"He was not!"

"The hell he wasn't." I turned left in the second row, veering us toward our cars, parked side by side. "And that was on school grounds, in full view of anyone who happened to walk by. He must be getting desperate. Or ready to quit at Eastlake and find another campus to prey on."

"Kaylee, I really don't think he'd do that," Emma insisted. I rolled my eyes. "Shake it off, Em. He's the bad guy."

"Unless…maybe…Sabine misread him, or maybe we misinterpreted the evidence."

"Emma…" I started, frowning at her.

"Sorry. I know. He just doesn't feel bad."

"What does he feel like?" I could understand the attraction—I had eyes, after all—but not the obsession. His charm didn't work on me.

"He feels...addictive." She hugged her own stomach, and her backpack swung to one side, but she didn't seem to notice. "When he looks at you, you feel really, really good. Like an afterglow that's not...after. You want things, and you know he can give them to you, and when he looks away, it feels like the spotlight left you to shine on someone else, and you'll do anything to bring it back. To feel that heat." Em stopped walking and frowned at me, like she couldn't believe what she was about to say. "I hated you when you came in," she confessed, like it hurt to say the words. And I have to admit, it kinda hurt to hear them. "I hated you, just a little bit, when he looked at you instead of me."

"I don't want him, Em. And neither do you." And listening to her talk about him like that—about a teacher she'd hardly ever spoken to outside of class before—gave me chills so deep my bones could have been carved from ice.

"But I do. I want him, Kaylee. That's the scary part." She started walking again, and her next words floated back to me. "I know better, but it doesn't matter. I still want him."

"Emma." I pulled her to a stop again and looked straight into her eyes. "You have to resist it. He's the honey, you're the fly. Or maybe he's the Venus flytrap. Either way, you're the fly, and the fly never wins."

She frowned. "So, what are you?"

"I'm the vinegar. Or the lawnmower, depending on the metaphor. Either way, I'm taking him down. And I'm not leaving you alone with him again."

Emma blinked and her gaze seemed a little clearer. Her forehead scrunched up, like she was trying to remember a fading dream. "Speaking of which, did you just do what I think you just did? Back there?" She nodded toward the building, and Beck's classroom.

"If you think I implied that you and I would have a three-way with our evil math teacher...then yeah. That's what I did."

"Imply, nothin'!" She dug her keys from her purse with one hand. "You practically promised! Damn, Kaylee, I didn't think you had it in you."

"Things have changed." I started walking again, and she jogged to catch up with me.

"What things?"

"Nothing..." I pulled my own keys from my pocket as we neared our cars, at the back of the lot.

"Nuh-uh. Don't even try that." She clicked the bauble on her key chain to unlock her doors, then pointed at the passenger seat. "Get in. You can tell me all about these changes on the way to the theater. I'll bring you back for your car after work." Emma tossed her backpack and purse into the backseat, then stood watching me, waiting.

"I'm not going to work, Em."

"Okay, that's it." Emma slammed her door and folded her arms over the roof of the car. "What's going on with you? Multiple detentions, no homework, blowing off work, freaking out at lunch, propositioning a teacher on behalf of both of us... I know he's an *evil* teacher, but that's just not your style. You're acting like...Sabine."

"That's not funny."

"That's my point. What going on, Kaylee?"

I took a long, deep breath, then met her gaze over the car. "If you want the detailed version, you're gonna be late for work."

Emma shrugged. "If you're not going, I'm not going."

I started to argue, then changed my mind. Who was I to

lecture her about responsibility? So I opened her passenger door and sat down, wedging my backpack between my feet on the floorboard.

"Nash and I just broke up," I said, as she slid into the driver's seat and closed the door.

"Again? Why?" Em looked surprised, but not as surprised as I'd expected her to be. But then, she didn't know everything yet.

"I kind of...kissed Tod."

"You *kind of* kissed Tod?!"

Aaaand...there's the surprise.

"Okay, I *really* kissed him. Then he kissed me back, and Nash and Sabine saw it. As did most of the Mathletes, several softball players and anyone else who happened to be in the hall. It was kind of a public spectacle. And now I don't know where I stand with Tod, but I'm sure Nash hates us both, and Sabine's probably doing mental cartwheels to celebrate. And that's not even the worst part."

"It gets worse?"

"Yeah." I took another deep breath. "I'm gonna die, Emma."

"You mean eventually, right?" She blinked, and I could tell it hadn't sunk in. "Please tell me you're making some kind of big-picture philosophical statement about the inevitability of death and the transient nature of human existence."

"Not eventually, Em. Sometime on Thursday. I don't know exactly when, and I don't know how, and I don't know where. I don't even know who's coming to reap my soul, because Tod just took the reaper who had that job and fed him to Avari. All I know is that it's hard to motivate myself to go work for a paycheck I'm never gonna cash or do homework that's never gonna get graded. But I am *hell-bent* on taking Mr. Beck down before I die."

Emma leaned back in the driver's seat, hands limp in her lap, keys dangling from one bent finger. "Okay, I'm going to need a minute. That's a lot to process."

"I know."

She took a couple of deep breaths, then rolled her head on the headrest to face me. "I was only in Beck's classroom for, like, an hour, right?" she asked, and I nodded, though it had felt like much less to me, in the Netherworld. "And in that time, you dumped your boyfriend, kissed his dead *brother* and found out you're going to *die?*"

I stared at my hands, nervously fiddling with my keys in my lap. "Actually, I already knew that last part."

"You already knew?" Em's voice sounded strained, like when her feelings were hurt and she didn't want me to know. I looked up to find her frowning at me. "How long?"

"Since Friday night," I admitted, a thick undercurrent of guilt flowing in to supplant my good intentions in not telling her earlier.

"Five days? You knew *five days ago,* and you didn't tell me?"

"I'm sorry, Emma. I didn't want you to have to dwell on it, like I have."

"Did it ever occur to you that I might *want* to dwell on it? Or at least know that it was coming?" Her eyes filled with tears, and her lower lip began to quiver. "How serious is this, Kay?" She blinked and wiped tears from her face with one hand, making an obvious effort to compose herself and her thoughts. "I mean, I know it's death, but you've already died once, and I've died, and, hell, even Sophie's died, so that's less of a permanent state than I used to think it was."

"This time it's permanent." And just saying the words triggered a new wave of fear inside me, beating at my spirit like waves against the cliffs, constantly eroding until there would soon be nothing left of me.

Emma shook her head, denying the inevitable. "But Tod? He can use his reaper connections to get you another extension—or whatever. Right?"

"No, Em." I gripped the door handle so hard my fingers ached. "He can't get me another exchange. No one gets more than one exchange. No exceptions." And even if there *were* exceptions, Tod wasn't in any position to secure one. He was still a rookie reaper, only two years dead, and still on the bottom rung of his afterlife.

"Wait, Tod can't fix this?" Her bottom lip shook, and I knew that the reality was starting to sink in. "You're seriously telling me you're going to die in two days? For real? Like, gone forever?"

It wasn't any easier to hear coming from her mouth, but I nodded, fighting to keep the facts closed off in some dark corner of my head with the other mental cobwebs I didn't want to deal with. And suddenly I realized that my mind was becoming a very messy place.

"Does everyone else know? Nash and Tod?" she asked, and I nodded miserably. *"Sabine?"* Em demanded, and when I nodded again, a new layer of hurt swept over her features, like the curtain on a stage.

"I had to tell her to get her to help me with Mr. Beck," I tried to explain, but I knew nothing I could say would help.

"So, I'm the only one you left out?"

"I wasn't leaving you out. I was trying to spare you from anticipating it. And I didn't tell Nash—my dad did. And Tod's the one who told him. So, really, the only person I've told is Sabine."

"What part of that is supposed to make me feel better?"

"None of it. *None* of it can make either of us feel better, which is why I didn't want you to know. Hell, I wish I didn't know. Em, I'm getting scared." And suddenly there were tears.

From nowhere. I'd known Emma longer than anyone else in my life, other than my uncle. I'd known her longer than I'd known my own father, and somewhere in the process of telling my best and oldest friend that I was going to die, I came to understand the truth of it for myself.

"Oh, Kaylee…" She dropped her keys in the center console and pulled me into a hug that shoved her water bottle into my ribs and my knee into the gear shift, but I wouldn't have let go for anything in the world.

"I've been trying not to think about it, and that's mostly been working, because nothing ever seems normal around here anymore," I sobbed, half-choking on my words as they ran together and my tears soaked into the shoulder of her shirt. "But every time I close my eyes, or take a deep breath—every time things get quiet for just a second—there it is again. Waiting for me. It's like my heart is a watch, and I know it's going to stop ticking on Thursday, and every single beat shoves me a second closer to death, and I try to dig in, or grab on to something, but it keeps pushing me, and I keep sliding, and there isn't much more space before I'll just…fall off the edge." By the end, I was sobbing, and squeezing her so tight she probably couldn't breathe, but she kept holding on.

"Okay, take a breath, Kaylee," she said at last, when my sobs finally began to fade. I let go of her to wipe my face with a dried-stiff paper napkin from her dashboard. "First of all, you should have told me. But in light of the circumstances, I'm gonna let that one slide. And second…what the hell are you even *doing* here? Why aren't you skydiving, or mountain climbing, or on a plane to some fabulous city you've never seen before. Your dad would totally make that happen, if you asked him. Why would you want to spend your last two days on earth at school?"

I blinked and wiped my face on my sleeve. "Em, I have to get rid of Beck."

"No you don't! Let Nash and Sabine handle it. Tod and Alec can help. Or hell, tell your dad and let him do it!"

"I'm telling my dad tonight—I would have already, but he's been so stressed out trying to find a way to exchange my date, which isn't going to happen. But I seriously doubt Tod and Nash are going to be working together on anything in the near future. And even if they were, none of them know what to do any better than I do. I need to know this is handled before I die, Emma. Especially after what I just saw in there." I nodded toward the school building. "Do you honestly think you could have told him no?"

"Yeah." She shrugged. "The problem is that I didn't want to. I *still* don't want to."

"And that's why I have to do this. I want to know that you're going to be safe before…you know."

Emma looked at me for a second, then sighed. "You have to let it go. Let someone else handle it this time. You can't save everyone, Kay. You can't control everything."

"You sound like Nash," I said, and as his name faded from my tongue, another wave of guilt crashed over me. Em must have seen it on my face.

"How did he take it? About Tod, I mean."

"Not well, but that's my fault. He hates me, and I can't blame him, and now I'm the reason he hates his own brother. And Nash thinks Tod's using me to hurt him because he's jealous that Nash is still alive."

Emma shook her head. "I don't blame him for being upset, but that's not it. Tod's been pining over you for months. Frankly, I'm impressed that you held out for so long."

"You knew there was…pining?"

Emma actually smiled, and that felt good, after all the tears.

"We all knew, Kaylee. Hell, I bet even your dad knew. I didn't think Tod would ever say anything, though, because of Nash."

"He didn't. I mean, he told me Nash and I were wrong for each other, and he's been hanging around a lot since Nash went into recovery, but he's always been a flirt, so I didn't really think anything about it until a couple of days ago. Then I saw him feed my reaper to Avari, and it just kind of... clicked. He did that for *me*."

"He did what? What exactly does that mean, feeding someone to Avari?"

"The reaper who was supposed to end my life on Thursday—his name was Thane, and he was kind of stalking me. So Tod found him, beat him up, hauled him into the Netherworld, and gave him to Avari. He just...fed my reaper to a hellion. He could have gotten in serious trouble, Em. He still could. But he did it anyway."

I glanced at Emma to find her watching me, her gaze half out of focus, but intense, like she was hanging on every word. "I can't get a guy to sit through an entire movie before he starts groping me, and Tod *killed* someone for you. And you're not even a couple. Are you?"

I exhaled deeply in frustration, trying to make sense out of the tangled knot my thoughts had become. "I don't know, Em. What would be the point? I'm not even going to be here in two days, but Nash will, and they'll still be brothers, and he hates Tod now as it is. How much worse is that going to be if this turns out to be more than just a couple of kisses?" The echoes of which I could still *feel*. Was it possible to be haunted by a kiss?

"I don't know," Em said. "I'm sure Nash is upset, and pissed off, and I don't blame him. But these aren't exactly normal circumstances. Maybe if you told him what you just told me, he'd understand. Eventually."

But I had my doubts.

I closed my eyes and rubbed my forehead. We'd hurt Nash from both sides—as his brother and his girlfriend. It wouldn't be fair of us to make that worse, just for two days of something that could never go any further. Would Tod even want to? Did he want to be with me badly enough to hurt his brother? Did I want him to? *Should* I want him, too?

"Okay you're obviously overthinking this," Emma said. "So just answer this one question. If Nash didn't care—if it truly wouldn't bother him to see you with his brother—what would you do?"

"But he *does* care…"

"That's not the point. Just for the next minute—for the sake of argument—pretend there is no Nash," she said, and I nodded slowly, trying to imagine something so impossible. "Now, since there's nobody to get hurt, no matter what you decide, what do you want to do?"

I closed my eyes, and in my head, I saw a set of bright blue ones staring back at me. "I want to kiss Tod again."

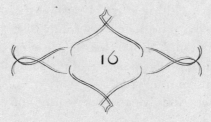

16

I followed Emma back to her house, and we spent the next two hours overanalyzing my ill-fated love life and ignoring her older sister's unsolicited advice about that ill-fated love life—which she understood very little of. We didn't talk about my impending death. In fact, we avoided the subject at all costs, by mutual, unspoken agreement.

Emma seemed to understand what I would have had to explain to anyone else—that I wanted just a couple of hours of normal with my best friend, before I returned to the maelstrom of bizarre the rest of my life had become. What little life I had left, anyway.

But when it was time for me to go, I accidently left my keys in her room, and when I went back for them, Emma was crying, facedown on her bed. Hard enough that she heard neither my footsteps, nor the rattle of my keys as I slid them into my pocket. My heart broke for us both as I snuck out again, so she wouldn't know I'd seen.

Five minutes later, I opened my front door to find a huge bowl of popcorn on the coffee table, and I could tell from the scent and the way some of the kernels were shriveled that they were drizzled with real butter.

"Hey." My dad stepped into the living room from the kitchen with two tall, clear glasses, topped in thick cream-colored foam.

"Is that what I think it is?" I pushed the door shut and dropped my keys into the empty candy dish, then took the glass he handed me. "Coke floats?" He used to make them when I was little—that was one of the few memories I had from before my mother died.

"None other. And I've got sour worms and Milk Duds for dessert."

"So this is dinner?" I dropped onto the couch and grabbed a handful of greasy popcorn.

"Unless you want pizza." My dad plopped onto the couch next to me and stuck a bendy straw into my float. "I happen to know the local delivery boy can be here in thirty seconds or less."

I laughed, because that's what he wanted to hear, but the mention of Tod made my heart ache, with a confusing combination of excitement and guilt. "No, this is fine. This is great."

"Good." He set his glass on the end table and picked up the remote control. "It looks like the movies recorded, but I'll be damned if I know how to make them play."

I swallowed my first mouthful of Coke and melted ice cream, then took the remote from him and pulled up the guide menu. "You know, you're going to have to learn to do this for yourself, at some point. I'm not going to be around to program the DVR forever…"

I meant it as a joke, but my dad looked like I'd just stabbed him in the heart. Repeatedly.

"Sorry. Just kidding." I shoved another handful of popcorn in my mouth to keep from making it worse.

"It's okay," my dad said, though it was clearly anything but.

"However, I reserve the right to wallow in denial for as long as I see fit. And on that note, how was school today?"

Another sip from my glass, and I was ready to play along. "Well...I embarrassed Sophie at lunch, failed to turn in five homework assignments, lied to my French teacher, saw Tod feed my personal reaper to Avari in the Netherworld, broke up with my boyfriend, then propositioned my math teacher." I shrugged and tried on a nervous grin. "Nothing worth writing home about."

My father leaned back on the couch, holding his float in both hands. "I swear, Kaylee, sometimes it's hard to tell when you're joking."

"Is this part of that whole wallowing in denial thing?" I reached for another handful of popcorn. "'Cause I was serious. All that really happened."

His brows rose and his gaze narrowed on me. "The father of a non-emancipated minor might be a little overwhelmed right now."

"A non-emancipated minor would never have told her father most of that."

My dad sighed. "I don't even know where to begin." I started to make a suggestion, but he cut me off. "Oh, wait. Yes I do. Why the hell would you proposition your math teacher? And what exactly do you mean by 'propositioned'?"

"I don't think you want details on my definition of that word, Dad. But it wasn't for real. Our math teacher is an incubus, and Em and I were trying to get him where we want him, so we can take him out. By...putting ourselves in the line of fire, tomorrow, at Emma's house." Before he could form a response—and his struggle with that was obvious—I pushed the play button on the remote. "How 'bout some *Alien?*"

"How 'bout some *answers?*" He grabbed the remote and pushed several buttons, and when he couldn't get the movie to stop, he finally stood and stomped across the room, then slammed his whole hand down on the power button.

Dramatic, but effective.

"Okay, I'll give you the short version," I conceded. "But then I demand some serious *Alien* carnage." My dad made a "go ahead" gesture, then reclaimed his seat next to me. "Mr. Beck is Mr. Wesner's replacement, and last week we discovered he's not human. He's an incubus. And he's in heat—or whatever. I would have told you, but that was the same day you and Tod told me I was going to die, and then everything started to pile up, and you were always gone trying to save my life. And as it turns out, there's just never a good time to tell your dad you're doing battle with an evil lust demon posing as your math teacher. Right?"

His pause was too long to precede anything good. "Is this what your little powwow this morning was about?"

"Yeah. We were pooling information and trying to come up with a viable game plan. If you want to help, we *really* need to know how to get rid of a possibly ancient incubus."

"By letting your father *kill* him for even *thinking* about touching his little girl."

The ache in my chest was warm and kind of wonderful, in the weirdest way. "Yeah, that'd be really awesome, if you could do that. 'Cause we actually don't know how to kill him, and I need to make sure he's gone before I die, 'cause he's going after Emma next."

"Next?"

"He's already impregnated three girls that we know of. He's also killed one woman and left another in a coma. But I'd bet there are others we don't know about yet." And with that thought, my appetite dried up like sweat on a Texas sidewalk.

"Damn it." My father scrubbed his face with both hands,

and I felt awful for adding to the stress he was already under. "Harmony warned me it could get crazy around here, with Avari living in the high school. But I never saw this incubus thing coming."

"Yeah, me, neither. It's not one of the things you typically worry about, in suburban Texas."

"Okay, if memory serves, your uncle Brendon ran up against an incubus once. I'll call him later and see what he can tell me. But just to make me feel marginally involved in your life, what happened with you and Nash? Not that I disapprove of the outcome, but this seems like an odd time to dump your boyfriend."

Oh, here we go... "Nash saw me kissing Tod."

My father's stare was almost vacant, and just when I was starting to wonder if he was still in there, he blinked. "I should have mixed something stronger than Coke floats."

We only made it through the first *Alien* movie before my dad's patience shattered beneath the cluster bomb I'd dropped on him and he excused himself to go call his brother. I couldn't blame him. Even our rare, about-to-expire father-daughter bonding time was outweighed by the threat of an incubus preying on the local coed populace.

Dad made the call from his room, so I sat on my bed with my door open, trying to hear what he obviously wanted to chew over privately before passing on to me. But he was hard to hear through his closed door.

"No, we're short on specifics, and even shorter on time," my dad said. He'd told my uncle Brendon about my expiration date, and they'd planned a family dinner for the next night, Wednesday, possibly my last night in the land of the living, and the night I'd planned to lure my evil incubus teacher to his death. I couldn't imagine how awkward that meal would

be, though, considering my cousin Sophie's complete ignorance of all nonhuman matters.

"She doesn't know his real name or how old he is…" My
father's words faded, and I assumed my uncle was speaking
on the other end of the line. "Math. You should ask Sophie
if she has him."

But she didn't. I'd verified that the day we found out what
Beck was.

"I know, but let's not borrow trouble till we're ready to pay
some back." My dad's mattress creaked and I could picture
him sitting on the edge of the bed, hunched over and stressed.
But I didn't hear anything after that because my phone buzzed
in my pocket. I dug it out to find a text from Tod.

Can I come over?

Suddenly my chest burned like my lungs were on fire. Like
when I was a little girl on the playground swing set, and that
plummeting feeling made me feel scared, and excited, and so
alive.

Yeah. In my room.

An instant later, Tod stood in the middle of my bedroom
floor, and I realized that the courtesy text before just popping
in was only one of the things that had changed.

"Hey," he said, hands shoved into his jeans pockets, watching me carefully, like he didn't quite know how to act around
me now and would be taking his cues from me. Which
sucked, 'cause that was my plan, too.

"Hey." I sat up on the bed and folded my legs beneath me,
itching to touch him, or somehow acknowledge what had
happened between us. Yet I felt guilty for that impulse—for
wanting something that would hurt Nash.

"I need to tell you something." He glanced at the floor,
looking more conflicted than I'd ever seen him, and that

burning in my chest became a steady smolder of resignation and disappointment I had no right to feel.

I knew where this was going. Nash was his brother—his flesh and blood. And Nash would be here for the next three hundred years or so, long after any memory of me faded from both of their minds. Of *course* he would choose his brother over me. How could he not? And part of me knew that was the right thing to do. How could I not want peace between them, especially considering that aside from Harmony and potentially Sabine, they *had* no one else. Tod and Nash would probably never be best friends, but they would always be brothers, and who was I to get in the way of that?

Tod exhaled slowly, and I could only watch him, waiting for the inevitable heartbreak. Could a person actually die of a broken heart? Was that how I would go?

"I'm not supposed to want you, Kaylee. Not like this," he said, the blues in his eyes churning with disparate emotions, and my stubborn heart beat harder. "I made a decision two years ago and gave up the right to want *anything*."

I wasn't sure what that meant, but I wasn't going to interrupt him, because no one had ever spoken to me like this. As if whatever he was trying to tell me was so raw and painful it had to come straight from his soul.

"I'm not supposed to have a life, or a future beyond helping preserve the balance between life and death. My humanity is supposed to fade. They want us that way. Empty, so it's easier to take life, day after day. Sometimes it becomes too easy, and reapers get bored. Desperate for something—anything—to break up the monotony."

He was talking about Thane; I understood that much. I was Thane's entertainment—his break from monotony.

"That's not supposed to happen, but neither is this."

"This" was me. *I* wasn't supposed to happen to Tod. My

next breath burned in my throat, and he shifted onto one foot staring down at me like he wanted to sit, but couldn't let himself get comfortable until he'd said what he had to say.

"They were starting to get what they wanted from me. I stayed close to my mom and Nash, and that worked for a while, but it wasn't enough. Only two years dead, and it was getting harder for me to feel…anything. I was starting to slip into the darkness. The numbness. And the worst part is that it wasn't even scary. I was losing myself, and I didn't even care.

"Then I met you, and at first I didn't understand what had happened. What had changed. All I knew was that I wanted to be near you. Then you helped me with Addison, even though it nearly got you killed—*I* nearly got you killed—and I started to understand how special you are. But by then, you were getting serious with Nash. With my *brother*—one of few people in the whole world I still gave a damn about. So I tried to stay away. I tried so *hard*." His voice cracked on the last word, and my heart cracked with it. Tears stood in my eyes, but I was afraid to let them fall. I was afraid to even breathe for fear of missing a single word.

"But you kept pulling me back. You're the brightest thing I've ever seen, Kaylee. You're this beautiful ball of fire spitting sparks out at the world, burning fiercely, holding back the dark by sheer will. And I always knew that if I reached out—if I tried to touch you—I'd get burned. Because you're not mine. I'm not supposed to feel the fire. I'm not supposed to want it. But I *do*. I want you, Kaylee, like I've never wanted anything. Ever. I want the fire. I want the heat, and the light, and I want the burn. But…"

He left that word hanging. The most hated word in the English language. And I knew what was supposed to follow it.

"But Nash…" I finished for him, and my tears fell in scorching trails down my cheeks.

Tod nodded miserably. "He's my brother. He can hate me his entire life, but that won't change the fact that he's my little brother, and I'm supposed to protect him, not hurt him."

"And we hurt him." I couldn't get Nash's face out of my mind, how betrayed he'd looked standing in the hall. When he saw us.

"Yeah. We did."

"Why...?" I started, then had to suck in a deep breath to continue. To control the heartbroken, angry tears that wanted to flow again. I stood and turned away from him while I wiped my face, and my frustration built. "Why did you say Nash and I aren't right for each other, if you didn't want to hurt him?" I demanded, turning on him again. "Why the hell would you show me that if it wasn't going to lead to anything?"

"Because it's true. Even if you were both scheduled to live forever, eventually he would have messed up again and hurt you. Or you would have broken his heart. But I won't deny that I had selfish reasons for saying it, even though it was the truth."

"So you wanted us to break up."

"Hell *yes,* I wanted you to break up," he said, and for one horrible, wonderful moment, relief almost overwhelmed my guilt. "But I didn't want to be the catalyst. I wanted you to realize he was wrong for you, *then* realize that I might not be. I'm so sorry it all came out of order, and if I could undo what he saw and go back and do this the right way, I would. He's my *brother.*"

I sniffled back more tears and sank onto my comforter again. "So, you're here to let me down easy?" This was the part that would kill me, two days early. I could feel it.

"No," he said, and I looked up, sure I'd heard him wrong, or I was missing something. "I'm here because I couldn't stay away from you. I'll spend the next three hundred years trying to make this up to Nash, if that's what it takes. But I'm going to spend the next two days with you. If you want my company."

My next breath was so shallow I hardly had the air to speak. "I want that so, so much."

Tod sank into my desk chair and a slow, relieved smile formed on his face. "I was sure that after all that, you'd decide this was too much trouble."

"This?"

"Us," he clarified, rolling the chair closer to the bed, one foot at a time.

I scooted toward the edge of the mattress to meet him, my pulse rushing so fast just breathing felt surreal. "There's an us?"

"As far as I'm concerned…" He leaned forward, his mouth inches from mine, and my pulse spiked. "There's nothing *but* us." His lips met mine, and he kissed me slowly, deeply, like we had all the time in the world. And in that moment, that's exactly what it felt like.

When I finally pulled back to catch my breath, my head was spinning. Or maybe the whole damn room was spinning. "I think that was even better than the first time," I whispered.

"There's no one gawking at us now."

But that reminded me of the public spectacle our first kiss had become, and why we'd been there in the first place. And of the questions I still had to ask, as badly as I hated to ruin the moment. "So…Thane's gone?" I asked, and Tod nodded. "What does that mean, exactly?"

"It means that Levi will be scrambling to replace him."

"Does he know what happened?"

Tod leaned back in my desk chair. "He knows that Thane had an unfortunate run-in with everyone's least favorite hellion and that he won't be rejoining the workforce. But he *might* not be entirely clear on how Thane and Avari happened to meet."

"Are you going to get in trouble for this?"

He shrugged, like it didn't matter. "I'm dead. What more could they do to me?"

But I wasn't buying his nonchalance. They could demote him back to reaping on the local nursing home circuit. They could transfer him to another district, away from his family. They could recycle his soul and end his afterlife.

The thought that Tod could die—for real this time—because of me made me want to vomit my junk food dinner all over my comforter. "The truth. How bad could this get?"

Tod exhaled slowly, then met my gaze with a heavy one of his own. "Levi wanted to make an example out of Thane and he's pretty pissed that I messed that up. But he likes me—as much as a reaper his age can really like anyone—and he's the one who left the information around for me to find in the first place. I think he'll leave it alone as long as he can claim plausible deniability. But if anyone over his head finds out I acted against another reaper—one who outranks me—without permission or evidence…well, let's just say there'll be a sudden opening at the pizza place."

My nausea swelled into bone chilling horror. Tod could still die—again—for what he'd done for me. But he hadn't hesitated to do it.

"So he hasn't replaced Thane yet?" I said, trying not to think about how badly this could end for Tod. There was nothing I could do to change that. I couldn't make him take back what he'd done, and even mentioning it would sound ungrateful.

"Not that I know of."

I didn't know what to say to that. Knowing that Levi was

looking for someone to kill me—though inevitable—was creepy and beyond bizarre.

Though it hadn't even happened yet, my death was already hurting people, in spite of my best efforts to make it easy on everyone. I should have told Emma earlier. I'd thought that by not telling her, I'd be sparing her several days of advance grief, but it turns out, I was denying her the chance to come to terms with my death.

And Nash…

"I should have taken your advice," I blurted out, with no conscious warning from my brain that I was even going to speak.

Tod took one look at the pain that must have been swirling in my eyes and he put on a teasing grin as easily as most guys would put on a baseball cap. "About the pizza? I told you, goat cheese is no joke."

"No." He was going to make me say it. "About Nash. I should have let Sabine have him six weeks ago. You were right—if I'd let him go then, he would have moved on by now, and whatever's going to happen on Thursday wouldn't be so hard for him." And, of course, he wouldn't have been blindsided by me kissing his undead brother in the middle of the math hall.

Tod exhaled heavily, and when he looked up, the soft swirl of blue in his eyes caught me off guard. And suddenly my heart felt bruised in advance of whatever he was going to say. "I lied, Kaylee."

Okay, not the best opening… But not the worst either, considering his last big announcement was that I was going to die. "About what?"

"About Nash," Tod said, and though he looked uncomfortable with the very concept of making a confession, he didn't look particularly sorry about the offense itself. "I don't think he would have gotten over you this quickly."

"Then why did you say it?" Why would he lie to me—even if I was the pot to his black kettle?

"Because you don't belong with him! I tried to tell you that, but you wouldn't listen, and I thought if you understood that he'd be better off without you, you'd break up with him for his own good. So I...exaggerated how easy it'd be for him to get over you, with Sabine there to step in. But I underestimated how *incredibly* stubborn you are."

"I prefer to think of it as dedication..." I mumbled.

"Whatever you want to call it. The harder Sabine pulled on him, the harder you pulled back, just so she couldn't have him."

"That's not why!"

"Not consciously, no," Tod agreed, taking my hand in his. "Which is why you couldn't see what I was trying to show you. But then you saw, and you kissed me, and that changed everything for me, and now I only know two things for sure."

"What things?" I couldn't get enough air, no matter how fast my lungs pulled it in, and I couldn't think beyond waiting for whatever he would say next.

"I know that you and I belong together. And I know that it's too late for that to matter."

My heart cracked open, and pain leaked out. "That's the problem, Tod. It's too late for anything to matter. That's why I kissed you," I admitted, challenging myself to hold his gaze during my own confession.

"You kissed me because it wouldn't matter?" A flicker of hurt swirled in his eyes. "You really think it doesn't matter?"

"That's not what I meant." That kiss had meant a lot to several different people. To Nash. To Tod. Hell, even to Sabine. And I wasn't going to deny what it changed for me. "I meant…I'm going to die in less than two days, and you should know better than anyone what that means. It's scary, and surreal, but in a way, it's also like the ultimate freedom. Does that make any sense?"

"Yeah." Tod brushed a pale curl from his forehead. "You can do whatever you want, because you're not going to be here to suffer the consequences. Right?"

"Right."

His brows rose over a new shine in his eyes. "So what you're really saying is that kissing me is one of those things a girl shouldn't die without experiencing, right?"

"Wow, you have a healthy ego."

He shrugged. "Helps make up for the pallor of death. But you're avoiding the question."

"I didn't think you were serious."

"Dead serious." The reaper grinned over his own joke, and I groaned. "Humor me, Kaylee. Dead guys don't get much action—I'm gonna have to make this memory last a loooong time," he said, and it felt like someone had sucked all the air out of the room and left me gasping. He was going to make the memory last? The memory of me kissing him?

"Make it last, like, *forever?*" I whispered, and immediately wished I'd kept that question to myself.

"Yeah. Like mental movie footage." His mouth was grinning, but his eyes were serious. "Now I'm compiling the bonus features, including an interview with the kissee herself. So tell me, Ms. Cavanaugh, how long have you been dying to kiss me?"

I groaned. "More death humor?"

Another shrug. "It's kind of my shtick. Answer the question."

"I don't know." I sat up and played along, surprised to realize that for the first time in days, I wasn't tense and on alert, waiting for the proverbial scythe to swing—ironic, considering I was sitting next to a Grim Reaper. "It's not like I planned it, but I will admit that the prospect hasn't been especially distasteful lately."

"Not especially distasteful?" He pretended to think it over. "That ought to keep my ego in check."

I laughed. "Is that even possible?"

"Probably not. But I wouldn't put anything past you, Kaylee," Tod said, looking straight into my eyes. I looked back until the connection between us started to feel raw, and taut, and *vital,* in no way I could explain. I'd never felt so exposed and vulnerable, yet confident of my own safety. I felt like he could see past my eyes into parts of me no one had ever seen before. And he deserved the truth.

"Fine." I crossed my legs yoga style and picked at a bit of fuzz on my comforter. "I admit it. I didn't want to die without knowing what it was like to kiss you." I *might* have been thinking about that on occasion recently, since we'd been spending so much time together....

I don't know how I thought he'd react to that tender bit of truth, but his wary frown definitely wasn't what I'd expected.

Tod leaned back in my desk chair, putting a frustrating distance between us. "Like you didn't want to die without knowing what it was like to sleep with my brother?"

And that's when I understood my mistake—and damn, I'd made a lot of them.

"I didn't sleep with him, Tod. Thanks to you, ironically enough." Because he'd interrupted us with the news that Thane had been assigned as my reaper.

"That's not irony, Kaylee," he said, and his gaze never wavered. "It was careful timing."

I blinked, gaping at him in disbelief. "You knew...?"

"That you were about to have sex with Nash? Yeah." He

shrugged, like that was no big deal, but my irritation had just flared into a brutal emotional heartburn.

"You were here? *Watching?*" I shouldn't have been surprised. There was nothing to stop a reaper from being wherever he wanted, unseen by all. But knowing my privacy had been violated during one of the most intimate moments of my life sickened me like little I'd ever felt.

"Hell no, I wasn't here. I can't even stand to see Nash kiss you, much less...anything more. But here's what you really want to know—I don't spy on you, Kaylee. Not anymore." Tod was careful to let me see the cobalt twist of sincerity in his eyes.

"But you used to?" I refused to be placated by the past tense nature of the offense.

"Yeah, but it was nothing personal." He shrugged and crossed his arms over his chest. "I have a lot of hours to kill and nowhere to be when I'm not working. So I watch people. Most reapers do it out of boredom, but I've been hanging out at my mom's house ever since I died, because I don't know where else to go. It's not my home, because I never lived there, but it's always been *like* home, because my family's there."

I couldn't quite interpret the ache in my chest, but it tempered my anger, whether or not it should have. "When did you start watching me?"

"After what happened with your aunt." The week I'd found out I was a *bean sidhe* and started going out with Nash. "You were the only one other than my family who knew I existed, so I'd tag along when Nash came over and watch whatever you guys were watching on TV."

"Were we really that boring?" It was weird to see me and Nash through someone else's eyes.

Tod laughed. "Yeah. Thank goodness. But then you helped

me with Addy, for no reason except that I asked you to, and I started to come over here on my own, just to see you."

I was half creeped out, half fascinated, and all ears. "When did you stop?"

"When I realized I hated seeing you make out with my brother."

"I don't understand." But maybe I was beginning to, and that ache in my chest deepened.

Tod glanced at my comforter, then met my gaze again. "Okay, I'm starting to realize how creepy this whole thing makes me sound, but try to remember that until you, my whole afterlife was like a one-way mirror. I saw people, but they never saw me. There was no interaction. No involvement. No malice or creepy intent. I'm not like Thane—I never stalked people I was scheduled to reap. I was just… watching. Living vicariously, which is the only way I can live now."

"I'm with you so far…" And sympathy was starting to win out over the creepy factor. He must have been so *lonely*.…

"Good." The tension in his frame started to ease. "Anyway, I stopped watching you when we started hanging out together for real."

"After Nash started using?" I asked, and Tod nodded. I couldn't be around Nash while he was going through withdrawal. The wounds were still too raw, and the thought of seeing him hurt. But Tod had come over a couple of times during my otherwise lonely winter break, and we'd done… nothing. We'd just hung out, watching stupid YouTube videos and listening to music, openly avoiding the subject of Nash and his frost addiction.

Maybe that should have been my first clue.…

"Once I realized I wanted more than friendship from you,

it didn't seem fair for me to see you when you didn't know I was there."

My relief was almost enough to mitigate my irritation at having been watched in the first place. "So...if you weren't spying, how did you know...what Nash and I were about to do the other day?"

"Sabine called me."

I closed my eyes, resisting the urge to slap my own forehead. How had I not figured that out? I'd called Sabine for advice, then hung up when Nash arrived, and she'd probably had Tod on the phone before my voice even faded from her ear. *Damn* Sabine! But she wasn't working alone....

"What could possibly make you think what I do in private is any of your business?" I demanded, my voice low with anger.

"Sleeping with Nash would have been a mistake, and I don't want anyone to hurt you—including you."

"You don't get to decide what's a mistake for me, Tod."

He frowned, obviously confused. "Was I wrong? Do you wish you'd done it?"

"No." Especially now that Nash and I had broken up, and I could see the truth about my own motivations—I hadn't wanted to sleep with Nash so much as I'd wanted to lose my virginity before I died. "But that's not the point. I have a right to make my own mistakes, just like everyone else. Don't ever do that again."

"Fine." He recrossed his arms over his chest. "But I'm not sorry I did it. And neither are you."

I nodded slowly. "Fair enough. So..." I hesitated, not sure I really wanted the answer to what I was about to ask. "Were you and Sabine working together to break up me and Nash?"

"No. She tried to talk me into that when she first got here, but I told you, I didn't want to be what broke you two up."

"But you didn't mind her trying it, even though it's morally repugnant to intentionally break up someone else's relationship?"

Tod's brows arched in amusement over my moral outrage. "How is it wrong to put everything you have into getting what you want most in the world?" Which was exactly what Sabine had done.

Or was he talking about wanting me like that—more than anything else in the world? My pulse raced so fast my head started to swim. He wanted me more than anything? *Wait— focus...*

"It's wrong because you don't have the right to end someone else's relationship!" Had two years of reaping souls skewed his moral compass, or was he always like this?

"First of all, keep in mind that this is all hypothetical. I didn't try to break up you and Nash—that was Sabine." The reaper leaned forward, his eyes bright with interest, enjoying what he obviously saw as a recreational debate. "And second, if the couple shouldn't have been together in the first place, breaking them up is actually doing a good deed. So you're welcome. Hypothetically."

I didn't know whether to laugh or yell at him. "You don't get to *decide* who should be together and who shouldn't!"

"Are you saying I was wrong?" Tod's gaze narrowed on me in challenge. "Did you really think you and Nash belonged together for the rest of your lives, even after what he did to you?"

Damn it. "I did at first. I thought I could forgive and forget." I'd *tried* to. But the truth was that I couldn't make myself trust him again, though I'd probably never admit to Sabine that she was right about that. "But that's not the point."

"That *is* the point! Right and wrong aren't as simple as black and white. You and Nash would have done more damage to each other together than the breakup would have done to either of you, and just because you couldn't see that doesn't make it wrong for those who care about you both to point out the truth."

For one long moment, I could only stare at him in disbelief. "It's a good thing I'm *not* going to live long enough to go out with you, because you'd drive me crazy."

"There's a good kind of crazy, Kaylee," he insisted softly, reaching out to wrap his warm hand around mine. "It's the kind that makes you think about things that make your head hurt, because not thinking about them is the coward's way out. The kind that makes you touch people who bruise your soul, just because they need to be touched. This is the kind of crazy that lets you stare out into the darkness and rage at eternity, while it stares back at you, ready to swallow you whole."

Tod leaned closer, staring into my eyes so intently I was sure he could see everything I was thinking, but too afraid to say. "I've seen you fight, Kaylee. I've seen you step into that darkness for someone else, then claw your way out, bruised, but still standing. You're that kind of crazy, and I live in that darkness. Together, we'd take crazy to a whole new level."

My pulse whooshed in my ears so fast I could barely hear myself speak. "I only have—"

"Two days." He squeezed my hand. "So what? You can spend them feeling sorry for yourself, or you can let me help make them the best two days of your life, and my afterlife. So what's it gonna be?"

I stared into his eyes, like I'd never seen him before. And I hadn't—not like this. But he'd obviously seen me, better than anyone else ever had.

"Well?" Tod watched me, his hand still warm in mine.

In answer, I leaned forward and kissed him again.

17

"Hey, Kaylee," my dad called, as his door squealed open at the end of the hall.

I jerked away from Tod so fast the whole room seemed to spin around us, and when I looked up, I found my dad watching us from my doorway, surprised into a rare moment of total speechlessness.

"Hey, Mr. Cavanaugh." Tod swiveled to face him in my desk chair, and I could see my father struggling for a response.

"Tod, could you excuse us for a minute?" he said at last.

Tod gave me an amused look no one else could have interpreted. "I'll be in the living room." Then he disappeared, and the chair spun without him.

My father sighed and stepped into my room, closing the door behind him. "Could you please ask him to walk like a normal person when he's here?"

I shrugged. "He's not a normal person."

"Is this going to be a regular thing now?"

"I don't know how regular it could be, considering how little time I have left."

My dad sank onto the end of my bed and picked at one thumbnail before meeting my gaze again. "This is going to sound stupid, considering the circumstances, but don't you think this is happening kind of fast, Kaylee?"

Another shrug. "I guess that depends on your perspective. From Tod's, it's been a long time coming."

He seemed to think about that for a minute, then stared at his hands again and nodded. "Yeah, I guess it has."

I frowned at him in surprise. "You knew?"

"How he felt about you? It was pretty obvious, Kaylee."

To everyone but me, evidently. "Is that why you were always mean to him?"

"I wasn't mean to him. And I have to admit he's certainly grown on me this week, with everything he's tried to do for you. But yes. If things were different now—" meaning, if I were going to live "—I don't think he'd be a very good choice for you."

I laughed. "In all fairness, you should know that parental seal of approval is *not* a requirement for a boyfriend. In fact, it's usually a deal-breaker."

"Noted." He sighed. "Seriously, though, what kind of future can you possibly have with a dead boy?"

"I'm sixteen. Even if I were going to live, college is as far into the future as I've really thought so far, and it's not like the distance would be a problem for him." One of the advantages of the reaper mode of travel…

"Kay, you may not be thinking about the future—you might not be even if yours were going to be…longer—but he is. Tod is eternal, Kaylee. His future is probably all he *ever* thinks about."

"I don't know, Dad. I think he'd rather live in the moment, because he knows how much future he'll have. It must be overwhelming, facing forever. Don't you think?" Not that I'd ever know…

"I guess." He lapsed into a heavy pause, just watching me.

"But my point is that none of that matters now. Tod isn't my top choice for you, and if this were going to be a long-term thing, I'd insist that he follow all the normal social standards—no popping in anytime he wants, no popping into your room *ever,* and no visits after eleven. But this isn't a normal situation, and I want you to be happy."

"What does all that mean?"

My dad sighed and twisted to fully face me. "It means that Tod's welcome here. Well, not *here* specifically," he amended, glancing at the bed we both sat on for emphasis. "But he's welcome in our home."

"Thank you." And suddenly I wanted to cry again. "You know, for a dad, you're kinda awesome."

The sudden mixture of pain and regret twisting through his irises was too much for both of us, so he squeezed my hand, then changed the subject. "So...how's Nash taking all this, with you and Tod? Have you talked to him?"

"I don't think he'd answer if I called." I'd texted Sabine from Emma's, though, to check up on him. She'd reported that he was kind of drunk, and very pissed off, and that I should stay away and let him get over it.

My father sighed. "Well, I can't blame him there." And neither could I. "Kaylee, I have to go meet your uncle, and I don't want to leave you alone...."

"Dad, nothing's going to happen today," I insisted.

"You don't know that. I was going to see if Alec could come over again, but if Tod's already here and he's willing to stay..."

"I suppose I could clear my schedule..." Tod called from the living room, and I laughed out loud.

"Yeah, I had a feeling," my dad mumbled.

"Oh, hey," I said, jumping up from my bed when he headed for the door. "Take this to Uncle Brendon..." I plopped into my desk chair and pressed the space bar on my laptop to wake it up, then jabbed the print screen button. My printer whirred to life and spat out a black-and-white copy of the Crestwood faculty page, including the yearbook photo of one Mr. David Allan. "Maybe it'll turn out to be the same incubus he knew."

"I doubt that, but I guess it's worth a shot." My dad took the page I held out, with Beck's picture circled in red. "Don't make me regret leaving you two alone," he warned, as I followed him into the living room.

When the front door closed behind him, I turned to find Tod watching me, and I knew that if my father had seen the heat churning fiercely in the reaper's eyes, he never would have left the house at all.

"Well, he's right about that, I guess," Tod whispered into my ear as I wrapped my arms around his neck. "There's no more time for regrets."

I parked across the lot from Sabine's car on Wednesday morning and avoided Nash's locker on the way to class, but there was no way to avoid the rumors, and they were already buzzing by the time I got to school.

"*She* cheated on *Nash?*" a girl from my French class said, clearly unaware that I was walking behind her in the hall. "I would have thought it'd be the other way around. Who was the other guy?"

The girl next to her shrugged, hauling her backpack strap higher on one bony shoulder. "Never saw him before. But he was thoroughly covetable."

It was hard not to laugh out loud, thinking of Tod's potential ego boost. Too bad it came at the expense of my own self-image.

"So...does that mean Nash's up for grabs again?" the first girl asked, and I couldn't resist—what did I have to lose?

"Yeah, he's available, but you don't have a Popsicle's chance in hell," I said, falling into step beside them, enjoying their twin shocked expressions. "And if you even try, Sabine Campbell will kick your face in." Sabine was still fairly new, but already working on infamy. "She's got dibs."

Both girls stopped and gaped at me, and I smiled all the way to class.

"So, what happened last night? Did Tod come over?" Emma demanded in a whisper the moment I slid into my chair. And evidently the flush I could feel crawling over my face wasn't answer enough for her.

"Yeah. He stayed till his shift started at midnight."

"And...? Did you do it?"

"Shh!" I glanced around the classroom, cheeks burning even hotter, but no one seemed to have heard. "And no, we didn't."

"Is it because he's dead?" she whispered, leaning closer. "Is that a problem? Does his blood still circulate?"

"Em! No, that's not the problem." Was it? I hadn't actually asked. But he was warm to the touch, which seemed to indicate good circulation... "There's no problem. We've been together less than twenty-four hours."

Emma frowned, like I'd lapsed into Greek. "If there's ever been justification for an accelerated physical connection, this is it. He's been waiting for you for months, Kaylee, and you don't have much time left." The pained line across her forehead was the only indication of how upset she really was, in spite of an obvious determination to wear her brave face. "And, if I can indulge in a moment of selfishness, we're running out of time for the 'guess what I just lost' phone call. It's, like a rite of passage."

"You can't be serious."

She shrugged. "I'm not saying you should sleep with Tod

just so we can have one last best friend tell-all. But, should you go down that path, I solemnly swear not to judge you." She placed one hand over her heart. "And to provide the ice cream."

"I'll keep that in mind."

"That's all I'm asking. So...is it weird?" she asked, while the other students settled in around us, most staring at Mr. Beck as he wrote last night's homework problems on the board.

"Is what weird?" The fact that Tod was dead? The fact that I soon would be? The fact that a couple dozen people had seen my very public breakup with Nash, over a stolen kiss from his brother?

"Being *with* him, after thinking of him as a friend for so long."

"It's kinda weird," I admitted, not quite able to hide my smile. "But not because I already know him." In fact, that was kind of cool. We hadn't had any awkward getting-to-know-you moments, beyond his whole Peeping-Tom admission, which I'd decided to forgive, on the condition that it never happened again.

Now, if I could just get Nash to forgive me sometime in the next day or so...

"So, are you and Tod a couple now?"

"I don't know. It seems kind of pointless to put a label on it, considering that we've only really got one day together."

Emma's face crumpled, and I wished I could take the words back. Evidently that was one reminder too many.

"How can you be so casual about this?" she demanded in a fierce whisper, brushing tears from her eye with the side of one finger, like she was wiping off a smear of eyeliner. "It's like you don't even care."

"Everyone keeps saying that," I whispered back, leaning closer to keep from being overheard. "But I don't know how else I'm supposed to act. This isn't like dying of cancer, Em. I'm not sick, which is a huge plus, obviously, but I'm not going to linger for another month while I say my goodbyes. There's no wiggle room, and I can't tell the world that I won't be here after tomorrow. So I don't have any choice except to go on living for the next twenty-four hours, trying to distract myself from how mind-bendingly final the whole thing seems by bringing down our demon teacher." And by spending time with a living dead boy whose interest in me I'd discovered much too late to properly explore.

And by trying to explain to Nash why I'd kissed his brother, then asking him for forgiveness he had no reason to give either of us.

"I know. I'm sorry." Emma sniffled and pulled a tissue from the minipack in her purse. "It just feels like you're leaving me. Senior year's going to suck with no best friend."

"Yeah, sorry about that." But at least she'd *have* a senior year....

"I wish there was something..." Em began, but then the late bell cut her off, and Mr. Beck closed the classroom door.

Math sucked even more than usual that day, mostly because every single minute counted down by the clock over the door felt like a minute of my life wasted. And I didn't have that many minutes left to spare.

I watched Mr. Beck as he went over the homework I hadn't done, then called people up to the board to help him demonstrate the day's lesson. There was nothing inappropriate about him in class, and I had to keep glancing at Danica's empty chair to assure myself that I hadn't imagined the whole thing.

During the rush for the door after the bell rang, I caught Mr. Beck watching me and Emma—the very first overtly predatory look I'd seen from him—so I pretended to search through my backpack for something until we could reasonably be last in line for the exit. Then I threaded my arm through Em's and glanced over my shoulder, shooting Mr. Beck my best vixen smile, trying not to show the nausea churning in my stomach.

Emma spun to face him from the doorway and held up eight fingers, silently mouthing "eight o'clock." He nodded, anticipation firing in his gaze like sparks from a bonfire, and she tugged me into the hallway.

Where I almost ran smack into Nash and Sabine.

"Can I talk to you?" Nash asked, before I'd recovered from the near-collision, and that's when I realized he'd come looking for me. Neither he nor Sabine had any other reason to be in the math hall between first and second period.

"Yeah." We both had class in four minutes, but school had never mattered less. This might be my only chance to explain what had happened and why. To see for myself how he was handling the breakup. To ask him to forgive Tod, even if he couldn't forgive me—it was killing me that I'd come between brothers, and I wanted to clean up at least that part of the mess we'd made before I lost the chance.

"I'll see you later, Em," I said, and I couldn't help noting the fury on Sabine's face as she and Emma watched us walk off together toward the parking lot. But there was something more there, beneath her anger. She was…worried. About what? That I'd try to take him back?

Nash took an immediate left when the glass doors closed behind us and wound up leaning against the wall, just out of sight from the hallway. For nearly a minute, we both stared at the ground, and I assumed that, like me, he wasn't sure how to start this conversation. So I jumped in.

"I'm so sorry about yesterday," I said, through the lump that had formed in my throat. "I didn't mean for that to happen. Any of it." Though my lame apology couldn't possibly make things okay between us, any more than his apology was able to fix things when he'd messed up.

"I was kind of hoping you'd say that." Nash leaned with one shoulder against the bricks, facing me from a foot away, and I couldn't quite interpret the intense swirl of greens and browns in his irises. "I don't want to fight, Kaylee. Especially now. I don't want you to die mad at me, or thinking that I'm mad at you. So if you say it meant nothing, I'll believe you. It's Tod I'm pissed at anyway, not you."

The second period bell rang, and my head rang with it, and it actually took me the length of that clanging to figure out what he was really saying. And when it finally sank in that he wanted to get back together, my guilt was almost too thick to breathe through.

"Nash, I…" I glanced at the ground, at a complete loss for words. He didn't know Tod and I had moved beyond that first kiss, and he'd obviously come to school assuming that if he forgave me, we could pick up right where we'd left off. "Things aren't the same anymore."

"I know," he said, before I could decide how to continue. "Everything must feel so weird for you now, knowing it's all going to end. I don't even want to *think* about you being gone. I just want to spend this last day with you, and we can forget about what happened yesterday. That's not important now. What's important is salvaging what time we have left together."

Crap. I'd never felt more guilty in my life, and it was worse knowing that he wasn't mad at me when he had every right to be, and if I weren't about to die, we both knew he *would* be.

"Nash, I really appreciate that—" *Lame.* "—and I know you're just trying to make sure that my last day on earth doesn't suck." *True*. "But we can't get back together just because I'm going to die tomorrow. That's not a real reason."

"We shouldn't have broken up in the first place," he insisted, and I realized he was only hearing what he wanted to hear. Competing vines of unease and guilt wound slowly up my spine, tightening as he continued. "When I messed up, you forgave me. Now I'm forgiving you. You were scared and confused—who wouldn't be in your position—and he was there, like he's *always* there." Nash shrugged. "I'm still gonna kick his ass the next time he has the balls to face me, but today's about us. You and me. So let's get out of here and have some fun. This may be our last chance."

He reached for my hand, but I pulled away before he could touch me, and an irritated twist of green shot through his irises, piercing stubborn composure to reveal something stronger and darker than mere determination.

Uh-oh.

"Nash, I need you to understand something," I said. "Tod was the catalyst for our breakup, but he wasn't the reason. He's not the source of our problems. Nothing's been the same between us since the winter carnival." Since the thing we didn't talk about. It was always there between us, making him too cautious and putting me on edge. "You know that."

"That's not true." He shook his head firmly, stubbornly. "We moved on. We were fine. It was working."

"No it wasn't. Not like it used to." I was always afraid he'd slip up, and it would happen again—even Sabine had told him that. Hell, he had trouble trusting himself half the time. "I've tried to put it behind me. I tried so hard, and I didn't realize it wasn't really working until I felt something that *did* work."

"What are you saying?" He looked like I'd just smacked him in the head with a two-by-four—like he didn't know whether to cry or strike back.

Why was there no greeting card for letting a guy down easy the day before you're scheduled to tumble into the dark hereafter? "I'm sorry for what I did. I'm sorry for how this happened. And I'm so, so sorry that I didn't see the problem sooner. I didn't want to see it, because I wanted us to work." My vision blurred with tears and I had to swallow the lump forming in my throat. I didn't want to say what needed to be said, but it wasn't fair to either of us to leave this hanging. "But we don't work. Not as a couple. Not anymore."

Nash shook his head, frowning, more frustrated than surprised now. "Yes we do."

"Nash, you need someone with more than I have to give you. More than I'd have, even if I were going to live." Someone who didn't have to talk herself into trusting him. "You need someone who understands the way you think and sees into your soul."

"That's you."

"No, it's not. I don't understand what's going on in there most of the time." I glanced at his chest, where his heart beat beneath his shirt, then back up to his face. "I don't know what you want from life. I don't know where you want to go to college. I don't know where your father's buried. I don't even know how you feel about losing Scott and Doug. You don't tell me any of that."

"Because I don't want to scare you!"

"That's my point. You need someone you aren't worried about scaring."

"He's not getting it," Sabine said, and I whirled around to find her walking toward us, from the direction of the quad, her sneakers silent on the spring grass. How long had she been there? "Maybe because you're leaving out one important detail." She stepped onto the sidewalk and aimed an angry, challenging look my way. "Why don't you tell him what this is really about?"

"Go away, Sabine." My pulse spiked, and I realized with one glance at her that she knew what he didn't want to hear and I didn't want to tell him—that Tod and I weren't a once-kiss mistake. That we'd gotten together for real after Nash and I broke up—either because she'd read my fears, or she was just plain perceptive. Or both. "This is none of your business."

"What is this really about?" Nash glanced from her to me with dread twisting tight coils of brown and green around his pupils.

"She's talking about Tod, but this isn't about him. He's not what went wrong between us."

"What about Tod?" Nash demanded through clenched teeth.

I exhaled slowly. "He and I...kind of...got together last night."

Nash's irises went still, and the only interpretation I had for that was that he didn't know what to feel. Then the colors in his eyes burst into furious motion—a true storm of color. "What the hell does that mean? You *slept* with *my brother?*"

"No! You know, there are entire moments in *some* people's lives that aren't about sex!"

"You were the one pushing the issue this week, Kaylee," he snapped, jaw tight, forehead deeply furrowed.

"I know. And that was a mistake."

Too late, I realized what I'd said, and how he would misinterpret it. "Sex with me would have been a mistake?" He bristled with anger, but the wound went deeper than that, and we all three knew it. "Why? Because you're so pure and spotless, and I might have tarnished your shine?"

"That's not what I—"

"That *is* what you meant." He was getting louder, and I

was afraid someone would hear him, but there were no windows on this side of the building, and the doors stayed closed. "You're purity personified, and I'm one big moral question mark. So I guess you're really doing me a favor. Maybe I won't look so bad when you're not standing next to me," Nash snapped, and my face stung, like he'd slapped me. Tears formed in my eyes, but I blinked them away, clinging to anger as I faced the death of any hope I'd had for us parting on good terms.

"What is *wrong* with you?" He'd never spoken to me like that before. He *wouldn't*.

"I caught my girlfriend making out with my brother in front of half the school!" He was shouting now, his hands curled into fists at his sides. "I think that entitles me to a little anger."

"Yeah, it does." I wasn't going to deny that. And I'd been pissed when I'd caught him kissing Sabine, even though he hadn't initiated that. "But I don't know what else you want me to say. I've never been sorrier about anything in my life. Tod feels so bad he's prepared to spend the rest of your life trying to make it up to you."

"But he wasn't sorry enough to keep his hands to himself last night, was he?" His eyes shined with angry tears, even as his irises churned with pain. "You let him touch you?"

"Oh, hell…" Sabine mumbled. "Don't answer that."

I glanced at her in surprise, and she seemed to be trying to tell me something without actually saying it. Some kind of warning. But by then I could hardly see through my own anger.

"That's none of your business," I said softly. Yet I could feel myself flush.

Nash blinked, openly wounded for a second before fresh

fury rolled over him, straightening his spine, squaring his shoulders.

"Fine," he said through clenched teeth, and the bright green coil of malice twisting in his eyes seemed to suck the air straight from my lungs. "I guess I should have seen this coming. I mean, you two have so much in common, like death, and lies, and spying on people you claim to care about. He's the cold corpse to your frigid bitch."

His words stung so sharp and deep that at first I couldn't breathe. Even Sabine looked surprised by the venom in his tone, and in the second it took me to recover, I realized something was truly wrong. Nash wouldn't talk to me like that, no matter how mad I made him, or how badly I hurt him. He wasn't that kind of guy.

"Give me your hand." I reached out for it when he refused, and when he tried to step back, I lunged forward and caught his fingers.

They were ice-cold.

No. "Damn it, Nash." I turned to Sabine without letting go of him. "He's using again." And it was all my fault. Again.

"What do you care?" Nash pulled his freezing fingers from my grasp and leaned against the brick wall. "You'd rather be with the living dead than with me, so why don't you two just go haunt someone and leave me alone."

I didn't know what to do. I couldn't decide whether to yell at him or wrap one arm around him and take him somewhere safe until he came down from his bitter high. I didn't know whether to hate him for giving in again, or hate myself for driving him to it.

Finally I whirled on Sabine with a furious insight. "Did you know about this?"

She shrugged, but looked distinctly unhappy. "Harmony caught us with a bottle of Jack last night and kicked me out. I left to feed, then went back after she left for work, and he was like this, but I couldn't find his balloon. He finally fell asleep early this morning, so I left him for half an hour to grab a change of clothes, and he was high again when I got back. But he insisted on coming to school to talk to you."

"Shut up, Sabine," Nash snapped, but she ignored him.

"Why didn't you tell me?" I demanded.

"Why should I? He's not your problem anymore."

I gaped at her in disbelief. "Breaking up with him doesn't mean I don't *care* about him!" Nash and I had been through too much together for that to ever be possible. Our parents were close. His mom was the only mother figure I had. He was the only other *bean sidhe* my age I'd ever met. And my feelings for his brother would have kept me and Nash in each other's lives, even if none of the rest of that were true. At least, they would if I were scheduled to live past Thursday. "And it definitely doesn't mean I want to watch him die!"

Sabine rolled her eyes. "He's not going to die. I'll take him home with me until he comes down, then I'll make sure it doesn't happen again. That's the difference between you and me—I'm not going to run from his problems."

That wasn't fair. But it was true.

"Both of you *shut up!*" Nash brushed past us and stomped into the parking lot. "I'm nobody's problem but my own."

I rushed after him with Sabine on my heels, and we caught up with him just past the first row of cars. "Nash, go home with Sabine. She'll make sure you don't kill yourself."

"Why bother? I have to be dead to get your attention, right?" He took a left in the first aisle, and I had to jog to catch up. "What are you, some kind of necrophiliac? 'Cause that's really sick."

"*Damn* it, Nash." As Sabine caught up with us, I grabbed his arm and spun him around to face me before he could take another step, trying to ignore the cold that seeped through his sleeve and into my fingers. "I don't expect you to understand about me and Tod, and I'm so sorry that we hurt you. I can't justify what I did and I can't explain what I feel for him, and I honestly don't know where it would go, if I were going to be here past tomorrow. All I know is how good I feel when I'm with him, and how I want to be with him when he's gone, and how, when he looks at me, I get this feeling in the pit of my stomach, like I'm falling, but I can't remember jumping, and I don't think I'll ever hit the ground."

Nash jerked his arm from my grip. "I do understand—that's how I feel about you. But that doesn't matter, does it? It wouldn't matter even if tomorrow never comes and you get to live forever."

"Nash, tomorrow will come, and I *will* die. And you can't deal with that like you're dealing with this. No more frost. Promise me."

"You can't make out with my brother, then ask for promises from me. Not that any of that matters now, considering we're both going to lose you in a matter of hours," Nash said. "But you're an idiot if you can't see what Tod's really doing. He's clinging to you for the same reason he hangs around me and Mom—he thinks if he has something to keep him anchored in the human world, he won't lose his humanity. That's all you are to him, Kaylee. You're just another anchor helping him cling to what he can't let go of."

"That's not true." Unshed tears burned in my eyes and behind my nose, and I refused to let them fall. "Why would he bother? What kind of anchor am I going to be for him when I'm dead?"

Nash huffed in disgust. "Sabine was right—you only see what you want to see. It's easier for you to cast him as the hero and me as the villain, 'cause then you can justify running away when I needed you. I *needed* you, Kaylee, and you weren't there. And now look what's happened." He spread his arms to indicate his own frost high, and guilt and anger buzzed inside me like a swarm of wasps in my chest.

"I never cast you as the villain, Nash. You're doing that to yourself." My openhanded gesture took in his entire body, currently full of Netherworld poison, and Sabine bristled.

"You know this is at least partly your fault," she snapped.

"I know." It bruised something deep inside me to see him on frost again, and it hurt even worse to know I'd driven him to relapse. Frost—Demon's Breath—was more dangerous to humans than to *bean sidhes,* but Nash couldn't dodge permanent damage forever. While he was high, the drug would magnify his emotions—in this case, heartbreak and anger. It would also amplify any aggression—true even in the most even-tempered users—and compromise his judgment. But the long-term effects—insanity and potentially death—were much scarier.

I couldn't just leave him like that, knowing it might be the last time I ever saw him. "What can I do? You want me to call your mom?" Harmony knew how to help him through this. She'd done it before.

"No." Something dark and determined stirred in his irises, and an uneasy pressure settled into my chest. "Can you just… give me a ride home?" he said, and Sabine stiffened on my left.

"*I'll* take you home!" she insisted, but he shook his head.

"I need to talk to Kaylee. Spend the day with me," he said, holding my gaze with one so intent I couldn't look away. "Keep me company."

My heart tripped unevenly and I glanced at Sabine to find her jaw clenched, her eyes dark with something stronger than fear, more dangerous than anger.

"Both of us?" I wouldn't go without her. I couldn't do that to either of us.

Nash shook his head. "Just you and me. One last time." When I hesitated, he sighed. "Please, Kaylee. I just want to talk."

"She doesn't want you!" Sabine shouted, and we both turned to her in surprise. "Not like that. She can't trust you, but she was scared to admit it and you were scared to face it. But now it's out, and you both need to just *move on*."

"Sabine, let it go," Nash said, and I could feel the seductive warmth of his Influence, which sent chills skittering up and down my spine, even though it wasn't directed at me. "I just want more time," he said, and though he was looking at her, Influencing her, he was really talking to me. "A chance to say goodbye."

"Stop it!" Sabine spat, visibly shaking free of his words, sunlight glinting off the ring in her upper ear. He couldn't control her unless she wanted to be controlled. For her, his Influence was a game, and today she wasn't playing.

Nash reached for me, and when I stepped back, I bumped into the side of a dusty blue sedan. "Just come talk to me. We don't have to go to my house. We can go to the lake and feed the geese."

My pulse spiked with a bolt of old fear. I couldn't be alone with him while he was using. He would never intentionally hurt me, but he wasn't himself when he was on frost, and things had gotten out of control before.

"Nash, I can't," I said, drowning in my own guilt. "Go home with Sabine. Let her take care of you. I promise I'll check on you later." With Tod, whether he was visible or not. "I'm sorry." I edged around the blue car and had taken several steps toward my own when Nash shouted behind me.

"You owe me!"

I flinched, but I didn't stop. Yes, Tod and I had made a mistake, and yes, we felt horrible about it, but I'd done my best to explain and I'd apologized from the bottom of my soul more times than I could remember. But Nash was asking for something I couldn't do.

When I didn't answer, he shouted again. "Come back!"

Confliction burned in my chest for a single instant before

his Influence rolled over me in a white-hot wave of compulsion, and suddenly I *wanted* to turn and walk back to him.

Panic tightened my throat, threatening to choke me. I fought him in my head, but my feet turned and carried me back to him, even as angry tears formed in my eyes. *This isn't happening.* He'd *sworn* he'd never Influence me again!

"*Nash*…" Sabine said, but he ignored her, staring straight into my eyes.

"Give me your keys," he said, and my hand slid into my pocket slowly, as the first tears fell.

Fighthimfighthimfighthim…!

But I couldn't fight, because I *wanted* to give him my keys.

"Come with me." He took the keys, then wound his freezing fingers around mine, and I *wanted* to follow him toward my car, even though I knew that if he'd just *stop talking,* I wouldn't want anything but to run far enough away that I couldn't hear him.

"Stop," I said, using all the willpower I had left to halt my steps and voice my objection. "You promised you wouldn't do this."

"You're not leaving me much of a choice. I just want to talk." And every word he spoke washed away a little more of my objection, blurring my thoughts until they were hazy at best.

"Where are we going?" I asked, as my pulse swooshed sluggishly and my feet carried me farther and farther from the school building.

"Somewhere private," he said with another warm pulse of Influence, and suddenly I wanted to be alone with him—all except for the thin voice of protest in my head whispering that this was a very bad idea. But the rest of me knew better. The rest of me knew that Nash could take care of me and make me happy. And all I had to do was let him.

Sabine grabbed his arm. "Nash, let her go!" She looked scared for only the second time since I'd met her, and I knew I should understand her fear, but it was *just* out of my grasp. "This is insane. You can't make her want you. You can't talk her into loving you." Sabine flinched, like each word she said actually hurt, and I felt bad for her. She needed someone to make her happy, like Nash made me happy.

"My memories of her are empty, Sabine. The images are there, but I can't *feel* anything when I think about them. I can't feel what Kaylee and I used to be like together. I know that's my fault, and I'll never forgive myself for giving that part of her up. But I *need* today with her. I need new memories of her—*good* ones—or after she's gone, I will truly have lost her. All of her."

He jerked free from her grasp and we were walking again. "I need you to understand that, and give us this one day." He stopped next to my car and pulled open the passenger's-side door, but Sabine stepped in front of him, blocking the car, her face a raw display of determination, her eyes dark with bitter pain.

"You're high," she said, and he tried to brush her aside, but Sabine wouldn't go. "Listen to me, Nash. You're not thinking clearly. You're hurt, and angry, and you're already mourning her, and the Demon's Breath is making all that worse. But I'm telling you right now that she's gonna hate you for this. And so will Tod."

"Screw Tod!" Nash shouted, and I jumped, startled. I blinked, and everything looked a little clearer. The world felt a little sharper. "He shouldn't have been anywhere near her in the first place."

"Fine. But this isn't going to fix that. You can't talk forever, and as soon as you stop, she's going to realize what you're doing, and she'll die hating you. Is that what you want?"

Fear slipped into the vacuum that the departing mental haze left in my head, and my hands started to shake. Something was wrong. I didn't want to go…wherever he wanted to take me.

"I just need her back, for one day. This is my last chance to make that happen." Nash pulled her out of the way and pushed me closer to the car. "Get in," he ordered, and the pain in his voice almost rivaled the Influence.

But by then I understood. This was wrong, and I should fight it.

I watched him through my own tears, struggling to keep my legs locked. To stay standing. "If you ever loved me, you won't do this…" I whispered, with all the volume I could manage.

"I do love you. Everything's going to be fine, I promise. Now get in the car."

"She doesn't want to go with you!" Sabine pulled him away from me, but he jerked free of her hold.

"Yes she does. Ask her." And he was right. I wanted to go wherever he wanted to take me, and that fact scared me so badly I could hardly breathe, because I knew I shouldn't want to. "Sit, Kaylee."

My legs gave out and I fell onto my own passenger seat, as the first tear trailed down my cheek.

He tried to close the door, but Sabine held it open. "Nash, don't make me do this…"

"Get out of the way. You know I'd never hurt her. I just want to talk to her," he said, face flushed with irritation, irises swirling in an uneven, complicated mix of grief and determination.

"That *is* hurting her." Sabine punched him in the stomach, and he doubled over from the blow. And suddenly I was free.

While he coughed, I sucked in a deep, clean breath and stood on shaky legs, tears falling steadily now, backing away from him in horror.

"Thank you," I whispered to Sabine, and I realized from the bruised look in her eyes that she was hurting, too. Maybe more than I was.

"Just go away, Kaylee." She handed me my keys and slid one arm around Nash to hold him up. "You did this to him, and the sooner he's over you, the better off we'll all be."

The ache in my chest was a steady throb of guilt, and fear, and worry. I slammed my open door, and backed away from them both, then around the car. "Are you sure you can handle him?" I asked as I sank into the driver's seat.

"Yeah. I'm stronger than you are. And I know how to work off misplaced aggression."

The truth of both statements pissed me off, but I wasn't going to argue. "Keep him away from me. And keep him clean." Then I started the car and drove out of the lot, fighting more tears.

I texted Emma to tell her I was going home, and that she should stay away from Nash for a while, and that I'd call her after school to explain. Then I took several deep breaths and called Harmony from the road.

"Kaylee?" Harmony said into my ear, her voice still groggy from sleep. And I burst into tears.

"Kaylee, what's wrong?" Bed springs creaked, and she sounded more awake. "What happened?"

The road blurred beneath my tears, so I pulled into the nearest parking lot and turned off the engine. "Remember when you told me to watch out for *bean sidhe* brothers?"

"Yes…" She sounded both relieved and wary to realize my

call had nothing to do with my impending death, and every-thing to do with her sons' hearts.

"I didn't watch out well enough."

Harmony's sigh seemed to carry the weight of the world. "Does this have something to do with why Nash and Sabine were drinking last night?"

"Yes. But it's so much worse now. And I'm so sorry for what I did, and now everything's messed up." And telling Harmony was almost as hard as telling Nash, because she was the closest thing I had to a mom, but she *was* their mother, and I'd torn her real family apart.

"Okay, calm down and tell me what happened. Where are you? Do you need me to come get you?"

"No, you have to go get Nash. You have to help him."

"Why? What happened to Nash?" She was on her feet now—I could hear the floorboard creak over the line, be-tween my own ragged, tear-choked breaths.

"I kissed Tod, and Nash saw it, and we broke up. But then he came to school today and wanted to get back together, but he's high on frost and he's out of control. He tried to make me leave with him, and Sabine had to hit him, and everything is so messed up, and I don't know how to fix it."

Harmony took a deep breath, and I envied her ability to simply institute calm whenever she needed it. If I were going to grow up, I'd want to be just like her. "Is Nash still with Sabine?"

"Yeah. They're in the school parking lot."

"Okay, I'm going to let you go so I can call her and see about Nash."

"Okay." I sniffled one more time, then wiped my face with the tail of my shirt. "Harmony, I'm so sorry."

"So am I, sweetie. I'm sorry for all of us."

She hung up, and I took several more deep breaths to make

sure I wouldn't sound like I'd been crying. Then I called Tod from the road. He answered on the first ring.

"Hey, shouldn't you be in class?"

"No. Definitely not. Can you come over?" I would have asked him to bring pizza, but it was only nine-thirty in the morning, and the pizza place didn't open till eleven.

"I'll meet you at your house." But, of course, he was already waiting on the porch when I got there.

Inside, I pulled him close for a hug I never wanted to end. He felt good, his shoulder solid beneath my cheek, his arms around me, hands clasped at the base of my spine. Tod felt strong, and warm, and wonderful, and I wanted to hold him—to be held by him—for the rest of what little life I had left. "I really needed that," I said, staring up at him when I finally let go. "I might need another one."

"I live to serve. Except for the part about living…" He leaned in for another hug, but stopped with one good look into my eyes. "What's wrong?"

Instead of answering, I tugged him toward the couch, then pulled him down next to me.

"Kaylee, what happened?"

"I talked to Nash at school today, and it didn't go so well."

"Not so well, meaning…?"

"He was high. And upset. I had to tell him about us, and that made it worse."

"Damn it." Tod let his head fall against the back of the couch. But he didn't look surprised.

"You knew he was using again?"

He sat up when I twisted to sit cross-legged facing him, with my spine against the arm of the couch. "Um…yeah. I caught him with a full balloon last night. Don't worry, though. I popped it."

Which was why Sabine hadn't been able to find it. "Why didn't you *tell* me?"

"Because I knew you'd blame yourself." He shrugged, like keeping something that important from me was okay.

"Yeah. Because it's my fault!"

"No." Tod took my hand and intertwined his fingers with mine. "Kaylee, no one feels worse about what Nash is going through than I do. I don't regret a single second I've spent with you, but I regret how we got here, and I hate that us being together makes my brother miserable. But you aren't responsible for how he reacts to pain and anger, and this isn't the last time he'll have to face either of those. Nash makes his own decisions, and you can't blame yourself for how he's chosen to cope with this."

"But—"

He cut off my protest with a kiss that lingered, and deepened, and ended with a satisfied sound from deep in his throat as he leaned his forehead against mine.

"Cute." I couldn't resist a small smile, but it faded almost immediately. "Seriously, though, he saw us together, and now he's high and miserable. We're the reason he started using again."

"No." Tod shook his head, and that stray curl fell over his brow. "We're the reason he's upset enough to want to get high. But Kaylee, it's not like a balloon full of Demon's Breath just appeared in his hands, and you certainly didn't give it to him. He made a conscious decision and an active effort to go find one."

"How? Where would he get Demon's Breath, if he can't cross over? How would Avari even get it into our world?"

"Where there's demand, there will always be someone willing to supply. There are a hundred different ways Avari could be off-loading his product. Assuming it's even him." Tod rubbed his forehead. "The only supplier I know of specifically is the balloon animal guy who hangs out near the zoo. His black balloons aren't for kids. But I know how to take care of him."

"What are you going to do?"

"Is that something you really want me to answer?"

Was it? "No. But if he's really Nash's new source, just… make it stick. Whatever you do." I felt a little sick to my stomach, knowing I'd just given my blessing for Tod to do something I didn't even want to think about. To another human being. But anyone peddling frost was a murderer in my eyes, and Tod wouldn't kill him—he would never reap off the record. Though the balloon animal guy might soon *wish* he were dead.

"It'll stick. And I want you to stop worrying about Nash."

"But—" I started, and Tod cut me off with another kiss. "Is this the routine now?" I asked, as his hand tightened around mine and my heart lodged in my throat. "I argue, and you cut me off with a kiss?"

"Not all arguments. In general, I like it when you argue. You get all fiery and passionate. But stupid arguments?" He somehow managed to raise both brows and frown sternly at the same time. "Yeah. I'm gonna shut you up. Like this." He kissed me again, and that one lasted.

"Mmm… Best punitive system ever."

"That's kinda what I thought."

"For real, though, you have to tell me stuff like that. No secrets."

Tod frowned down at me. "I should tell you about bad things that you can't fix, even when I know you're just going to blame yourself for them and have a miserable last day of life?"

Well, when you put it like that… "Yes." I nodded firmly.

"Fine. I'll keep that in mind, should I find another opportunity to ruin the rest of your life."

"That's all I'm asking."

"I don't want you to worry about Nash, though. When he fell asleep, I took his balloon and popped it in the Netherworld, so he should be fine, at least until he finds another one." Demon's Breath was stored in and dispensed from latex party balloons, an idea I'd accidentally given to Avari, who turned out to be a rather enterprising hellion. "And we can worry about that in a couple of days."

"I won't *be* here to worry about that in a couple of days."

"Exactly. See, even death has a bright side."

But I couldn't let it go. "When did you get rid of Nash's balloon?"

"Last night, after I left here. Sometime after midnight."

"Sabine said he was trashed when she picked him up this morning, and his hands were freezing during second period. How is that possible?"

"It's not, unless he restocked, or had more than that one balloon in the first place." Tod closed his eyes and let his head fall back again. "Shit."

"And you don't feel even a little bit responsible for this?" I asked softly, wishing I could absolve him of guilt, even as I demanded that he accept some of the responsibility.

"I didn't say that. I said *you* shouldn't feel responsible." The reaper sighed and ran one hand through his short curls. "Okay, I gotta go find the rest of his stash. You wanna come with me or meet me after?"

"Actually, I think it can wait. He's with Sabine." In some ways I'd never truly be able to trust her. But I trusted her to keep Nash safe—especially after she'd seen him lose control in the parking lot. "And your mom's probably there by now."

"You called my mom?"

"She can help him, Tod."

"I know. I was just hoping she wouldn't have to know this time. But it sounds like he picked up right where he left off, so yeah, I guess you had to tell her."

"I'm sorry. I told her about us, too. I hope she doesn't hate me for coming between the two of you."

"She could never hate you, Kaylee. I'll probably get an earful, though." He grimaced at the thought. "But enough about that. How do you want to spend your last full day?"

"I don't know..." I held up our joined hands. "This is nice." Tod's hand fit so well in mine that I didn't want to go anywhere or think about anything but him, and us, and the fact that we hadn't even considered turning on the TV, because we didn't need it for entertainment. And he made me smile. Even knowing that Nash was back on frost, my demon math teacher wanted to impregnate my best friend and my lifeline was scheduled to end the next day, Tod could make me laugh.

"Yeah, it is." His gaze went out of focus, like he was looking at something I couldn't see. "I can't remember the last time I actually got to touch someone I care about, just for the sake of touching and being touched. For human contact that demands nothing."

"You and Addy didn't...?"

"Get back together?" he said when I wasn't sure how to finish my own sentence, and I nodded. "No. Seeing Addy again was like going back in time, to before I died. But I don't think she thought of me like that. Not this time, anyway. She had more important things on her mind." Like reclaiming her sister's sold soul, not to mention her own. "And then she died, and I couldn't stop it." He was looking at me again by then, and I knew what he was thinking.

"This is different, Tod." I put my free hand on top of the one that held his. "I still have my soul, so I'm not just moving into the Netherworld for an eternity of torture. Dying for me will be more like a release, right? It's everyone else I'm worried about."

"Your dad and uncle are working on the incubus issue, and I'll do whatever I can to help, so you don't have to worry about Emma. The worst part for her will be missing you. And your dad's going to be fine, now that Thane's out of the picture."

"Thank you so much for that." I picked at a worn spot on the denim over his knee. "I don't know how to tell you how much that meant to me." Though evidently that one fateful kiss was worth a thousand words.

"That was truly my pleasure. In fact, it was so much fun I'm not even going to add it to the running total of rescues you owe me."

"How gallant of you."

"Does that mean I've earned my shining armor? 'Cause I don't see how I can slay the dragon without it." When I didn't smile, his frown deepened. "If you're still worried about Nash, you know Sabine and I will watch out for him."

"I know. I just hate that I'm going to die with him hating me." Because how could he not? I closed my eyes and rubbed my forehead, trying to draw my scrambled thoughts into focus. "From the moment you told me I was going to die— okay, from the moment I came to terms with that—all I've wanted to do was put everything in order. Make sure everyone I care about would be okay after I'm gone. But I messed that up, and now Nash has to live with the consequences of what I did."

"What *we* did," Tod insisted.

"Either way, he hates us both."

"He's spent half his life hating me. Hell, he thinks I'm trying to make him miserable as a punishment for living. He's upset and confused, but he'll understand eventually."

"You really think so?"

Tod shrugged, but couldn't quite hide his own doubt. "We're brothers—a three-hundred-year life span is a long time to hold a grudge."

Three hundred years. That's what I should have had, give or take. And Tod had eternity, though I couldn't accurately describe his post-death existence as a life span. Still, compared to the mere hours I had left, eternal un-death was looking pretty good.

"How did you die, Tod?"

He couldn't—or didn't—hide his surprise. "Nash didn't tell you?"

"I never asked." It honestly hadn't occurred to me. Tod had been dead long before I met him, and I rarely thought of him as ever having been alive, as obvious as that conclusion seemed in retrospect.

"Well, I guess that's just as well." He stroked the back of my hand with his thumb. "He doesn't know the truth anyway. No one does, except my mom and Levi."

"Is it some top secret reaper thing? No one can know how you entered the afterlife?" I joked, but Tod looked so solemn my smile died on my face.

"No. I asked my mom and Levi to keep what really happened a secret. To protect Nash."

"You know you can tell me, right?" I ducked, trying to draw his gaze up to my face again. "I'm not going to tell anyone, and after tomorrow, you're right back where you started, with just two people knowing."

"It's not that I don't want you to know—I'd answer any question you asked me, Kaylee, even if you were scheduled to live forever." He frowned, and a rare look of uncertainty flickered over features I'd nearly memorized. "It's that I've literally never told anyone what happened—not since I told my mother."

A tingling began deep in my stomach and traveled up my spine, bringing with it a warmth like I'd never known. Tod was giving me a first—a very important first—and he was trusting me to keep a secret he'd never told anyone else, except his mother. And though I'd accepted my fate days ago, suddenly the injustice of my own death seemed unbearable for a whole new reason.

I wanted more firsts with Tod.

But all I had left was a handful of lasts. My last day. My last hour. My last minute. My last words. And my last breath.

"You sure you want to hear this?" Tod asked, eyeing me in concern—my eyes probably gave away my every thought. "We *are* allowed to talk about something other than death."

"I wanna know. You're the only person I know who's survived death." Other than Emma and Sophie, who didn't remember anything. "I want to know what I'm in for."

Tod frowned. "Your death won't be like mine, Kaylee. No two deaths are the same, but mine was more different than most. I was recruited by the reapers—before I died."

"Before you died? How does that work?"

"It's a blind choice. To be eligible for recruitment, you have to be willing to make a sacrifice for someone else, without knowing you could be rewarded with an afterlife."

"I don't understand." In fact, I understood less than I had before he'd started talking.

"Okay, here's the typical recruitment scenario…" Tod let go of my hand, so he could gesture with his. "Once the personnel request comes down, the local reaper district manager will start sorting through the potential recruits in his area. But he's not looking for someone scheduled to die. He's looking for someone who might be willing to die for someone else. That's how they weed through the power-hungry psychos—though Thane is proof that the system isn't perfect."

"No kidding." Whoever recruited him should be fed to a nursery of bloodthirsty Netherworld cannibal children. "Wait, does that mean you weren't supposed to die?" That tingle in my spine became an outright chill....

"Everyone's supposed to die. But no, I wasn't supposed to die *then*."

"What happened?" I felt like a kid at story hour, riveted by the tale unfolding in front of me.

"I was driving late on a Friday night, and some drunk asshole hit me head-on. I didn't see him till it was too late to get out of the way, 'cause he was driving without headlights."

No wonder my dad didn't want me driving in the middle of the night on weekends. Not that that mattered anymore...

"I was fine," Tod continued. "I hit my head, and the steering column came within inches of crushing my chest, but I would have lived. But my passenger wasn't buckled. He flew forward and cracked the windshield with his head, and died a couple of minutes later. It was too late to call for an ambulance, so I did the only thing I could think of. I begged the reaper to give him more time." Tod swallowed thickly, and I realized he was seeing something else again—maybe that dark road, more than two years in his past. "What he gave me instead was a choice. I could let the kid die—or I could take his place."

And he'd done it, of course. That part of the story was obvious. But... "Why would you do that? Why would you agree to die for someone else?" I mean, my mom had done it for me, but I was her flesh and blood...

And that's when I understood what Tod wasn't saying.

"It was Nash, wasn't it?" I whispered. Tod didn't answer,

but I could see the truth in his eyes. "Nash died, and you traded your life for his. And that got you noticed by the reapers."

"More or less."

"And he doesn't know!"

Tod shook his head. "He would have been all messed up if he knew he was the reason I died." He seemed to choke on a bitter laugh. "The joke was on me, though, because he blamed himself anyway."

"Why?"

"Because he was the reason we were out so late. On that road."

"You and I both died in car crashes..." I said, thinking out loud. "Do you think that means something?"

"I hope not, because you and *Nash* both died in car crashes," Tod pointed out. "I got my chest beaten in by a pint-size reaper eager to fill the opening in his district."

"If you hadn't, I never would have met either you or Nash. And if Nash had never told me what I am, eventually I would have wound up in Lakeside again. Which means I would have died in the mental health ward."

"Well, at least something good came out of the whole thing."

"A lot of good came out of it, Tod. You're like that guy on *It's a Wonderful Life,* only the opposite—if you'd lived, bad things would have happened to everyone around you."

Tod's pale brows rose in surprise, then he burst into laughter. "I'm going to miss you, Kaylee." His irises swirled slowly with an odd mixture of sorrow and wistfulness. "You have no idea how much I'm going to miss you."

"Good. Maybe I won't be out of mind as soon as I'm out of sight."

"I saw you in the hospital once. Way before you started going out with Nash."

"In the hospital…?" That was the day they checked me into Lakeside. It had to be. I hadn't been in the hospital for anything else.

"Yeah. You were the first *bean sidhe* I heard sing for someone's soul, other than my mom, but I didn't realize that was you when Nash first introduced us. Do you remember seeing me in the hospital that first time?"

I shook my head, searching my memory but coming up empty. I must have been medicated. Or… "Maybe you were invisible."

"I was. But you saw me anyway. You looked right at me, and the only way I've been able to explain that is that maybe I wanted to be seen by you—*just* you—even way back then." His hand tightened around mine, and it was hard to believe I was facing death, when I felt so incredibly alive in that moment.

"Will you be there when it happens?" I blurted, caving to impulse, and his smile faded slowly at the grim reminder. "I don't want my dad or Emma to see me die, but I don't want to be alone, either. So…will you stay with me until it's over? Please?"

For one horrible moment, I was afraid he'd say no. Afraid I'd asked too much from a relationship less than eighteen hours old. Then he leaned forward to kiss the corner of my mouth and whisper into my ear.

"Kaylee, I would do anything for the girl who granted my dying wish."

19

Tod called in sick to work, and we spent the next two hours on my couch, tangled up in each other both physically and emotionally. All at once, it felt like we were going too fast—like I was racing down the final hill on a massive roller coaster, determined to savor every intoxicated heartbeat—yet we couldn't go fast enough. Because there wouldn't be enough time.

I would never get to finish this ride with Tod—never fully explore this bond I'd discovered too late—and we both knew it. All we could do was live in the moment. So that's exactly what we did. We lived in every single electrifying moment of the connection consuming us both, but destined to burn out early.

Between kisses that echoed and scalded the length of my body, I told him what it was like to save a life, and he told me what it was like to take one. I told him I was afraid of losing control—of being devoured by someone else's will—but he already knew that. He told me he was afraid of being forgotten—of fading from humanity and simply ceasing to exist—but I already knew that.

Tod whispered his secrets, and I swallowed them whole,

then fed him with my own. My hands wandered and his explored, waking in me cravings and impulses like I'd never felt. I wanted things—I wanted *him*—not out of curiosity and deadline-driven determination, but out of a raw need to experience all of him. To know and be known like never before. To share everything I had and everything I would ever be with him. And for the first time, the strength of my own hunger didn't scare me. Because it *was* my hunger.

Then, finally, Tod groaned, pulling away to sit up on the couch, his hand splayed across my stomach, over the material of my shirt.

"What's wrong?"

"Not a damn thing." He brushed one curl back from his forehead, eyes churning with a craving that surely mirrored my own. "But I need a break."

"Why?" I sat up, frowning.

"Because you feel really good, and I haven't done this in a long time. Not since I died. So I kind of need to stop or...not stop."

Then I understood, and my face burned so hot my cheeks could have been on fire. "Oh. I'm sorry." Embarrassed, I put both hands over my face, but Tod pulled them down gently, and his blue-eyed gaze met mine.

"You're embarrassed by proof that I want you? If either of us should be embarrassed by this, it's me. But I'm not. I just need to cool down, so I can want you again in a few minutes."

The blaze in my cheeks turned inward, scalding a trail down my center to points lower, until I thought my body would roast itself alive if he didn't stop looking at me like that. Yet I hoped he'd never stop looking at me like that.

Tod laughed, and I groaned when I realized he'd seen what I was thinking—a twist of overheated blue?—in my eyes.

"How 'bout some lunch?" he said, and I stood, grasping at the offer of a distraction.

"I think we have some sandwich stuff..."

He followed me into the kitchen, and pulled open the fridge, then bent to investigate the meat drawer. "Just give me a minute. I'll think about cold cuts."

I burst into laughter. I couldn't help it.

"Cold cuts are funny?" He stood, and I shook my head, still laughing behind one hand.

"I was thinking about something else," I said, but he only watched me, waiting for an elaboration. "Em wanted to know if blood flow would be an issue for you, and now I can tell her that it's definitely not a problem."

Tod frowned, but good humor swirled lazily in his eyes. "I'm dead, not impotent. Nasty rumors like that must be quashed before they gain momentum. Feel free to emphasize how very functional I am."

I laughed again, setting a loaf of bread on the counter while he sniffed a package of sliced ham. "How functional are you? And on a completely unrelated subject, if I get kissed for stupid arguments, what would happen if I did something *really* bad?"

His pale brows rose, and his irises twisted faster. "How bad are we talking?"

"I don't know. Failing to correct inaccurate, sexually defamatory rumors?"

"That *would* be bad." Tod dropped the ham on the counter and pulled me closer, pressing me against the closed refrigerator door, and a spark shot up my spine and set fire to my lungs. "I think I'd have to take the situation in hand." His right hand found my left one and his fingers intertwined with mine. His skin was warm against my palm while the fridge was cold against the back of my hand. With him pressed against me—

all of him—I could feel how much he still wanted me. And that knowledge was exciting. Intoxicating.

"What if that wasn't enough to do the trick?" I whispered, made bold by the blatant need churning in his eyes. "What if I were *persistently* bad?"

"That might require a stronger approach." He leaned toward me and dropped a series of tiny, hot kisses down my neck, headed for my collarbone. I reached up with my free hand to feel his hair—the curls were *so* soft—and his left hand found the slight curve of my hip, fingers pressing into my skin beneath the hem of my shirt, like they wanted more than they could possibly find there.

"I don't think this is fixing your little problem," I whispered, as his hand wandered slowly over my waist and toward my ribs, over my shirt now.

Tod straightened and gave me a frown. "You should be careful, tossing descriptors like that around in a situation like this. My 'problem' isn't little. Unless you're drawing some pretty wild comparisons. Please tell me you're not drawing wild comparisons. Or blood-relative comparisons."

"Nope. No comparisons. That's one limb of your family tree I'm not going out on. Are you comparing me to Addison?"

"To Addy? Hell no. Genna, maybe…" he teased, and I frowned, though I had no idea who that was.

"So how do I stack up?" I asked, not sure I really wanted to know.

"Kaylee, you burn so bright that everyone else looks dim in comparison. You're all I see, and all I want to see, and I would be happy if this moment never ended. If I could spend the rest of my afterlife doing this…"

He leaned down again and started a new trail of kisses beginning at the hollow beneath my jaw, his hands flat against my lower back, like he couldn't touch enough of me, even if we'd had nothing but time.

We spent the rest of the day on my couch, ignoring a succession of movies in favor of each other, holding back my fear of death and incubi with the feel of him. With the stories he told and the questions he asked.

Hours later, someone knocked on my front door, and I came up for air long enough to glance at the time on my cell phone. Almost 3:00 p.m.

School was out, and that was probably Emma at the door, and I knew I should go answer it. But I wanted one more kiss. One more minute for just me and Tod, and this moment we'd stolen from eternity.

One more minute, then I would do the right thing. The mature thing. I would start learning how to let it all go....

"I thought Sabine wanted in on this," Emma said, helping herself to a cold soda from my fridge. She'd come over after school expecting our game plan powwow to include all four members of the Eastlake super league, but Sabine and Nash were, obviously, still MIA, and Tod had gone to check on them. And maybe to cool off again. "Don't tell me she's mad at you. She ought to be thanking you for finally giving her what she wanted."

"It's not that simple," I said, then decided I didn't want to spend any of what little time I had left rehashing that morning's catastrophe. "Here's the short version. Nash fell off the wagon—hard—and Sabine's babysitting him."

"What wagon?" She popped the top on her can and sipped from it.

"He's on frost again, Em." And Nash-on-frost was very different from sober-Nash.

"Ohh..." Emma dropped into one of the kitchen chairs and

pulled one knee up to her chest. No doubt she was remembering Doug, her boyfriend and one of Nash's best friends, who'd died of a frost overdose in December. "Is this because you broke up with him?"

"No," Tod said, appearing beside me out of nowhere, and that time I didn't even jump. "He's upset because she broke up with him, but he got high because he's an addict. He makes his own choices."

"Okaaay..." But Em looked unconvinced, and I couldn't quite quash the remnants of my own guilt.

Tod took my hand, his fingers winding around mine, and my chest tightened. Everything between us was new and shiny, a thrill that would never fade, thanks to my own imminent death, and the excitement was compounded by the fact that we were about to go fight evil together—like a one-up mushroom for our entire relationship. Yet Tod looked grim, even for a reaper. "Why didn't you tell me what he did to you?"

Crap. Sabine must have told him.

"What did he do?" Em sat up straight, eyeing us both expectantly.

"Because I knew you'd blame yourself?" I said, throwing his own words back at him, but all I got was a deeper frown.

"What happened to 'no secrets'?"

"I didn't tell you because I didn't want to talk about it. I was mad, and humiliated, and I just wanted to forget about it."

"Kaylee, you didn't do anything wrong. Sabine knows it. I know it. Nash'll know it, once he's thinking straight." His hand tightened around mine. "You have no reason to be embarrassed."

"What did he *do?*" Em repeated, losing patience now.

"If I were stronger, I could have resisted. Sabine can resist him."

"Sabine can just unleash his own fear on him and make him back down. You can't."

"What the hell did Nash *do?*" Em demanded, standing to get our attention.

"He tried to use his Influence to make her go somewhere private with him. Alone. So he could Influence her into taking him back."

"That son of a bitch!" Em looked like she wanted to punch him, too, only maybe lower than Sabine had aimed.

"It's more complicated than that. He was hurting. And anyway, it was the frost," I insisted. No matter how mad he got at me and Tod, he wouldn't have done something like that if he'd been clean. I was absolutely certain of that.

Tod was unconvinced. "It was him *on* frost."

"Is he okay?" Em asked, settling into her chair again.

"Sabine and my mom seem to have it under control, at least for the moment," Tod said. "But I don't think we should count on either of them for backup tonight."

"So, what, it's just the three of us?" Em asked, and I was relieved to hear a tremor of fear in her voice. The real trouble would come later, when Beck unleashed his charm on her again, and she forgot to be afraid.

"What, you don't think I can protect you?" I said, only half kidding as I ducked into the living room to grab my laptop from my backpack.

"I don't doubt your *bean sidhe* skills, Kaylee." Emma leaned back in her chair to see me around the kitchen doorway. "I just don't see how they're going to be any good against an incubus. I mean, we don't even know how to fight him, short of a good hard kick to the groin."

"You can't go wrong with that," Tod mumbled, looking distinctly uncomfortable at the thought.

"Except that by the time it's time to kick him, that's the last thing you're going to want to do. Which is where this comes in." I set my laptop on the kitchen peninsula and turned it on. "So far, we haven't had much luck fighting Netherworld evil with tips from the internet, but Alec says that because they need humans to breed with, as well as to feed from, incubi have a long, and presumably well-documented history in our world." And I was hoping that at least some of that history had made its way to the web.

"Ooh, I have mine, too, so I can double our efforts." Emma claimed the second bar stool and plugged her laptop in next to mine. While we searched with Google like madwomen, Tod stood behind us where he could see both screens, reading and pointing out anything he thought might be useful.

"Is this chick for real?" Emma asked, about ten minutes into the research, and I leaned over to glance at her screen. "She claims she's been communicating with demons that appear and disappear at night in her room since she was a kid, but now she's tired of them and wants to know how to get rid of them."

"Antipsychotic medication," Tod suggested, scowling at the screen. "The internet is full of crackpots claiming to have personal contact with 'demons' who bear no resemblance to any Netherworld creature I've ever heard of, except for hellions. And if hellions could cross the barrier into your bedroom, we'd have bigger things to worry about than one horny incubus."

"I wish you wouldn't throw that word around like it's harmless," I said, elbowing him in the ribs.

"Horny?" Tod grinned.

Emma laughed. "She means *crackpot*."

"Just because someone talks to things other people can't see or hear doesn't mean those things aren't there, and it doesn't necessarily mean she's crazy," I insisted. "She could just be having a series of bad dreams."

The reaper's brows rose in amusement over my automatic defense of the mentally unstable. "Or, she could have an over-active imagination and a pathological need to be the center of attention. With all due respect to those who've unjustly served time in mental institutions, people who are really hearing and seeing things they shouldn't either go crazy—in which case a coherent internet plea for help would be improbable—or they keep quiet about their so-called delusions to avoid look-ing crazy."

Tod spun my stool so that I faced him, then looked straight into my eyes, so I could see sincerity swirling in his. "You are none of the above, Kaylee, so you can quit worrying about that. But just because *you're* not crazy or looking for attention doesn't mean that—" he glanced at Emma's screen, then back at me "—DemonQueen87 is in possession of all her marbles."

"Okay, valid point," I said, when I couldn't find fault with his logic. "So, did DemonQueen get any advice we could use?" Just because her problem was probably bogus didn't mean all the answers would be.

"Yeah, I don't think so." Em scrolled slowly, reading aloud as her finger slid down the mouse pad. "'Banishing incanta-tions…'"

"Bullshit," Tod declared, rolling bright blue eyes. "Even if that wasn't a bunch of mumbo jumbo nonsense, incantations wouldn't work against something with a physical presence. You can't fight evil by chanting a few magic words."

"'Religious rituals…'" Em continued, without even look-ing up for his rant. "'Ceremony conducted by the high priest of a Wiccan church or a…Magickian'?" She looked up from the screen, frowning. "Is that even a real word?"

"Dunno." I shrugged. "Do Wiccans have high priests?"

"I have no idea." Emma leaned over to glance at my screen. "You having any better luck?"

"Not unless you believe that sleeping with scissors under your pillow will prevent midnight ninja incubus attacks."

"That's superstitious nonsense." Tod sank into one of the kitchen chairs, looking more frustrated than I'd ever seen him. "A long time ago, people used to blame fictional incarnations of incubi to cover up an affair or pregnancy out of wedlock. It was this whole, 'I was raped by a demon' defense that absolved the 'victim' of guilt and gave everyone something intangible to blame. That created this whole legend of ethereal demons that could seduce people in their sleep, like some version of a *mara* who would molest you instead of scaring you, thus tempting you to damn your own soul by committing sinful acts of sex. Unfortunately, that means that all the methods of fighting these 'demons' that come out of that era assume that the incubus has no true physical form."

"Which means they're useless to us, since we know incubi are actually thoroughly physical psychic parasites," I concluded, and Tod nodded.

"That kick to the groin method isn't looking so bad now, is it?" Emma said.

"Neither are the scissors."

"We'll call that plan B," Tod said, pulling open the fridge in search of another can of soda.

Two hours later, I was starving, and we'd still had no word from my dad or uncle about the family dinner, which I'd invited both Tod and Em to stay for. Nor were we any closer to a decent plan A. Evidently no one in the history of the internet had ever successfully annihilated a real live incubus.

"I think we're going to have to call it quits on the ambush," Emma said, closing her laptop with a soft click. "At least for tonight."

"No!" I refreshed my browser and typed in another variant of the same "banish kill incubus" keyword search I'd been scouring the internet with. "I'm not going to *have* another night!" And I didn't want to die without knowing Beck would be no threat to my best friend. "Besides, if we're not there when he shows up tonight, he's going to know something's up, and we'll have lost the element of surprise. And we—or *you guys,* since I'll be dead—won't get another shot at him if he knows you know what he is."

Emma shrugged, meeting my gaze reluctantly. "Maybe that's for the best, Kay. If he figures out what he's up against, maybe he'll just…move on."

"But that's just passing our problem on to someone else. Someone who won't know how to fight him."

"*We* don't know how to fight him," she pointed out, with infuriatingly sound logic. "The lack of information to the contrary suggests that incubi are probably immortal and practically invincible. So what choice do we have, Kaylee? You may be immune to the evil hotness, but I'm not, and I don't want to walk away from this pregnant with a demon fetus. Or dead because I knew too much."

"She's right, Kay," Tod said. "It's not fair to involve her in this. Not when we can't guarantee her safety."

"I know." I closed my laptop slowly, burning from the inside out with anger and frustration. "Maybe I could…"

"Not by yourself," Emma interrupted. "I know you're going to die anyway." She swallowed and closed her eyes in a longer-than-normal blink. "But that's not how you want it to happen, is it?"

"Besides, if Beck shows up at Emma's house and you're the

only one there—or at least the only one he can see—he's going to know something's up," Tod said.

I couldn't argue against their logic, but I couldn't give up the fight, in either my head or my heart. At some point, I'd started equating a "good death"—the only thing I had left to aspire to—with defeating Beck and protecting my school. I didn't want to die without knowing he'd gone first.

But before I could put any of that into words, my phone rang, and the display showed my dad's number. I held up a one-minute finger to Em and Tod, then flipped my phone open. "Hey, are you on your way home?" I asked, when I recognized road noise in the background. "Uncle Brendon and Sophie are probably already on their way."

"Kaylee, I didn't go to work today. I'm with Brendon, and we're not going to make it back for dinner. He's already called Sophie. I'm so sorry, honey."

Suddenly the kitchen felt too cold and goose bumps popped up on my arms. "Where are you?" I crossed into the living room and started to sit, until I realized I had an almost physical need to keep moving. To burn nervous energy. So I paced back and forth in front of the coffee table.

"On the way home from Tallulah."

"Tallulah, *Louisiana?!*"

"Um…yeah. Brendon spent all night tracking down that incubus he ran up against fifteen years ago, and we got lucky."

"You found him?" I asked, and Tod and Emma followed me into the living room, listening carefully, and dropped onto the couch.

"Yeah, his name is Daniel, and we set out this morning to pay him a visit."

"Hey, Kay-bear," my uncle called to me over the line.

"Hi," I returned, pausing in midstride to stroke Styx's head when she jumped into the recliner. "So…did this Daniel tell you how to take out an incubus?"

"Well, he wasn't very forthcoming with any information we could potentially use against him, but he did introduce us to his son—an eight-year-old incubus named Charles. It turns out that Charles is the only reason his father hasn't re-located or changed his name—he's trying to give the kid a stable childhood, at least until he comes into his psychic ap-petite, around puberty." Which seemed to be typical for most nonhuman species.

"Okay, hurray for Charles and his father-of-the-year." Un-fortunately, I wasn't hearing anything that would actually help us get rid of Beck.

"That's not all," my dad continued, in that "pay attention" tone. "Daniel is a very proud father, and he insisted on in-troducing Charles to us. Kaylee, the kid's eyes swirl, and that can only mean one thing. His mother was a *bean sidhe*."

"A *bean sidhe?*" I said, and on the edge of my vision, Emma turned to Tod in question. "I thought incubi had to breed with human women."

"That's what *I* said!" my uncle called, presumably from the driver's seat. "But Daniel said that inaccuracy is probably due to the fact that they usually *do* breed with human women for the simple ease of availability."

"But it's a bit of a trade-off," my dad added. "Humans have trouble carrying incubi babies—"

"Yeah, we've noticed," I said, thinking of both Farrah and Danica.

"—and even if they manage to give birth, the baby won't live more than a few minutes without a soul."

"Aren't babies born with souls?" I asked, thoroughly con-fused.

"Evidently not incubus babies," my uncle said.

"Okay, so how would a baby incubus get a soul?" I asked, far from sure I actually wanted the answer.

"Well, if the mother dies before the umbilical cord is cut, the baby just kind of…inherits its mother's soul. That's what happened with Charles's mother, although your uncle and I are far from convinced that this poor *bean sidhe* just *happened* to die the moment after she gave birth. She wouldn't have had the same trouble carrying an incubus fetus that a human woman would have."

Meaning that Daniel had killed the mother of his child, to keep the hard-won infant alive.

I stopped pacing in the middle of the living room, one hand over my eyes, trying to block out that mental image. "That is *beyond* messed up!"

"What's messed up?" Emma demanded, and I spared a moment to be grateful that she had decided on her own not to meet with Beck.

"It gets worse, if the mother's human," Uncle Brendon called over the traffic noise.

"Worse, how?" I asked, pacing again before I'd even realized my feet were moving.

"A human soul can't sustain an incubus body," my dad said, and I could hear the reluctance in his voice. "So if the baby is born from a human mother, there has to be some alternate source of a soul. And it needs to be ready and waiting, if the baby's going to survive."

Thoughts spun through my head fast enough to make me dizzy, and I struggled to bring all the facts into alignment. To make sense of the chaos.

Danica and Farrah were both human mothers, so how had Beck intended to keep his children alive after birth? Danica hadn't made it very far into her pregnancy, so he'd probably thought he had plenty of time to find a soul for her child. But souls can't be stolen from the living, which meant he must have been prepared to kill some poor nonhuman to donate his or her soul to his son.

And suddenly I was very, very grateful for the *dissimulatus* bracelets Harmony had given us, which had protected me, Nash and Sabine from notice.

Except that Sabine had read Beck's fears and creeped him out. Had he figured out she wasn't human? Had we painted a target on Sabine by sending her in to investigate? Would Beck be reluctant to leave Eastlake, if he knew there was at least one supernatural soul up for grabs there?

"Kaylee?" my father said into my ear, but I was too lost in my own thoughts—still pacing frantically—to answer.

What about Farrah? Her pregnancy had progressed the furthest, thanks to Lydia, and in two short months, he'd have to...

"Oh, *hell*," I whispered, as another little bit of understanding clicked into place in my head.

"What?" my dad asked, as Tod and Emma watched me expectantly.

"Lydia..." I dropped into the recliner, and hardly noticed Styx's squeal when I landed on her tail. "It's no coincidence they were rooming together."

"What?" my dad repeated over the phone, while Tod echoed the same question from the couch. But Dad didn't know about Lydia, and Tod and Em didn't know incubi babies were born in need of a nonhuman soul. I was the only one with all the pieces of that particular puzzle.

"I just...I think I figured out where Beck was planning to get a supernatural soul," I said into the phone.

"It's not...?" my dad started, obviously unable to actually say what I knew he was thinking.

"No, it's not me. He still thinks I'm human, thanks to the *dissimulatus*." I held my arm up to study the braided fiber that had kept me off Beck's radar—until I'd offered him a three-way with me and Em. "But I think he knows something's off about Sabine, and one of his earlier victims had a syphon for a roommate." And suddenly any doubt I'd had about the wisdom of breaking Lydia out of Lakeside was gone. Tod and I had saved not just her life, but her soul.

I wondered if Beck knew yet that his backup soul had flown the coop....

"In case it isn't obvious," my dad said. "I do *not* want you and Emma to go through with this idiotic plan to get your teacher alone tonight."

"It is obvious. And don't worry, we've already called that off. In fact, I think Emma should stay the night here, just in case."

"Good idea," my dad said, and Uncle Brendon piped up with something I couldn't quite hear.

"What'd he say?"

"He said you should try to get the rest of Emma's family out of the house tonight, too, just in case."

Especially considering that Beck had a track record of feeding from his victims' mothers, and Em's mom had been alone with Em and her older sisters for as long as I'd known them. The Marshall house was practically an incubus buffet.

"Okay, we'll come up with something," I said as Styx laid her head on my lap and closed her eyes. "What time will you be home?"

"We're still almost six hours away, but hoping to be home a little after midnight. I don't want to miss any of your last day."

"I'll wait up for you." My heart ached, and I couldn't quite separate sadness for his loss from my own fear. "I gotta go."

"Okay, see you tonight."

I flipped my phone closed, then leaned back in the recliner to slide it into my pocket.

"What are we coming up with?" Em asked, before I could organize everything I needed to tell them into anything resembling coherence. "And what was he saying about babies and souls?"

"It sounds like Beck's incubus children need a nonhuman soul to survive," Tod said.

"Yeah." I was impressed with how much he'd put together based on what little he'd heard. "If the mother's not human, the incubus will kill her to provide the baby with her soul. But if the mother's human, he has to find an alternate source."

Tod nodded grimly. "And you think Beck had something to do with Farrah and Lydia rooming together?"

"I think it's too much of a coincidence to have happened on its own," I said. Em still looked confused, but I'd have to explain in the car. It was almost six-thirty. Beck would come calling at eight, if not before. "We need to go get your overnight stuff and talk your mom and sisters into leaving for the night. Right now."

"Hey, Kaylee!" Ms. Marshall stuck her head out of the bathroom when I followed Emma down the hall toward her room. "What are you girls up to tonight?"

"Sleepover at Kaylee's," Em said, pulling her sleeping bag from the top of the hall closet.

"On a school night?" Ms. Marshall frowned, her lips outlined, but not yet filled in with lipstick. "I don't think so...."

"We're cramming for a big math test," I said, leaning against the door frame, where I could see them both. "And I swear we'll get plenty of sleep." *Lies, all lies...* When had my life become a series of disasters barely strung together with lies?

"Mr. Cavanaugh's fine with it, Mom." Em crossed her room and started pulling clothes from her dresser, as if her mother had already agreed. "And he'll be there the whole time. This is totally legit."

Yeah. Legitimately guaranteed to save Emma's life and keep her uterus unoccupied. Her mother should have been thanking us.

"Besides, you're going out with Sean tonight, right?" Em zipped her duffel. "This way you could stay the night."

"Emma!" Ms. Marshall stuck her head into the hall again, curling iron wrapped around a strand of hair all the way up to her skull.

"Oh, come on, Mom. I'm seventeen. I know what happens when the lights go out, and this way you won't have to drive home in the middle of the night and try to sneak in without waking anyone up."

Em's mom released her curl and set the iron down, seeming to consider. "Fine, go stay with Kaylee. But whether or not I spend the night with Sean is none of your business."

Em grinned. "Duly noted. Cara's staying at the sorority house tonight, right?"

Ms. Marshall gave her a puzzled look. "Yeaaah. Just like she has every night for the past two years. Why?"

"No reason." We just had to make sure. "What about Traci?"

"New guy!" Em's nineteen-year-old sister called from down the hall. "He's picking me up in fifteen minutes. But that does *not* mean you can raid my closet."

"Wouldn't dream of it…" Em lied, reaching around her mother to grab her makeup bag from the bathroom counter. How the three of them shared one bathroom was beyond me.

Five minutes later, we climbed into Emma's car and headed back to my house for what would surely be my last sleepover. Ever.

20

With our incubus-busting plans rightfully canceled and my
father still on the road, we decided to spend what would probably be my last evening on earth finishing the *Alien* marathon and eating junk food. Em and I hit the grocery store for
brownies and enough ice cream to overload our small freezer
while Tod left to procure pizza.

I'd just finished popping the first bag of popcorn when the
doorbell rang twice in rapid succession, then again before I
could get to the door.

I looked through the peephole to see my cousin standing
on the front porch, hands on her narrow hips, scowling at my
front door. Her new car was parked in the driveway behind
mine, shining in the streetlight, a fresh reminder that Sophie
had been unleashed on the world as a new driver—a fright-
ening prospect for all of humankind.

Swallowing a growl of frustration, I pulled open the door
and frowned at her. "What are you doing here?"

"Dinner, remember?" Sophie brushed past me into the living room, where she scowled at Emma, then at the spread of
junk food laid out on the coffee table. "I don't eat carbs or

processed sugar, so I hope you have something better than that."

"Sophie, dinner was canceled. And it was supposed to be two hours ago."

She shrugged. "I want to be here even less than you want me here." Though I had good reason to doubt that. "My dad said if I didn't come hang out with you for the rest of the night, then give him a ride home when he gets here, I'd regret it for the rest of my life. I said he'd never been more wrong. Then he said he'd donate my car to some charity I've never heard of and make me take the bus to school for the rest of my life if I wasn't at your house in ten minutes. So what is this?" She tossed her purse onto a chair and glanced at Emma, then back at me. "Fashion intervention or suicide watch?"

"It's gonna be the scene of a homicide if you don't put bitchy on the back burner," Emma snapped, and I laughed out loud.

"Seriously, Sophie, you don't have to stay." I crossed my arms over my chest. "Em and I are just studying for a test."

"You have enough junk food to feed the girls wrestling team and not a book in sight. Besides, my dad wouldn't send me over here just to crash a study session. I don't give a damn what you're really doing, but I'm not gonna risk my car just so you can do it in privacy. You're stuck with me till your dad brings my dad back." She dropped onto the couch and grabbed the remote control. "I hope you don't mind the TV, 'cause I'm not gonna suffer in silence."

I knew what my uncle was doing, and it was sweet of him to try to get Sophie to spend some time with me before I died. But even if she felt guilty after I was gone, I couldn't imagine her actually missing me, and I really didn't want to spend my last night on earth with my spoiled, bitchy cousin.

Unfortunately, she liked her new car more than she disliked me. Sophie wasn't going anywhere.

"Fine. But we're watching *Aliens*." I plucked the remote from her fist. "And if you want something more substantial than popcorn, there may be some carrot sticks in the fridge. But they're about a month old, so they may be more green than orange by now."

Sophie made a face. "It's a wonder you're still alive, the way you eat."

"Give it one more day," I mumbled under my breath, and Emma frowned.

"Okay, I got green olives on one side, 'cause I like green olives," Tod said, half a second after blinking into existence in the doorway between the living room and the kitchen.

Sophie jumped at the sound of his voice and whirled around fast enough to make my head spin. Her eyes widened at the sight of him, and for one irrational moment, I wanted to step in front of him so she couldn't even look at him. I might only have him for a couple of days, but he was mine. Completely. "Who the hell are you?"

Tod glanced at me with one brow raised in surprise, holding a grease-stained pizza box. "Who am I, Kay?"

I stood and took the pizza from him. "This is my...Tod."

"Your Tod?" Sophie frowned, then understanding brightened her eyes and she stood, eyeing him like she might assess him for quality control. "You're the guy from the math hall." She said it like an accusation. Then she turned to me, reluctantly impressed. "He's why you dumped Nash?"

Tod's eyes narrowed in anger. "You shouldn't talk about things you don't understand. Which should leave you pretty damn quiet."

Sophie blinked, and a flash of temper flared in her eyes. "You don't even know me."

"I know enough." Tod had seen Sophie die, and he'd helped reinstate her soul. He'd expelled Avari from her body when she was possessed. He'd seen her insult me and Emma over and over. "What is she doing here?" He asked, following me into the kitchen, where I set the pizza box on the counter and pulled a stack of paper plates from an overhead cabinet.

"Her dad sent her. I think he wants us to spend some time together."

"Then I'm forced to question his wisdom."

I handed him a plate, and as I turned to dig some sodas from the fridge, I heard Sophie whisper from the living room. "But who is he? And why the hell do hot guys keep throwing themselves at Kaylee?"

Tod blinked out of the kitchen, and before I could hiss for him to come back, he appeared behind Sophie's chair and leaned down inches from her ear. "Because she's nice. Maybe you should try it."

Sophie nearly jumped out of her own skin, and I couldn't help laughing, which ruined the stern face I tried to scold Tod with.

"How did you get back there?" she demanded.

Tod shrugged. "The usual way."

"I didn't see you…" She glanced up at the path he would have had to take to walk past her.

Tod shrugged. "Maybe you're losing it. I hear they make pills for that."

Em laughed and Sophie glared at him, and I was thoroughly amused to realize she was—for maybe the first time ever—speechless.

Emma started the movie, and Sophie ate the tomatoes and olives from her slice of pizza, but instead of watching *Aliens,* she watched me and Tod. Which made us both uncomfortable. He wasn't accustomed to being seen by people he didn't like, and I was sure she was watching us and thinking about Nash, and my guilt compounded under her scrutiny.

Four hours later, Sophie slouched over in her chair, asleep, and Emma fell into a food coma with Styx on her lap, chocolate on her breath, and Ripley fighting prison planet aliens on the TV. I decided to let her sleep until my dad got home, so Tod and I would have a little semi-privacy.

"Thanks for staying," I whispered to keep from waking Emma. "I can't think of a better way to spend my last night." Sophie, not withstanding.

"Beats the hell out of fighting an evil math teacher, doesn't it?" he said, curling the fingers of his free hand around mine. "Or keeping Nash from sneaking out to replace his stash."

"I wish there was something we could do for him."

"If there were, I'd be doing it. Sabine will call if she needs help," Tod said, and that reminded me of something I'd meant to ask him earlier.

"Did she tell you why I called her on Sunday?" I asked, sitting up so I could see his face. "Right before she called and told you to interrupt me and Nash?" When I'd asked her for advice about sex…

Tod's irises swirled in a twist of amusement, and I wanted to cover my face with both hands. "There's no shame in learning from the voice of experience," he said.

"Aggghhh!" I snatched a couch pillow and screamed into it, venting embarrassment, and only stopped when Tod pulled the pillow from my grasp, still smiling.

"Kay, I thought it was cute." He frowned, then rephrased. "Well, *now* I think it's cute. At the time…not so much."

"It's not cute!" I snapped, considering pulling the throw blanket over my head. "It's humiliating."

"You're cute when you're humiliated."

"I'm glad you think so." I ran my hands through my hair

to smooth it after the pillow incident. "That seems to be my perpetual state."

"Yeah, well, that's better than my perpetual state of not-really-alive, right?"

"I don't know, from where I'm sitting, facing actual death, dead-but-still-here looks pretty good."

"Well, it's not," Tod said, and I was surprised by his sharp tone. "Being with you today was beyond amazing. But it doesn't accurately reflect the rest of my afterlife. Being alone in a crowd with you is one thing. But being alone for the rest of eternity?" He shook his head slowly. "You don't want this, Kaylee. I don't want this for you. And neither would your dad."

Except that I wouldn't be alone, if I were a reaper, and neither would Tod. We'd be together. But… "Don't worry. I don't qualify, right?" Because I was actually scheduled to die. "The reapers won't even be looking at me." Except for Tod, and whoever they sent for my soul. "I'm actually going to die."

Tod started to respond—probably ready to convince me that true death was a mercy—but then his phone rang from his pocket, cutting off whatever he'd been about to say. "It's Sabine," he said, glancing at the display. "Shit."

An uneasy feeling settled into my stomach, worry for him amplifying my guilt.

"Go ahead," I said, when he looked unsure about answering. "She wouldn't call if she didn't need something."

Tod flipped open his phone, and though I only heard his half of the conversation, the gist of it was clear. Nash had become too much for her to handle, at least for the moment. "Okay, I'll be right there." The reaper hung up and met my gaze, irritation swirling slowly in his. "His temperature keeps dropping and he can't keep anything down. They need me to go get my mom." Because he could blink her home from work faster than she could drive.

"Isn't that a little severe? He's only been sober for, like twelve hours."

"The relapse seems to be hitting him harder than the original addiction. That could mean he's using a different source this time—not Avari—or that he's taking a stronger dose. Or that his body's less able to fight the physical backlash this time because none of this is new anymore."

The possibilities did nothing to lessen my fear for him, settling onto me like a physical weight. This was my fault, even if I hadn't popped a balloon in his face this time.

"I have to go," Tod said, and my hand tightened around his involuntarily while my heart thudded in my ear.

"I know. It's fine." But it wasn't. Not really. It was almost midnight. Almost Thursday. Almost the day of my death. My dad wasn't back yet, my cousin and best friend were sleeping peacefully without the crippling fear I couldn't shake free from, and death was looming over my shoulder, lurking in every shadow I glanced at, every panicked beat of my heart. "Nash needs you." I knew that. But letting go of Tod's hand was the hardest thing I'd ever had to do.

"I'm so sorry, Kaylee. I'll be back as soon as I can," he promised, confliction stirring the blue depths of his eyes, like a storm over the ocean.

I nodded mutely. It meant a lot to me that he didn't smile and try to pretend like everything was okay. Everything was almost *over,* and every breath I took brought that reality closer. Soon, I'd take a breath and it would turn out to be my last. And the world wouldn't care.

"Okay, then, I'll be back as soon as I can talk someone into taking my shift." He leaned in for a goodbye kiss, and I held him with one hand behind his head when he tried to pull away, determined to make this kiss last a while, in case it was my last. Because over his shoulder the microwave clock taunted me from the kitchen, blinking 12:04 over and over.

Thursday had come.

Today I would die.

With Tod gone, I curled up under the blanket, only half watching the movie while Emma slept beside me on two of the couch cushions, Styx snoring softly in the crook of her arm. In spite of my determination not to waste any of my last day, I was starting to nod off when Em's phone buzzed on the coffee table. She had a text.

I picked it up, debating waking her, and read the message on the screen, from her sister, Traci.

Got dumped. Need sugar. Where r u?

Crap. Traci was home alone. She'd probably be fine—surely Beck had come and gone hours ago—but I wasn't willing to take a chance with Em's sister.

Come to Kaylee's, I typed. **We have junk food.**

Traci's next text asked for the address, so I gave it to her. When she said she'd be right over, I unlocked the front door, then threw away the candy wrappers and half-eaten popcorn from our own binge, secretly kind of glad for the excuse to wake up Emma when her sister arrived.

Usually when Traci got dumped, she and her best friend would binge drink, bad-mouthing the new ex with drunken abandon, so the thought that she wanted comfort this time from her little sister and her sister's best friend was...unexpected. And the coincidental timing was...too much to believe. And Traci already knew where I lived...

I stopped halfway to the kitchen with three empty, sticky glasses. *That text wasn't from Traci...*

Shit! I set the glasses on the nearest end table and ran to the front door, where I twisted the dead bolt and threaded the chain lock through its channel. Then I raced across the living room and through the kitchen to double-check the locks on the back door, but even with the house relatively secure, I couldn't make my pulse slow into the normal range.

I rounded the kitchen table, glancing around in search of my phone, then stopped cold with one glance into the living room.

"Kaylee Cavanaugh." Mr. Beck stood in the middle of the room in snug jeans and a T-shirt, staring at me. No, *glaring* at me.

Fear raced along my spine and into every nerve ending in my body. I wiped sweat from my palms onto my jeans, and fought for enough calm to think clearly. "How'd you get in here?"

"Doors and locks aren't much of a problem for me." He'd come in through the Netherworld, which explained how he'd gotten in to see Farrah so many times....

Escape options flittered through my head, as worthless as a swarm of moths, mostly because Em and Sophie were still sleeping, and Beck stood between us. I couldn't leave without them. "I don't suppose you'd go away, if I ask nicely?"

"Not without what I came for," he said, his voice low, and angry, and very un-teacherlike. "My plan was to call your bluff this evening, but Emma's house was deserted. Any idea how that happened?"

"We know what you are," I said, unwilling to answer his questions and unable to quiet the cold foreboding swelling inside me.

"Yeah, I picked up on that during your little role-playing exercise yesterday, and at first I couldn't figure out how you knew. Then I noticed your bracelet." He glanced at my wrist, and I realized I was twisting the braided fiber nervously.

"And I noticed that Emma wore one, too. *Dissimulatus*, right? Which means you're trying to hide something. Your species, maybe?"

"Emma's human." That was the exception in my no-revelation policy. I wanted no mistake about the fact that she would *not* be the best walking incubator.

"Yes, I figured that out when I met her sister. And your other friend...?" He glanced at Sophie over his shoulder.

"She's not a friend. She's my cousin. And she's human, too."

"But *you're* not human, are you?"

"Where's Traci?" I demanded, glancing at the clock on the microwave. 12:10. My dad or Tod could show up anytime. I just had to stall....

"She's safe in her own bed." Beck stepped into the kitchen doorway, and I stepped back, and too late I realized I'd just blocked myself into the U-shaped kitchen. "And—not to flatter myself—it looks like she's going to sleep straight through till morning. At least. But on the bright side, she's forgotten all about that loser boyfriend."

Shitshitshit! "You...fed from her?" I could hear my own heartbeat echo in my ears, a cadence of fear and fury that had no outlet.

Beck leaned against the kitchen door frame, arms crossed over the lines of a perfectly sculpted chest barely hidden beneath his snug T-shirt. "I prefer to think of it as a mutual exchange of services. She was well compensated. Ask her, if you don't believe me."

His meaning sank in, and revulsion crawled over me like an army of flies buzzing beneath my skin. "She's alive?"

"She is. And whether or not she stays alive depends on you."

I blinked, running down the clock with my silence. Waiting for help, because I was in over my head. I couldn't fight an incubus. I didn't even know how. But I couldn't let Traci die, if there was any way I could stop it. And even if I was willing to leave Emma and Sophie—and I wasn't—I couldn't escape into the Netherworld because he'd only follow me. Or take my best friend or my cousin.

My gaze slid toward Emma, then Sophie, both somehow still asleep, and he glanced at them over his shoulder. "Don't worry. They're going to sleep for a while."

"You're feeding from them in their sleep?" How was that even possible?

"Just enough to keep them out of the way. Our desires don't sleep, even when we do, which makes sleepers the psychic version of fast food."

"I'll kill you if you hurt either of them."

Beck laughed out loud. "Do you know where I spent my evening, Kaylee? After I left Miss Marshall to her rest?" I shook my head, but he didn't seem to notice. "I went to check on a former student, who's been faithfully nurturing a precious little bundle of mine, in spite of her own failing health."

Uh-oh. "Farrah?"

He smiled, like I'd just performed a particularly impressive magic trick. "That's why you're such a good student, Kaylee—you do your homework."

I shrugged and took another glance at the clock. 12:12. Had time actually *stopped?* "How is Farrah?"

The glint of dark humor faded in Beck's eyes as they narrowed. "Farrah is dead. I took her to the Netherworld to give birth in peace, and she delivered my son with her last breath. He died in my arms, less than fifteen minutes later. Months of hard work and hope, gone." He stepped closer, and again I stepped back, until my spine hit the edge of the kitchen counter. There was nowhere left to go.

"Farrah was seven months pregnant," he said. "The infant

would have been viable—if I'd had a soul to give him." Another step toward me, and panic echoed in every whoosh of my racing pulse. "But when I took my newborn son to collect the soul kept warm for him in the body of a certain young syphon, she was *gone*. And my son died, staring up at me with blind eyes, empty for want of a soul." Fury blazed in his own eyes, like he was the bonfire and I was the fuel. "You wouldn't know anything about that, would you, Ms. Cavanaugh?"

"Lydia wasn't crazy," I whispered, then cleared my voice, determined to project both volume and confidence I didn't feel. "She shouldn't have been there in the first place."

"Yes, but she *was* there, and her soul was mine for the taking. You've cost me a soul, Ms. Cavanaugh, and you're going to make up for that loss tonight."

I burst into laughter, grimly, and maybe inappropriately amused by the irony. "You're out of luck, Mr. Beck." And the truth of that statement—the unexpected upside to my imminent death—rolled through me on a sudden surge of reckless courage. I braced my hands on the counter behind me and hopped onto it, my legs dangling in front of the cabinet doors, suddenly a bit more confident because of what I knew and he did not. "You can't get life out of me, Mr. Beck. I'm going to die today, so I'm no use to you. So why don't you just go away?"

Beck blinked, and I relished those short seconds of surprise. Then they died a swift, brutal death. "If I wanted you to carry my child, your expiration date would be a bit of a problem. Fortunately, that's not what I have in mind for you. My inherent charm works best on humans. The bitter irony in that is that humans are rarely able to carry an incubus baby to full term, and never able to provide the infant with a soul."

I shrugged, trying not to let him see my renewed fear. "Sucks for you."

He nodded solemnly. "Succinctly put. I can either breed with a human and look elsewhere for a soul, or I can try to force someone in possession of the desired soul to carry my child. And since I find physical force a repulsive way to start new life, I have no use for your body. I was going to have to kill you for your soul anyway." He shrugged, evidently satisfied with how fate had dealt the cards. "But on the bright side, at least you no longer have to wonder how you're going to die."

21

Panic swelled in my chest, numbing me to the point that I could barely breathe. I couldn't think fast enough to process what he'd just said. All I'd understood was that I was going to die because he was going to kill me. And take my soul.

"No." I slid off of the counter, terrified to realize that my legs no longer wanted to support me—they were shaky from shock. "I am *not* going to die without my soul."

"You'll be dead—what does it matter? It's not like you're going to be tortured for all of eternity. You're simply giving life to my son. Could be worse, right?"

"No. It couldn't." Call me crazy, but I didn't *want* to be reincarnated as the hell spawn of a lust-demon. "You don't need me," I insisted, edging slowly along the counter, silently counting the drawers my fingers skimmed over, headed toward the last one. "I'm not the only nonhuman girl in town, you know. I'm not even the only one in the school. This soul doesn't have to come from a girl, right?"

No, I wasn't selling out Nash and Sabine. But if I could get rid of Beck long enough to make sure Em, Sophie and I were safe, I could call Tod and he could get Sabine and Nash somewhere safe. We could call my dad and meet up for safety in numbers. Or something.

"Oh, I know." Beck's brows rose in mild interest. "This town has become quite the hotbed of nonhuman activity. But neither your *mara* friend— Sabine is a *mara,* right?" he asked, and I could only nod. "Smart girl, but a little too eager. I never would have figured out her secret if she hadn't tried to read my fears. But my point is that neither she nor your boyfriend will suffice. I haven't figured out what Nash is, thanks to the *dissimulatus,* but I can tell that he isn't pure, and neither is Sabine. They won't work."

"Pure?" That's all I could manage, from the litany of questions firing from my overloaded synapses like sparks from a dying flame.

"Oooh, missed that part of the homework, did you?" Beck stepped closer, cutting off my escape. "The baby's soul has to be pure. Untouched, in one way or another, because it comes directly from the source, without all the purification, sterilization, or whatever they do to souls that are turned in to the proper authority. And pure souls get harder and harder to find, with each passing generation."

"They do?" Pointless question. *Keep him talking...*

"Nash and Sabine have been around the block a few times—I can tell that even with their psychic shields. And your boyfriend's soul is bruised and battered from something else. Something dark that he tries to hide."

Addiction to frost, of course. That was a soul-smudge if I'd ever heard of one.

"And like every predator, Ms. Campbell drinks from the fount of life. Even if she were virginal and blushing, you can't just buff off a soul that survives by skimming from others."

But I couldn't think past Nash and Sabine, and the block they'd both been around....

"Virginity? That's what makes a soul pure?" Oh, the irony *stung*. My fingers found the last drawer and I pulled it open behind me, relieved when it rolled silently.

Beck shrugged. "It's among the qualifiers, as is a selfless desire to do what's right, despite the personal consequences. Ironic, isn't it, considering your soul will soon belong to a perfect little predator."

"A virgin sacrifice? I'm your *virgin sacrifice?* Seriously?" I couldn't get my hand into the drawer from my current angle. Not without him seeing.

"Oh, I'm quite serious. And grateful for how tightly you've clung to antiquated virtue. That couldn't have been easy, in today's world."

"Stay away from me!" I stepped to the side and grabbed the butcher knife from the open drawer, surprised by how steady my two-handed grip felt. I'd said I could kill in self-defense, but I hadn't really believed it until that moment. Until the thought of facing death with no soul scared me far beyond the loss of my own life.

"Most donors don't provide their own sacrificial weapon, so I hope you don't mind, but…I brought my own." Beck reached back and pulled a small, double-bladed wavy dagger, presumably from a sheath at his back.

My heart tried to beat its way out of my chest. I couldn't breathe.

Think, Kaylee! My dad wasn't home, Tod was gone, Nash was messed up, Sabine was taking care of Nash, and Emma and Sophie were unconscious, being drained as we spoke. I was truly on my own, for the first time ever.

Beck came closer, and I couldn't take my gaze off the double-bladed knife. My kitchen lights gleamed on old metal, still visibly sharp and etched with words I couldn't read, in some language I didn't know. Even if the shape alone hadn't told me, the writing would have: this was no ordinary blade. It meant something.

It meant my death, and the theft of my soul.

"Shouldn't the soul harvest wait until you have an actual baby to put it in?" I said, still clutching my own knife.

Beck shrugged, an oddly casual gesture, considering what he held and what he planned to do. "I'm willing to wait another eight or nine months. Those Marshall girls are quite a fertile brood."

Nooo. "Traci?" I fought nausea at the thought. "How is that even possible?" He'd only met her a few hours ago, at most.

"A little luck, fortunate timing and some very eager swimmers."

Ew, ew, ew…!

"Of course, it's too early to tell about gender—that'll take a few weeks at best—but it's never too early to start planning."

"Yes it is! It's *way* too early to start planning. Won't my soul, like, go stale or something between now and then?"

"Well, fresh is best, of course, but that's not always possible. Which is where this comes in." He turned the dagger over, and it reflected bright spots of light all over the room. "Handy little gadget I just acquired from one of the local hellions. Cost me an arm and leg—neither of them mine, of course—but well worth it. If I've learned anything from losing Lydia's soul, it's that a father can never be too prepared."

"What is that?" I whispered, trying to hide the tremor in my voice.

"Hellion-forged steel. So long as this is in your flesh when your heart stops beating, it'll collect your soul and hold it for up to a year. Like supernatural Tupperware."

Fighting encroaching panic, adrenaline burning in my veins, I edged to the right, along the counter, desperately wishing I hadn't blocked myself into the kitchen.

He reached for me, and I lunged to the left. But there was nowhere else to go—I was cornered by the cabinet and the fridge.

Beck grabbed my left arm and jerked me forward. I screamed and shoved my knife into his side, as hard as I could.

For one moment, neither of us moved. Each ragged breath seemed to burn my throat, all the way into my lungs. Something warm and sticky flowed over my hand, and I looked down to find blood pouring from his shirt and trailing down his pants.

I gasped and let go of the knife, scrambling backward until I hit the fridge. Blood dripped from my fingers onto the floor, and even when I closed my eyes, the pattern they formed remained on the insides of my eyelids.

Then Beck laughed, and my eyes flew open again. I stared in shock as he pulled the butcher knife from his stomach and tossed it into the sink, where it clattered into the popcorn bowl. Through the hole in his shirt, I could see the two-inch gash seal itself, like it was never even there. And if not for all the blood, I would have thought I'd imagined the whole thing.

"Stainless steel isn't much of a problem for me, either." In the next second, he was there, pinning me to the fridge, one hand around my wrist, the other pressing the dual dagger tips into my chest, just below my rib cage. "I think we're done with this now…" He slid one finger beneath the braided *dissimulatus* bracelet, tugging my arm toward the top dagger blade.

Every breath I took, every panicked beat of my adrenaline-flooded heart demanded action. Resistance. Struggle, at least. But I'd never fought anyone in my life. The closest I'd ever come was slapping Sabine, and if I was in over my head against Nash's nightmare of an ex-girlfriend, I didn't stand a chance against an incubus who healed his own wounds. Especially not with his knife poised to slide beneath my ribs, taking my life and my soul in one vicious stroke.

Beck lowered my arm against the dagger so that the top blade slid between my skin and the bracelet. The knife sliced through the braided fiber like it wasn't even there.

The bracelet fell from my arm, and Beck caught it without removing the dagger from my chest. He turned it over in his hand, studying it, eyes alight with interest. "Wonderful craftsmanship," he said. "Where did you get this?"

I said nothing, furious tears standing in my eyes, mercifully blurring a face most of my classmates had swooned over.

He wadded up the ruined fiber and tossed it across the kitchen, where it hit the far wall and fell to the floor, too far away to continue "jamming" my psychic signature and hiding my species. Then he stared down at me from inches away, studying me critically through narrowed eyes.

"Not a harpy..." he said, with a glance at my ears. "But then, *dissimulatus* wouldn't have hidden the pointy ears, would it?"

I didn't answer, and he didn't seem to care.

"Not a *mara*..." he said, studying my eyes, no doubt noting my complete inability to read and inspire fear with them. "Not alluring enough to be a siren, though that was my guess for Emma, and you're *definitely* not a succubus... Which only leaves a couple of possibilities, considering your human appearance and your psychic signature. So, maybe...*bean sidhe?*"

My eyes must have given it away, because he nodded decisively, eyes flashing in triumph. "Does it matter?"

"Only to verify that you are not, in fact, human. Though I must admit, I am curious—I've never met a *bean sidhe* before." Beck stared down at me almost longingly. "It's a shame that getting to know you properly would smudge that shiny purity. *Bean sidhes* are so rare, and you're not *bad*-looking..."

Evil and *flattering*. "Wow, who wouldn't want to be murdered by such a charmer?" I said, my mind racing along with my heart as he began to lightly trace the bottom of my rib cage with the lower blade.

Beck laughed, and his knife hand jiggled. I gasped as the point of the blade poked me through my shirt, almost firm enough to break my skin. "I like your spirit. But letting you go would be an unconscionable waste of resources."

"So you're just going to stab me in the kitchen?" I demanded, mining my terror for remaining fiery threads of anger to keep panic at bay. "Shouldn't you at least try to make it look like an accident? I mean, this whole stabbing thing sounds messy, and you'll never get all that blood out of the tile grout."

"I'll be done with your body before it even cools, and mine is the only blood I plan to dispose of." But he glanced around the kitchen, as if he were truly seeing it for the first time. "However, now that you mention it, the kitchen does seem a bit...cold. Why don't we take this to your room? You'd like to die in your own bed, right?" he said, and chill bumps burst to life on every inch of my body. "Then your dad can find you, and it'll look like a crime of passion. Maybe they'll even blame Nash. Didn't the two of you have a big, public fight the other day?"

Oh, nooo. Beck was right. The whole world had seen me kiss someone else, then seen Nash stomp out. Em and Sabine would know he hadn't killed me, and our families would believe him, obviously. But if he couldn't stay off frost, the police would know he was messed up on *something,* and even if they couldn't pin down the actual substance, he'd look unstable, at the least.

"No." I felt my eyes go wide, but Beck only grinned in return, clearly enjoying my misery. "Please, no, Mr. Beck. Nash didn't do anything to you. You can't let people blame this on him."

"Oh, I think that wraps things up nicely, and it'll throw the school into fear and chaos, which should keep the local hellion population happy." He grabbed my arm in his free hand and before I could blink, he'd spun me around, the twin knife points now poking into my back, on either side of my spine. "It never hurts to pay tribute to the local hellions, if you ever plan to revisit their haunts."

"You're paying tribute to Avari?" Terror tightened my throat, and I could barely force the words out, but I had to keep talking. Keep trying to distract him long enough to… do something drastic.

"You know him?" Beck pushed me forward, and I didn't dare resist, with death so close at my back. Where the hell was my dad? Or Tod?

I held my arms stiff at my side, wondering if I could grab a makeshift weapon before he could shove the knife through my spine… "I know he's going to be pissed if I die and he doesn't get my soul."

On the dusty mirror over the couch, Beck's brows rose, and he glanced at me in sudden interest. "Well, then, it's a good thing I'm planning to leave him a tribute, huh?"

Crap. Had I just given him another reason to blame Nash? "No!"

"Shh. I don't think you want to wake Emma and your cousin." Beck pushed me across the living room and into the hall, where I took one last look at my best friend, still passed out on the couch, before he shoved me toward my room.

"Sit." Beck nodded at my desk chair as he marched me

through my own door—it hadn't been hard to find in a two-bedroom house.

Huh? But I sat, the knife now pressed into my side, only more confused when he leaned over me to open my laptop. I hadn't shut it down when I closed it, so it flared to life instantly, my email inbox greeting me with unnerving normalcy while I sat with a mystical two-bladed knife pressing into my ribs.

"You're going to send Nash an email, begging him not to come over. Tell him to calm down, and you'll talk to him tomorrow, at school, but you're not going to let him in while he's this angry."

My teeth clenched together so hard my jaws ached in protest, and I had to force my mouth open to speak. "No."

"Do it. It has to be in your own words, with only your prints on the keyboard."

I craned my neck to look up at him, wishing he could see the fury surely raging in my irises. "You want to kill me? Fine. Kill me. But I'm not going to help you frame Nash."

Beck leaned so close I felt his breath on my ear. The tip of one blade bit into my skin. I gasped at the sharp pain and couldn't help wondering how much worse the real thing would hurt. "You're going to do it, or when I'm done with you, I'll take Emma and your cousin back to Emma's house and we'll have a little fun while your soulless corpse cools."

A bitter, black pain settled into my stomach, and threatened to swallow me whole. "Don't touch them," I whispered furiously, with all the volume I could manage.

"You have my word that I won't, if you do exactly what I tell you to."

Hellions can't lie; did the same thing go for incubi? I didn't know, but I had no doubt that if I didn't write the email, he'd do to Em and Sophie what he'd done to Danica. Or maybe what he'd done to her mother.

He was making me choose. Nash or Emma and Sophie.

If I wrote the letter and the police found it—no doubt Beck would leave it open on my laptop—Nash would probably spend the rest of his life on the run. As would Harmony, because she and Tod wouldn't let him go down for my murder.

But if I didn't write the letter, Emma and Sophie would die, either from the energy Beck would drain from them, or to give his demon children life.

I couldn't let them die. Not again. Not because of me. So I started typing.

Tears blurred out the screen. I blinked, and they trailed down my cheeks in hot rivers of my own terror, and anger, and remorse. But I did what I had to do. I begged Nash not to come over. I promised I'd talk to him at school, but not until he calmed down. And at the end of the letter, I told him he scared me when he was like "this," as Beck ordered. Tears dripped on the keyboard when I typed my name at the bottom of the screen. More dripped from my chin while my pointer hovered over the send button.

"Do it," Beck whispered into my ear, and I could hear his breathing escalate, like he was turned on by what he was making me do. By the pain and chaos he was creating. "Do it, or I swear they will die screaming in both pleasure and pain. Tonight."

My entire body shook with sobs. But I clicked Send. And ruined everything, for everyone I'd ever loved.

"Good girl…" Beck crooned, pulling up on my arm until I had to stand. My legs almost refused to hold me. Shock settled over me, blurring things. Numbing me. I couldn't think through the fog swirling in my head, like my brain had given up and crossed over into hell without the rest of me.

"Sit down," he murmured, and I only realized I'd sat on the bed when I felt the mattress sink beneath me.

I may as well have killed him. I'd ended Nash's life just the same, with the press of a few buttons and a single click of the mouse.

"Here, let's take your shirt off—just a little scene setting. Small-town cops usually need it spoon-fed to them, and we don't want to leave any doubts."

Would Tod forgive me? He'd never know why I did it, but he'd know it wasn't true. Would he hate me for eternity for what I'd done to his brother? To his mother?

I barely felt Beck unbutton my shirt, but vaguely I was aware that he did it one-handed, because those twin points of pain—promise of an end to this new misery—never left my side.

"Lie down now…" There was gentle pressure on my bare shoulder, and the bed rose up to meet me. I was drowning in guilt, so cold and bitter I could no longer feel the fear I'd been living with for the past five days. Fear didn't matter any-more—I was going to die whether I was afraid of death or not.

The only things that mattered were the people I loved, and I'd just betrayed every last one of them. My life was a series of small lies, but my death was the biggest one of all.

Beck leaned over me, his head backlit by the light on my ceiling. His cheek brushed mine, an intimate invasion I hated, even on the verge of death. "This'll only hurt for a minute," he promised. "And since you're not going to make a last con-fession, maybe I should." He sat up then, and I forced my gaze to focus on the cruelty and joy shining in his eyes. "I'm still going to take Emma and your cousin. They'll die screaming my name."

I blinked, and my room roared back into focus, so sharp

and crisp my eyes burned. Rage blazed through me, igniting my every nerve ending, sparking in every synapse. And suddenly I realized I had nothing left to lose.

"The hell they will." I smacked his knife hand away from my chest, and one blade sliced across my left palm. Blood flowed, and the pain was sharp, but I'd caught him by surprise. I sat up, my right fist already flying, and through sheer luck, the blow actually glanced across his chin.

Stunned, Beck reached for me. I dropped beneath his grasping hand and rolled off the other side of the mattress, reaching for Nash's bat. But it had rolled too far under the bed, and Beck was there in an instant, my incompetent fighting skills no match for his supernatural speed. He threw me against the wall, one hand around my neck. Gagging, I tried to shove my knee into his groin, but he blocked the blow with the fist still clenching the knife.

"No..." I croaked, desperate for a breath—just enough to wail my way into the Netherworld. Beck would follow me, but at least then I'd be running, and I could lure him away from Emma and Sophie. At least then, I'd have a chance. But Beck only tightened his grip.

"You stupid little *bitch*," he spat, swinging me away from the wall by my throat. "You couldn't just play nice, could you? I was going to make it fast—both blades straight through your heart. But now I think I'll let you suffer."

My vision darkened. My throat burned. My terror knew no limits.

Beck pushed me backward, his fingers flexing around my neck until my ears rang. The backs of my legs hit the mattress, and he kept pushing until I had to sit, clawing at his fingers with both hands.

He shoved again, and I fell onto my back with him straddling me. But finally his grip on my throat loosened, just enough for me to suck in a shallow, unsatisfying breath—not enough to scream, just enough to live. The fresh air burned all the way down, and Beck clucked his tongue. "Can't let you suffocate," he said, raising the double-bladed knife for me to see, twisting it so that the light overhead glinted off every shiny surface. "You have to die by hellion-forged steel, or you're no good to me." The knife disappeared from sight, and an instant later I felt both tips press into my skin, in the center of my stomach. "Any last words?"

He relaxed his grip on my throat a little more, just enough that I could croak out a couple of words. And a couple was all I had for him.

"Fuck—" I gasped, ignoring the pain "—you."

"Well said." His right arm flexed. My pulse roared in my ears. And the blades sank slowly, steadily into my stomach, bringing with them a fiery pain like nothing I'd never felt.

I gasped, and his hand fell away from my throat. My world shrank to encompass nothing but the agony spreading out from my center, spilling from my flesh in warm rivers of blood.

Beck crawled onto the bed next to me, on his knees, watching in fascination as I blinked up at him. My hands shook as they reached for my stomach, hovering over both the devastating damage and the hated instrument.

"Does it hurt?" he asked, eyes shining with eagerness.

I pulled in an agonizing breath and licked my lips with a tongue that was suddenly dry. "You tell me." Then I grabbed the hilt and pulled, screaming as the blades slid free of my flesh. And with the last of my strength, I shoved the dual dagger up beneath his rib cage, straight into his heart.

22

Beck's eyes went wide. He gasped, and that sudden intake seemed to last forever. Blood poured from his chest, sluicing over the hilt of the knife to soak my comforter.

"Hellion-forged steel, huh?" I whispered, with all the volume I could manage. *Guess I found something that will kill an incubus.* The question was, would it capture his soul?

Beck blinked one more time, his eyes already losing focus. I forced myself up on one elbow, my other hand clutching at my own wounds, blood pouring through my fingers. He fell backward on the bed, his head hanging off the edge. And while I watched, paralyzed by the burning pain spreading out from the core of my body, a dark aura developed around him, darkening by the second.

He was dying. I'd killed him. But Beck's death wouldn't prevent my own.

I lay back on the bed, terrified by the feel of my own blood pouring through my fingers, racked by pain I could never have imagined. There was so much blood between us, I could practically taste it in the air, and the thick, coppery scent made me gag with each breath.

Desperate now, I dug in my pocket with my free hand,

horrified by the darkness growing on the edges of my vision. That wasn't Beck's death aura—that was me losing consciousness. I was dying. Was my reaper already here? Tod had said I wouldn't see him....

I flipped the phone open and held it up long enough to press and hold the number four. Then my hand fell back on the mattress, useless.

While the phone rang, I turned my head, my left cheek pressed into the mattress. Beck lay inches away, and as I watched, the phone still ringing faintly from my open palm, I saw his soul struggle up from his body, like it wanted to rise. And almost as fast as it appeared, it began to trail toward his chest, like smoke pulled up a chimney by an unseen draft.

His soul was cloudy and streaked with dark ribbons of smut, and as Tod answered his phone with a greeting I didn't have the strength to answer, Beck's soul seemed to soak into the hilt of the dagger until a second later there wasn't a trace of it left.

"Hello?" Tod said again. "Kaylee? Are you all right?"

I opened my mouth but what came out wasn't a real word. I could only manage a hint of sound riding a pain-laden sigh. Then my eyes closed, and I was alone with the sound of my own irregular breathing.

"Kaylee?" Tod sounded closer now, and when his hand brushed hair back from my face, I would have jumped, if I'd had the strength. "No...! Kaylee, wake up. *Please* wake up."

Tod was crying. I'd never heard him cry before.

I forced one eye open, and there he was on his knees by the bed, still clutching his own phone. "So sorry," I mouthed, but the words carried no sound. I was so sorry for what I'd done to Nash, but I couldn't tell him. And that meant he couldn't tell Nash.

"You're gonna be okay." Tod dropped his phone and slid

one arm beneath my shoulders, the other beneath my knees. "Can you put pressure on the wound?"

But I couldn't even shake my head in answer. I couldn't move.

"I'm taking you to the hospital, but I can't go that far in one shot carrying you, so we'll have to stop a couple of times on the way. Okay?"

I couldn't answer, but that didn't matter. I closed my eyes, then opened them almost immediately when something cold and wet fell on my face. It was raining softly, and I was outside, in a parking lot I didn't recognize. The lot faded, and the next instant Tod stood in a park, still clutching me to his chest, still crying.

My eyes fell shut again, and a second later, a familiar, antiseptic scent burned my nose, while bright lights rendered the world red and veiny through my closed eyelids.

I blinked, and the hospital came into view. A hallway, full of beeps, and voices, and the steady metallic clink of carts wheeled on linoleum. Tod laid me on a stretcher and pressed something to my stomach. It didn't hurt anymore, and that should have scared me, but nothing scared me more than seeing him cry.

Reapers don't cry. They *don't*. But I'd made Tod cry. And he didn't even know what I'd done yet.

"They're going to fix you, Kaylee," he said, leaning down to whisper in my ear. "I promise."

I shook my head, but Tod stepped back anyway, pulling his hand out of mine. He glanced down the hall, toward the source of most of the noise. "Hey, somebody help! This girl's bleeding!"

"My dad…" I mouthed, when I couldn't force any more sound, and Tod nodded. Then he disappeared.

A second later, footsteps pounded toward me, and the

first nurse appeared from around the corner, clad in Looney Tunes–print scrubs. "Holy—" She yelled something else I couldn't focus on, and more people came running. They wheeled me past a long desk and into a room full of equipment, and someone started cutting my remaining clothes off.

Minutes later—or seconds; I'd lost all sense of time—Tod reappeared with my father in tow.

"Kaylee!" my dad shouted, and a man in scrubs held him back. "That's my daughter!"

"Sir, how did you get in here?"

My dad threw one punch, and the nurse hit the floor. In the next instant, he was at my side, and someone was yelling that he could stay, if he stayed out of the way.

"Kaylee…" Tears trailed down his face as he brushed hair back from my head. Someone pushed him aside and an oxygen mask was lowered over my face, then he was back and Tod was with him.

They watched me, tears standing in their eyes, and every time I blinked, it became a struggle to open my eyes again. I didn't hear the questions, the slosh of liquids, or the crackle of sealed packages being opened. I didn't feel the needles, or the sterile solution, or the pulse monitor clipped over my finger. I only saw Tod and my dad. The men who loved me. I wished I could tell them how sorry I was that I'd ruined everything.

Then I blinked, and the world dimmed. And suddenly a little redheaded boy was there, completely out of place in an E.R. operating room. He pulled Tod away from the bed and said something I couldn't hear.

Levi.

It was time. Levi had come to reap my soul.

But instead, he handed Tod a slip of paper, watching solemnly as he read it, and Tod gaped at him. Then shook his head. Levi repeated whatever he'd said, then gestured to me with one open hand. Tod crossed his arms over his chest and held his ground. And finally I understood.

Levi wasn't my reaper. Tod was. By bringing me to the hospital, Tod had put me on his own reaping list. And he was refusing to kill me.

I glanced up at my dad, but he was still crying, still stroking my hair, and he saw nothing else.

The boy frowned up at Tod, like he was waiting for something. For the reaper he'd recruited and trained to concede logic and give in. But Tod only shook his head, one last time.

Levi's frown deepened, and he reached up toward Tod's chest with one small hand. Tod's blue eyes widened, and his mouth fell open. His soul streamed out of his body and curled around Levi's tiny fist like a handful of incorporeal cotton. Tod glanced at me and blinked once. Then he disappeared.

He was just...gone.

No...! I screamed, but no sound came out. The pain in my heart swallowed the pain in my stomach like the ocean devours a single drop of rain. Thoughtless, wordless agony washed over me, a loss like I'd never felt before. I was hollow, empty of everything but pain, and the ghost memory of blue eyes watching me, seeing me like no one else ever had. Those eyes would never look at me again. They would never blink, or swirl, or shine. They were gone. Tod was gone.

My entire world was pain.

I couldn't see through my tears, and when they finally fell, Levi stood next to my father, heedless of the nurses and doctors who stepped through him to get to me. "I'm so sorry, Kaylee," he said. "He didn't give me any choice."

Then he placed one hand over my eyes, and the world went black.

I don't know what happened while the world was gone, but when it came back, the light was too bright to bear, even with my eyes closed. I blinked, and that brightness intensified beyond my threshold for pain, like a bolt of lightning through my brain. I blinked again, and my eyes began to adjust.

And my brain finally caught up.

"What the hell...?" I whispered, surprised by how rough my voice sounded, until I remembered what happened.

"This isn't hell, Kaylee. Far from it."

I jerked in surprise, then sat up so fast my head swam. A woman stood in front of me, wearing a brown suit jacket and skirt. Her hair was short, and her nose was long. Before I had a chance to ask her anything, I realized I was naked from the waist up. And sitting on a cold, metal table.

Mortified, I grabbed the plain white sheet that had fallen when I sat up and clutched it to my chest. Then I stared at the wall of stainless-steel drawers to my left. And the three other metal gurneys on my right.

I was in the morgue.

"Did I die?" I asked, my voice virtually toneless with shock.

"Yes," a familiar voice said from behind me, and I turned to watch Levi circle my table. "But Madeline has asked for an audience with you. Please give her your full attention."

Before I could process that, Madeline cleared her throat, and I glanced at her automatically. "Kaylee, we'd like to offer you the opportunity to—"

"No." I clutched the sheet tighter and stared her right in the eyes. "I don't want to be a reaper." Not after what had happened to Tod. How could they ever think I'd work for them after they killed him?

Her left brow arched dramatically. "That's not what we want, either. I work for the reclamation department, and we could use your services."

"Doing what?" I frowned, glancing from Madeline to Levi, then back to her.

"Reclaiming souls from those they don't belong to."

"Stolen souls? From hellions?" *Shouldn't my heart be pounding?* The very thought terrified me. But my heart refused to beat. Because I was dead.

"No, you would be working here, in the human world. As a female *bean sidhe,* you're uniquely suited to what we do. And frankly, we're drastically understaffed."

"Can you…make me alive again?"

"No, not like you were." Madeline glanced at her hands, clasped in front of her. "Unfortunately, no one can do that. But we can do almost as well."

"You'd exist in form similar to that of a reaper," Levi supplied. "But with a different skill set."

Like a reaper. Like Tod, who'd had a physical form whenever he'd wanted it. Who'd been able to stay with his family. Until I'd gotten him killed, and Nash framed for my murder.

"No," I repeated, eyeing Madeline steadily. "I've seen how you reward people cursed with an afterlife. No way."

"I don't think you understand the opportunity you're passing up, Kaylee." Madeline crossed her arms over her suit jacket. "Not just for you, but for everyone you care about. As things stand now, your best friend is devastated and your father is inconsolable. And your boyfriend…"

"Ex…" Levi supplied, laying one arm on the gurney, over the sheet that covered me.

Madeline began again. "Your *ex*-boyfriend is sitting in a jail cell, sick with withdrawal from a very powerful substance and about to be charged with your murder."

"But that's not possible." My hands clenched around the cold sheet in frustration and anger. "I killed Mr. Beck. They must have found his body. They have to know he killed me." Yet I couldn't quite wrap my mind around the sentence I'd just spoken.

Levi watched me in what may have been sympathy. Or possibly impatience. "Kaylee, you and the incubus were stabbed with the same instrument, seconds apart, on your bed. At the moment, the police believe that Nash found you there together, and that he killed you both in a jealous rage."

I shook my head, clinging to denial. "Fingerprints. His fingerprints aren't there."

Levi shrugged. "They'll say he wiped them off. He's a smart boy. Smart enough to wrap your dying hands around the hilt of the knife."

"No!" My dad would know better, as would Harmony, Emma and Sabine. But no one had actually seen Beck stab me—Em and Sophie had already been asleep when he'd arrived—and thanks to her criminal record, Sabine would make the world's worst alibi for Nash.

Nash could actually go down for this. And without Tod to break him out, he would spend the rest of his life in jail. Because I'd helped Beck frame him.

I couldn't let that happen.

"You're saying that if I do this thing for you, this job, you'll help Nash?"

Madeline frowned, and I knew I wasn't going to like whatever came next. "It's more than just this one job, Kaylee. It's a commitment to work for the reclamation department. In exchange, you'll be granted an afterlife with certain physical privileges—and a few unavoidable limitations—for as long as you remain in our employ."

"Limitations?"

She lifted one brow in what may have been amusement. "Most people are more interested in the advantages."

"Fine," I snapped. "What are those?"

"Immortality, of course. Agelessness."

"Those sound like limitations to me. Who wants to be

sixteen forever?" And alone, at that. I didn't want to watch my friends and family age and die. I didn't want the world to move on without me. I didn't want to face eternity on my own.

And she must have seen that on my face.

"And, of course, the biggest advantage is the chance to help Mr. Hudson."

She meant Nash. But I couldn't help thinking about Tod, too. He'd died—again—for me.

"Would you really let Nash go down for my murder, knowing he's innocent?" I demanded.

"Would *you?*" Madeline's gaze held steady. Based on her eyes, I knew she had a soul, but based on her cold, hard demeanor, I'd guess she hadn't recently found use for her heart. "We can't intervene on behalf of every innocent man sent to prison, Kaylee. The reclamation department is only willing to expend its resources on Nash's behalf if we'll be getting something in return—your services. It's your choice."

"What could you do for him?"

"As a signing bonus, if you agree to work for us, the reclamation department will arrange for Mr. Hudson's escape from police custody."

"So he can be on the run for the rest of his life? No way." I shook my head firmly, desperately hoping I wasn't pushing my luck. Hoping they needed me as badly as it sounded like they needed me.

"How long since I died?" I asked. If Nash hadn't been charged yet, it couldn't have been that long.

"Only a couple of hours," Madeline answered.

"But..." That didn't make any sense. "It took you guys more than a week to bring Tod back as a reaper after he died." He'd actually been buried and everything.

Madeline glanced at Levi with a small, arrogant smile, then

met my gaze again. "Reapers are a dime a dozen, Kaylee. The reclamation department has considerably more resources and, in this case, much stronger motivation. We need your help with something very important, and we need it soon. So we expedited the process."

I nodded slowly, still thinking. "You have to make it go away, or my answer's no."

"You want us to clear Nash's name?"

"No, *I* want to clear his name." I'd dragged him into this; I had to get him out of it. "I want you to make the *crime* disappear. No murder. I was attacked by my math teacher—to which I'm willing to testify—but I survived, and Nash had nothing to do with it."

"Kaylee, we can't reverse your death."

"I know." I sucked in a deep breath, relieved that my lungs seemed to work, even if my heart didn't. "But you can cover it up. If I work for you, I get to keep my body, right? Like Tod did?"

"You can become corporeal at will, yes," Madeline said slowly, obviously starting to follow my train of thought.

"Then who says I died? I haven't been buried. I haven't been autopsied..."

"Kaylee, you died in a public hospital," Levi pointed out. "Your death has been documented. It was witnessed."

I shrugged, still watching Madeline. "So make the paperwork go away. The news stories could just be false reports of my death. That's happened before, right? And you can make the witnesses forget, can't you? People see things. It's inevitable. So someone must be cleaning up after them, right? You must have someone who can make them forget..."

Her frown deepened, but I could see the possibility in her eyes. "Kaylee, what you're suggesting is quite complicated and would require considerable resources...."

"But you can do it, right?" I held my breath—or rather, I stopped breathing—waiting for her answer, hoping I was right.

Madeline glanced at Levi, and he shrugged. Then she turned to me again. "Yes. It's possible. But only at great expense, and I'm not convinced your services are worth what you're asking for."

"Really?" I lifted my eyebrows, resisting the urge to cross my fingers. "So, you have other female *bean sidhes?* You already have someone who can call out to the soul you want reclaimed?"

I knew I'd won when her gaze narrowed and her jaw clenched.

"Fine. It'll take a couple of hours to set up, but…you never died. You were transferred to a private hospital to recover, and you'll be rejoining your classmates in a couple of weeks. After you've finished this first job for us." I nodded, trying not to visibly gloat. "But Kaylee, that won't last," she warned. "You can finish school—you might even make it through college—but eventually people are going to notice that you don't age. You're going to have to disappear."

"I know." But that was no big deal—if I'd lived, I'd have looked thirty on my one hundredth birthday. I'd always expected to have to disappear eventually.

I took a deep breath, then let it out slowly. "There's one more thing.…"

Madeline blew on my signature to dry the ink, then handed me my copy of the contract. I'd read the whole thing, and even understood most of it. And thanks to Addison's mistakes, I knew to demand my own copy.

"We're so pleased to have you on board, Kaylee," she said, folding her copy of my contract into thirds while I folded the hospital gown and laid it on the empty bed, glad to be wearing real clothes again, even if they'd been "borrowed" from some other patient. "We'll be in touch very soon about your first assignment."

I didn't care that she was pleased. I didn't give a damn about the assignment. I just wanted to go home.

"Are you ready?" Levi asked, watching me closely through his dead child eyes, and it occurred to me for the first time how much he and I had in common. I'd lived longer, but he'd been dead longer. And someday I might catch up to him.

"Yeah." I accepted the hand he held out, then took one final glance around the empty hospital room we'd appropriated for my statement to the police. "Get me out of here."

I closed my eyes and waited for the dizziness and disorientation that usually accompanied reaper-travel. But I felt nothing. The first indication I had that we'd left the hospital was the change in temperature. Then the whisper of hushed voices.

I opened my eyes, still holding Levi's hand. We stood in Nash's kitchen, alone, but I could hear movement and voices from the living room. And crying. Everyone was here, because my house was the scene of a double homicide, my mattress still soaked with two types of blood—one of them mine.

"How much do they know?" I asked, still invisible and inaudible as long as I held his hand.

"Only that Nash has been released. I thought you'd want to tell them the rest yourself."

I nodded. "Thanks." Then I let go of his hand.

"Good luck, Kaylee," Levi said. Then he disappeared.

I took a deep breath. Then I took another. I'd figured out quickly how to make my lungs work, but the process was no longer automatic, because it was no longer necessary. But breathing made me feel more…normal, so I took one more breath, then pushed open the swinging kitchen door and stepped into the living room.

Emma was the first to look up, from an armchair in one corner, while my dad and Harmony held one another, her head on his shoulder, their faces red and tear-streaked.

It broke my heart to see my father cry.

"Kaylee?" Emma said. Her jaw dropped open, and Harmony sat up straight, staring at me. Then my father's gaze met mine, and I burst into tears.

"Kay?" He was there in an instant, feeling my arms, holding my face. Trying to convince himself that I was real. I couldn't say anything—couldn't think of what to say—so I hugged him instead, squeezing him as hard as I could, breathing him in until he clutched me back, finally convinced.

"What happened?" he asked, on the tail of the most relieved sob I'd ever heard. "You died. I saw you die." They hadn't fixed his memory—I'd asked them not to.

"I made a deal, Dad. I had to, to make things right."

"What kind of deal?"

"Aiden," Harmony said from behind him, and her voice was so somber, so heartbroken, that I let go of him and looked up to find her watching me, blond curls in disarray, blue eyes so full of grief I could hardly stand to look at them. She didn't know about Tod yet—not for sure. Not if Levi hadn't told her. So was she grieving for me? "She signed on with the reapers."

"Did you…?" my dad asked, turning back to me in horror, and I shook my head.

"Not exactly. I'll explain it all later, but for now, can we just…" But I didn't have any way to finish that sentence.

"But you're back, right?" Emma asked, still standing across the room. She looked pale, and confused, and a little scared. "However you did it, you're really back?"

"Not quite as good as new, but yeah. I'm back." I held my

arms out and she ran into them, squeezing me so tight I was almost glad I didn't need to breathe.

"I woke up, and he was on your bed, and Sophie was screaming!" she sobbed into my hair. "And there was so much blood, and you were gone!"

And Emma and Sophie were all alone with a dead incubus, and they had no idea what had happened. They must have been terrified.

"Beck's dead," I said, holding her while she cried. "Everything's going to be fine. Different. But fine." That's what I'd been telling myself over and over for the past few hours, while I waited for Madeline to get everything set up. While I waited for word from Levi, which never came. "How's Sophie?" I asked my dad, without letting go of Emma.

"Traumatized, but she'll be fine. Your uncle's decided to tell her everything. The secrets have become too much for them both."

I nodded. It was overdue.

Harmony watched me over Emma's shoulder, arms wrapped around her own stomach, like something hurt deep inside. I wanted to hug her, but I wasn't sure she'd want to touch me after what I'd done. I wanted apologize for what I'd put her through. For what I'd let happen to her sons, after she'd already lost so much. But I didn't have the words to make either of us feel better.

"They were supposed to release Nash..." I said finally, when Em let me go.

Harmony nodded. "Sabine went to pick him up from questioning half an hour ago. He...he didn't want me to come." She glanced at the ground, then back up at me. "They said he'd been cleared, but they didn't say how."

"I gave a statement to the police. There's going to be a story about it on the news tonight. They're going to say there was a mix-up at the hospital and that the reports of my death were made in error." That was almost a direct quote, from Madeline. As was the next part. "Arlington Memorial is telling reporters I was transferred to an undisclosed hospital for privacy, because of the high-profile nature of my case." A sixteen-year-old girl attacked and nearly killed in her own home by a male teacher... Evidently that was a brow-raiser. "And I'm going to be fine."

Before anyone could come up with a response beyond utter, speechless surprise, a car rumbled to a stop outside, and Harmony leaned over the couch to peek out the front window. "It's Nash..." She rubbed her hands on her jeans nervously, then opened the front door. A minute later, Sabine led Nash in with one arm around his waist. He looked sick and exhausted, like he was the one who'd almost died.

Nash froze when he saw me, and anger raged in his eyes. He let go of Sabine and glared at me, and I felt my father at my back, a silent, solid presence, which Nash didn't even seem to notice. "What the hell did you do?" he demanded, his voice low and rough, but blessedly free of Influence.

"I told them you didn't do it. I cleared you," I said, unable to quash the guilt I was drowning in with every word.

"You framed me for a double murder," Nash spat, and Sabine glared at me from his side, her eyes dark and even scarier than usual. "Why, Kaylee?"

"I'm *so* sorry," I said, tears filling my eyes. But there was nothing I could do or say to make things right between me and Nash. Not now. Not after everything we'd done to each other. How was it possible that a relationship I'd once thought was meant to be could have spawned so much pain? Addiction. Lies. Betrayal. Unfaithfulness. Manipulation by Influence. And now suspicion of two murders. We couldn't have hurt each other worse if we'd been *trying*.

"I'm so sorry, Nash," I said again. Because I had to try. "Beck made me. He had a knife, and he was going to—" But I couldn't finish that thought. I didn't want Emma to know what Beck had threatened to do to her and Sophie. Ever. "I'm so, so sorry." And I'd be paying for what I'd done to him with every single day of my afterlife.

"Nash, she *died*," Emma said softly. "That bastard stabbed her and tried to steal her soul."

Sabine's eyes widened, and I could see some of her anger fade, but Nash...

"What soul?" Nash stomped past me unsteadily on his way to his room, and we all stared after him.

"He doesn't mean that," Harmony said, and my father wrapped one arm around her in sympathy. "He's...not himself."

I nodded. It was my fault Nash wasn't himself, but I couldn't quite believe that he didn't mean it. Wouldn't I hate him if he'd framed me for murder? Hadn't I hated him just a little, after what happened in the parking lot? And that was nothing, compared to what I'd done.

"Kaylee..." Harmony said, and I could see the question in the slow, pain-filled swirl of pale blue in her eyes, demanding—yet dreading—to know the extent of her loss. "Where's Tod? He's not answering his phone."

Tears filled my eyes again, and my dad pulled me close.

"Harmony..." he began, and I realized then that he knew. He'd either seen Tod die, or he'd figured it out. But he hadn't told her yet. "Tod refused to reap Kaylee's soul. I'm so sorry."

Harmony's hands flew to her mouth, and her eyes watered. She dropped onto the couch and squeezed her eyes shut, but the tears leaked out anyway.

"I tried..." I whispered, as my own tears fell. "I tried to get him back, but Levi said there was nothing he could do."

"And if you'd waited another hour, that would have been true."

I froze in my father's arms, and if my heart had been beating, surely it would have stopped at the sound of Tod's voice. Harmony stood, red eyes wide, and I turned slowly.

Tod stood in front of the kitchen door, his arms crossed over his chest, his lips turned up in a half smile. He spread his arms, and I ran into them, and they closed around me, and I could feel him, warm and solid, and very real.

"Levi says, 'Surprise,'" he whispered, and I pulled away just enough to look into his eyes. "I take it I have you to thank for this?"

Tears poured down my face and I was vaguely relieved to realize that I could still cry. "He said it was too late. He said he'd already turned your soul in," I sobbed. "I thought you were gone...." I hugged him tighter—couldn't get close enough—and he rubbed my back.

"He didn't want to promise something he wasn't sure he could deliver." Tod stepped away so he could see my face. "Thank you, Kaylee," he said, and I laughed at the absurdity, and the irony, and the inexpressible giddiness of getting a gift—a surprise, at that—from the very agent of death who'd taken my life.

"Does this make us even, Reaper?" I asked.

In answer, Tod kissed me.

And finally, my heart began to beat.

★ ★ ★ ★ ★

Acknowledgments

Thanks, as always, to my critique partner Rinda Elliot, who listens (and believes me) every time I swear that this one is the BEST ONE YET!!!

Thanks to my editor, Mary-Theresa Hussey, for unwavering enthusiasm for the Soul Screamers series, and for never even flinching at what I've put Kaylee and her friends through.

Thanks to Natashya Wilson, for input and encouragement.

Thanks to everyone behind the scenes at Harlequin Teen. You've made this possible. Kaylee and I thank you.

And, of course, thanks to #1, who puts up with me and with the multitude of fictional characters who take up most of my time and attention. Someday, more of both will be yours. I swear.

Netherworld Survial Guide

A collection of entries salvaged from Alec's personal journey
during his twenty-six year captivity in the Nether...

COMMON HAZARDOUS PLANTS

Note: Flora in the Netherworld is eighty-eight percent carnivorous, ten percent omnivorous and less than two percent docile. So keep in mind that if you see a plant, it probably wants to eat you.

Razor Wheat

- **Location**–Rural areas with little foot traffic.
- **Description**–Fields full of dense vegetation similar to wheat in structure, ranging in color from deep red stalks to olive-hued seed clusters. Over six feet tall at mature height.
- **Dangers**–Razor wheat stalk shatters upon contact, raining tiny, sharp shards of plant that can slice through clothing and shred bare flesh.
- **Best Precaution**–Complete avoidance.
- **Second-Best Precaution**–Long sleeves, full-length rubber waders and fishing boots, metal trash-can lid wielded like a shield.

Crimson Creeper

- **Location**–Anywhere it can get a foothold. Creeper can take root in as little as a quarter-inch-wide crack in concrete and will grow to split the pavement open. It grows quickly and spreads voraciously, climbing walls, towers, trees and anything else that can be made to hold still.
- **Description**–A deep green vine growing up to four inches in diameter, bearing alternating leaves bleeding to crimson or bloodred on variegated edges. Vines also sport needle-thin thorns between the leaves.
- **Dangers**–Though anchored by strong, deep roots, which have hallucinogenic properties when consumed, Creeper vines slither autonomously and will actually wind around prey, injecting predigestive venom through its thorns. The

vine will then coil around its meal and wait until the creature is slowly dissolved into liquid fertilizer from the inside out.

- **Best Precaution**–Complete avoidance.
- **Second-Best Precaution**–Crimson Creeper blooms can be made into a tea which acts as one of two known antidotes to the Creeper venom; however, the vine blooms only once every three years. Blooms can be dried and preserved for up to two decades.

COMMON DANGEROUS CREATURES

Note: Whether it intends to consume your mind, body or soul, fauna in the Netherworld is ninety-nine percent carnivorous, in one form or another. So keep in mind that if you see a creature, it probably wants to eat you.

Hellions

- **Location**–Everywhere. Anywhere. Never close your eyes.
- **Description**–Hellions can look like anything they want. They can be any size, shape or color. Their only physical limitation is that they cannot exactly duplicate any other creature living or dead.
- **Dangers**–Hellions feed from chaos in general, and individual emotions in particular. But what they really want is your soul—a never-ending buffet. Since souls cannot be stolen from the living, a hellion will try to bargain for or con you out of it. If you refuse—and even sometimes if you don't—the hellion will either kill you for your soul or torture you, *then* kill you for your soul.
- **Best Precaution**–Complete avoidance.
- **Second-Best Precaution**–Pray.

Harpies

- **Location**–Found in large numbers near thin spots in the barrier between worlds, but individual harpies can live anywhere they choose, in either the human world or the Netherworld.
- **Description**–In the human world, harpies can pass for human at a glance, as long as they brush hair over their pointed ears and hide their compact, batlike wings beneath clothing. In the Netherworld, harpies appear less human, with mouths full of sharp, thin teeth, claws instead of hands and birdlike, clawed talons instead of feet.
- **Dangers**–Harpies are snatchers. Collectors. They will dive out of the air with no warning to grab whatever catches their eye, which can be anything from broken pots and pans to shiny rings—often still attached to human fingers. Also, they're carnivores and they don't distinguish between human and animal flesh.
- **Best Precaution**–Complete avoidance.
- **Second-Best Precaution**–Stay inside or keep one eye trained on the sky and get ready to run.

Escape and Evasion

Note: The best way to escape a Netherworld threat is to leave the Netherworld, though that won't keep certain species, such as harpies, from crossing into the human world after you. If you are incapable of leaving under your own power, eventually something *will* eat you. But to help put that moment off as long as possible, here is a list of the most effective evasion tactics:

Find a shelter in rural areas. Netherworld creatures are attracted to heavily populated areas, where the overflow of human energy they feed from is most concentrated.

Fibers from the *dissimulatus* plant can be woven together and worn to disguise your energy signature and keep predators from identifying you as human and thus edible.

New York Times Bestselling Author

JULIE KAGAWA

THE IRON FEY

"Julie Kagawa's Iron Fey series is the next *Twilight*."—*Teen.com*

Book 1

Book 2

Book 3

Available November 2011!

www.TheIronFey.com

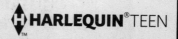
HARLEQUIN®TEEN

HTIRONFEY3BKREVTRR2

FROM *NEW YORK TIMES* BESTSELLING AUTHOR

GENA SHOWALTER

Book 1

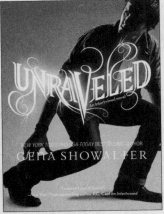

Book 2

Aden Stone should be dead—but when his vampire girlfriend, Victoria, saves his life, she puts everything they care about at risk. Aden grows stronger, but so does the darkness inside him—a darkness that may consume him, his friends, and all the paranormal creatures he has drawn to Crossroads, Oklahoma, as a final showdown looms.

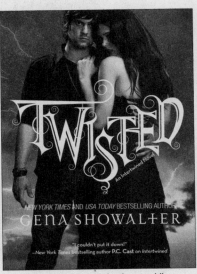

Available wherever books are sold!

www.HarlequinTEEN.com

HTGS2010REVTRR2